P. P. Bliss, D. W Whittle

Memoirs of Philip P. Bliss

P. P. Bliss, D. W Whittle

Memoirs of Philip P. Bliss

ISBN/EAN: 9783337093167

Printed in Europe, USA, Canada, Australia, Japan

Cover: Foto ©Andreas Hilbeck / pixelio.de

More available books at **www.hansebooks.com**

MEMOIRS

OF

PHILIP P. BLISS.

EDITED BY

D. W. WHITTLE:

CONTRIBUTIONS BY

REV. E. P. GOODWIN, IRA D. SANKEY, AND GEO. F. ROOT.

INTRODUCTION BY D. L. MOODY.

A. S. BARNES & COMPANY,

NEW YORK, CHICAGO, AND NEW ORLEANS.

1877.

PREFACE.

THE kind indulgence of the reader is asked for the imperfections that may be discovered in these Memoirs. The Editor is a novice in work of this kind. It was undertaken by him at the solicitation of friends who desired, if a life was to be written, a correct and reliable narrative of the facts which, from past association, he could seem to give better than others, and who were willing, in receiving the narrative, to overlook the crudeness of its literary performance.

It is not expected that the work will fall into the hands of many outside of those in some way acquainted and in sympathy with the loved friend of whom it speaks, and whose simple desire in reading the book will be to know him better—to know all that can be known of the man and his work. To all such the interest in the subject of the memoir will lead them to overlook its faults. To all others, it can only be said that no claim is made for the book, except that it is a loving and faithful attempt to truthfully narrate what could be recalled from memory, and gathered from all reliable sources, of the life of Mr. Bliss. Much could undoubtedly have been profitably omitted, and no one could feel more keenly than the writer that *much* could profitably be added to make a complete picture of this variously-gifted, large-hearted, consecrated Christian man. What is presented will seem to his dearest friends but fragments of glass, through which will be caught glimpses of the man they knew. This is all that it seems to the writer.

But one other word of apology remains to be presented to the general public for the issuing of the book to them. The profits arising from its sale are to be devoted to the mother and such of the family of Mr. Bliss, other than his children, who were dependent upon him for maintenance. The impression has been made by statements as to the response to Mr. Moody's appeal, that an abundant provision has been realized for his family. So far as the orphan children are concerned, this is happily true. The children of the Sabbath schools have sent in, up to the present time, penny contributions amounting in the aggregate to about $9,500. This money is in the hands of trustees for the purpose mentioned in the appeal, viz., the erection of a monument and the education and maintenance of the children. It cannot be diverted from this object.

All collections, so far as known, are for the same definite purpose. The estate of Mr. Bliss is in the hands of an executor, who is under legal responsibility to administer for the benefit solely of the heirs-at-law, the minor children. Whatever may be realized from the railroad company, from insurance, from copyright interests, must be kept and accounted for to the minor children when of age. It will thus be seen that while a fair provision is made for the boys, other objects, dear to the heart of both Mr. and Mrs. Bliss, are left wholly unprovided for. Mr. Bliss left a will which stipulated that $200 a year should be paid to his mother; but in probating the will it was ruled that, as he had changed this clause since the will was dated, and the change was without attestation, the original clause, which was $100 a year, was all that could be allowed. In addition to this mother, there were sisters and nephews who were constant recipients of his assistance, and for whom he had plans of future aid that would have been realized to them had he lived.

This statement is not made as the basis of any appeal for a continuation of contributions. No solicitations are made that the book should be bought as an act of charitable donation. The facts are stated to justify the publication of the book as giving friends who desire the privilege, the opportunity of creating a fund to be used in carrying out in some measure the plans of Mr. Bliss for his family. By assignment with the publishers, all copyright profits will be paid over to Rev. E. P. Goodwin, H. G. Spafford and D. W. Whittle, as Trustees.

Acknowledgments and thanks are hereby tendered to the friends who have kindly assisted in the preparation of this book, by furnishing letters of Mr. Bliss and giving incidents connected with his life and work.

The obligations that the writer and all friends are under to Messrs. John Church & Co., Mr. Bliss's publishers, and the owners of the copyrights upon the words and music of his songs and hymns, for permitting without cost the use of the words and music compiled in this work, and the contributions of Mr. Bliss from the Song Messenger, are hereby gratefully acknowledged.

The composers, whose chapter of songs, as a memorial to their loved brother and companion in labor, constitutes so attractive and valuable a feature of the memoirs, are cordially remembered for the cheerful assent they have rendered to the request made for their contributions.

That God may add His blessing, and that His children who read this book may be quickened in spiritual life, and that some unsaved one may be led to the acceptance of the Lord Jesus Christ by a word or sentence here read and applied by the Spirit of God, is the highest ambition and sincere prayer of the writer.

D. W. WHITTLE.

CHICAGO, Feb. 19th, 1877.

INTRODUCTION.

I HAVE pleasure in giving a word of introduction to the work of my friends, Major Whittle and Doctor Goodwin, in presenting to the public the memoirs of my dear friend and brother, P. P. Bliss. I regret the little time at my disposal prevents my writing more fully concerning the man and his work. I could probably add nothing to the facts of his life that are here compiled, but I would like to tell something of how I loved and admired him. I believe he was raised up of God to write hymns for the Church of Christ in this age, as Charles Wesley was for the church in his day. His songs have gone around the world, and have led and will con tinue to lead hundreds of souls to Christ. In my estimate, he was the most highly honored of God, of any man of his time, as a writer and singer of Gospel Songs, and with all his gifts he was the most humble man I ever knew. I loved him as a brother, and shall cherish his memory, giving praise to God for the grace manifested in him, while life lasts.

D. L. MOODY.

BOSTON, February 19th, 1877.

CONTENTS.

CHAPTER VI.

CHAPTER VII.

CHAPTER VIII.

CHAPTER IX.

CHAPTER X.

CHAPTER XI.

CHAPTER XII.

CHAPTER XVII.

CHAPTER XVIII.

CHAPTER XIX.

CHAPTER XX.

CHAPTER XXI.

CHAPTER XXII.

CHAPTER XXIII.

CHAPTER XXIV.

CHAPTER XXV.

CHAPTER XXVI.

CHAPTER XXVII.

CHAPTER XXVIII.

BLISS' LAST HYMNS

SET TO MUSIC BY HIS FRIENDS.

LAST SONG OF P. P. BLISS.

MEMOIR OF P. P. BLISS.

CHAPTER I.

I COPY the following from a memorandum found among Mr.
Bliss's papers, endorsed " P. P. Bliss, 1861," and containing
the genealogy, memorial and statistics of the Bliss family, obtained
from his father, uncles and " The Seventh-day Baptist Memorial:"
" The earliest notice of our ancestors that we have is contained in
the will of Governor Arnold, dated 1677, in which he gives to his
daughter, Damaris Bliss, wife of John Bliss, a parcel of land in the
precincts of Newport. Governor Arnold also mentions the name
of George Bliss as one of whom he had bought land, and whom he
named as one of the first purchasers of the island of Quononicut :
Beginning, then, with John Bliss—who, with his brother George
Bliss, and, tradition says, one other brother, came from Wales with
their widowed mother and were early settlers of Connecticut—we
have the following genealogical table, which, with one exception,
we know to be correct : John Bliss married Damaris Arnold, 1670.
Josiah Bliss, their son, died 1748. William Bliss, son of Josiah,
born 1728, married Barbara Phillips, October 20th, 1750. They
had seven sons and five daughters. The third son, John Bliss, was
born January 17th, 1760, and was the grandfather of the writer.
He learned the trade of a shoemaker, and on the fourth day of
November, 17—, married Reliance Babcock, of Dartmouth, Mass.
In 1788, he moved to Greenfield, Saratoga County, New York, and
purchased a farm of one hundred acres ; there being at that time

but one log hut at Saratoga Springs, situated near High Rock Spring, seven miles from his house. In February, 1801, he walked from Greenfield to Newport, Rhode Island, for the purpose of submitting to the ordinance of baptism.

"John Bliss had sixteen children. Twelve were sons, but only two of them survived. My father, Isaac Bliss, was one of twins. He, with his brother Josiah, was born April 29, 1797. He was married to Lydia Doolittle, June 7, 1831. They had five children: Phebe, born May 27, 1832; Reliance, born May 14, 1834; Philip Paul, born July 9, 1838; Elizabeth, born May 1, 1842; James D., born July 10, 1846. Reliance died November 4, 1847; James D., February 15, 1847."

Under date of January, 1864, in Mr. Bliss' diary is this note: "January.—Pa Bliss died, the best man I ever knew." Mr. Bliss had great affection for his father, and dearly loved his memory. I have often heard him speak with great tenderness of his simple, child-like faith. "He lived in continual communion with his Savior; always happy, always trusting, always singing. Mother used sometimes to say to him, laughingly, that all his hymns commenced with the word 'come;' and I can remember many of them that he used to sing. There were 'Come, ye sinners, poor and needy;' 'Come on, my partners in distress;' 'Come, ye that love the Lord.' He was always a poor man, but early in the morning, and after the toil of the day, in the evening, sitting in the porch of his humble home, his voice would be heard in song, and I can almost hear him now, singing upon the other side, 'Come to that happy land, come, come away.' He was a diligent reader of the Bible, and had the most implicit faith in its teachings, and a deep reverence for its commands. My first recollection of him is his daily family prayer. Devout, tender and child-like; repeating over and over again, year after year, about the same words, until we all knew them by heart, his prayers were very real, very holy to me in my childhood. It was very hard for father ever to punish us children, and when he did, he suffered more than we. He would talk to us with great solicitude, and when we would say we were sorry, and would do better, he would be full of joy, and would say, 'That is right; that is right.'"

In addition to this testimony of Mr. Bliss, all the recollections of his sisters and neighbors go to show that he was a man of lovely simplicity and tenderness of nature, and of devoted piety. His character and example had much to do in moulding the character of his son. This father died at Rome, Pennsylvania, in the home of Philip, and was buried in the village cemetery. His wife, Lydia Bliss, and her two daughters survive to mourn over the loss, to them, of the son who had taken for many years the place of husband and father, but also to rejoice that father and son, who were so dear to each other on earth, are reünited in Heaven. The last words of the dying father were, "Philip, take care of your mother;" and most unselfishly was the charge fulfilled until death called him away, and most fitting does it seem that the writer of these lines should be penning them to fulfill the loving task from which the son is forever removed in bodily presence, but which shall still be performed by his memory, cherished and perpetuated in these pages. The work is thrice hallowed in the memory of the dying father's charge, the tender associations connected with this dearly loved brother and friend, and the privilege of a ministry of love to "his mother and mine."

Philip Paul Bliss was born in Clearfield County, Pennsylvania, July 9, 1838, in the usual log home occupied by the early settlers of the mountain and forest region of Northern Pennsylvania. In February, 1844, the family removed to Kinsman, Trumbull County, Ohio, where they resided for three years. In 1847, they returned to Pennsylvania, residing in Espeyville, Crawford County. In November, 1848, they removed to Tioga County. During these years of his boyhood, Philip had few advantages in the way of schooling. Moving from place to place and in sparsely settled regions, he had to take such teaching as he could get. His father's singing and praying and reading the Scriptures, his mother's daily lessons, with the contact of the grand scenery around his home, the mountains, valleys, forests and streams of which were ever dear to him, made up, for the most part, the influences that were brought to bear upon his first ten years of life. He early developed a passion for music, and would sit and listen with delight to his father singing, when but a child, and very early sang with him. He would readily catch up a tune, and whistle it or play it upon some rude musical instrument of his own manufacture.

Mr. Bliss has told me of the impression made upon him, when he was about ten years of age, by the first piano he had seen. He was a large, overgrown boy, and one day, down in the village, as he was passing by a house, he heard music, sweeter than anything he had ever before listened to. The door stood open and he was irresistibly drawn toward the sweet sounds that came from within. He was barefoot, and entered unobserved and stood at the parlor door, listening, entranced, as a young lady played upon the piano. As she ceased playing, he exclaimed, with an intense desire, " O, lady, play some more." She looked around, surprised, and with no appreciation of the tender heart that had been so touched by her music, said, " Go out of here with your great feet," and he went away crushed, but with the memory of harmonies that seemed to him like heaven.

In 1849, at the age of eleven years, he went away from home to work upon a farm. His sister says : "I remember well the morning he left. All of his clothing was done up in a handkerchief and carried in his hand. When he went out of the gate, he threw back to us children two pennies and went on down the road and would not look back."

In 1851, he had this memorandum : " Worked on farm for Marvin at nine dollars a month." He was then only thirteen years of age. The next year, he was in a lumber camp, on Pine Creek, as assistant cook. In 1853 he was on Dyer's Hill, in Covington, cutting logs. The next year, he worked in a saw-mill in Portage, New York. Thus five years of his life, from the age of eleven to sixteen, passed on the farm and in the lumber camp, in toiling for bread. With a great desire for education, a portion of the seasons during this period was passed in school, and every opportunity that presented for improvement was eagerly taken advantage of.

In 1850, while at school near Elk Run, a revival commenced among the scholars, conducted by a Baptist minister, and he at that time made his first public profession of Christ. A short time after, he was immersed in the creek near his own home, some four miles from the school, by a minister of the Christian Church, who was at the time holding meetings in the neighborhood. He became connected with the Baptist Church near the school. His own relation of his Christian experience has always been that he never had any marked period of conversion ; that he could never remember the time when he did not love the Savior—when he was not sorry for his sins, and when he did not pray. He undoubtedly experienced regeneration in answer to the prayers of a godly father at a very early age, and all through life manifested that he was a child of God.

In 1855, he spent the winter in a select school at East Troy, Bradford County, Pennsylvania. In 1856, he worked on a farm in the summer and taught school in the winter, at Hartsville, Allegany County, New York. He was then but eighteen years of age, and his quickness of mind for learning, and his industry in the improvement of opportunities, are in a marked way indicated by the fact that he was fitted to become a teacher. It was, to be sure, a humble position, but still it was *a position*, and indicated aspiration. The place sought him because, in the judgment of the School Board, he was the man for the place.

The following winter he passed at Towanda, Pennsylvania, and at Towner Hill. Here he met for the first time Mr. J. G. Towner, who was afterward associated with him in concerting, and received that winter, in Mr. Towner's singing school, his first systematic instruction in music. The same winter, he attended a musical convention at Rome, Pennsylvania. This was the first convention he ever attended, and it did much to strengthen his growing passion for music, and to develop his native talent in harmony. In the providence of God, the convention was in charge of W. B. Bradbury, then in the commencement of his life-work as a composer of sacred music for the children. From the time of this meeting, Mr. Bliss cherished a deep affection for Mr. Bradbury and a reverence for the gifts God had bestowed upon him as a composer. How much this meeting had to do with the moulding of his future life, in the turning of his thoughts, almost unconsciously to himself, in the direction of a work similar to Mr. Bradbury's, we can never know. How appropriate now to Mr. Bliss is the song written by him upon the death of the lamented Bradbury :

WE LOVE HIM.

We love him, though his friendly hand
  Has never clasped our own ;
His gentle voice and loving smile
  We never yet have known.
We love the sweet, the blessed songs
  That he to us has giv'n ;

We know he loved us here on earth;
We love him though in heaven.

> CHORUS.—We'll roll the chorus of praise along,
> Till " Over the River " we go;
> He'll lead us then in more beautiful songs
> Than ever we knew below

We love the sparkling " Golden Chain,"
The " Shower " of beauties rare;
The " Censer " full of joyous praise,
" Fresh Laurels," green and fair.
We love to sing his songs of heaven,
Of Jesus and His love;
They make us happier here below,
And raise our thoughts above.

We love the things that he has loved;
We love his earthly name;
And when we know his angel form,
We'll love him just the same.
We'll love each other better then,
We'll love " Our Father " more;
We'll roll a sweeter song of praise
Along the " Golden Shore."

CHAPTER II.

IN 1858, Mr. Bliss was at Almond, New York, and in the winter
of that year he taught in the Rome Academy at Rome, Pennsylvania. The previous year, his musical gift had brought him
into an acquaintance with the family of Mr. O. F. Young, a thrifty
farmer and a devout Christian man, who, some thirty years before, had come into the valley to teach school, and had married
one of his pupils, the daughter of Peter Allen, a leading citizen of
Rome, and was now the head of a happy family, consisting of
Grandma Allen, her daughter his wife, with their five children,
two sons and three daughters. The whole family were singers,
and Mr. Young being one of the School Board, Mr. Bliss was
invited to make their house his home, and soon became as one of
the family. He brought here his younger sister, that she might
attend school and be with him for the winter.

The descriptions given of Mr. Bliss by his friends, and a daguerreotype taken at this time, indicate that he was possessed of
unusual personal attractions. Of large frame and finely proportioned, a handsome, frank, open face, with fine, large, expressive
eyes, and always buoyant and cheerful, full of the kindliest feeling,
wit and good humor, with a devout Christian character, and of unsullied moral reputation, he became a universal favorite among
young and old. Among his pupils were the children of Mr. Young,
who became his most intimate friends. The eldest daughter, Lucy,
then about eighteen years of age, was the associate and companion
of Mr. Bliss' sister, and thus these young people were thrown much
together. During the winter, the singing school, the spelling
class and the choir meetings went on as is wont in the country

villages of the East, and these two "kept company," and found
ere long that they were necessary to each other's happiness. So,
one beautiful morning in the following spring, June 1, 1859, with
Pa and Ma Young accompanying, they went in a very quiet way to
the little town of Wysocks, six miles down the valley, and were
married by the minister, in the parlor of the minister's house.

It is a beautiful ride down the valley of the Wysocken. The
hills rise up grandly on either side; the brook flows rapidly by,
its babbling and murmurings heard from the road, hidden sometimes in deep dells by overhanging trees, and gleaming in the
light through open fields. The woods were filled with wild flowers
and singing birds, that June morning, and the world was full
of poetry to these two dear friends as they rode to their wedding.
Happy in the love of God, happy in each other's love, how rich
they were! Of money they had absolutely none. Mr. Bliss did
not possess at this time fifty dollars' worth of worldly goods. Mr.
Young derived a comfortable support from his farm, but had nothing wherewith to endow the young couple, beyond the warm welcome
to the old homestead of the loved daughter and the one whom he
had long loved as a son. They came back to the home, and Mr.
Bliss, taking off his Sunday clothes, went out to work on the farm,
and Lucy went into the kitchen to help her mother.

I find in his diary this mention of this event in his life: "June
1, 1859—Married to Miss Lucy J. Young, the *very best thing* I
could have done." And looking back upon the eighteen years they
have lived together on earth, and all they were to each other, in
the experiences of joy and sorrow, of poverty and prosperity, that
they passed through, no one who knew them but would acquiesce
and recognize the providence of God in bringing them together.
Mrs. Bliss was in many things the opposite and the complement
of her husband. He was by nature poetical, impulsive, demon-
strative, easily moved; she strongly practical, steady, reticent, and
with great adherence of purpose. She was both wife and mother
to him from the first of their union. She was of a deep nature,
loving, tender in her affection, beyond what most who knew her
gave her credit for. His buoyant, joyful, affectionate, warm-hearted
demonstrativeness naturally made her more reserved manner seem
constrained; but all who learned to know her loved and admired her, and thanked God that Philip Bliss had such a wife. At

the time of her marriage, she was a member of the Presbyterian Church in Rome, having made profession of faith in Christ at the age of sixteen. Mr. Bliss, about the time of his marriage, became connected with the same church, and labored efficiently with them in church work, being for some time the Superintendent of a Union Sunday School in the village, and is remembered by many of the grown-up people in this connection.

The year after his marriage, Mr. Bliss worked upon the farm for his father-in-law, and received for his support thirteen dollars a month, the amount usually paid to farm hands. That winter he commenced teaching music in Bradford County, at two dollars an evening "and found." The year 1860 he ever reckoned as a memorable one in his history. The little knowledge he had obtained of music made him feel deeply how little he knew, and gave him the most burning desire to prosecute a thorough study of the art. His soul was filled with that which he longed to express, but the future looked dark to him. He had no means and no prospect of being able to secure any further education. For a time he became burdened and depressed with these thoughts.

In July and August of that year, a Normal Academy of Music was held in Geneseo, New York, under Perkins, Cook, Bassini and others. It was the great event of the period among the musical people of the surrounding country. The advantages to be offered in training and culture were unusual, and of the utmost value to those desiring to cultivate music. Poor Bliss obtained the programme, and eagerly pored over the inducements and opportunities it offered. It was just what he needed. It would be such a joy to him to meet these masters in the art—such a help to him for all the future ; but the expense was far beyond his means. He had not a dollar in the world. It was impossible for him to go. He was almost heart-broken about it. He threw himself upon the old settee in the sitting-room one day, when no one but Grandma Allen was in the room, and he says, "I just cried for disappointment. I thought everything had come to an end ; that my life must be passed as a farm hand and country schoolmaster, and all bright hopes for the future must be given up." Grandma was full of sympathy, and wanted to know all about the trouble. After she had been told about the academy, she said, "Now, Phil., what does that cost ? " " Well, Grandma," he said, "it would take as much as thirty dollars." "Well, thirty **dollars is a good deal of** money," **said the kind old lady ;** "I have an old stocking that I have been **dropping pieces of** silver in for a good many years, and I'll just see how **much there** is. Perhaps there are thirty dollars, **and if there are, why, you can take it and go** to the Normal." The stocking **was brought** out and found to contain more **than** the thirty dollars, and Bliss spent **six weeks of the** hardest study of his life **at the** Normal. God bless dear old Grandma Allen. The world owes her interest compounded a hundred times over as long as she lives, and a grateful remembrance after her death, for what she did that day for P. P. Bliss.

In the winter **of** 1860, **Mr. Bliss** formally **took up** the business of a professional music teacher. In his diary he says : "Old Fanny (a horse) and a twenty-dollar melodeon furnished by **O. F. Young** set me **up in the** profession." **The next three years were** passed in and about Rome. He was quite **successful as a teacher,** and during the winter months had plenty of employment. **In the summer he worked** upon his father-in-law's **farm,** and **again attended the Normal** Academy in 1861, and **in 1863. In 1861, he writes :** "**Summer** at Geneseo, New York, **T. E.** Perkins, **T. J. Cook and Pychowski,** faculty this season." In 1862, there is this memorandum : "Worked on farm. **Did not go off to** school **this summer— partly on account of** my **health and partly on account of** my wealth ! **Winter, Honesdale, Pennsylvania, made the** acquaintance of I. Brundage, a good **Rev. and** singer." To be a *good* minister and a *good* singer **was to occupy a** large place **in Mr. Bliss'** affections, **and he ever esteemed Mr.** Brundage **as a** very dear friend. Indeed, long **before** he **entered upon the life of an** evangelist, **while** following the profession **of music, he had scores of** warm-hearted personal **friends among the ministers** of the Gospel. He had a great respect for **their** calling—**a desire to** be helpful to them in their work, **and a love for them** individually, which all who came to **know** him most cordially reciprocated. From no other class of persons **have so many and so** tender expressions of love for his **memory and sorrow at his death been received** as from the ministers.

During these years at Rome, Mr. Bliss' **pastor was Rev. Darwin Cook. Mr. Bliss** esteemed him very **highly, and ever spoke of him** with affection. He has often said **that it was Mr. Cook's** encouraging words, more **than** anything **else, that stimulated** him to excel in his profession, and particularly turned his attention to the composition of melodies for Sunday school songs. Mr. Cook is still living, and participated in the funeral exercises of Mr. and Mrs. Bliss in Towanda, and writes as follows of his recollections of Mr. Bliss :

MERRYALL, January 31, 1877.

MAJ. WHITTLE :

Dear Bro.—I am sorry that I can't help you more. I went to Rome in 1850, and left in 1858. About 1855, I first met P. P. Bliss in the church at Rome. He stood in the choir and sang. In our little company he could not fail to be observed. Therefore I said to Mr. O. F. Young, my chorister, "That young man's voice is worth a thousand dollars a year. Perhaps he does not know it." Mr. Young took him home with him to dinner, and afterward gave him his daughter. Mr. Bliss afterward said that remark of mine was the first hint he ever received that he had any competency or any possibilities more than ordinary. From that time, I occasionally met him while he was holding singing conventions. He began to compose laughable medleys, and to sing money out of the pockets of the penurious.

I well remember that on one occasion such a man gave five dollars to some benevolence, if Bliss would sing his medley. I heard him sing his "Little Willie," at a fortieth wedding anniversary, when the thought struck me, what a power has song to impress the Gospel. I went to him and told him the thought. I mentioned the remark of one who said, "Let me make the songs of a nation, and I care not who makes its laws." I instanced a case at hand then and there, in which his song, in five minutes, had effected more than eight years of preaching.

He was married in June, 1859. At the tenth anniversary I met him again, and was greatly pleased at his evident rapid development. When Mr. Bradbury died, I wrote to him, that if his (Mr. Bradbury's) mantle had fallen on any one, he (Mr. Bliss) must be the man. After the loss of his first child, he wrote to me, and indeed kept me informed of his doings and progress, and when he and Major Whittle were in the South, he had forwarded to me a daily, now and then, to tell me of his work. He had not united with the church when I left Rome, in the spring of 1858, and I do not know the precise date of that union.

I am thankful that I ever met that man, and that I was permitted to give him encouragement in the right direction. He stated publicly in a large congregation "that this man had done him more good than any other man." I don't now recall anything very important in his religious development. We only met occasionally after 1858.

His wife grew up in our Sabbath school, was strong, bright, active, promising, with a good musical talent. It was quite natural that the two should be drawn together. I always esteemed her very highly.

Yours in the Lord,

DARWIN COOK.

Merryall, Bradford Co., Pennsylvania.

In 1863, Mr. Bliss writes: "Geneseo again. Perkins, Bassini and Zundel. A very good term for me. Winter, taught at Castile, New York. Boarded at D. Bovee's. A pleasant winter, only my wife, Lou, was at home; so I was only half a man, *if half.*" The instructors of Mr. Bliss at these Normals all speak in the highest terms of his unusual intelligence and remarkable proficiency. Bassini, at his first Normal, selected him as his most intelligent pupil, and in that and succeeding years took unwonted interest in him, in giving him private lessons upon the use of the voice. Much of his remarkable power in this respect, he felt, was due to the careful and scientific instruction received from Bassini. With a quick apprehension and a thinking mind, Mr. Bliss desired to be intelligent in his profession, and was always wishing to be taught, ever ready to receive, and careful to retain instruction. He never felt that he himself was a master, and ever preferred to be a scholar rather than a teacher.

During this period of his life at Rome, from the proceeds of his singing schools, he saved up a few hundred dollars, and bought a little cottage, to which he removed his parents, and for a time set up housekeeping. The dear old father, who had passed most of his days in humble homes in the backwoods, was now sixty-five years of age. The little cottage in Rome was a better home than he had ever lived in. Many months his children, "Phil" and "Lou," had planned the surprise that awaited him. They had saved in every possible way to buy and plainly furnish the little home. When all was made ready, Father Bliss was sent for. The day of his arrival in Rome, he stopped at Father Young's for dinner. In the afternoon, the happy children took the gentle, laughing, gray-haired old Christian in the wagon, and riding along the one village street, asked him to pick out the house that they had selected to be his home. Two or three times he essayed to express his choice, picking out the humblest, and each time taking a poorer one, until at last he gave up, a little troubled that he might have been too ambitious. When the happy Phil, almost too full to contain himself, turned the team, and driving back up the street, stopped at a pretty little cottage, a neat piazza in front, a large yard filled with blossoming lilacs and budding apple trees, it looked very beautiful; and as the strong man lifted his father from the wagon, it was a very happy hour to him, as he said,

"This is your home, father." The dear old man sat down in a chair placed for him upon the stoop, and, with tears running down his cheeks, said, "Phil, I never expected to have so good a home on earth as this."

Here the last months of the life of the old saint passed away sweetly, peacefully and happily. The remembrance of these, his last days, were always exceedingly precious to Mr. and Mrs. Bliss. The burden of life in some degree rolled away, and he entered more into the sunlight that awaited him in fullness in the life beyond. "The first time I ever saw Father Bliss," Mrs. Bliss once told me, "he reproved me for laughing on Sunday." Brought up by a Puritan father, living in communion with God, drinking daily from the Bible, the only book he ever read, life was to him very solemn, and everything around him was related to God and to eternity. His children all felt this atmosphere in their association with him, and none of them drank in more of the father's sense of the *reality* of eternal things than did his son. There is a root and stalk for every beautiful flower that blooms, a spring for every flowing stream ; and all that has given power on the earth to Philip Bliss' songs finds its root in the Bible of the Hebrews, its stalk in the living characters developed by that Bible among the Puritans. The stream of melody that flowed through him, making glad the people of God, had its spring in the intense reality of spiritual things that came down to him from a godly ancestry.

During these months with his children, the father laid aside everything of austerity that had ever associated itself with him, and was like a happy child. Mr. Bliss often thanked God for his goodness in permitting him to have the joy of making his dear father happy, and of being with him in his last days. In January, 1864, after only a few months in the home he thought so much better than he was entitled to, the father died, and was taken to his Heavenly home, to meet the great surprise of knowing what "God hath prepared for them that love Him." There can be no more fitting close to this chapter than the song of Mr. Bliss, written, much of it, from personal recollection, and which he usually prefaced, in singing, by a few remarks about his father, and by saying, very devoutly, "I thank God for a godly ancestry."

MY GRANDFATHER'S BIBLE.

A CENTENNIAL SONG.

The Sabbath day—sweet day of rest—
  Was drawing to a close;
The summer breeze went murm'ring by,
  To lull me to repose:
I took my father's Bible down—
  His father's gift to him—
A treasure rare, beyond compare,
  Though soiled the page, and dim.

"**Old friend**," said I, "if thou couldst tell,
  What would thy mem'ries be ?"
And **from the Book there** seemed **to come**
  This evening reverie:
"Good will to men, Peace **be to thee!**
  My mission aye hath been,
To tell the love of Him who **died**
  To save a world from sin.

"**A** hundred years ago I sailed,
  With those who sail no more,
Through perils dread; by land and **sea**,
  I reached **New** England's shore;
There, **on a** soul-worn, faithful band
  This **soothing** psalm did fall:
Lord, Thou **hast been our** dwelling place,
  In generations **all**.

"Year after year, in temples rude,
  Upon the desk I lay,
To teach of Him, the Great High **Priest** ;
  The Life, the Truth, the Way.
And multitudes who listened there
  To God's life-giving word
Are resting from their labors, now,
  '**For ever with the** Lord.'

"Anon a lowly **home** I found,
  But Love and Peace were there. . .
The children with the father read,
  And knelt with **him** in prayer;

And through the valley, as one passed,
  I heard her sweetly sing:
O Grave, where is thy victory?
  O Death, where is thy sting?

Hold fast the faith," the old Book said;
  " Thy father's God adore. . . ;
And on the ' Rock of Ages ' rest
  Thy soul forever more."
" Amen," said I, " by grace I will,
  Till at His feet we fall,
And join the everlasting song,
  And crown Him Lord of All.

CHAPTER III.

THE first composition of Mr. Bliss, so far as is known, was in
the year 1864, while in his own house at Rome. He writes
in his diary : "1864.—Lived in Rome, Pennsylvania. Worked on
farm some ; wrote music some ; housekeeping some ; taught in
Nunda, Castile, etc. Saved one hundred dollars this year." Mr.
James McGranahan, for years a musical friend of Mr. Bliss, was,
during the summer of 1864, a clerk in the country store and post
office of Rome. He says : " I well remember Bliss' first published
composition. He sent the manuscript to Root & Cady, and after
a time he received back a proof in *print*. He brought in the copy
to show me and ask my opinion as to corrections. I had had one
or two pieces printed, and knew just how he felt, and we had a
very pleasant time over his first piece. It was a great pleasure to
him, and yet he had a great deal of wonder that anything he had
written was worth publishing. The name of the piece is " Lora
Vale," copyrighted by Root & Cady in 1865, and published as
sheet music. Before sending to Root & Cady, he had forwarded
it to Bradbury, and by him it had been refused, much to Mr.
Bliss' disappointment, but he was encouraged by friends to send
it to Mr. Root.

LORA VALE.

SONG AND CHORUS BY P. P. BLISS.

Calmly fell the silver moonlight
Over hill and over dale,
As with mournful hearts we lingered
By the couch of Lora Vale.

She was dying, gentle Lora ;
  She was passing like a sigh
From a world of love and beauty
  To a brighter world on high.

CHORUS.—Lora, Lora, still we love thee,
      Tho' we see thy form no more,
      And we know thou'lt come to meet us,
      When we reach the mystic shore.

Brightly dawned the morrow's morning,
  Over hill and over dale,
Still with mournful hearts we lingered
  By the side of Lora Vale.
She was almost at the river,
  When the light broke from the sky,
And she smiled and whispered faintly,
  "I am not afraid to die."

Softly through the trellised window
  Came the west wind's gentle breath,
But she heeded not its mildness,
  For she slept the sleep of death ;
And beyond the silver moonbeams,
  Aye, beyond the stars of night,
Now she dwells, our darling Lora,
  In the home of angels bright.

This was the commencement of the exercise of his gifts as a
composer. The style of the song will show that the conception of
the use of song as conveying Gospel truth had not yet come to
him. It is a song of sentiment, of a kind good in its way, but
which it would have been impossible to have got him to write
during the last years of life. The song became popular, and
enjoyed a sale of several thousands. Let the reader place in con-
trast the words of this song, sweet in its sentiment, but purpose-
less in teaching, and without specific mention of Christ, and the
words of the two latest—so far as is known—hymns that he ever
wrote, found in this book, and some correct idea of his development
can be obtained.

From 1864 to 1876, twelve years, his pen was busy in giving
expression to the songs that came thronging through his soul. All
of his work was done during these years. He was twenty-six years

old when he wrote his first song, and thirty-eight when he wrote
his last.   In the year 1863 or '64 he first met Mr. George F. Root,
of Chicago.   The acquaintance then formed became an intimate
friendship, and was one of the links in the chain of providences that
led him into a larger field of usefulness, and finally into the place
God was preparing him for, of a Gospel singer.   Mr. Root thus
writes of his first impressions and memories of Mr. Bliss:

My acquaintance with Mr. Bliss did not begin very early in his life, though
it might have been near the beginning of his musical career.   He had attended a term or two of a normal musical institute, had taught some, and had
given some concerts near his home, when he wrote his first letter to me.
This letter contained an early — perhaps his first — musical composition, a
song entitled Lora Vale.

The song was promising, but the letter was more so, as indicating an individual entirely out of the common run of literary or musical aspirants.   I
think this letter, with many other mementoes of Mr. Bliss that would now be
useful, was in my office and was destroyed at the great fire of Chicago, Oct. 8
and 9, 1871: at any rate, they cannot now be found.

We published Lora Vale, and this led to further correspondence.   And our
interest constantly increased in this many-sided " country-boy," as he called
himself.   His curious conceits, so piquant and varied, his beautiful penmanship, his bright nature, that could not seem to see anything unhappy or
unbeautiful in life, attracted us strongly, and led often to letters on my part
that were not needed for business purposes, but were for the sake of the
answer they were sure to bring.   The deeper nature of the man did not show
then, but that which did appear was " pure and lovely, and of good report."

Whether the proposition to come to Illinois was out of the whole cloth
from us, or whether he intimated, as our correspondence progressed, that he
would like to come, I do not remember; but about 1863 or '64 he did come,
and pleasant was our surprise to find that our bright and attractive letter-writer
lived in a " house " every way worthy of him.   It is rare indeed to find both
mind and body alike so strong, healthy and beautiful in one individual as they
were in him.   He went to work, first about the State, holding musical conventions and giving concerts and attending to the interests of certain parts of our
business; sending to us occasional communications for our musical paper and
occasional compositions.   I do not recall particulars about these compositions.
I only know that it was my pleasure to look them over and suggest, if I
could, improvements, or hint at faults now and then, especially in the earlier
ones.   I say my pleasure, for never had teacher so teachable and docile a subject for criticism (I can hardly say pupil, for I never taught him regularly),
nor one who repaid with such generous affection the small services that were
in this way rendered to him.   His modesty as well as his generosity always
inclined him to give to others much of the credit that belonged to his own

Heaven-sent gifts. A favorite signature in his letters to me was " Your Poor Pupil Bliss."

I do not know of his modes or habits of composition, but do know of his wonderful fertility and facility. His responses to the calls for the many kinds of literary and musical work that we soon found he could do always surprised us as much by their promptness as by their uniform excellence. It is probable that with every topic that entered his mind there came trooping multitudes of congruous ideas, images and words, and he had only to take his choice ; and his choice was always happy, always appropriate and often strik-ing in its originality and beauty. As Mr. F. W. Root, in a recent number of the *Musical Visitor*, says of Mr. Bliss: " His faculty for seizing upon the salient features of whatever came under his notice amounted to an unerring instinct. The one kernel of wheat in a bushel of chaff was the first thing he saw."

It was lovely to see how near to all he did was his religion. There was for him no line on one side of which was a bright face and on the other a solemn one. His smile went into his religion and his religion into his smile. His Lord was always welcome and apparently always there in his open and loving heart. It was this that made his liveliness so irresistibly sweet and attractive. You constantly felt its sphere of innocence. This hymn, by a kindred spirit, is a most true expression of his constant condition :

> Thy happy ones a strain begin ;
> > Dost not Thou, Lord, glad souls possess ?
> Thy cheerful Spirit dwells within ;
> > We feel Thee in our joyfulness.
>
> Our mirth is not afraid of Thee ;
> > Our life rejoices to be bright ;
> We would not from our gladness flee,
> > We give full welcome to delight.
>
> Thou wilt not, Lord, our smiles deny ;
> > Dost thou not deem them of rich worth ?
> Our cheer flows on beneath Thine eye ;
> > We feel accepted in our mirth.
>
> We turn to Thee a smiling face,
> > Thou sendest us a smile again ;
> Our joy, the richness of Thy grace,
> > Thine own, the cheer of this glad strain.

In speaking of himself in a lecture before a State Sunday School Associa-tion, this pleasant insight occurs. After making the remark, "Let song *develop* feeling and then do not fail to use it to direct and purify affection," he goes on : " I well remember a loving, large-eyed lad who in the day school could scarcely sing the old song of

> A, B, C, D, E, F, G ('Haste thee, winter'),

but that the tears would **fall and mark the time.** The lad knew not why he wept, but the faithful Christian **teacher** turned **this** mighty motive **power to heavenly purposes, and** gave these outflowing sympathies wholesome **food.** So the love of song grew **and** prevailed, so the channel of the affections widened, and so the lad, though taller grown, stands here to plead for song."

In another article in his correspondence with our musical paper, he **speaks** in a characteristic way of the death of a friend who had **written** some poetry **for** him ; but other extracts from this article are **so** illustrative **of his** every-day life that we also insert **them here** in their order.

He begins with speaking of a "general association **of ministers," in which** he conducted the **music, thus:**

There was **a deal of mighty fine** *talking*, **a** *few* earnest *prayers*, **but** very little hearty *singing*. **Why is it that so few ministers sing ? Wouldn't** it improve their voices, and *hearts* too ?

But please don't put me down as fault-finding. I think *Sunshine* and its author had a full **share of attention.** On the other hand let me tell this. During the convention in Burling**ton,** Iowa, a few weeks since, which, by the way, was a "real good one"—though the first **since** W. B. Bradbury was there, fourteen or fifteen years ago—it was my good fortune to be **a** guest of Dr. Salter, Pastor of the Congregational Church, and to hear at family worship such solid **tunes** as *Duke Street, Peterboro, St. Martin's*, etc., sung by *all the household*, all singing soprano in a spirited manner, making a lasting impression on my soul.

I don't believe ministers' and deacons' families are a whit worse than other folks,—N. **B. My father** was never even a sexton—but I do believe that every Christian family should **be** a praise-giving band, and, if possible, 'psalm-singers.'

Since Burlington, I have sung in Waukegan and Milburn, within forty miles of Chicago, **and the** statistics show that *not one-half* of the children of that county (Lake) are **in** Sunday **School, nor in any way** 'hear the Gospel sound.' Surely there is work enough to do!

An event worthy to be recorded and never to be forgotten is the departure—I can't say **death—of** *Kate Cameron*. Her name was *first* on a list of thirty to unite with our church the **very day she received the welcome to the Church above.**

She has **written many sweet spiritual songs, but** none more beautiful, I think, than "That City," written for *The Joy*, and sung at her own funeral :

> " You tell me of a city
> That is so bright and fair,
> Oh, why do not the friends I love
> Talk more of going there ?"

Sure enough, I wonder why we don't ?

And here again —**after we had** suggested **that he** occupy a certain place regularly in the paper. **This was** among **the last** things before increasing work on his part and new business relations on ours caused a loving separation, **after** a nearly ten years' connection.

P. P. BLISS, HIS COLUMN.

SELECTED EDITORIAL.

In assuming editorial charge of this column, we make our editorial bow (wow), etc.

The editor fondly hopes, etc.

In our treatment of those vast and vital issues of the momentous future, we shall endeavor to maintain a persistent, etc.

In view of our past editorial experience, we can confidently promise—etc.

Our old friends and acquaintances need scarcely to be told that they may expect us to pay —o, etc., etc.

EDITORIAL CORRESPONDENCE!—AHEM!

OMAHA, Neb., July 15, 1873.

Just five hundred miles in twenty-four hours—and you'll see the center of the world! No, not quite. We call it, "Away out West," but it lacks thirty miles of being the middle of Uncle Sam's farm! [I was tempted to go the thirty miles further, so I could say I'd been half-way across.]

And the programmes said, " The Fifth Annual State Sunday School Convention." Though as to numbers and results 'twas called the beginning of things.

" Elaborate and elegant," was the unanimous verdict on the church decorations; " Cordial and complete," the welcome ; " Harmonious and helpful" all the exercises.

The success of the *music* department is the subject of this article. Saml. Burns, Superintendent of the M. E. S. S., of Omaha, in behalf of the Executive Committee, sent on for fifty copies of the book to be used, and had two or three weeks' practice: so much for preparation.

Professor Nightingale, President of the Convention, was, as you'd know by his name, a musical spirit, and gave the singing its proper place and time in each session, so that music seemed to be one of the exercises, and not a mere pastime. So much for selection.

Dr. J. H. Vincent, of New York, father and founder of the "*Berean Series*" and " *S. School Journal*," being the prominent speaker, aided the singing materially, not only by his kindly words concerning it, but by engaging heartily in it, both its chorus and quartette. So much for sympathy.

Mr. F. J. Hartley, of London, Eng., also a live worker in S. S., manifested a wonderful interest in everything pertaining to American institutions, and complimented the style of our S. S. songs and the manner in which they are rendered, as worthy of imitation. So much for Christian charity

The Children's Mass Meeting of course was a grand success, and the speeches and songs " splendid !" Among the pieces sung were: " Hold the Fort," " Daniel's Band," " More to Follow," " Heaven for Me," " Pull for the Shore," and " Remembered." (At that time recently issued.)

Something about an " Old Piano " was sung and apparently enjoyed, but *some folks* might consider " sacred " songs only appropriate, and perhaps nothing had better be said about " profane " songs in such a solemn convention. (?)

All in all, a more social convention (ice cream included) could not be imagined. And in the years to come, Nebraska will be a bright star in the Sunday School firmament.

That her Sunday School singing may be as popular as the U. P. R. R., and her Christian charity be as broad and inviting as her blooming prairies, is the wish of

SUNSHINE.

The Joy is a good name for a singing book. Don't you think so ? The name was discovered, as a great many other good things are yet to be, in the Bible. Turn to Jeremiah, 33d chapter and 11th verse—and you will find it. Though, as it may not be convenient to turn just now—people seldom turn to look up a quotation—it may be well enough to print it here.

" The voice of joy, and the voice of gladness ; the voice of the bridegroom, and the voice of the bride ; the voice of them that shall say, Praise the Lord of Hosts: for the Lord is good ; for His mercy endureth forever."

Dear Bliss and dear Mrs. Bliss, I cannot think of you without a pang and a longing, but I know they will gradually wear away, and nothing but joy will remain for our next meeting.

GEO. F. ROOT.

The article by F. W. Root, in *Church's Musical Visitor* for January, 1877, quoted from by Mr. Geo. F. Root, is so excellent in its appreciation of Mr. Bliss that it is given entire :

I have just been looking in our charming little holiday gift-book, illustrating Mr. Bliss' poem, "Hold the Fort," written upon an incident familiar to all, which occurred in our civil war. I consider this work an extraordinary combination of effects, a striking cluster of pure gems of sentiment. The first element in it is an appeal to love of country; our patriotism stirs mightily within us as we read of the gallant struggles of our soldiers at Altoona Pass —of their heroic endurance and final deliverance by General Sherman. Then we see the thrilling story idealized and glorified by being put to a spiritual use by the evangelist, Major Whittle. Next comes Mr. Bliss' strong, epigrammatic poem, crystallizing the parallel drawn by his fellow-laborer, and pointing it with Gospel truth that it may strike home to every hearer. The pictures, however they be considered from a technical standpoint, stimulate the imagination to a more vivid apprehension of the allegory, and then comes the music touching the whole with Promethean fire and giving it wings that it may fly to the uttermost parts of the earth and to the innermost recesses of the soul. A man must be without patriotic enthusiasm, without religious sentiment, and without æsthetic sensibility who can look upon this work unmoved; and especially will he be affected if he mourns with us the untimely death of the poet-musician, who contributed such important elements to it. If ever a man seemed fashioned by the Divine hand for special and exalted work, that man was P. P. Bliss. He had a splendid physique, a handsome face, and a dignified, striking presence. It sometimes seemed incongruous, delightfully so, that in one of such great size and masculine appearance there should also appear such gentleness of manner, such perfect amiability, such conspicuous lack of self-assertion, such considerateness and deference to all, and such almost feminine sensitiveness. He had not had opportunities for large intellectual culture, but his natural mental gifts were wonderful. His faculty for seizing upon the salient features of whatever came under his notice amounted to an unerring instinct. The one kernel of wheat in a bushel of chaff was the first thing he saw. And his ability to control words and phrases so that they should realize a thousand odd conceits of his imagination seemed unlimited. I know that he sometimes met adverse criticism upon the rhymes which he threw off upon local subjects; but by far the greater number of these little effusions sparkled with wit and appropriateness, and his shortcomings were remarkably few for one who was obliged to make an airy, fantastic muse conform to the circumscribed requirements of a monthly magazine. Examine the work which really enlisted his whole soul, and you will see nothing but keen discernment, rare taste, and great verbal facility. His Gospel hymns contain no pointless verses, awkward rhythms or forced rhymes, but, on the contrary, they glow with all that gives life to such composition.

Mr. Bliss possessed wide human sympathies, and had a strong social instinct: his acquaintances immediately became his friends, as a natural consequence of his many-sided attractiveness. The last time I saw him for more than a passing moment was at his home, a beautiful little town among the hills of the Upper Susquehanna valley, far enough away from railroads, telegraphs, and the other great auxiliaries of driving care and tumultuous traffic to allow the imagination to escape from the world. He, with his wife and little boys, together with a number of relatives, spent a clear sunshiny Saturday of last summer, surrounded by congenial friends from the neighborhood and from a distance, all feeling conscious of living a delightful little pastoral, around which was thrown a peculiarly graceful halo of friendly intercourse. At the close of this golden day, just before taking our departure, four of us, including our host, stood out under the twining branches of the grove in which we were assembled, and sang from memory the little quartette, " The Two Roses "—two roses that were there in radiant bloom have been gathered!—after which Mr. Bliss, full of the glowing happiness which had been evident with him throughout the day, exclaimed : "O, dear friends; why can't you all stay over till to-morrow? We would then have as good a *Sunday* time as we've had a *Saturday* time to-day!" Mr. Bliss' voice was always a marvel to me. He used occasionally to come to my room, requesting that I would look into his vocalization with a view to suggestions. At first a few suggestions were made, but latterly I could do nothing but admire. Beginning with E flat, or even D flat below, he would, without apparent effort, produce a series of clarion tones, in an ascending series, until having reached the D (fourth line tenor clef) I would look to see him weaken and give up, as would most bass singers ; but no, on he would go, taking D sharp, E, F, *F sharp and G*, without weakness, without throatyness, without a sound of straining, and without the usual apoplectic look of effort. I feel quite safe in saying that his chest range was from D flat below to A flat above, the quality being strong and agreeable throughout and one vowel as good as another. He would have made name and fortune on the dramatic stage had he chosen that profession and studied a more scientific class of music than that in which he chose to work. The lavishness of natural endowment may be also seen in his musical compositions, though in not so high a degree. He never composed upon large designs, and so never expanded his natural gifts into any very comprehensive creative ability. But I find enough in his melodies to justify myself in saying that he had the instincts of a musical composer. " When Jesus Comes " deserves to live by the side of the best songs of the church ; its intellectual side is well enough, and its emotional element is to me irresistible. And I venture to say that it will live, unless I am also mistaken in the belief that the religious progress of to-day (of which this song is an outgrowth) is giving deeper consideration to the things of the heart than has been given in any epoch known to history hitherto, or, indeed unless certain Gospel singers kill the piece by a very mistaken way of rendering it. Mrs. Bliss was so thoroughly devoted to her husband, that her life merged in his. There is a melancholy satisfaction in the thought that this dire calamity did not part this most devoted couple.

In 1865, Mr. Bliss writes : "Summer, concerted with J. G. Towner. A pleasant singer, honest partner and lively companion. Made a hundred dollars in two weeks. Drafted in the United States Army two weeks." Mr. Bliss reported for duty at Carlisle barracks after being drafted, and after two weeks' service was discharged, it being evident that the war was at an end, and that no more men would be needed.

He again writes : " About November 1st, George F. Root wrote to ask us if the 'Yankee Boys' would come West and engage with Root & Cady. The 'Yankee Boys' very readily consented in consideration of a guaranteed salary and expenses paid. Came to Chicago, November 21st, 1865. December, 1865, 'Yankee Boys,' not succeeding in the concert line, tender their resignation to Root & Cady, who gracefully accept, but propose to retain 'Mr. Bliss' in their employ 'if he will stay.' Answer, he will stay. Thus Root & Cady very kindly disengage me from a life which is becoming irksome. They offer me a hundred and fifty dollars a month and expenses of self and wife. On settlement, our receipts were so small that I told Mr. Cady I would ask only a hundred dollars a month, which he *allowed*." At the close of 1868, the firm advanced his salary both for the preceding and succeeding year.

From this time on for eight years, Mr. Bliss' occupation was the holding of musical conventions and the giving of concerts, and private instruction in music in towns through the Northwest. For four years his conventions were held under his arrangement with Root & Cady ; after that, by independent appointment. He was very popular as a musical conductor and teacher, and was much sought after for convention work. During the first of his engagement with Root & Cady, Mrs. Bliss was employed as clerk in Root & Cady's store, then in the Crosby Opera House Building, on Washington street, Chicago. This position she filled for about six months, and then accompanied her husband in all of his travels, to assist in his concerts and convention work. Every summer they would return to Rome to visit the old homestead. During these visits to his home, in the rest and peace he enjoyed there among the hills, many of Mr. Bliss' sweetest pieces were written. Their home, during these years, they considered as being in Chicago. About one-fifth of their Sundays were probably passed here. They boarded, for some years, with musical companions, Mr. and Mrs. O. Blackman, and were always deeply attached to these dear friends. In February, 1868, he remained in Chicago some weeks, writing music for a book published by Root & Cady, called "The Triumph."

On December 28th of the same year, he writes : "Bought my gold watch—a hundred and sixty dollars." At the close of this year, he writes in his diary : "Thus the overruling Providence has led me by unmistakable evidences to see and recognize His dealing with me all through life's journey. Truly we have much to be thankful for. My dear wife, my greatest earthly treasure, joins in the opinion that we are and ever have been highly favored of Heaven ; that we find our greatest enjoyment in each other's society, when striving to make each other happy, and our highest aim is to be useful to ourselves and others, and to 'glorify God that we may enjoy Him forever.' "

The sentiment of gratitude that ever actuated Mr. Bliss is shown in these lines. His first impulse, in every good thing that came to him, and in all his joy and happiness, sometimes, to others, arising from comparatively trifling causes, was to fall on his knees and thank God. The sentiment of deep attachment to his wife that pervaded his life is also shown. They were indeed inseparable and fond of each other and helpful to each other, in all the relations of life here and hereafter, beyond the conception of many who bear the relation of husband and wife, even though they profess that the relationship is sanctified in Christ. May the example of these dear friends in this respect be owned of God to make more happy many a Christian home where they were known and loved, and where what is here feebly represented is known to be true of them.

During 1869, Mr. Bliss wrote songs and tunes for "The Prize," a Sunday School book published by Root & Cady, and also wrote some pieces, which were published as sheet music. He held conventions at Bushnell, Carthage, Randolph, Hamilton, Mason City, Lamoille, Delavan, Secor, Washington, Momence, Peoria and Havana, in Illinois, and in Brockton, New York—thirteen conventions in all, running in time from one to four weeks. While at his home in the summer (Rome, Pennsylvania,) he writes : "June 1, celebrated our tin wedding." "June 5.—To Boston for the Jubilee. Stopped in New York and heard Parepa at Steinway Hall ; also Levy, the great cornetist, Campbell, the base, and at Boston, Ole Bull, Arbuckle, Gilmore and Co." "June 20.—To Brooklyn to hear H. W. Beecher preach." He closes his memorandums for the year with an acknowledgment of blessings received. Notes his settlement with Root & Cady, and mentions that he has "plenty of convention engagements at one hundred dollars for four days." He adds: "In daily contact with G. F. Root, J. R. Murray, Balatka, O. Blackman, W. S. B. Mathews, D. C. C. Miller, H. R. Palmer and other good musicians."

This brief mention of his life for one year will show that he was a busy man. He had very little idle time. He had established a reputation and was regarded as successful in his profession, and with a bright future before him as a musician.

During this year, 1869, an event occurred in his history, that he regarded of the same pivotal nature in its results to him as was the loan of Grandma Allen, that enabled him to go to Geneseo, and the meeting with Mr. Root, that led to his coming west. This event was the meeting with and forming the acquaintance of Mr. D. L. Moody as narrated in the following chapter.

CHAPTER IV.

IN the special manifestation of the power of the Holy Spirit in the Church of Christ, it has often, and perhaps usually, been that the instruments He may have chosen to use have a very intimate connection with and relationship to each other, which it is permitted us to trace, and, in so doing, more fully recognize His presence in and with the church, and His overruling providence in the life of every child of God.

In the summer of 1869, Mr. Moody was holding Gospel services in Wood's Museum, near the corner of Randolph and Clark streets, in Chicago. For half an hour preceding his theater meeting, he was in the habit of speaking in the open air from the steps of the Court House near by. Mr. Bliss has told me of this meeting as follows : " I had been nearly four years in the West, at that time, and had passed a good many Sundays in Chicago, returning from the country where I was occupied holding Musical Conventions ; but I had never met Moody. One Sunday evening, my wife and I went out for a walk, before going to church, and passing up Clark street, we came upon the open-air meeting. I was at once attracted by the earnestness of the speaker, who, I was told, was Moody, and, waiting until he closed with an earnest appeal for all to follow him to the theater, we decided we would go, and fell in with the crowd, and spent the evening in his meeting there. That night Mr. Moody was without his usual leader for the singing, and the music was rather weak. From the audience I helped what I could on the hymns, and attracted Moody's attention. At the close of the meeting, he was at the door shaking hands with all who passed out, and as I came to him he had my name and history in about two minutes, and a promise that when I was in Chicago Sunday evenings, I would come and help in the singing at the theater meetings. This was the commencement of our acquaintance. I sang at the theater meetings often after that, and, making longer stops in Chicago in connection with writing music, I was often at the noon meeting, and was frequently made use of by Moody in his various gatherings."

How little did either of the two men who met that night at the theater door realize what God was preparing them for, and the relation they would in future years sustain to one another in the work of winning souls.

The following year, in May, 1870, I first met Mr. Bliss. I had heard his name mentioned by Mr. Moody, several times, as having sung at some of his meetings, and of his having asked Root & Cady "where in the world they had kept such a man for four years, that he hadn't become known in Chicago." Mr. C. M. Wyman (since deceased) was at that time in Chicago, working with Mr. Bliss in making songs. He, with Bliss, was an earnest Christian, and both came to Moody's meetings when they could. I think the first impression Mr. Moody received of the power of solo singing in Gospel work he obtained from these two men ; at all events, such impressions as he may have had were crystalized by his use of them. He had a sense of personal loss in his tone, as he would say, " to think that such a singer as Bliss should have been around here for the last four years and we not known him."

At the time mentioned, I received an invitation from my friend, Mr. Talcott, of Rockford, to come out and address the Winnebago Sunday School Convention, and, if possible, to bring a singer with me. I consulted Mr. Moody about a singer and was referred to Wyman. I called upon Wyman, and found that a previous engagement would prevent his going. While talking with him, Bliss came in, and, after an introduction, he was solicited by us both to go. He cheerfully and pleasantly consented, and met me at the depot the same afternoon. I was much impressed at this convention with Bliss' power as a singer, and was won toward him from the first as a lovable man.

A few days after our return, Mr. T. M. Avery was asking me if I knew who could be obtained to take charge of the singing of the First Congregational Church, then about to move into their new building on the corner of Washington and Ann streets. I told him of my experience with Mr. Bliss, and the opinion Mr. Moody had of him, and that I should like to have him meet him. An appointment was made for a day following, and Mr. Bliss was brought into communication with the people of that church, with the result narrated by Dr. Goodwin. My residence, at the time, was only one block from the church, and as Mr. Bliss wished to be near his new field of labor, he and his wife became inmates of my family, where they remained until they commenced housekeeping in November of the same year. It was at this house, No. 43 South May street, that he wrote, "Hold the Fort," "I am so glad that Jesus loves Me," and other of his popular pieces. The memory of those days is very pleasant, very sacred to us. A dear old father—since passed into glory—my dear friend and Mr. and Mrs. Bliss' dear friend, Charles Severance, a noble, manly young man, loved by us all, who died the following spring, were then with us. What precious seasons of family worship; what animated discussions of Bible truth with my father; what interest in talking over songs and sermons, Sunday schools and plans of work! How kind and tender dear Bliss was to my invalid father! How he would cheer him in his joyous, hearty way, and in the singing of his favorite songs! How welcome he always was when he came home from his conventions; how sorry we always were to have him go. In all the time he was with us, he was always the same kind-hearted, cheerful, loving and lovable man. Of his Christian work at this time the following, contributed by Dr. Goodwin, will furnish the most complete record:

In July, 1870, Mr. Bliss became leader of the choir of my First Congregational Church of Chicago, and a few months later, the Superintendent of the Sabbath school. He continued to hold both of these positions for something more than three years, resigning his superintendency only when he had fairly entered upon his work as a singing evangelist. As may be supposed, I saw him very often during all this period, and came to know him well; and the memory of the friendship that grew up between us, and interlocked our hearts more and more as the fellowship of worship and work went on, is and will ever be a perpetual joy. His was a nature to invite confidence and to keep it Thoroughly frank and unsuspecting, with not a thought of policy or craft, intensely sympathetic and outspoken, with a heart overflowing with kindness of spirit, a conscience quick to hear and imperative to heed every call of duty, a devotion to the service of the Master that never seemed to falter or grow cold, he drew me to him from the first as a brother and yoke-fellow to be exceedingly beloved and rejoiced in; and the better I knew him the more I admired the unaffected simplicity and beauty of his character—the more I felt impressed with the depth and earnestness of his piety—the more I leaned upon and valued his coöperation.

Few pastors, I am persuaded, are privileged to have in their choristers such gifted, sympathizing, efficient helpers. Too often, it is to be feared, the pulpit and the choir gallery are out of harmony as to the ends proposed, or the methods by which the ends agreed on shall be sought; and the cases are not few, nor hard to find, where in the handling of choir-leaders and those who abet them, the Lord's house is turned into a concert hall, the service of song made largely a device for filling and renting pews, and the minister compelled to sandwich his part in between performances that suggest anything but the worship of God or the salvation of men. Sometimes, indeed, he has to come to his duties in the pulpit after the world and the flesh and the devil have, through the fingers and lips of an unconverted organist and choir-leader, set things moving to their liking, and then turn the service over to them after the sermon, to be finished up as they may elect. Doubtless the devil likes that way of conducting Sabbath services. If he can only get people's heads full of waltzes, and operas, and sonatas and what-not else, before the preaching comes, and then have a chance to follow it up with a march or an aria of his own selection, the preacher's thirty minutes of Gospel will not greatly damage his interests. Little wonder that preaching in such circumstances saves few souls. It is like expecting harvest with the enemy invited to go before the toiler, sowing tares, and to follow him gathering up and snatching away the seed.

To those who knew anything of P. P. Bliss, it will not be needful to say that he had no sympathy with any such idea of the music of the sanctuary. He shared to the fullest extent my feeling, that the disposition to make the song and service of God's house showy and entertaining was an abomination in God's sight. He held, as I did, that all music in connection with worship, whether by instrument or voice, should be consecrated and worshipful. In his conception, he who led at the organ should be one to come to the keys fresh from his closet, one who should pray, as his hands swept over the manuals, that the power of God might, through him, constrain the people's hearts to worship in spirit and in truth. So he believed that all who led in the service of song should sing with grace in their hearts; that the music should be strictly spiritual music—not selections made on grounds of taste, high musical character, but selections aimed at honoring God, exalting Jesus Christ, magnifying His Gospel—music, in a word, that God's Spirit could wholly own and use to comfort, strengthen, and inspire God's people, and lead unsaved souls to Christ. Accordingly the highest devotional character marked all his selections, all his rehearsals, all his leadership in the Lord's house. It was his invariable custom to open his rehearsals by prayer. He often invited me to lead in that service, and to address the choir on the subject of the singing adapted to worship; and few weeks passed without his impressing the spiritual idea as the all-controlling one, and one never to be forgotten by those who were to lead the praises of the congregation.

As Mr. Bliss stood in the choir gallery, partly facing the singers, during his leadership, there was exactly in front of him, in the center of the eastern window of the transept a large crimson cross. Many times during rehearsals he would point thither, saying, "I am glad we have the cross always before us. Let us forget everything else when we sing. Let us seek to have the people lose sight of us, of our efforts, our skill, and think only of Him who died thereon, and of the peace, comfort, strength, joy He gives them that trust Him." It is not strange that, with such a chorister in charge, all solicitude about anthems and voluntaries vanished from the preacher's mind. Whatever the selection, I knew it would be full of worship alike in the sentiment and the rendering, would prepare the way for the Word of God ; and when the sermon was ended, no matter what the final thought, whether admonition, encouragement or appeal, I always felt sure that the chorister's heart was one with mine, and that I could commit the closing service to him, as I sometimes did, with perfect confidence that the impression sought to be produced would be deepened.

This was preëminently true of Mr. Bliss' management of the singing in all gatherings for prayer. He was a royal helper here. He loved such fellowship, could not bear to have things drag and grow listless and stupid, as they sometimes do. His sunny, buoyant nature could not tolerate such an atmosphere, his warm, fresh feelings brought him at once to the rescue. He would break out at such times with one of his ringing songs that would go through all hearts like the blast of a bugle, and set everything astir. He was especially fond of songs that magnified the name and grace of Christ, and urged to larger trust and consecration and engagedness in His service. "Free from the Law," "More Holiness give Me," "I gave My Life for Thee," The Half was never Told," "Hold fast till I Come," were among his favorites, and they would sometimes scatter the gloom and despondency, or coldness of a meeting, as a sudden burst of sunshine through a thick sky puts to rout clouds and fog. Indeed, a stupid, lifeless meeting with P. P. Bliss in it would have been a marvel. All through his songs and his words of witness breathed the spirit of absorbing devotion. With him the coming of the Lord was a Scripture truth, so real and vivid that his life felt the inspiration of it in everything he said or did. He felt profoundly that the Bridegroom might come at any moment, and it was hence his intense desire to have his work done, his lamp trimmed, and to be ready to enter into the marriage. During the last two years while engaged as an evangelist, he was rarely present in the prayer-meetings ; but whenever he was there, almost invariably before he spoke or sang, he gave expression to the feeling that possibly he might be witnessing for the last time. The very last evening when he met with us, he came forward near the close of the meeting, uttering this thought, sang as a word of counsel and encouragement to all young converts, a number of whom had been testifying during the evening, the song whose chorus is :

> Hold fast till I come,
> Hold fast till I come ;
> A bright crown awaits thee ;
> Hold fast till I come.

In his Sunday school relations, he was especially happy and beloved. It is safe to say that no school ever had a superintendent who held larger place in the children's hearts than he ; and it is easy to see why. He was an enthusiastic lover of children. It never cost him any effort to meet children on their level. for he lived there. He knew a child's nature by instinct, or rather he possessed such a nature, and could no more help gathering about him the little four and five-year-olds of the infant class, and talking to them in a way that every one of them understood wherever he was, than a florist could help gathering roses and japonicas and fuchsias about him, and talking to them day by day. And the same of older children. The consequence was, that whenever he appeared before the school, every face brightened instantly. Every eye was intent, every ear eager. He never had to ring for order while he was talking ; never had any rough, turbulent boys whom he could not interest and control. The look of his eye, the sound of his voice was all-potent. The members of his school, young and old, felt him to be a personal friend, and so he was. He knew very many of them by name. He entered keenly into all their childish experiences ; was always ready to listen to the unbosomings which they were eager to pour into his ears ; to answer their questions and give the counsel they sought. It was marvelous to see how completely and without effort he possessed their confidence, and how supremely he swayed them by his opinion. Whatever he said was law and gospel in the fullest sense ; and wherever he went, as it was his delight to go, among the children's homes, especially those of the humbler sort, in times of sickness, his sunny presence and cheery words and stirring songs were better than all medicines. Patience, courage, hopefulness always followed his visits ; and parents were as glad to see him as the children, and often as much helped by his coming.

Mr. Bliss' ability to teach children to sing was amazing, and it was compensation for a long pilgrimage to see him handle a school when training it musically. From the moment he named a piece, he seemed to inspire all with his enthusiasm. Not an eye would wander, not a face be dull. He would say a few pithy words, explaining the sentiment of the song, a few more, possibly, about the music and how to render it ; sing a strain or two alone, and then, after two or three repetitions, the school would march through and ring it out as if they had been familiar with it for months. It was as if he had the gift of infusing music into everybody. No matter how little musical culture or skill teachers and scholars had, no matter how out of key or out of time, they were naturally inclined to sing. Somehow when Mr. Bliss led, the difficulties and irregularities and discords seemed to disappear, and there was one grand thrill of feeling, one royal burst of harmony.

The best thing about this singing was that, like that of the choir gallery, it was never for show. Mr. Bliss would have abominated any attempt at musical display, or anything simply entertaining as truly on the part of children as adults. With him the Sunday school and all the departments and appliances of it meant salvation. He believed with his whole heart in the early conversion of children. He was wont to say that he could never remember the time when he did not trust in Christ as his Savior and desire to serve Him. He felt profoundly that when Jesus said " Suffer the little children to come unto Me and forbid them not, for of such is the kingdom of heaven," He meant to have parents and all understand that He was the children's Savior, and that in their tenderest years the little ones might know renewing grace and become the children of the Kingdom. He greatly coveted such early trust in Christ, and with increasing devotion brought to bear all the agencies at his command to secure it. Next to the word of God, he felt the instrumentality of song to be most potent and used it mightily. Praying before he sang, praying while he sang, and exhorting all others to sing prayerfully and in the spirit, he led the school. Many times he would stop in the middle of a song to lift up the cross, emphasize the love of Jesus, and urge every heart to immediate decision on the Lord's side. He often did it with tears—tears in his eyes and tears in his voice ; and time and again, as, with that wonderful pathos and sweetness of which he was such a master, he poured forth his soul in the affectionate entreaties of " Calling Now," or " Almost Persuaded," all hearts would melt as if touched of God, and the solemn hush that followed seemed like a moment of universal prayer and consecration.

God richly blessed this dear brother's songs and labors in the school. During his connection with it there was rarely a communion season without some of its members coming forward to unite with the church ; and if the names of all whom he helped by word and song to accept Jesus Christ as Savior, while he was Superintendent, could be called, there would rise up a great cloud of witnesses. Doubtless much of the seed sowed proved like that in the parable, seed by the wayside, in stony ground, among thorns, and came to naught. But there was left, nevertheless, a generous portion that brought forth, some thirty, some sixty, some an hundred fold ; and the harvest among the children from his sowing is only begun.

We saw but little of Mr. Bliss after he entered upon his work as an evangelist, but what we did see made us all feel that more and more the spirit of anointing was upon him. Whenever he could, he came back for a visit to the old place of toil and prayer, and never without stirring all our hearts by some word of cheer, or of incitement to larger devotion in the Master's service. Often he would set the blood bounding by a new song rendered as only he could do it ; and very likely he would follow this with a prayer, whose childlike simplicity and earnestness and pathos revealed how intimate his communion was with God, and how he longed to be more and more used in winning souls. It is not too much to say that during these last years Christ was in all his thoughts ; as one of his later songs expresses it :

My only song and story,
Is Jesus died for me ;
My only hope of glory
The cross of Calvary.

Would that the spirit of such a discipleship might pervade all our singers, our Sunday School superintendents, our teachers, our church members. Then there would be singing in the spirit, praying in the spirit, working in the spirit, and heaven would be kept jubilant over souls rescued from sin. May God help all who read the record of this consecrated life to enter into the secret of its joy and its power—to be determined not to know anything save Jesus Christ and Him crucified.

E. P. GOODWIN.

CHAPTER V.

DURING the winter of 1873-4, Mr. Bliss received many letters from Mr. Moody, then in Scotland, urging him to give up his business, drop everything and sing the Gospel. Similar letters came to the writer, urging that we should go out together and hold meetings. Mr. and Mrs. Bliss were ready for this, if they could see it as the Lord's will. Mrs. Bliss' characteristic remark was : "I am willing that Mr. Bliss should do anything that we can be sure is the Lord's will, and I can trust the Lord to provide for us, but I don't want him to take such a step simply on Mr. Moody's will." There was much prayer and much hesitation on Mr. Bliss' part in approaching a decision upon the matter. He doubted his ability to be useful in the work ; doubted whether the drawing he felt toward it was of the Lord or his own inclinations. Mr. Moody continued to write. One of his sentences I remember was : "You have not faith. If you haven't faith of your own on this matter, start out on my faith. Launch out into the deep." A solemn providence of God that occurred at this time, and very deeply impressed both Mr. Bliss and myself, is linked in the chain that drew us into the work. In November, 1874, my Christian brother and dear personal friend and nearest neighbor, Mr. H. G. Spafford, received a telegram from England announcing the drowning of his four dear children in the loss of the " Ville de Havre." His wife, who accompanied the children, had been rescued and sent the despatch. These friends were dear to Mr. Bliss and myself, and their affliction was a deep personal sorrow.

Mr. Spafford left at once for Europe, to bring home his wife, and while there had a conference with Mr. Moody relating to Mr.

Bliss going with me into Gospel work. Upon his return, he urged the matter upon us, and his words and representations were used of God in bringing us both to regard it as probable that we should respond to the call. Shortly after this return of Mr. Spafford, and while we were waiting for some opening to indicate the Lord's will, an interview on the cars with Rev. C. M. Saunders, of Waukegan, Illinois, led to our arranging to go there for three or four evenings, as an experiment. If the Lord blessed us and souls were converted, we would take it as indication of His will, that He called us into the work. Through Mr. Saunders I am furnished with copies of the following letters concerning these meetings :

ELGIN WATCH Co., CHICAGO, March 16th, 1874.

Bliss, Cole and myself, God willing, will be with you Tuesday, Wednesday and Thursday evenings, next week, March 24, 25 and 26.

D. W. WHITTLE

CHICAGO, March, 14, 1874.

Dear Brother Saunders : Bro. Whittle will write you that he and I are coming to Waukegan, Tuesday, 24th inst. I know that you and all God's people will pray for the Spirit's power to accompany the effort. Solicit the singers to come and assist me in the singing. Would like a good organ and all the " Sunshine " in town. * * Organ in front of congregation, if possible, and good light all over the room, I venture to suggest. Every time you think of our coming, offer a prayer that it may be purely for God's glory. Amen. Wife and brother unite in love to thee and thine.

Sincerely,   P. P. BLISS.

The Tuesday evening meeting was not an encouraging one, as to attendance, and had no marked result, except in the very powerful impression upon the minds of Bliss, dear brother Cole and myself, that the Lord was with us. The next day it rained and we looked for a still smaller audience, but it was twice as large. Before the meeting closed, there were blessed indications of the work of the Holy Spirit upon the people. The place became very solemn, and as dear Bliss sang " Almost Persuaded," every word seemed filled with power. In different parts of the house, sinners arose as he sang, presenting themselves for prayer, and souls that night rejoiced in Christ. Our hearts were very full, and a great responsibility was upon us. The next afternoon, we all three met in the study of the Congregational Church, where our meetings were held, and spent some hours in prayer. Bliss made a formal surrender of eve.ything to the Lord ; gave up his musical conventions ; gave up his writing of secular music ; gave up everything, and in a simple childlike, trusting prayer, placed himself, with any talent, any power God had given him, at the disposal of the Lord, for any use He could make of him in the spreading of His Gospel. Dear Cole united with us in this consecration. It was a wonderful afternoon. As I think back upon the scene in that little study, and recall Bliss' prayer, and the emotions that filled us all in the sense of God's presence, the room seems lit up in my memory with a halo of glory.

This meeting of consecration was followed by a wonderful meeting in the evening. Some twenty or more accepted Christ, and a spirit of deep conviction was upon many souls. We returned to Chicago in the morning, praising God—Bliss to find substitutes for his conventions, and I to resign my business position. From that Wednesday, March 25, 1874, up to December 15, 1876, when I parted from him no more to meet on earth, I never heard Mr. Bliss express a regret that he made this surrender, that he gave himself to God for His work. His income from his business at this time was good and growing. His reputation as a composer was recognized, and he looked forward with his wife to soon being in a condition where he could settle down and be at home, giving up his convention work. His decision involved the giving up of income, the simple trusting God for all means of support, the relinquishing of all plans for ever settling down in a home, a lowering of his reputation in the eyes of many well-meaning musical friends, who recognized his ability to become a leader in the art, and the taking up of a laborious, self-denying calling—a calling in which it is not possible for one to abide unless laborious and self-denying. None of these things that he gave up did Bliss ever speak of. He was as silent about them as the disciples in the Gospels, when, with their eyes on the Lord, they followed Him over Palestine, are silent about the boats, nets and fishes they left by the sea of Galilee. I think Bliss truly counted these things nothing compared with the joy of being a servant of Jesus Christ, and the gladness of being used to impart life by the Gospel to dead souls. On our way to Waukegan, that morning, he selected a verse which, said he, " let us keep as our watchword in the work." The verse is in Hebrews xii, 2 : " Looking unto Jesus, the Author and Finisher of our faith ; who, for the joy that was set before Him, endured the cross, despising the shame, and is set down at the right

hand of the throne of God." Many and many a time has his cheery
utterance of the words "Looking unto Jesus" chased away despondency, and given grace and courage for the trials of the way. There
is a strange silence on the earth to me, as the thought comes that
I am never to hear that voice here again. May my memory of
it ever be connected with these words, so dear to him, and may the
thought that he is up there forever with the Lord be to us all, by
the power of the Holy Spirit, a greater inspiration than was the
voice so loved, so missed.

It is not necessary that I should enter into any detailed account
of Mr. Bliss' work while an evangelist. The memorials printed
in this book are sufficient evidence of the acceptance of his labors to
the church of Christ, and of his endorsement by the ministers of
the Gospel of all evangelical denominations as one approved of
God. In the chapters devoted to his songs will be found such incidents as I can recall connected with his singing the Gospel. The
towns and cities he visited in the work were as follows : In 1874—
Waukegan and Turner Junction, Illinois; Geneva, Wisconsin ;
Elgin, Illinois ; Whitewater, Wisconsin ; Detroit, Michigan ; Pittsburgh, Pennsylvania. In 1875—Chicago; Louisville and Lexington,
Kentucky ; Nashville and Memphis, Tennessee ; St. Paul and Minneapolis, Minnesota ; Milwaukee, Wisconsin. In 1876—Racine and
Madison, Wisconsin ; St. Louis, Missouri ; Mobile, Montgomery
and Selma, Alabama ; Augusta, Georgia ; Kalamazoo and Jackson,
Michigan ; Peoria, Illinois—twenty-five in all. From all of these
places there will be *some* to meet him in glory and to recognize him
as the one through whose personal influence they were led to accept
salvation.

As memory runs back over the audiences assembled in these
various places to hear him sing, and who were often moved by his
melodies as the breath of wind moves the bending grain, now weeping, now exulting, now thrilled by the Christ exalted in his song,
I offer the fervent prayer that all who ever heard him sing on earth
may sing with him in Heaven ; and that any before whom these
lines may come, whose memory, with mine, runs back to meetings
where they were "Almost Persuaded," and almost rose as accepting
Jesus, as he sang, but are still unsaved, may now at once decide
and give themselves up to Christ. May all the singers whom he
loved and so often prayed for be ready, as he was, for the sum-

mons home, and may they join that choir of blood-washed ones on high, where he and his dear wife are now singing, "Saved by the Blood of the Crucified One." May all the dear ministers in these places, who loved him and prayed with him, and for him, be anointed with power from on high, to win souls, laboring as those who know not, as he knew not, how short the time may be.

During the last year of his life, Mr. Bliss had an increased desire to work for the children and young people. He conducted a daily meeting for them, and with most blessed results. Hundreds of them, I believe, have been led to Christ, intelligently and savingly, in his meetings. In Peoria, he expressed to me very decidedly his determination to work more earnestly in that direction. His tenderness of nature and sympathy fitted him specially for reaching the hearts of the young. They were drawn to him because they knew he loved them.

A little incident that occurred in Peoria will illustrate his sympathy for children. It was just before Christmas, and Mr. and Mrs. Bliss were busy each day in procuring presents to take home to little Paul and George, and to Grandma, and all at home. One day Bliss was on the street and noticed, as he was passing, a little girl, poorly clad, standing in front of a toy-store window, gazing intently and longingly at the dolls displayed in large numbers and in a pretty arrangement from large to small, in the window. He stopped at once, and kindly and earnestly said, "Now just pick out the one that you want, and you shall have it. I will go in and buy it for you." He would have been delighted to do so, he said—had already done it in his own mind—but the child looked around at him with a painful expression of distrust and unbelief, and, gathering her shawl over her head, hurried away, not heeding his repeated assurances that she could have a doll if she wanted it. "That is just the way sinners treat Christ," said he, as he told me about it. "I was real grieved that the little one wouldn't let me do for her what I wanted to, and that she distrusted me, when I just wished with all my heart to make her happy. I think I understand a little better how the Lord feels at our unbelief of His precious promises."

I wish all the dear young people and children who have ever attended Mr. Bliss' meetings to know how sincere and tender an interest he had in their welfare. He very much prized the testimonies of the children given to him on cards, or in little notes, and many of them are filed away among his papers. He had a faculty for interesting the children in the Scriptures, and secured their participation in the meetings by giving out texts and asking each to bring a verse upon the text and recite it. "Love," "Peace," "Grace," "Faith," "Believe," "Heaven," and other texts were used by him. Of course the singing was made a specialty of in his meetings. He sang a great deal with the children, and some *for* them. He always secured their attention to the sentiment of the hymns and the truth taught in them, before singing, and would have them pray with him for God to bless the singing. The singing was thus taken up out of the place of mere entertainment too often assigned it in meetings, and was made a spiritual power in worship and in preaching the Gospel. When he prayed, he usually had the children follow him audibly. After singing and prayer, he would have the texts repeated, and request that any who wished to confess Christ as their Savior should do so, after they had repeated their verse. Many a grown person has been led in this manner, in his meetings (for as many adults attended them as children), to overcome their timidity, and to know the joy that comes from obeying the word in Romans x, 10, by "confessing with the mouth the Lord Jesus." After recitation of texts and singing, he would give them a ten minute lesson from the word. The following are some of his outlines for these lessons :

HEAR AND REMEMBER.

Matt. xv, 10.	"Hear."	John xv, 20.	Remember.
Matt. xvii, 5.	"Hear *Him*."	Matt. vii, 12.	Do.
Mark iv, 24.	"*What*."	John ii, 5.	Do it.
Luke viii, 18.	"Now."	John xv, 14.	Do.

ILLUSTRATIONS.

"The man who loved music."
"The broken arm."
"Two girls who 'loved.'"

COME.

Gen. vii, 1.	Come *thou*.
Isaiah i, 18.	Come *now*.
Matt. xi, 28.	Come *unto me*.
Rev. xxii, 20.	Come, Lord Jesus.

Upon the blackboard he would have

<table>
<tr><td>C</td><td rowspan="3">O</td><td>M</td><td rowspan="3">E</td><td>Come.</td></tr>
<tr><td>H</td><td>M</td><td>Home.</td></tr>
<tr><td>L</td><td>V</td><td>Love.</td></tr>
</table>

"I AM."

John viii, 12. Light.
John x, 9. Door.
John xi, 11. Good Shepherd.

ILLUSTRATIONS.

"Know *Him*."
"Mr. Homer Book."
"Mute speaking Father."
"Sick boy told to *eat*."

"ALL THINGS."

2 Cor. iv, 14. For your sakes.
2 Cor. v, 17. Are become new.
2 Cor. v, 18. Are of God.
2 Cor. vi, 4. Approving ourselves.
2 Cor. vi, 10. Possessing *all things*.

These are given as illustrating his preparation for his meetings, and his method of using the Scriptures. I have wished to give them, and to briefly sketch his manner of conducting meetings, for the benefit others may derive as to methods of interesting the children in religious services, and also to have Mr. Bliss remembered as something more than a singer, in the evangelical work in which he was engaged. He was much used of God in preaching the word in the manner above set forth, as well as in singing. The services he has conducted alone in various parts of the country, which he used to call "praise meetings," have been much blessed, and were abundant evidence of his ability for the general work of an evangelist. It would be an injustice to his memory to think of him as a singer only, and to consider that the part he has borne in the work which has been owned of God was simply that of singing. We pray to the Lord of the harvest to raise up the *singer* to take his place in singing the Gospel; but shall we ever have again singer, poet, composer, preacher, all combined in one of like character with Philip Bliss? If necessary for the church, yes. By the grace of God he was what he was. But it seems to many of us that "take him for all in all, we ne'er shall look upon his like again." He has been given to us to show how beautiful the gifts of God may become when shining out through a Christian life, from a soul consecrated by the blood of Christ, and sanctified by the indwelling of the Spirit of God.

CHAPTER VI.

THOUSANDS of people who never saw Mr. Bliss feel that they knew and loved him through his hymns. To them and to the generation to come, the principal interest in his life will center around these productions of his pen. It is proposed to collect in this and following chapters such facts in regard to the composition and use of the best known and most widely used of his songs as will be of interest to the world.

The first song Mr. Bliss wrote, that was used in Sunday schools or Gospel meetings, is the piece found in Gospel Songs, entitled "If Papa were only Ready." He caught the song from reading in a religious paper of a little boy dying and telling his father, just before death came to take him away, that he was afraid "he would not come to heaven because he couldn't leave the store." He wrote the words and music in May, 1867, at Rome, Pennsylvania, and sent it on to Mr. Root, who was much pleased with it and caused its immediate publication. The following are the words:

IF PAPA WERE ONLY READY.

I should like to die, said Willie, if my papa could die too,
But he says he isn't ready, 'cause he has so much to do;
And my little sister Nellie says that I must surely die,
And that she and mamma—then she stopp'd, because it made me cry.

But she told me, I remember, once while sitting on her knee,
That the angels never weary, watching over her and me;
And that if we're good (and mamma told me just the same before),
They will let us into heaven when they see us at the door.

There I know I shall be happy, and will always want to stay ;
I shall love to hear the singing, I shall love the endless day ;
I shall love to look at Jesus, I shall love Him more and more,
And I'll gather water-lilies for the angel at the door.

There will be none but the holy—I shall know no more of sin ;
Though I'll see mamma and Nellie, for I know he'll let them in,
But I'll have to tell the angel, when I meet him at the door,
That he must excuse my papa, 'cause he couldn't leave the store.

Nellie says, that may be I shall very soon be called away ;
If papa were only ready, I should like to go to-day ;
But if I should go before him to that world of light and joy,
Then I guess he'd want to come to Heaven to see his little boy.

The books of songs by Mr. Bliss are as follows : "The Charm,"
1871 ; "The Song Tree," a collection of parlor and concert music,
1872 ; "The Sunshine," for Sunday Schools, 1873 ; "The Joy,"
for conventions and for church choir music, 1873 ; "Gospel
Songs," for Gospel meetings and Sunday Schools, 1874.

All of these books are copyrighted by John Church & Co., and
it is by their permission that the selections of Mr. Bliss' poetry,
given herewith, are taken, for the most part, from these books.
In addition to these publications, in 1875 he compiled, and in connection with Mr. Sankey edited, " Gospel Hymns and Sacred Songs,"
and in 1876, his last work was the preparation of the book known as
Gospel Hymns No 2, Mr. Sankey being associated with him as
editor.   These last two books are published by John Church & Co.
and Biglow & Main jointly—the work of Mr. Bliss in them, under
the copyright of John Church & Co.   Very many pieces of Mr.
Bliss' appear in the books of Geo. F. Root and H. R. Palmer, and
many were published in sheet music form.   A large number of his
popular pieces were published in " The Prize," a book of Sunday
School songs, edited by Geo. F. Root, in 1870.

From the above it will be seen that he was an industrious
worker.   From 1870 to 1876, six years, his pen was very busy.   The
above seven books, forty or fifty songs in sheet form, many pieces
in books of others in exchange for what they had furnished him,
with much miscellaneous writing as contributor to a musical journal,
and in other directions, and all this in connection with his convention, choir and Sunday school work up to 1874, and from that

time constantly in evangelistic work, make us marvel that he found time to do so much. It can only be explained by an admission of his wonderful gifts, that made his song writing not so much a matter of labor as a delight—an outflow of melody that *must* find expression, and a careful and laborious training of *fit methods* of expression of words and harmony for the melody with which his soul was filled. He was a very systematic and orderly man in all of his surroundings. Scrupulously neat in person and apparel, and with the sensitiveness of a woman in matters of taste, and a shrinking from all suggestion of vulgarity in anything in him or around him, his study or place of work, wherever he might be, partook of the nature of the man. His books and papers were in order, his desk or table usually clear, and his work prosecuted in a business-like manner. It pained him to have things in a "helter skelter" way about him. A misspelled word in a letter, or the wrong pronunciation of a word in an address, was to him like a note out of harmony in music. His penmanship was very neat, and his letters and manuscripts, as completed by him, are without blots or erasures. He never liked to write a letter with a pencil, and would always copy over a piece of music if possible, rather than to send it to his publishers with erasures. And yet none of his friends will remember him as being one known as a *precise* man, in a manner to make others *feel* preciseness in his company. His joyous nature, and happy and good humored way of noticing others' defects, and of carrying out his rules, kept away any uncomfortable feeling on the part of any one associated or brought in contact with him. His tenderness was such he would not have injured the feelings of a child for worlds.

Mr. Bliss' best songs were never studied themes connected with the Sunday school lessons of those years. *They* were studied pieces, and, he himself often said, were not a success. They did not have inspiration in them. He could not sit down at any time, and upon a given theme write a given song that would be a success. Sometimes a melody would come to him, and he would work it out and write it down and wait for words. Sometimes the lines for a chorus would be the first suggestion of a hymn. Sometimes the last verse of a hymn would form in his mind and would be written down, and hymn and tune be worked up from it. More often the whole hymn, in theme, structure of words, chorus and tune, would be born at

once, and all written out together. This, he has told me, was true
of the hymns that have been most sung. "Hold the Fort,"
"Down Life's dark Vale we Wander," "More to Follow," "Jesus
Loves Me," "Windows open toward Jerusalem," were written in
this manner. His own soul was full and was thrilled with the
themes that took possession of him. My most vivid recollections
of him will always be of his entire self abandonment of joy in the
consciousness of being used of God in bringing out in song some
precious Gospel truth, some exalting view of Christ. He has come
to me often with the theme of a hymn, and with his face shining
and eyes moist, explained his plan and purpose as in his mind, and
asked me to thank God and pray with him that God might bless the
song. He never felt that the songs *originated* with him. They
seemed to him to come *through* him from God. As he grew in the
knowledge of God's word, he would marvel at the truth he had
expressed in his songs without knowing it. At the time of writing
"Hold the Fort," he had no clear views as to the testimony of the
Scriptures, that the attitude of the Christian should always be the
daily expectation and desire of the personal return of Jesus Christ.
When this truth came in power into his soul, he recognized the
purpose of God in his writing the hymn, and that its use by the
church all around the world was on account of its harmony with
the word of God, upon a truth intended to arouse Christians.

   After his consecration to Christ for His service in saving souls,
Mr. Bliss' experience crystalized more and more into an apprehension of a personal Savior. Christ risen—Christ ever present
with us—Jesus, the real, living, personal Jesus of the Gospels,
came closer and closer to him. His communion with Christ was
uninterrupted. And his songs in these days abounded with Christ.
The last year of his life, nearly all the songs he wrote contain the
three themes of Gospel testimony, Christ died for our sins, He
lives for our justification, He is coming again in a glory which we
are to share. He did not *plan* these hymns with any *purpose* to
teach these truths, and was surprised himself when his attention
was called to the fact of the uniformity of their testimony in these
directions. He simply wrote of what filled his own heart and had
come to his own soul. "The Half was never Told," "No other
Name is Given," "Hallelujah ! what a Savior," "Are your Windows open toward Jerusalem ?" "Hallelujah ! He is Risen," "At

the Feet of Jesus," "Hallelujah ! 'tis Done," all of which appear in Gospel Hymns No 2, are examples of the truth of this statement. It is also very suggestive to notice the character of teaching, in words furnished by other authors with music written by him, that appear in this same work. I am sure that he did not *contemplate* any test of this kind in making his selections from scores of manuscript songs that were monthly sent to him; he simply set music to the words that inspired music in his soul. I do not think he ever exchanged a word with any one as to any distinctive character of teaching in the songs selected ; but all these words that he selected convey the same leading truths. " Look away to Jesus," " Hold fast till I Come," "Out of the Ark," "Till He come," " It is well with My Soul," etc., are examples. Mr. Bliss' songs can only be understood and appreciated by an understanding of the *reality to him* of the truths they convey, as connected with a personal Christ. The words he sang so grandly—

> Christ Jesus is my all in all,
> My comfort and my love,
> My life below, and He shall be
> My joy and crown above—

just filled his soul. I believe he had no more thought, in singing them, of doing anything for the entertainment of people, or to excite admiration, than the meadow lark mounting to heaven, singing as it soars. He sang from an overflowing heart to the praise of his Savior. The last words that I know of his writing were the two pieces, " My Redeemer," and " I've passed the Cross of Calvary." Nothing that he ever wrote made him more happy. I can see him now, as he came into my room at Peoria and stood by my table, with the words of the latter piece written in pencil, and I can hear his earnest voice as he read the verses and called my attention to the " *empty tomb* " and the " *vantage ground ;* " and the tears filled his eyes as he stood for a moment and spoke of the risen Christ, the acceptance we have in Him, and the victory over sin and over the flesh that faith in such acceptance gives the believer. Now he said, " If the Lord will give me a tune for this, I believe it will be used to bring some souls on to the mountain." The Lord gave him a tune during the last week of his life at Rome. He sang it to the family with inspiring effect, but the written music then used was burned at Ashtabula. It was one of a few pieces that he placed in his satchel, to look over during his journey. The family are all musicians, but cannot recall the melody that inspired them that evening, and we shall not hear it as he sang it until we stand with him in the rapidly-hastening-on resurrection morning, and know, with him, the fullness of Christ's resurrection power. I think that then, among the voices of the redeemed, we shall distinguish his, and hush our praises for a moment to listen to the tune the Lord had given him as he sings—

> Oh, glorious height of vantage ground,
> Oh, blest victorious hour!

God grant to all who read a part in that first resurrection.

In writing, Mr. Bliss had a marvelous command of words and facility in selecting the very happiest phrases to express his thought. A favorite entertainment with him was to have a word selected, and each of the party present make as many words as possible from the letters contained in the word chosen. After each had written out all the words he could conjure, and lists were compared, it would always be found that he had two or three words the most. He loved to make adjectives and alliterations of words, commencing with the same letter, as in the lines,

> "Earth's *fairest flowers* will *droop* and *die*.
> Life's dearest joys *flit fleetest* by."

He had all the gifts of a natural poet in instinct and imagination, and the faculty of expressing his thoughts in fitting musical words and sentences. There was a charm in the nicely balanced, sensitive criticism which he would in a deprecating way give upon verses submitted him for criticism, or which he himself had written, that is very pleasant to recall.

The pieces that contain most of the true genius of poetry, in the latest edition of Gospel Hymns, as viewed by those of critical taste, would probably be the hymn "Eternity," by Miss Ellen Gates, and "Arise and Shine," by Miss Mary Lathbury ; and no words that he ever set to music ever so inspired Mr. Bliss, or so satisfied his poetic instincts. He could not read or sing the words without enthusiasm. Indeed, the music he wrote for them shows how keenly in sympathy with the words he must have been. Never did music more aptly express the heart that beats, in living words, than the inspiring melody of "Arise and Shine," and the sweet, solemn strains of "Eternity," as completed by him.

It is not claimed for Mr. Bliss that the works he leaves behind him would give him a reputation as a *great* poet. He was very far from classing himself in the list of poets at all. But it is claimed that he possessed the true poetic genius in a far more than ordinary degree, and that, had his life been spared, he would have given expression to poetry equal to the very best of our sacred hymns. There will be many who will claim this for some of the pieces that he has left behind him. Let the hymns speak for themselves, and may his prayer be answered, that the gifts, the style and the person of the author be lost sight of in the theme they present.

It has been stated that Mrs. Bliss wrote several hymns which were published in Mr. Bliss' books under the name of "Paulina." This is a mistake. So far as is known, Mrs. Bliss never wrote any hymns or songs. Two pieces of very popular music were suggested by her to Mr. Bliss, and were written out by him and published as her compositions. One of them was "I will Love Jesus;" the other, "Rock of Ages." Both melodies are very beautiful, and were Mrs. Bliss' suggestion. The words, "I will Love Jesus," were written by Mrs. Dr. Griswold, of Chicago, for many years a friend of Mr. Bliss, and the writer of many popular hymns set to music by Mr. Bliss, George F. Root, and other composers. Her *nom de plume* has always been "Paulina." The above and three other pieces written by Mrs. Griswold, viz., "We're going Home To-morrow," "Hold Fast till I Come," "Who is on the Lord's Side?" with music by Mr. Bliss, appear in Gospel Hymns. The name "Paulina" was associated with Mrs. Bliss in the Memorial Services held in Chicago, and the impression there given that she was the writer of the hymns credited to that name.

Several pieces known as Mr. Bliss', and made popular by his music, will be missed from this collection. They are omitted because the words were not written by him. Several of them were changed by him to adapt them to the music. Many of them have an entire verse or words for chorus added by Mr. Bliss; but no pieces, so far as could be known, have been printed in his memoirs, except those of which he was the sole author. Among popular pieces known as

Bliss' hymns, the following, with the names of the authors of the words, are given :

" Only Remembered,"	Dr. H. Bonar.
" What hast Thou done for Me ?"	Miss Frances Havergal.
" I bring My Sins to Thee,"	Miss Frances Havergal.
" What shall the Harvest be ?"	Mrs. Emily L. Oakey.
" Look Away to Jesus,"	Rev. Henry Burton.
" Precious Promise,"	Nathaniel Niles.
" Crown of Rejoicing,"	Rev. J. B. Atchinson.
" Eternity,"	Ellen H. Gates.
" Arise and Shine,"	Mary A. Lathbury.
" Waiting and Watching for Me,"	Unknown.
" Till He Come,"	Rev. E. H. Bickersteth.
" The New Song,"	Rev. A. T. Pierson.
" It is well with my Soul,"	H. G. Spafford.
" Go bury thy Sorrow,"	Unknown.
" He Knows,"	Alice Carey.

The latter piece was found in manuscript, set to music, among Mr. Bliss' papers, and was supposed, by friends, to have been written by him, and has been so spoken of. It was certainly among the last pieces that he set to music, and the thoughts it expresses, so appropriate to what awaited him, were vividly upon his mind in changing the words and arranging the music during his last days. It can thus truly be regarded as his last song. But the sweet poem he used was from the pen of the gifted Alice Carey. All of these corrections and the giving of credit to whom it is due are so in accordance with the spirit of Mr. Bliss, that the writer takes pleasure in making these remarks.

CHAPTER VII.

IN writing of the last days of Mr. Bliss, his own words near the close of 1876 are recalled, and naturally introduce what comes to the mind, and lead to a brief resumé of the work of the whole of the last year of his life. He counted it a year of *special* mercy and blessing. He had been permitted to carry out his plans as to places he would like to visit, and as to songs he would like to publish, and had had his prayers answered in the conversion of friends, and deeper spiritual experience for himself and others. The reader can but notice, as he follows him through the year, that, by the mercy of God, his work rounded out to completion, and it was a year passed very much as he would have liked to have had it, had he known that upon the very last day of the year his friends would have been searching for his body, and that his work on earth was to end with 1876.

In January of that year, Mr. Bliss was at Racine and Madison, Wisconsin, and was much blessed and very happy in Gospel work. Christians were much revived, and many unsaved in both places were led to Christ. In the latter place he became much attached to Rev. Mr. Bright, pastor of the Baptist Church, who, a few months later, fell dead in his pulpit from disease of the heart. Mr. Bliss was much impressed by the news of his sudden death, and expressed himself as wishing just such a departure.

In the latter part of January, Mr. Bliss went to St. Louis, where he remained until March, singing in the Gospel meetings held in the Rink, and holding a service of his own for the young people in Dr. Ganse's (Presbyterian) Church, which was largely attended, and will be long remembered by scores of the young people in St. Louis.

5

He sang the Gospel Hymns in the Jail and Reform Schools and in nearly all the reformatory institutions, while there. In March, he went
to Mobile, Alabama, to fill an appointment for a Gospel meeting.
The route chosen was by rail to Vicksburg, Mississippi, and from
thence by steamer to New Orleans, and by rail from there to Mobile.
Mrs. Bliss accompanied him, and the trip was a great source of pleasure to them both. The new section of country, the scenes of interest connected with the war, the rapid entering into spring, as they
traveled south, all conspired to make the journey a delightful one.
In the evening upon the steamboat, Mr. Bliss entertained the passengers for half an hour or more in singing at the piano ; and at the
close, when Captain and all who could come in to the cabin were
collected, he would sing a familiar hymn, and then very pleasantly
propose and lead in worship. The visit to Mobile was a delightful
one. The pastors, the Mayor (an excellent Christian man), and
Christian people generally, manifested the utmost cordiality and
kindness, and did all in their power to make the visit a happy one,
and the meetings a success. God was pleased to add His blessing
upon the efforts put forth, and many were impressed by Gospel
truth, and many were led to confess Christ. The meetings of Mr.
Bliss for young people, held in the Baptist church, were much
blessed. The church was crowded each afternoon, and very many
were led to the Savior by his preaching of Christ in song, in Bible
instruction, and personal appeal.

Never did his singing seem more effective than in one of the
meetings held in this city, on Sunday evening, in the Opera House.
The audience was composed entirely of men, and crowded every
part of the house. He sang as solos, " Pull for the Shore," " Nothing but Leaves," " What shall the Harvest Be ?" and " Memories
of Childhood," with great power. A solemnity came over all who
listened as his deep, sweet voice took up the mournful cadence,
" Nothing but Leaves," and when he sang the " Trundle Bed,"
there was hardly a dry eye in the audience. Nearly two hundred
men sought an interest in the prayers of Christians, that they might
be saved. Mr. and Mrs. Bliss were very happy in the work in
Mobile, and cherished pleasant memories of the friends there.

After ten days in Mobile, Mr. Bliss went to Montgomery, and
sang in the meetings held in the City Hall. Great interest was at
once manifested, and the meetings were largely attended. The

pastors and people here, as at Mobile, were most hospitable and cordial in the welcome extended to their Northern brethren. Here, as in Mobile, special pains were taken to hold services for the colored people, and arrangements made for their attending the general meetings. Mr. Bliss' singing was greatly enjoyed by the colored people, and he in turn was much moved by their wild and plaintive melodies. When he had been singing the song of his composing, "Father, I'm Tired," they would be broken down in uncontrollable emotion. His labors at Montgomery were owned of God, and closed in a meeting participated in by all the pastors, and where scores of souls confessed to a hope in Christ.

From Montgomery Mr. Bliss went to Selma, having as fellow-passengers General Tom Thumb and family. Upon arriving at Selma, a crowd was found gathered at the depot to see the General. Mr. Bliss found it difficult to get off the steps of the car, and while standing for a moment before the staring crowd, said solemnly: "Gentlemen, you are mistaken, I am not Tom Thumb." The people with a hearty laugh made way for him. Selma has become well known in Christian circles throughout the country, for the consecrated activity of a band of Christian laymen, who, under the inspiration of Hall and Cree, some five years ago, organized there the first Young Men's Christian Association of Alabama. These dear brethren made Christian work in their city a delight to their visitors. Their hearts and homes were wide open—their enthusiasm and zeal in the work unbounded. An immense cotton warehouse was cleaned up and seated for the meetings; ladies and gentlemen from the church choirs came in to supply a fine chorus; the sainted Rev. Alfred Morrison—taken to heaven just a little before Mr. Bliss—and all the pastors, gave a hearty support to the effort, and a blessed work was enjoyed. Here, as in Montgomery and Mobile, Mr. Bliss conducted young people's meetings, with precious fruit for Christ.

Mrs. Bliss returned to Chicago from Selma, to arrange for closing up their house for a summer's removal to Rome, leaving Mr. Bliss to fill an appointment at Augusta, Georgia. The trip to Augusta was made via the Selma and Dalton Railroad through Rome, Georgia, and from thence to Atlanta, to give Mr. Bliss an opportunity to visit Kenesaw Mountain, where occurred the incident that gave rise to the song, "Hold the Fort." He stopped at

Marietta on a beautiful April morning, and, after dinner with the writer, rode out two miles to the mountain. The carriage left us about three-fourths of a mile from the summit, and we pursued our journey on foot. The violets were just in blossom, and we paused frequently to stoop and gather them, or to cut canes from the young hickory trees, by the side of the path. Upon the summit, the ruins of the earthwork near which General Polk was killed, and part of the framework of the signal station from which Sherman had the message signaled to "hold the fort," were found.

It was a bright, clear, sunny day, and the landscape for miles in every direction was before our view from this remarkable elevation. Altoona Mountain, where the fort was held, could be plainly seen twenty miles to the north ; and the intervening valley across which Sherman hurried his troops was at our feet.

Bliss enjoyed the scene to the full. He took in all of its beauty and all of its inspiration. We read the passage concerning the coming of our Lord from heaven—knelt in prayer and consecration—and then sang "Hold the Fort," looking out upon the distant mountain, looking up to the clear blue sky, and hoping and almost expecting that Jesus might then appear, so near He seemed to us that April day. I thank my Heavenly Father that I was led to so urge my friend and brother to make that mountain visit. He reckoned it, while he lived, as one of his blessed days, and the memory of it to me is, and will continue to be while life lasts, a transfiguration scene. How little did we think that day, that ere the year should close, for *him* the battle would be won, and he be taken to the mountains of glory, to signal for his Lord to the soldiers in the valley, "Cheer, my Comrades, Cheer." May the voice that rang out so grandly from the summit of Kenesaw that glorious afternoon still go ringing on around the earth in the same message there sung, "I am Coming," hastening the appearing of the Lord and the glad day when we shall be caught up with living and departed loved ones, "to meet the Lord in the air ; and so shall we ever be with the Lord." "Amen. Even so, come quickly, Lord Jesus."

We conclude this chapter with Mr. Bliss' glorious hymn, "Hold the Fort," with the story which suggested it.

During October, 1864, just before Sherman began his famous march to the sea, while his army lay camped in the neighborhood of Atlanta, the army of Hood in a carefully prepared movement passed the right flank of Sherman's army, and gained his rear, commenced the destruction of the railroad leading north, burning blockhouses and capturing the small garrisons along the line. Sherman's army was put in rapid motion, following Hood, to save the supplies and larger posts, the principal of which was located at Altoona Pass, a defile in the Altoona range of mountains, through which ran the railroad. General Corse, of Illinois, was stationed here with a brigade of troops, composed of Minnesota and Illinois regiments, in all about 1,500 men, Colonel Tourtelotte being second in command. A million and a half of rations were stored here, and it was highly important that the earthworks commanding the Pass and protecting the supplies should be held. Six thousand men, under command of General French, were detailed by Hood to take the position. The works were completely surrounded and summoned to surrender. Corse refused, and sharp fighting commenced. The defenders were slowly driven into a small fort upon the crest of the hill. Many had fallen, and the result seemed to render a prolongation of the fight hopeless. At this moment, an officer caught sight of a white signal flag, far away across the valley, twenty miles distant, upon the top of Kenesaw Mountain. The signal was answered, and soon the message was waved across from mountain to mountain :

"Hold the Fort; I am coming.   W. T. SHERMAN."

Cheers went up ; every man was nerved to the full appreciation of the position ; and, under a murderous fire, which killed or wounded more than half the men in the fort—Corse himself being shot three times through the head, Colonel Tourtelotte taking command, though himself badly wounded—they held the fort for three hours, until the advance guard of Sherman's army came up. French was obliged to retreat.

No incident of the war illustrates more thrillingly the inspiration imparted by the knowledge of the presence of the commander, and that he is cognizant of our position, and that, doing our utmost, he will supplant our weakness by speedy reinforcements. So, the message of Sherman to the soldiers of Altoona becomes the message of the Great Commander, who signals ever to all who fight life's battle, "Hold the Fort."

In May, 1870, Mr. Bliss accompanied me to Rockford, Illinois, to sing at a Sunday School Convention. He there heard me relate the above incident as an illustration of the inspiration derived by the Christian from the thought of Christ as our Commander and of His coming to our relief. The song was born at once in his mind, and on his return to Chicago, while at my house, he wrote it out and published it in sheet music form.

HOLD THE FORT.

Ho! my comrades, see the signal
  Waving in the sky!
Reinforcements now appearing
  Victory is nigh!

CHORUS—"Hold the fort, for I am coming,"
    Jesus signals still.
      Wave the answer back to heaven,
      —"By thy grace, we will."

See the mighty host advancing,
  Satan leading on;
Mighty men around us falling,
  Courage almost gone:

See the glorious banner waving,
  Hear the bugle blow:
In our Leader's name we'll triumph
  Over every foe.

Fierce and long the battle rages,
  But our Help is near;
Onward comes our Great Commander
  Cheer, my comrades, cheer!

CHAPTER VIII.

MR. BLISS remained in Augusta but five days, but was much used of God during that time. His singing made a deep impression on the people, and his earnest words of testimony were owned in the conversion of many to Christ. On Easter Sunday he sang in the open air, at a meeting held in the court-house square. Between three and four thousand people were present, and gave the most rapt attention as he sang "Hallelujah, He is Risen," and other Gospel songs. His afternoon service was crowded with people, and much religious interest immediately developed.

April 17th, Mr. Bliss left Augusta for Chicago. Here he packed away books and papers, and made arrangements to store away furniture until he and his family should return at the close of the year to again make a home. The books then put away he was never to see again. It was to him a final disposition of his earthly effects. With wife and children he left Chicago, May 1st, for Rome, Pennsylvania, the old home, intending here to pass the summer in rest and in writing songs for the winter campaign, and commencing the work again in October. It was a very happy summer to him. The little invalid George was greatly benefited by the change of air and scene, and rapidly grew well and strong. Old friends came to visit them, and many dear familiar scenes and friends were visited by them. During the summer, a Normal Institute was held in Towanda, and one beautiful Saturday, all the singers came up in carriages to Rome, and passed the day with Mr. Bliss. He was happy as a child, with the pleasure of the meeting with old-time friends, and the singing under the trees of the old-time songs. He attended for

.a few days the Sunday School Parliament conducted by Rev. W. F.
Crafts, at "Thousand Island Park ;" visited the Philadelphia Exposition ; sang at the Chautauqua Assembly, and greatly enjoyed its
sessions and the intercourse with Christian friends there, and passed
a week, that he counted a very delightful one, at the home of Mr.
Moody at Northfield, Massachusetts.   Mrs. Bliss was his constant
companion during the summer, at all of these places.   Mr. J. H.
Vincent, conductor of the Chautauqua Assembly, thus writes of
Mr. Bliss' services there and his personal recollections of him :

The fearful tragedy of last Friday evening sent a thrill of horror throughout the country, before the names of the unfortunate victims had been announced.   But what was the consternation and grief of the American church,
when the telegraph made known the fact that among the unrecognized or un-
recovered passengers was the evangelist and singer, P. P. Bliss, who, through
his many songs, and especially through his association with Major Whittle in
evangelistic labor, was so well and so widely known.

Mr. Bliss was on his way to Chicago to engage in special labors.   I have the
impression that he had been summoned there to assist in the meetings of the
week of prayer.   He was accompanied by his lovely and devoted wife, who
went down with him in the fated train, and who with him entered the Fa
ther's house.

According to the report of one of the rescued passengers, Mr. Bliss, after
the accident, escaped from the car, and then returned to save his wife.   Finding
that she could not be brought out, he resigned himself to her doom, and they
perished together.

Mr. Bliss was one of the noblest and one of the gentlest of men.   He had
the delicacy of a woman and the strength of a man.   His physique was magnificent.   I think he was one of the most handsome men I ever met.   Large,
well proportioned, graceful, with a fine, manly face, full of expression.   That
body of his was a grand instrument of music, and from its strength came forth
sweetness and power.   His voice was deep, of wonderful compass and pathos.
As it rang out through the woods at Chautauqua, the most thoughtless would
stop and listen.   Its marvelous magnetic charm was intensified by the energy
of the Divine Spirit, which so thoroughly possessed the body and soul of the
sweet singer.   To the utmost transparency of his pure and simple character he
added a fervent and childlike faith.   He was a rare Christian.   He knew and
believed and enjoyed and lived and preached and sang the Gospel of Christ.
His songs were for the glory of Christ.   I never knew a man more thoroughly
imbued with the Christian spirit.   He had one aim and one work in life.   He
was always on the look-out for souls.   He coveted, above everything else, spiritual results.   At our "Sunday School Assembly," in private conversation, in
the prayer-meetings, in the eventide conferences, on the platform, everywhere,
he seemed absorbed in this one great work.   Last evening I received from a

personal friend and Chautauqua Sunday School worker a letter in which the
following allusion to Mr. Bliss will illustrate the impression he made :

"I do not know how it has appeared to you, but I have been impressed with
the idea that Brother Bliss grew very rapidly in grace the last year. I noticed,
for instance, a great difference between the Syracuse Convention of 1875 and
your Chautauqua meeting of last summer. He came to the Lake full of the
Holy Ghost and of faith, and all his work was accompanied by divine power.
You may not have noticed it, but I saw a change from his very first utterance
on the platform ; and I certainly never knew one more happy in his selections,
suggestions, etc. I remember, in one of the deeply impressive meetings when
a soul said he would '*try* to seek the Lord,' quick as thought Mr. Bliss said to
him ' spell it—t-r-u-s-t.' In the meetings you assigned to me I found him a
helper indeed from the time he reached the grounds, prompt, unassuming, but
most decided, and with that earnest, serious manner befitting the winner of
souls. The felicity of his hymn and tune selections is generally known, but the
force of his Christian character, his directness, energy and downright devotion
should be emphasized now that we have lost him."

One of the holiest, Mr. Bliss was one of the cheeriest of men. His was not
a somber piety. There was no touch of asceticism in his nature. He was as
simple as a child, and full of genial humor. His personal letters overflow with
playfulness, puns, rhymes, and personal thrusts of the wittiest but always of
the most generous character. He lived in the light. It was the light of the
Lord, and that is the light of love. He never had anything but good to say of
his brethren. He never carped nor criticised. He saw in others what he had
most of in himself. He "took to" people. He loved his fellow men.

I am not competent to speak of Mr. Bliss as a musician. No doubt many of
his songs lack the fire of true poetry and the ring of the immortal music, but
when he sang them the words became poetry, and the melodies the very soul
of music. Many of his productions have real merit, and will live and be sung
for a hundred years to come. They are charged with the sentiment and the
force of the living Gospel. "I am so glad that our Father in Heaven" will be
a child-song in the church of the future. "If there's only one song" of his
that remains, it will be that one. His "Almost Persuaded" has the solemnity
of eternity in it. Many a soul has been led by it to immediate decision. "Still
there's More to Follow," has kindled the faith of the believer and led him to
seek more of the wondrous " grace" and " love" and " power" which are the
burden of it. "The Light of the World is Jesus" is a song which derives peculiar significance from the tragic end of its author. Did he sing at the last:

No darkness have we who in Jesus abide ?

That the prayer of the song " When Jesus Comes," was fulfilled in his last
moments I cannot doubt.

Oh, let my lamp be burning,
When Jesus comes.

I can hear him sing again, out of the tempest in which his earthly bark was foundered, as his redeemed spirit looked upon the shores of the glorious land just beyond:

> Bright gleams the morning, sailor, uplift the eye,
> Clouds and darkness disappearing, glory is nigh !
> Safe in the life-boat, sailor, sing evermore,
> " Glory, glory, hallelujah ! pull for the shore."

Mrs. Bliss was in every way worthy of the noble companion of her life and death.   Like him she was remarkably pure and simple.   She was his helper in couventions, and she encouraged him to put forth his earliest efforts as a musician.   How her rich alto voice would pour forth its volumes of music as they stood together on the Chautauqua platform !   I have heard them again and again sing at night to an immense concourse of people, and amidst the stillness of the grave the people would hear these voices of the Lord calling to them as out of eternity.

And the orphaned children !   How often in our travels together have those dear parents talked of the treasures of heart and home.   May the Father of the fatherless be the protector of the little darlings !   I sincerely hope that Mr. Moody's call for a penny collection in all the Sunday Schools of the country, January 14, will receive a prompt and liberal response.

The circumstances combined to render the disaster of the Friday evening— that fearful holocaust—the most horrible of all modern accidents.   The terrible crash of eleven cars as they fell seventy feet, the howling winds, the crushing ice, the freezing waters, the drifting, blinding snow, the raging fires, and the black, starless skies !   What agony did the victims experience !   No mortal tongue can describe it !

But that tempest was to our dear Bliss and his wife the "whirlwind" in which they were caught up, as by a "chariot of fire," into the kingdom of the Eternal.   Whether killed by the fall, or the waters, or the fire, it mattered little to them.   Whether the struggle was for but a moment, or protracted for many minutes, it was for them to look the dear Lord in the face—the Lord whom they had trusted and loved so long—and all was well.   And all now is well.

How can we account for such a wonderful visitation ?   Are good men so plentiful that the Lord can remove one so useful just at the time of his largest promise ?   What *does* it all mean ?

Well, we are not called upon to explain it.   God does not require His servants to account for or to defend His administration.   But we do see a few things in the visitation which give us some light and consolation.

1. The departed brother and his wife were ready.   They were ripe for heaven.   Why should we mourn or wonder when the chorus of the skies is made stronger and sweeter ?

2. The songs our dear brother wrote are still with us.   And they have received a new sweetness and significance and power by the tragic end of the singer of them.

3. This death has startled into new activity and consecration the workers

in all the churches.   Who can estimate the intensified convictions, the strength-ened purposes, the redoubled diligence among that blessed brotherhood who are at work in America—and all this, under God, caused by this solemn call.

4. By the peculiar method of. the divine providence in the present case, a holy Christian life is brought before the public.   Brother Bliss now preaches with a tongue of fire to the millions.   Tens of thousands who had never seen nor even heard of the departed are now brought face to face with his lovely character, and with the Christ he so faithfully proclaimed.

5. But is there no ministry in the sphere to which he has been removed, for such a royal soul as his?

Dear Bliss!   The memories will come—his face, his noble form, his gentle manners, his fervent prayers and appeals, his deep absorption in the one beau-tiful work of his life!   Farewell, dear friend!   Our hearts bleed at the thought that we shall see him no more here!   The world seems lonely without him! But we shall meet yonder!

J. H. VINCENT

Plainfield, N. J., January 4, 1877.

While at Northfield, in September, Mr. Bliss accompanied Mr. Moody to Greenfield, Brattleboro, Keene and adjacent towns, and sang at meetings Mr. Moody conducted.   He writes : "September 18, 1876.—Just returned from a week with Bro. Moody, in his home at Northfield, driving one hundred miles over Vermont, Massachu-setts and New Hampshire hills, and holding *eleven meetings.*" He greatly enjoyed this visit, as did also Mrs. Bliss, although both would laughingly mention Mr. Moody's habit of making the best use of his visitors that he could, as manifest by his using them at eleven meetings in a week.

October 1st, Mr. Bliss arrived in Chicago, and was present at Moody and Sankey's opening service.   He was the guest, at this time, of Mr. H. M. Thompson, of the Brevoort House, and here com-pleted several of the songs that appeared in Gospel Hymns No. 2. He did not participate in any of the Chicago meetings in a public way, but for three weeks was a constant attendant, and was greatly blessed in the remarkable services that opened Mr. Moody's work in Chicago, and in the personal contact with Mr. Moody and Mr. Sankey, with the latter of whom he spent most of his time, remov-ing for a couple of weeks to Mr. Sankey's hotel, that they might be uninterruptedly together.   Until this time they had never been much together in the work, but had arranged for their hymn books mostly by correspondence.   Now, they had what both had long desired—a season of personal conference, that cemented more closely the bonds of brotherhood between them.

The hundreds of those who have compared and criticised these two men, and, judging of what is in us all *by nature*, have thought of them as in any manner envious or jealous of one another, would have a clearer apprehension of what the grace of God in the heart can do, if they could have known the loving relationship that existed between them. It was a scene long to be remembered, to be with them alone for an hour in the room at the Pacific Hotel, as they compared and tested and criticised the songs to be used in their meetings. First, one would be at the organ rendering a song, then the other, and both laughing, crying and praying together over their work. They rejoiced in each other's gifts, and praised God for the honor conferred upon them in being used in His service. Mr. Bliss would never listen, if he could avoid it, to depreciation of others, and in all the writer's fellowship with him, he cannot recall an unkind or envious expression or act toward those whom he may have esteemed better singers or of greater reputation than himself. God answered to him in a remarkable degree his prayer,

> Only an Instrument, ready His praises to sound at His will,
> Willing, should He not require me, in silence to wait on Him still.

He could sit and listen to the singing of others, and pray for them, and rejoice in God's using them, without a thought to mar his communion with God. During this sojourn in Chicago, many precious gatherings of brethren consecrated to evangelistic work were enjoyed by Mr. Bliss. Needham and Stebbins, Moorhouse, Charles Inglis, Rockwell, Morton, Jacobs, Farwell, Spafford, Dean and others were frequently together in those days, dining with Moody, and discussing Gospel truth or plans of work, or in Bliss' room listening to some new song. These brethren and others engaged in the work were all dear to Mr. Bliss, and were many times mentioned by name in his prayers. He delighted to hear of the blessing of God upon their labors, and to see of their own growth in grace.

October 21st, the brethren separated for their different posts near Chicago. Mr. Bliss went to Kalamazoo, Michigan, Mrs. Bliss accompanying him. The evening of their arrival, they were entertained at Rev. Mr. Spencer's, where, with thoughtful hospitality, all the pastors of the city were gathered to give them welcome. It was a very pleasant and profitable meeting, and both Mr. and Mrs. Bliss often recurred to it as having given them much pleasure. The meetings held here were participated in by all the ministers, and from the first were much blessed. Mr. Bliss conducted a young people's meeting here as in other places, and with happy results. Many there look upon him as the instrument in God's hands of leading them to Christ. He sang in the young ladies' seminary, and at the Baptist College, and in many private residences to the sick and invalid ones. The dear friend there, who for seven years or more has been confined to his room, will well remember the sunshiny day, when Mr. Bliss came and sang to him the "Ninety and Nine," "Hallelujah, what a Savior," and how, in the seasons of prayer and reading the word that followed this visit, he gave his heart to the Lord. In a little while, he will cross the tide, and will know in its fullness the truth, "Hallelujah, what a Savior." The dear young man who met Mr. and Mrs. Bliss in the singing room, grown reckless from repeated failures in his *experiments* at becoming a Christian, will never forget the pressure of the hands that were so kindly placed upon his shoulders, or the earnest, loving look from the eyes that met his, or the words so earnestly spoken, telling him that his failure had come from *his experiments*, and urging him now, without experimenting, to trust Christ fully for all things, and make a full commitment to Him. Very earnestly did both these dear friends pray for this young man. Very faithful was dear Mrs. Bliss in her encouragement and counsel to him, and very happy were both of them when, the day of their departure, they took their leave of him, an intelligent, decided, happy Christian. Never will dear H. forget the interest taken in his conversion by Mr. Bliss, nor the sympathy and faith of Mrs. Bliss with his dear parents, when they were praying to God for his salvation. H. has sent me a copy of a letter received from Mr. Bliss, which speaks his heart, and tells of his personal interest in his Lord's work:

JACKSON, MICH., 20th November, 1876.

God bless you, my dear friend H., or Brother "Fred," as I prefer to call you. It is just as I expected. Your letter didn't surprise me a bit.

Welcome to the ranks. Now "forward, march," in the service of our Captain. You are not the man to sit still and prosper. And I'm so glad, Fred, that you've begun in time to put in a full day's work. So here's my heart's "Good Cheer," and I expect to see you take both hands and pull with a will.

The *kind* of a "Christian" you are to be will be largely determined in the next few months, I might have said weeks.

Lend a hand to that score or more of your associates and the college boys. Pull them in shore before they drift down to the rapids. Help some weak friend by a lift on his burden.

Oh, how the world needs happy, singing, *joyful* young Christians!

I congratulate you upon the good times you are going to have in the service of the Lord. If the Devil knocks you down occasionally, you'll fall on your knees; and then he'll soon leave you. Good is the Lord. Amen.

Should have replied sooner, but hoped to see you. We all go to Chicago to-morrow night. Love to father, mother and sisters.

Yours in Galatians ii, 20,

P. P. BLISS.

Just beginning to get hold here. Pray for us.

One evening, at Kalamazoo, while on the way to the service, this verse was repeated and became a favorite with us from that on, and was almost daily quoted:

In peace I go; no fear I know
Since Christ walks by my side.
His love to me my joy shall be,
His words shall be my guide.

Among the papers found in his trunk was a slip with that verse written upon it. "*Whatever comes*, let us just stick to that," he would remark, and it truly expressed the atmosphere in which, in those days, he seemed to be walking. Each day the Master gave him some special work, some special blessing. Some years before, he had given a concert in Kalamazoo, and was entertained for the night by a gentleman who a little time after had died. Mr. Bliss sought out the family, and found a representative of them in a daughter who had married a well-known business man, but neither of them Christians. God used his visit to them, and both were led, before the meeting closed, to accept Christ, and were very happy in His love, and are now among the most active Christian workers of the place.

Another letter, received from a young lady in Kalamazoo, and given below, will tell its own story as to the faithfulness of Mr. and Mrs. Bliss to *individual* souls—the simple secret of all success in evangelistic work, from the time that Jesus talked with Nicodemus by night and the woman at Samaria at noon, to the present hour.

Faithfulness in private work with individuals must keep pace with service in public to the crowds, or that will be no power.

KALAMAZOO, MICH., February 10, 1877.

MR. WHITTLE:

DEAR SIR—I was baptized last Sunday, and while I realize that " with God all things are possible," still it does not seem to me that any one but Mr. Bliss could have induced me to take this step.   I am a minister's daughter and have been a constant attendant on divine worship, and have attended many revivals where sinners flocked to Christ, but they always left me just outside the fold. When Mr. Bliss sang " Only Trust Him," it touched my heart.   Then he was so sympathetic, and he said that he did not know the time when he was converted.   He left *feeling* entirely out of the question ; and while others made " great the mystery of godliness," with him it was " Only Trust Him."

I promised Mrs. B. that I would write to them at Jackson, but was very busy with my studies, and, as I told Dr. Hodge, I waited too long ; but he thought that in heaven they would rejoice with far greater joy than they could on earth. But heaven seems a great way off, and there are a great many passages in the Bible I cannot understand, and when I heard of their death it seemed to me that God did not care for His children ; but with all such thoughts I see again the glorious singer, and hear in sweetest accent, " Only Trust Him."   There was no one, excepting my dear papa, mamma and sister, whose death I would have regretted so much.   I can scarcely realize that I knew them only three short weeks.   I spent the afternoon with them at their rooms here.   They were the happiest hours of my life.   Mrs. Bliss gave me her photograph, but the only one I have of him hangs on memory's walls, and it shall never be obliterated. I have a beautiful letter that they wrote me while they were here.   I am very glad that you came to Kalamazoo.   I pray for you that God will make you very successful in winning souls to Him.

I gave Mr. Bliss " Bunyan's Complete Works," and wrote on the fly leaf, " I go to prepare a place for you—that where I am there ye may be also ; " but little did I think he would so soon be there.   The last night they were here we were the last ones to leave the church.   At the door, Mr. Bliss turned around and said, " Good bye, old Methodist Church, I shall not see you again ; " but to me he said, " I will just say good night to you ; we shall meet again in the morning."   He won the love of all.   Heaven seems nearer and dearer now that they are there ; but how we miss them here ! Mr. Bliss said to me some time before he left, " I shall watch for you in heaven."   I know they are waiting for me at the beautiful gate.   Will you pray for me, Mr. Whittle, that I may be a *happy*, devoted Christian and meet them there ?

Yours in the blessed hope of John vi, 47,   **** ***

The afternoon Mr. Bliss left Kalamazoo, the young men, many of them new converts, surprised him by gathering at the depot and singing him a farewell from Gospel Songs.   The last song, which closed as the train came up to the station, was " We're going Home To-morrow."

CHAPTER IX.

FROM the 11th to the 21st of November, 1876, Mr. Bliss was in Jackson, Michigan, in union meetings. He was much used here, and was in an unusual degree anxious to talk personally with the unsaved. The first Sunday evening he conducted a meeting of his own in the Rev. Mr. Maile's church, and with much blessing. A dear friend, employed by the railroad company, with his wife, was present that evening, and both remained for personal conversation with him. They were singers and were glad to have him talk with them, and before he left them, both accepted Christ. That friend is now leading the singing in the church where he was converted, and is spoken of by the pastor as one of his most active workers.

The Michigan State Prison is located at Jackson, and on both Sunday mornings of Mr. Bliss' stay in the city, he conducted service for the eight hundred inmates there. The most tender, eloquent, and earnest appeal that could have possibly been made to sinners to accept the love of Christ was made by him at his last meeting with these dear men, Sunday morning, November 19th. He spoke of their homes, and of the little children, who missed their papas; told them of his own dear little Paul going around the room, and kneeling at the different chairs and praying for his papa and mamma; then turned all their awakened sympathies to Christ, by speaking of how impossible it would be for him to give up his dear little boy to die for others, and to die a death of great suffering, and those for whom he died to be his enemies. "Oh, friends," he said, with tears, "I could not do it, but this is what God did for you. He loved you and gave His Son to die for you." The Spirit of God was upon Mr. Bliss that morning in that prison, and as he spoke and as he sang, the hearts of those hardened men melted like wax. Defiant faces softened, and grew beautiful with earnest, tender, sympathetic feeling. The animal and sensuous expression predominant in many faces passed away, as they looked upon that earnest face, and saw the tears falling as he plead with them of Christ's love, and then sang, as if singing for God alone :

> Man of Sorrows. What a **name**
> For the Son of God, who **came** .
> Rebel sinners to reclaim.
> Hallelujah! what a Savior !

Two-thirds of the men there seemed quite broken **down by the** reality of the things of **God.** They never will forget **the service of** that hour. A strange feeling of **the sense** of the presence of **Jesus** Christ came over **the writer while Mr. Bliss was talking, and the** expression upon **the faces of the men was softening under his words.** It seemed to be an explanation **of the words spoken of Christ: "** Then drew near **unto Him publicans and sinners, for to hear Him."** He was filled **with sympathy and love, and his dear servant** that day **was near** enough **to the Master to reflect His spirit.**

. Here, as at Kalamazoo, **Mrs. Bliss accompanied** her husband to **nearly every meeting, and sang once or twice with** him every evening. His personal interest in **the unsaved was** made manifest **by** an incident that occurred in **Jackson.** Late one evening, at the close of a meeting, he went to the telegraph office in **the** depot, **to send** a message. While writing his dispatch, an operator **came in, and,** without noticing Mr. Bliss, commenced speaking **to the two or three** railroad men who were in the room, about the meeting. His first words, as laughingly reported by Mr. Bliss to the writer, were,: " Well, I've been to church, and if I couldn't preach better than that man, I'd quit the business. The singing though, was good. I think Bliss knows how to sing and I'll go again, perhaps, to hear him." Stepping up to the counter and **taking up** Mr. Bliss' dispatch, he at once recognized him, and **in a manly** way said : " Well, no offense **intended. I** didn't **know you** were here ; but I don't take back a word, except **the swearing.** I don't believe a word Whittle said." Without entering **into an** argument, Mr. Bliss presented the Gospel to him, and urged **upon him** the one **way** of salva-

6

tion. The young man objected very strongly to a statement in the sermon, that, no matter how sincere people were in their belief, they were lost if they rejected God's truth. "Well," said Mr. Bliss, "isn't it like this? If a man wants to go to Chicago to-night, and he makes a mistake, and when the Detroit train comes from the west, he takes it and goes east. Thinking very sincerely that he is on his way to Chicago won't help him a bit. He must believe what the conductor tells him, that he is wrong, and face about or he will never reach Chicago." The railroad men chimed in an assent to this illustration. "Just what happened on my train, the other day," said a conductor. "A man was going east, when he wanted to go west, and I had hard work to make him believe he was wrong." It was late and Mr. Bliss was very tired, but for some time he remained speaking to this friend. Nor did he forget the interview. Each day he prayed for this young man, and the very last person he spoke to in Jackson was this operator, urging him to accept Christ and take his stand as His follower.

The stay in Jackson was a very brief one, but blessed of God to many souls. The closing meeting, held in the Methodist Church, Bliss often referred to as one of the best of the year. After the preaching of the Gospel, Mr. Bliss sang, "I have a Savior—He's pleading in glory," with its sweet refrain, "For you I am praying. I'm praying for you," as found, with music by himself, in Gospel Songs. He sang this piece a great deal, and poured out his heart in real prayer as he sang it. During his singing, those present who desired the prayers of God's people were invited to rise, and how happy he would be, as he sang, to see them respond. While singing it one evening, his heart going out for sinners, he added this verse, not found in the song as printed in Gospel Hymns:

> And Jesus is calling, how can you reject Him?
> He says He loves sinners, so then He loves you.
> O friend, *do* believe it, *arise* and accept Him,
> Give Jesus your heart, while I'm praying for you.

That night in Jackson, as he sang, a hundred or more arose, and the Spirit of God was felt in power in the meeting. After his singing, prayer was offered, asking that those impressed might then and there decide and fully accept Christ as their Savior, as presented to them in the word. Mr. Bliss then sang "Hallelujah, 'tis Done;"

and all who would accept and were willing to confess Christ and promise to commence His service were given the opportunity of so doing by arising. Nearly all who had arisen for prayer again arose, and the singer's face fairly shone with joy as he sang:

> There's a part in that chorus for you and for me,
> And the theme of our praises forever will be:
>> Hallelujah, 'tis done! I believe on the Son!
>> I am saved by the blood of the Crucified One!

The meeting in Jackson closed November 21st, and Mr. and Mrs. Bliss came to Chicago to attend the Christian Convention called by Mr. Moody. During the session he made an address upon the use of song in worship, and sang at the prayer meeting of ministers in Farwell Hall, presided over by Mr. Moody, on the morning of November 24th. Over a thousand ministers were present, and the intense spiritual feeling prevailing found fit expression through Bliss in song. After he had sung "Are your Windows Open toward Jerusalem?" his own soul thrilled by the conscious presence of the Holy Spirit, one dear minister cried out, "God bless Mr. Bliss for that song;" and scores of amens came from as many earnest, tender hearts. This was the last time he sang in Chicago. None who were present in Farwell Hall that forenoon will ever forget the power with which he sang. Mr. Moody leaned forward in his chair, occupied with the song and the singer, and overcome by the feeling produced by the music and the sentiment of the hymn. It was the last time he was to hear him this side of the River. When next he hears his voice, it will be in the Heavenly choir.

"ARE YOUR WINDOWS OPEN TOWARD JERUSALEM?"

> Do you see the Hebrew captive kneeling,
>> At morning, noon and night, to pray?
> In his chamber he remembers Zion,
>> Though in exile far away.

> CHORUS:—Are your windows open toward Jerusalem,
>> Though as captives here a "little while" we stay?
> For the coming of the King in his glory,
>> Are you watching day by day?

> Do not fear to tread the fiery furnace,
>   Nor shrink the lion's den to share;
> For the God of Daniel will deliver,
>   He will send His angel there.
>
> Children of the living God, take courage;
>   Your great deliverance sweetly sing,
> Set your faces toward the hill of Zion,
>   Thence to hail our coming King.

The foregoing was suggested to Mr. Bliss while attending a Sunday service at the State Prison in Joliet, Illinois, where he had gone to sing. Mr. H. G. Spafford, of Chicago, addressed the prisoners, and used Daniel in Babylon, as an illustration to them of Gospel truth, and asked the question in closing—" Are your windows open toward Jerusalem ?"

CHAPTER X.

ON the 25th of November, Mr. and Mrs. Bliss, with the writer, left
Chicago, for Peoria, Illinois. It was of our Father's goodness,
that we should all be together, while there, in the hospitable care of
our dear friends, Mr. and Mrs. Robert Grier. Our rooms joined and
were connected with each other, and we were thus constantly together. Had we known that the separation was so near, we could
not have planned for ourselves, for the fullest enjoyment of the few
days remaining, as our Heavenly Father planned for us. Both of
us had long known and loved Reynolds, Tyng, McIlvaine and other
Christian workers in Peoria, and it was a joy to meet with them
and their families and to work with them for souls. In no place
were the dear brothers of the ministry more cordial and kind in
their welcome and fellowship. A hearty support was given to the
meetings by all the churches, and Rouse's Hall was kept full from
night to night with people brought in by the faithful visitation of
Christians to hear the Gospel. Mr. Bliss had many musical friends
in Peoria, and under the direction of Messrs. Bacon and Pitt he
found a choir ready to assist him, that gave him much delight.
Very earnest and faithful were they all, and very highly did Mr.
Bliss appreciate and enjoy their services.

While in Peoria, our dear brother, Mr. R. C. Morgan, of London, England (whose article upon Mr. Bliss, taken from *The
Christian,* will be found in the chapters devoted to memorial services), paid us a visit, and passed some days with us. His immediate object in coming was to talk with us about a visit to England.
This was proposed to us before he came, by Mr. Moody, but was
now to be considered. Mr. and Mrs. Bliss were both favorably inclined to the proposition, but desirous of knowing and doing the
will of the Lord in the matter. I find in our diary, under date of

December 4th: "To-day Bliss, and wife and I united in special prayer that God would guide as to our future movements. Moody has spoken about our going to England. We expect Brother Morgan of London here, this week, to suggest this to us. The pastors meet in Chicago, to-day, to consider inviting us there after Mr. Moody leaves, and calls are before us from various places. We know not what is best, but trust we are all willing to be led, and we ask the Master to plan for us and to keep us. We had rather go anywhere else than to Chicago, and shrink much from following Mr. Moody there. May God give us wisdom to know His will."

Mr. Bliss, from the very first, had an almost unaccountable aversion to the plan proposed of his returning from his Christmas visit to his children, to Chicago, and work there. He desired to remain in the East, working in New England, while Moody and Sankey were in Boston. The expression in his last letter before coming west is explained by this reluctance. The subject of conversation during these days at Peoria naturally turned much upon the proposed trip to England. Mrs. Bliss was disposed to leave her children in this country. She said, "They are under as good care with sister Clara as they could possibly be. They love her now as much as they do me, and I believe it would be better for them and better for us in the work, if they are left in Rome." In commenting upon this, the remark was made that if accident should occur and we were drowned, the children would be safe. Her reply was, "Well, I shouldn't think of that. If we ask the Lord to guide us, and it seems best for all to go, and we are all drowned, it is all right. It is the Lord's will, and it will be best. We should all go together." When Mr. Burchell's dispatch, stating that "Bliss, wife and children were among the dead," was shown me, these words of Mrs. Bliss came very vividly to my mind.

In Peoria Mr. Bliss held his children's meetings each afternoon, at the Methodist Church, and became more interested than ever in the work for the young, and earnestly expressed his determination to more and more labor in that direction. A number of very interesting conversions in his meetings gave him much pleasure. One dear little German boy, a manly little fellow of eight years old, interested Mr. and Mrs. Bliss very much. He was an intelligent boy, and had a business-like way of speaking of his having accepted Christ, that commended him specially to Mrs. Bliss, who was always repelled by affectation in young or old, and was, perhaps unconsciously, a little unsympathetic toward children on this account. It was during a conversation suggested by her speaking of her confidence in this boy, that Mr. Bliss said, "You do not understand the child **nature.** You never had a childhood, but were always a mother **child."** Since their death the following letter was received from **their little** Peoria friend. **It is given verbatim :**

PEORIA, Ill., January 27.

DEAR BROTHER WHITTLE:

I saw a piece in the *Standard* of you and Mr. Bliss. I saw that you **and the** Rev. Mr. Morgan, of London, were getting up a book of the **life** of Mr. and Mrs. Bliss, and wanted to have letters from those who have been blessed or converted by his songs. I can say that I was converted when they was singing the second hymn, "Hallelujah, 'tis Done." In singing the chorus of it, I thought do I believe on the Son? and so, as you gave the first invitation for all that were not Christians and wanted to be prayed for to rise, and then asked how many wanted to settle it now to rise, I was among that lot that rose as there were forty or fifty, you said. I saw five or six that rose that were right behind me. I attended all of Mr. Bliss' children's meetings, as also I attended all of yours. It was Thanksgiving **night, at** the Centennial Hall, in which I was converted. I expect you know **me.** I am eight years **old.** I remain, as **ever, your friend,**

WILLIAM **B.** HERSCHBERGER.

It was a very sad day for me when I received the news of brother Bliss' death. As there was crying and sobbing when we heard it, as my brother kept asking **what** was the matter. I hope you will pray for our family and for me, as I will continue to pray for you.

This letter fully justifies Mrs. Bliss in **her opinion of her little** friend William.

Mr. Reynolds writes from Peoria, in connection **with Mr.** Bliss' labors, that over fifty scholars in his Sunday School testified that they attributed the influence leading to their decision for Christ to the special labors of Mr. Bliss. In the evening meetings for adults, God gave him also many souls in Peoria. One night he was the last one home, and as he came home and hung up his coat in the hall, he remarked, in his happy way, "My last inquiry meeting was at the gate. Three **dear** young men, all hungry for the Gospel, and two of them have taken Christ."

Our last visit together to the afflicted was made in **Peoria.** He sang for one who was under peculiar bereavement, and who longed for release from life's burdens, his hymn, " Father, I'm Tired." The frail girl to whom he sang seemed much nearer that day to " crossing the tide" than the strong singer who so cheered her with his song ; but she still lives, and may for many a day, to praise the grace that can sustain and bless in the deepest affliction, while *he* has gone.

Among the many precious meetings in Peoria that come thronging to the mind, none, as connected with these loved ones, is more clearly remembered than the Thanksgiving morning prayer-meeting, in Dr. Edwards' church. Dear Bliss was full of the spirit of praise, and, as always, when upon that theme, he lifted us all into sympathy with him. He sang the song of his own composing, called " Grandfather's Bible," prefacing it by remarking how much he had to praise God for in having had a godly ancestry ; and very full of tender reminiscences to all were the old tunes woven in to tell the story of the Puritans' Bible. He loved to sing the old time tunes, and the hymns his father and mother taught him, and very sweetly he sang them that morning, causing the tears to flow from the eyes of many children " of parents passed into the skies."

Thanksgiving Day we spent with the kind friends who were entertaining us. After dinner, Mr. and Mrs. Bliss sang. He had written many very popular songs that he never sang after he went into Gospel work, and that I knew nothing of. One of these, called " Jolly Jonathan," I had heard of his singing at Northfield for Mr. Moody, and greatly to the latter's delight, and I wished to hear it. He had refused several times in Kalamazoo and Jackson, on our Saturday rest days, and upon this occasion I was the more importunate. Mrs. Bliss finally said, " Well, Mr. Bliss, you had better let the Major hear what it is ; but, Major, Mr. Bliss is through making and singing that kind of songs, and he doesn't like to have people remember him as singing them." I appreciate now, as I did not then, how out of sympathy he had become, in the habitual tone of his mind, with all that was not connected with Christ during these last days.

JOLLY JONATHAN.

Haow du yu du, my naburs? I'm glad tu see yu all,
Just make yerselves tu hum, I say; I'm tickled with your call,
I guess you'll find Columby a purty place tu stay;
I kalkelate you never see a land so fair and gay.
Ameriky, Ameriky, Ameriky, Hooraw!
Ameriky, Ameriky, Ameriky, Hooraw!

Aw, beg you pawdon, mistah; a chawming land I see,
But, aw, acwas the watahs wide a lawdly land theah be—
A land we call Old Hingland, magnifithent and grand;
A higheh awdeh Bwiton, hath, a wich, a noble band.
Britannia, Britannia, Britannia, Huwaw!
Britannia, Britannia, Britannia, Huwaw!

Och, bother, shtop yer blarney, just let Ould Ireland shpake;
A blessid darlin' koonthry, too, she is, and no mishtake,
Sich gintlemanly pigs, oh, sich praties there are raised,
Wid niver once a shnake, ye mind, Saint Patrick's name be praised!
Ould Ireland, Ould Ireland, Ould Ireland, Hoorah!
Ould Ireland, Ould Ireland, Ould Ireland, Hoorah!

Nix komarouse der Deitchland, das is der land for me;
Mit shootsenfest, mit sangerbund und sauerkraut so free;
Yaw, yaw, das is der koontry, mein faderland so dear,
I love, oh, my! I feels so pad, I'll dake some lager bier.
Der Deitcherland, Der Deitcherland, Der Deitcherland, yaw, yaw!
Der Deitcherland, Der Deitcherland, Der Deitcherland, yaw, yaw!

CHAPTER XI.

THERE seems now, in looking back over our intercourse in Peoria, a foreshadowing of approaching separation. One day while taking a walk that was almost a daily one with Mr. Bliss and the writer, up the Bluff, we spoke that the time might be near at hand, when one of us would be walking alone, and thinking of the departed one in places where we had been together. He, always inclined toward "the hope," said : "Just as probable that Christ may come and we all go together. What a beautiful day this would be for Him to come." We had talked of the sudden death of our friend Samuel Moody, Mr. Moody's brother, and in connection with that event and the view we had of the Lord's return, our minds were often turned toward what now recurs as almost premonitory of what was to come. On the 14th of December, we held our last meeting. From 8.30 A. M. to 5 P. M., with intermission at noon, we held a Christian Convention. Mr. Bliss sang through the day, and spoke with his usual earnestness and emphasis upon the use of song in worship. In the evening, accompanied by Brother Morgan, who had spent the day with us, we went to Rouse's Hall. On the way, Mrs. Bliss remarked : " Major, if you want us to sing ' Waiting and Watching,' to-night, you must not say anything before asking us to sing. It is all that I can do to control my feelings anyway, when we do sing it, and if you introduce it by remarks, I shall break down." They sang this piece, and "I Know not the Hour that My Lord will Come," that evening—the last I ever heard them sing together. Mr. Bliss sang " Eternity" alone.

That evening we left for Chicago. We breakfasted and dined with Mr. Moody at the Brevoort House, and arranged that we should

take up the work in Chicago, Sunday, December 31 ; I going back
to Peoria, and Bliss going to visit his children until that time.
After the Lord was through with us in Chicago, we were to go to
England. Bliss yielded about coming to Chicago, but to the last
was unconvinced as to its being best.

They left that Friday afternoon by the 5.15 Michigan Southern
train. Before leaving the hotel, we met for a few moments of
prayer in Room 13, and I parted with them there, never again to
meet on earth. He passed the following Sunday in Towanda, Pennsylvania, with his mother and his sister, Mrs. Willson. Three
letters that he wrote from there all speak of the joy he felt at the
meeting with the mother—of his thankfulness for the peace that
seemed to be filling her soul and the blessing her prayers and faith
had been to him. Monday, December 18th, he rode by stage to
Rome, and the parents were with their dear little boys again. All
of the associations of home for both of them clustered around Father
Young's house in Rome, their frequent happy resting-place on life's
journey ; they came with joy to it now, both almost as merry as
their little boys. They had been purchasing and making articles
for Christmas presents for weeks, and came with a trunk full of
surprises for the approaching holiday. ' When Christmas came,
Mother Bliss was sent for, and all the family circle within reach
were gathered at the old home. Mr. Bliss was the Santa Claus.
On Saturday he went out on to the hillside and cut the Christmas
tree, and with his own hands arranged it in the parlor and hung his
surprises. Saturday evening, the presents were distributed and
" the happiest Christmas he had ever known," as he said, was quickly
passed. He had surprises for everybody and spent the day in making everybody happy. From Grandma Allen down to little George,
everybody in the entire circle was remembered, and portions were
sent outside the circle to all of whom he could learn in the village
as being in want. He himself was not without his surprises. Gifts
from the wife and other loved ones, and a magnificent music box
from his loved friend and publisher, Mr. Church, added to his
happiness. This Christmas was to him the crowning joy and mercy
of a year of joys and mercies. His heart overflowed with thankfulness to God and with earnest desire to do more in the service of
Christ. He visited nearly every day among the neighbors, and urged
the claims of Christ upon the personal attention of those unsaved.

He attended nearly every meeting, and sang and gave Bible readings, and made personal appeals to his friends to at once decide for Christ. All testify that they never knew 'him so earnest. Grandma Allen says : " Why, that man would come in and say, ' Grandma, I wish I could see every person in this valley a Christian.'" The dear old Grandma is very quaint and original in her way, and " Phil," as all at home called him, loved to draw out her odd sayings. The little account Grandma gave me of one of his home meetings with them, on one of the last days, when they gathered for a Bible talk and sing, will illustrate the enjoyment she gave him. She said : " He had been asking them all around where they had rather have seen Jesus, when He was on the earth, if they had to select one place. They all selected different places, and he said he would rather have seen Him as He went up into heaven from the Mount of Olives ; and then he asked me where I had rather have seen Him, and I told him that I had rather have seen Him when He was a little helpless baby, there in the manger, among the oxen, and helped take care of Him, and he just cried about it."

God blessed Mr. Bliss' testimony and labor during this last week to the conversion of many old friends and neighbors, and some score or more feel that they owe their decision to his influence, and that the light they have received from the Son of God came through him.

Mr. Bliss' last meeting was held Wednesday evening, December 27. He was full of the Holy Spirit, and sang with more than usual power. Among the pieces that friends remember as sung that night are : " Alas ! and did my Savior Bleed ? " to the tune of Dundee ; " Happy Day," and " In the Christian's Home in Glory." He sang as solos " Eternity," " Father, I'm Tired," and as a closing song, " Hold Fast till I Come." In singing " Father, I'm Tired," he took occasion to speak of his companion in the work, and of his affection for him, and that he would sing the piece because it was one of his favorites. The last song, probably, that he sang on earth was " Hold Fast till I Come." He prefaced his singing it by saying that it was one of the first occasions of its being sung, and that it might be the last song he should ever sing to them.

On Wednesday, a letter came to me from Mr. Bliss, in which he wrote :

" I hear nothing from you definite as to my being wanted in

Chicago next Sunday. Unless I hear from you, I shall not leave this week." This letter came in the morning. He had been advertised to sing in Mr. Moody's Tabernacle the following Sunday afternoon. It was necessary to telegraph him to come. But evening came and found me at my home and the telegram was not sent. I had not forgotten it, but did not want to send it. I did not know then, I do not know now, why. All day long, it was upon my mind and was spoken of to friends that Bliss must be telegraphed for, and that I did not like to take the responsibility of doing it. Late in the evening, the dispatch was forwarded.

Thursday morning, he took his little boys into a room by themselves and prayed with them, bade good-bye to all, and, standing upon the threshold for a moment, said : "I would love to stay. I would far rather stay than go, if it were God's will ; but I must be about the Master's work." He wrote back from Waverly, New York, a station on the Erie Railroad, the same afternoon : "Tickets for Chicago, via Buffalo and Lake Shore Railroad. Baggage checked through. Shall be in Chicago Friday night. God bless you all forever."

Taking the afternoon train at Waverly, he expected to be in Buffalo at twelve o'clock that night, and connect with a train that would arrive in Chicago Friday evening. Ten miles from Waverly (as I learned from the conductor, in tracing him up), the engine of the train broke, and they were detained three hours. Their connection with this train was thus lost ; and upon arriving at Hornellsville late in the evening, they evidently decided to wait over, and have a night's rest, and arrive in Chicago Saturday morning at nine o'clock—for at Hornellsville they left the train, and are registered at the hotel, which they left Friday morning, taking the train which connected at Buffalo with the Chicago train, wrecked at Ashtabula, Ohio. The children were not with them, but had been left at Rome, Pennsylvania, in the care of grandparents and aunt.

The story of the disaster by which these two precious lives were lost will be found in another chapter. What experience they passed through, that night of fear and pain, we shall not know until we meet them on the other side. We may confidently believe that God gave them abundant grace for all they met of suffering, and that Christ was consciously near to them in their moment of need.

The time was shortened for the elect's sake and they were soon at home. From all the evidence that could be gathered from the testimony of survivors, it is believed that the Buffalo and Cleveland parlor car, in which they were seen by Mr. Burchell, a lady passenger, and by the newsboy of the train, struck first upon the ice after the fall of the bridge, and that another car fell upon it, crushing and probably instantly killing the passengers within. The floor of this car was identified in removing the wreck, and lay flat upon the ice, with the water that had come from the melted snow and ice, mingled with ashes and cinders frozen over it, substantiating the above theory.

Saturday morning, December 30th, when I read the report of the disaster, my heart sank within me, and I feared the worst. I immediately telegraphed to Rome to know if Mr. Bliss had left. But about three o'clock in the afternoon, before any reply from Rome, Mr. Burchell's telegram came, and we were face to face with the awful fact of their death. The next morning we were at Ashtabula, and remained for three days, until all the wreck had been removed, searching first for their bodies, then for anything that could be identified as having been connected with them. We found nothing ; and up to this time nothing has been found. Their watches, sleeve buttons, chains, keys, rings, not one thing connected with them has come to light. Scores of such articles have been raked up from the bottom of the river, but none of them are theirs. They have gone, as absolutely and completely gone, as if translated like Enoch.

Of the meeting with the stricken households, and the dear orphan boys, and the days of mourning passed with them, I cannot speak. God graciously manifested Himself in the comfort vouchsafed to the aged parents, and to brothers and sisters who shared their grief, and it was better indeed to be " in the house of mourning than the house of feasting." Some of the number there gathered were led to consecrate themselves to the work of Christ, and are now engaged in prosecuting the work of the dear departed brother in singing the Gospel. Many at the funeral service held in Rome were led to accept of Christ, and from all over the land has come testimony that Christ has been magnified in the death of His child as in his life. Scores, by the very fact of his death, have been impressed and turned to God. Hundreds will receive the truth through the pathos of memory of his death, giving new meaning to the truths of his songs. "God's ways are always right." No mistake has been made. We bow in submission to His will, and pray that this afflictive providence may be sanctified to us by the Spirit of God and that, "with windows open toward Jerusalem," we may live day by day, ready for "the coming of the King in His beauty," or for our departure to be with Him. "Amen, even so, come quickly, Lord Jesus."

The following lines, printed upon a leaflet, were found in Mr. Bliss' trunk. He carried the leaf for a long time in his pocketbook, until creased and worn, and it was placed among his papers. God in grace grant to writer and to readers, that the message may be as appropriate as a voice from us, when we depart to be with Christ, as it surely is in every line from him.

A VOICE FROM HEAVEN.

I shine in the light of God,	*Rev.* xxi. 23.
His likeness stamps my brow,	1 *John* iii. 2.
Through the shadows of death my feet have trod,	1 *Cor.* xv. 55.
And I reign in Glory now!	*Rev.* xxii. 5.
No breaking heart is here,	*Matt.* xxvi. 38.
No keen and thrilling pain,	*Job* xxxiii. 19.
No wasted cheek, where the frequent tear	*Rev.* xxi. 4.
Hath roll'd and left its stain.	*Ps.* xliii. 3.
I have found the joys of Heaven,	*Is.* xxxv. 10.
I am one of the angel-band :	*Heb.* xii. 22.
To my head a crown of gold is given,	1 *Pet.* v. 4.
And a harp is in my hand !	*Rev.* xiv. 2.
I have learn'd the song they sing,	*Is.* xxxviii 20.
Whom Jesus hath set free ;	*John* viii. 36.
And the glorious walls of Heaven still ring	*Is.* lx. 18.
With my new-born melody !	*Rev.* xv. 3.
No sin, no grief, no pain—	*Is.* xxv. 8.
Safe in my happy home !	*John* xiv. 2.
My fears all fled, my doubts all slain,	*Acts* vii. 55.
My hour of triumph come !	*Rom.* viii. 37.
O friends of mortal years,	*Prov.* xvii. 17.
The trusted and the true !	1 *John* i. 7.
Ye are walking still through the valley of tears,	*Heb.* x. 36.
But I wait to welcome you.	*Luke* xvi. 22.

Do I forget?—Oh no!   *Mal.* iii. 16.
  For memory's golden chain   2 *Pet.* i. 15.
Shall bind my heart to the hearts below,   1 *John* iv. 7.
  Till they meet and touch again.   1 *Thess.* iv. 18.

Each link is strong and bright,   *John* i. 51.
  And love's electric flame   *Dan* ix. 21.
Flows freely down like a river of light   *Rev.* xxii. 1.
  To the world from which I came.   1 *John* iv. 9.

Do you mourn when another star   1 *Cor.* xv. 41.
  Shines out from the glittering sky?   *Dan.* xii. 3.
Do you weep when the raging voice of war   *Deut.* xxxii. 1.
  And the storms of conflict die?   *Mark* iv. 39.

Then why do your tears run down,   *Luke* viii. 52.
  And your hearts be sorely riven,   *Prov.* xiv. 10.
For another gem in the Savior's crown,   *Is.* lxii. 3.
  And another soul in Heaven?   *Luke* xxiii. 43.

Farewell, dear friend and brother, **true** yokefellow in the service of Jesus Christ. The path is often lonely without you, and as they sing the songs you used to sing, and we listen in vain for the voice so wedded to the music, and music so wedded to the words, our hearts ache as the echoes die away, and a strange silence is on the air, as if the song itself mourned for the singer. No resting place beneath the sod can receive the tears we would shed, or the flowers we would bring to tell how we loved thee. We turn from the earthly memories to the heavenly realities. The days are fast passing by; soon upon the other shore we shall greet you, and you shall lead our praises to Him who hath redeemed us from our sins by His shed blood, and in His risen life hath given us resurrection hope, and to whom, even Jesus Christ our Lord, we now give all the praise for every sweet memory and for every precious anticipation of future joy connected with you.

CHAPTER XII.

THE following, of Mr. Bliss' compositions, were published in "The Prize," a collection of Sunday School hymns, etc., by George F. Root, issued in 1870, and the words are used by permission of the publishers, Messrs. John Church & Co., Cincinnati, Ohio:

PRESS FORWARD.

Press forward, press forward, press forward to the prize;
While life's bright morn, with rosy hue,
Bedecks the flowers that, bathed with dew,
Salute thy waking eyes,
Press forward to the prize,
Forward, forward, press forward to the prize,
Forward, forward, press forward to the prize.

Press forward, press forward, press forward to the prize;
When in the morn of life thy heart
From heaven's high calling would depart,
And doubts and fears arise,
Press forward to the prize.

Press forward, press forward, press forward to the prize;
When morn and noon of life are past,
And evening shadows lengthen fast,
And swift the daylight flies,
Press forward to the prize.

Press forward, press forward, press forward to the prize ;
  Though sweet the songs we sing below,
  A richer Prize will heaven bestow,
    And there our treasure lies,
    Press forward to the prize.

HAIL, HAPPY MORNING.

Hail, happy morning, hail, holy day !
Calling from earthly labors away ;
Sweet words of wisdom, glad songs of joy,
Now be our best employ.

CHORUS.—Sing once more the happy, happy song,
    While the golden moments roll along,
  "Come to the temple, come, come away,"
    "Hallow the Sabbath day."

Emblem of heaven, sweet day of rest,
In thy "remembrance" may we be blest.
So may our songs and lives ever say,
  "Hallow the Sabbath day."

Rest from our labors, rest from our cares ;
Rest in our praises, rest in our prayers ·
So the commandment would we obey.
  "Hallow the Sabbath day."

PETER'S DENIAL.

In the garden, boldly,
  Peter would have fought :
Now he answers coldly,
  "Nay, I know Him not."

CHORUS.—I would stand forever
    Near my Savior's side,
  Lest to glory yonder
    I should be denied.

LORD, SAVE ME.

Though life's stony pathway
  Be with dangers fraught,
Let my falt'rings never
  Say, " I know Him not."

Though long years of sorrow
  Be my earthly lot,
Let my murm'rings never
  Say, " I know Him not."

In the dark temptation,
  Vows and prayers forgot,
Let my yielding never
  Say, " I know Him not."

So, in toil or pleasure,
  Deed or word or thought,
Let me never, never
  Say, " I know Him not."

LORD, SAVE ME.

Winds are boist'rous, waves are high,
Midnight gloom o'erspreads the sky ;
Fearful, sinful, sinking down,
Peter's prayer I make my own.

CHORUS.—Mountain waves of sin I see,
        In Thy mercy, " Lord, save me,"
        Mountain waves of sin I see,
        In Thy mercy, " Lord, save me."

Lord, Thou bidst me come to Thee,
Thou alone my help must be ;
On the treach'rous waves I stand,
Savior, hold me by Thy hand.

Lord, my feeble faith forgive,
Help divine may I receive ;
All my guilty fears remove,
Wherefore can I doubt Thy love.

ONCE MORE WITH MOURNFUL STEP.

Once more with mournful step and slow,
Across the murm'ring brook they go;
Once more beneath the olive's shade,
The garden's well known paths they tread;
A Savior's sorrows we may mourn,
For surely He our griefs hath borne.

Each brow is sad, each heart with woe
Is breaking, since He said, "I go."
And see, a warlike band appears,
And fainting hopes are crushed with fears:
Alas, our guilt His sorrow made,
On Him was our transgression laid.

Though all forsake the Lord and flee,
Again He answers, "I am He."
Again the falt'ring foes arise,
The bitter cup He drinks and dies.
A Savior's love behold revealed,
And with His stripes we now are healed.

NAUGHT TO CHARGES FALSE.

Naught to charges false replying,
  In gentle mood,
Hearing all, but naught denying,
  Our Savior stood.

CHORUS.—Gentle, lamb-like would I be,
    Savior, more and more like Thee.

Priestly rage and perjured story,
  In vain are brought;
So, the mighty Lord of glory,
  Now answers not.

While "Away with Him" they're crying,
  His cross they raise;
On that shameful cross, while dying,
  For them He prays.

THE ASCENSION.

" Wait in Jerusalem together,"
    Wait, said the risen Lord ;
Wait for the promise of the Father
    Ye from Me have heard.

Wait for the power of His glory,
    Wait for His high commands ;
Then shall ye spread abroad the story,
    In all distant lands.

Thus, while the chosen who believed Him
    Gazed on the face of Love,
So, from their sight a cloud received Him,
    Up to Heaven above.

And while toward Heav'n they steadfastly gazed,
    Behold two men in white apparel
Who said unto them :

Ye men of Galilee, why stand ye gazing?
Why are ye sorrowful?   Why do ye weep?
As ye have seen your Savior ascending,
So in His glory shall He appear, He appear.

BETHESDA.

Near the healing pool Bethesda, day by day,
Where the gentle breezes through the porches play,
Many weak and weary, halt and withered lay,
    Waiting for the moving of the water.

CHORUS.—Weary waiting at Bethesda's side,
        For the moving of the healing tide,
        Lord, from Thee be all my strength supplied,
            While waiting for the moving of the water.

So in helpless misery and sin I lie,
Hearing not the footstep of the angel nigh,
Trembling, hoping, fearing lest at last I die,
    Waiting for the moving of the water.

Jesus knows the mourner's grief and hears his sighs,
Sees the look of anguish and the streaming eyes,
Kindly speaks and bids the weary sufferer "Rise,"
    Waiting for the moving of the water.

Loving Savior, all my weakness Thou dost see,
Still Thy tender mercies, Lord, bestow on me,
Speak the word, and let me stand complete in Thee,
    Waiting for the moving of the water.

THERE'S A LIGHT IN THE VALLEY.

Through the valley of the shadow I must go,
    Where the cold waters of Jordan roll;
But the promise of my Shepherd will, I know,
    Be the rod and the staff to my soul.
Even now, down the valley as I glide,
    I can hear my Savior say, "Follow me!"
And with Him I'm not afraid to cross the tide,
    There's a light in the valley for me.

CHORUS.—There's a light in the valley,
      There's a light in the valley for me,
      And no evil will I fear while my Shepherd is so near,
      There's a light in the valley for me, for me.

Now the rolling of the billows I can hear,
    As they beat on the turf-bound shore;
But the beacon light of love, so bright and clear,
    Guides my bark, frail and lone, safely o'er.
I shall find down the valley no alarms,
    For my Savior's blessed smile I can see;
He will bear me in His loving, mighty arms,
    There's a light in the valley for me.

HOSANNA! HOSANNA!

From the Mount of Olives descending,
    See the multitude draw nigh;
Low before the Holy One bending,
    Hear them all with rapture cry:

CHORUS.—Blessed is he that cometh in the name of the Lord,
    Hosanna, hosanna, hosanna, in the highest.

Some, their highest honor bestowing,
  Spread their garments in the way ;
Others leafy branches are strewing ;
  All, rejoicing, **shout and say** :

All around the city are crying,
  " Who is this ? " " What priest or king ? "
While within the temple replying
  Hear the children sweetly sing :

We our truthful worship would give Thee,
  Humbly at Thy feet would fall,
In our hearts would gladly receive Thee,
  Jesus, Savior, Lord of all.

SAFE WITH THE MASTER.

Where is now our loved one ?
  Where, O where ?
Not where the living weary,
  Not where the dying moan ;
Not where the day is dreary,
  Not where the night is lone ;
Not in a home of weeping,
  Not in a darkened room ;
Not in a graveyard sleeping,
  Not in a silent tomb,
      No, not there ; **no, not there !**

Where is now our loved one ?
  Where, O where ?
Safe in a land immortal,
  Safe in a country rare,
Safe in a heavenly portal,
  Safe in a mansion fair.
Safe with the joys supernal,
  Safe with the bless'd to bow,
Safe with the Love Eternal,
  Safe with the Master now,
      There, yes, there ; there, yes, there !

THE BEGGAR BY THE WAYSIDE.

By the wayside, near the city,
Sits a beggar, poor and blind;
Who can pass him without pity?
Who so careless and unkind?
Now his sightless eyes upturning,
Shaded by the leafy palms,
Tears his wrinkled cheeks are burning,
As he faintly asks for alms.

CHORUS.—Oh, **we** love the wondrous story,
How the blind received their sight;
May the Lord of life and glory
Lead us into heavenly light.

Lo, the multitude draws near him;
" What means this ?" we hear him cry;
How the answer seems to cheer him.
" It is Jesus passing by."
Hear him crying " Mercy, mercy,"
Though rebuked by those before,
" Jesus, Son of David, mercy,"
Hear him crying more and more.

Now **the** blessed Master, standing,
Hears the beggar's earnest cry,
While in gentle tones commanding,
" Bring the blind Bartimeus nigh."
" What wilt thou ?" He asks, while o'er Him
Falls a halo golden **bright**;
Low the beggar bends before Him—
" Lord, that **I receive my sight.**"

Hush ! the multitude are bending,
Breathless in the fading light,
While, his "saving faith " commending,
Jesus says, " Receive thy sight !"
Joy ! he sees ; and, upward gazing,
Hails the glorious light of day,
And rejoicing, singing, praising,
" Follows Jesus in **the** way."

I MUST ABIDE WITH THEE.

Through the crowded streets of Jericho, see
  The Holy Nazarene go,
Hear the shout of praise from the happy ones there
  Who His healing virtues know.

CHORUS.—Praise ye the Lord, His mercies show,
      Ever in His love confide.
    More than we ask will He bestow,
      Willingly with us abide.

In the friendly shade of a sycamore tree,
  The joyful publican see ;
Hear the Master's voice saying, " Zaccheus, come,
  For I must abide with thee."

Like an earnest little Zaccheus, I
  Would fain the Holy One see,
I would haste with joy at the blessed command,
  " For I must abide with Thee."

AND YET THERE IS ROOM.

" Go forth," said the Master, " and make no delay ;
  Invite to the banquet, invite all to-day ;
  The chosen have tarried, bring hither the blind,
  The poor and the needy ; leave no one behind."

CHORUS.—Now all things are ready, the Master says, " Come,"
      The whole world is bidden, " and yet there is room."
      The whole world is bidden, the whole world is bidden,
      The whole world is bidden, " and yet there is room."

Then quickly the servants went out from their Lord,
His message they published with joyful accord.
From highways and hedges they called to the feast,
And welcomed with rapture each wondering guest.

O, wayworn and weary, despise not the call,
Reject not that mercy, 'tis free—free to all ;
Thy Father is waiting to welcome thee home ;
Oh ! haste to the banquet while " yet there is room."

REMEMBERED.

Fading away, like the stars of the morning
  Losing their light in the glorious sun ;
So let me steal away, gently and lovingly,
  Only remembered by what I have done.

CHORUS.—Ever remembered, forever remembered,
        Ever remembered while the years are rolling on ;
      Ever remembered, forever remembered,
        Only remembered by what I have done.

So let my name and my place be forgotten,
  Only my life-race be patiently run ;
So let me pass away, peacefully, silently,
  Only remembered by what I have done.

So, in the harvest, if others may gather
  Sheaves from the fields that in spring I have sown ;
Who plowed or sowed matters not to the reaper—
  I'm only remembered by what I have done.

Fading away like the stars of the morning,
  So let my name be unhonored, unknown ;
Here, or up yonder, I must be remembered—
  Only remembered by what I have done.

FOLLOW ME.

Hear the blessed Savior say,
  Follow Me, follow Me,
In the darkness and the day, follow, follow Me.
Follow, though the torrents pour,
Follow, though the lions roar,
Follow, I have gone before ;
  Follow, follow Me.

CHORUS.—Oh, hear Him saying,
        Follow, follow, follow, follow, follow, follow Me.
        Blessed Savior, may we ever follow, follow Thee.

When the tempter's voice is heard,
  Follow Me, **follow Me,**
Rest upon My **Holy Word,** Follow, etc.
All thy doubts **and** fears I **know,**
All thy **weariness** and **woe;**
Forward humbly, boldly **go.**
  Follow, etc.

Never shall **thy** foes prevail,
  Follow Me, follow Me,
Never shall My promise fail.   **Follow, etc.**
Follow Me, let naught allure,
Follow Me, thy rest is sure,
Follow Me, it shall endure.
  Follow, etc.

LOOK AND LIVE.

Look to Jesus, weary one,
  Look and live, look and live ;
Look at what the Lord has done,
  Look and live ;
See Him lifted on the tree,
  Look and live, look and live ;
Hear Him say, " Look unto Me,"
  Look and live.

CHORUS.—Look ! the Lord is lifted high,
        Look to Him, He's ever nigh,
        Look and live, why will ye die?
        Look and live.

Though unworthy, vile, unclean,
  Look and live, look and live ;
Look away from self and sin,
  Look and live.
Long by Satan's power enslaved,
  Look and live, look and live ;
Look to Me, ye shall be saved,
  Look and live.

Though you've wander'd far away,
   Look and live, **look and live** ;
Harden not your **heart to-day,**
   Look and live.
'Tis thy Father calls thee home,
   Look and live, look and live ;
Whosoever will may come,
   Look and live.

------- ◆◆ -------

ONLY BELIEVE.

Earnestly the ruler **on the** Lord did **call,**
Tenderly entreating at His feet did fall ;
"My little daughter near to death doth **lie,**
Come, Lord, and heal her, or she soon must die."
"Trouble not the Master ;" soon they came and said,
"Trouble not the Master, for thy daughter is dead."
Sweetest words of comfort then did Jesus give,
"Be not afraid, only believe."

CHORUS.—Call on the Lord, His mercies still endure ;
      Call on the Lord, His promise still is sure ;
      Life, life eternal all may now receive.
      Be not afraid, only believe.

In the darkened **chamber** bends the **mother low,**
O'er her only **daughter,** with a mother's woe :
Darkened now forever is **her once** bright home ;
Tearfully she falters, "Has the Master come ?"
"Wherefore are ye weeping?" 'tis **the** Master's voice !
"She is only sleeping," doth the mother's heart rejoice ;
Trustingly the father says, "**We will** not grieve.
Be not afraid, only believe."

Quietly the Master **bids** the mourners go ,
All a parent's tenderness His actions show;
Ah, what holy rapture, oh, what glad surprise,
At His gentle voice commanding, "Maid, arise."
Courage, fainting mother, trust a loving Lord ;
Courage, fearful brother, rest forever on His word ;
Tender youth and age, in Him alone can live ;
"Be not afraid, only believe."

WHAT SHALL THE HARVEST BE?

Words suggested by D. HAYDN LLOYD.   Music by P. P. BLISS.

Sowing their seed by the dawn-light fair,
Sowing their seed in the noontide glare,
Sowing their seed in the fading light,
Sowing their seed in the solemn night,
  Oh, what shall the harvest be ?

CHORUS.—Sown in the darkness or sown in the light,
          Sown in our weakness or sown in our might
          Gathered in time or eternity,
          Sure, ah sure, will the harvest be.

Sowing their seed by the wayside high,
Sowing their seed on the rocks to die,
Sowing their seed where the thorns will spoil
Sowing their seed in the fertile soil,
  Oh, what shall the harvest be ?

Sowing the seed of a lingering pain,
Sowing the seed of a maddened brain,
Sowing the seed of a tarnished name,
Sowing the seed of eternal shame—
  Ah, sure will the harvest be !

Sowing their seed with an aching heart,
Sowing their seed while the tear-drops start,
Sowing in hope till the reapers come,
Gladly to gather the harvest home.
  Oh, what shall the harvest be ?

LOOK NOT UPON THE WINE.

Though its ruby blush so fair
  In the silver cup be cast,
Of the deadly "serpent's sting" beware, beware,
  'Twill pierce thy soul at last.

CHORUS.—Look not thou upon the wine when it is red ;
          When it moveth itself aright,
            All the light and beauty now around it shed
            Soon will end in sorrow's night.

'Tis a "mocker," luring on,
    With its "raging," fiery breath,
And its burning work is never, never done,
    Its flames are flames of death.

Tarry not, resolve to-day
    From the blighting curse to flee ;
'Tis the voice of wisdom calls away, away ;
    Be bold, be firm, be free.

----•◆•----

THE SPIRIT TREE.

" By their fruits ye shall know them," the Savior's words we read,
    And He looks from His mansions above,
And He knows if our hearts have received the precious seed,
    For the fruit of the Spirit is Love.

CHORUS.—Oh, the fruits of the Spirit are pure,
        May they all be found in me, in me,
        May my heart and my life ever yield the golden fruits
        Of the beautiful Spirit Tree.

Though the dark clouds of sorrow surround us as they may,
    And the pitfalls of passion annoy ;
Still believing, rejoicing, we onward press our way,
    For the fruit of the Spirit is Joy.

Though on seas of affliction our little bark be tossed,
    Though the high rolling billows increase,
Still with hope for our anchor we never can be lost,
    And the fruit of the Spirit is Peace.

Other fruits in their season we never fail to find,
    If with eyelids unsealed we can see ;
All that's gentle and tender, long-suffering and kind,
    Is the fruit of this beautiful tree.

In the sunlight of heaven the waving branches glow,
    Shedding perfume and gladness around ;
Naught of evil or danger the dwellers 'neath it know,
    For with Goodness its branches are crowned.

Sometimes, trembling and doubting, our home seems far away,
  And the leaves of the tree dry and sere ;
But the sweet fruits of Faith on the topmost branches sway,
  Bringing joys of the better land near.

Bringing hope to the weary and comfort to the sad,
  Bearing promise of heavenly birth ;
Making joyful the lowlands, the desert places glad,
  For " the meek shall inherit the earth."   ·

Naught impure or unholy the Spirit Tree can bear ;
  Evil trees evil fruits only show ;
No profane or intemp'rate the purer life can share,
  Or the fruits of the Spirit Tree know.

BEAUTIFUL RAIN.

Hear the music of the rain falling down
On the roof and window pane, falling down.
Murmur not, it seems to say,
For our Father's love to-day
Orders only in our way
    Good to fall,
Like the gentle falling rain
Over mountain, lake and plain,
Will His tender care remain
    Over all.

CHORUS.—Hear the music of the rain, beautiful rain,
        As the pearly drops in showers pattering fall.
        Hear the sweet subdued refrain,
        On the roof and window pane,
        Of our Father's tender love for all.

Hear the music of the rain falling down,
On the roof and window pane, falling down.
What a lesson does it bring,
What a chorus does it sing,
    What a message from our King of His love.
And we seem to hear Him say,
Come, ye children, learn My way,
    From My fold no longer stray.   Look above.

Hear the music of the rain falling down,
On the roof and window pane, falling down.
So our Father, kind and true,
Showers of blessings, ever new,
  On the good and evil, too, still doth send ;
And a cheerful song we raise,
To His honor and His praise,
  For the love that crowns our days to the end.

CHAPTER XIII.

IN 1871, "The Charm, a Collection of Sunday School Music, by
P. P. Bliss," was published. By permission of the publishers,
Messrs. Church & Co., Cincinnati, we print the following hymns
by Mr. Bliss :

MY SAVIOR'S CHARMS.

Charms in choral numbers,
  Charms in martial strains,
Charms in social chorus,
  Charms in glad refrain.

CHORUS.—But no other charms can be
  Like my Savior's charms to me ;
    Lovely charms
    Lasting charms,
Are my Savior's charms to me.

Charms in sanctus holy,
  Charms in festal lays,
Charms in freedom's anthem,
  Charms in childhood's praise.

Charms in harp and organ,
  Charms in reed and string,
Charms in trumpet pealing,
  Charms in everything.

LET THE LOWER LIGHTS BE BURNING.

ON a dark, stormy night, when the waves rolled like mountains and not a star was to be seen, a boat, rocking and plunging, neared the Cleveland harbor. "Are you sure this is Cleveland ?" asked the captain, seeing only one light from the light-house. "Quite sure, sir," replied the pilot. "Where are the lower lights ?" "Gone out, sir." "Can you make the harbor ?" "We *must*, or perish, sir !" And with a strong hand and a brave heart, the old pilot turned the wheel. But alas, in the darkness he missed the channel, and with a crash upon the rocks the boat was shivered, and many a life lost in a watery grave. Brethren, the Master will take care of the great light-house: *let us keep the lower lights burning !*—D. L. MOODY.

Brightly beams Our Father's mercy
From His Light-House evermore ;
But to us He gives the keeping
Of the lights along the shore.

CHORUS.—Let the lower lights be burning !
Send a gleam across the wave ;
Some poor, fainting, struggling seaman
You may rescue, you may save.

Dark the night of sin has settled,
Loud the angry billows roar ;
Eager eyes are watching, longing
For the lights along the shore.

Trim your feeble lamp, my brother,
Some poor sailor, tempest-tost,
Trying now to make the harbor,
In the darkness, *may be lost.*

JERUSALEM SO FAIR.

O, Jerusalem, the golden—city bright and fair ;
All the sanctified, the purified, the glorified are there ;
There the Savior we shall see, and His glory we shall share,
In Jerusalem so bright and fair.

CHORUS.—O Jerusalem, so fair ! O Jerusalem so fair !
All the sanctified, the purified, the glorified are there ;
There the Savior we shall see, and His glory we shall share,

O Jerusalem, the golden—city of the blest ;
Where the glory beams eternal on thy towers in beauty drest ;
Where the wicked cease from troubling, the weary are at rest,
In Jerusalem so bright and fair.

O Jerusalem, the golden—city fair and bright :
How thy pearly gates in splendor soon will burst upon our sight ;
How thy golden streets will glow, for the Lamb is all the light,
In Jerusalem so bright and fair.

HOW GOES THE BATTLE?

" Victory, victory ! " hear the angels say,
When a gentle word turns angry thoughts away ;
Though the stormy battle-field a little heart may be,
'Tis a mighty conflict, 'tis a glorious victory.

CHORUS.—How goes the battle, then, what news to-day ?
One side is gaining ground—one giving way !
Rally for the right, oh, battle manfully,
Let the blessed angel band shout the victory.
" Victory, Victory," Zion shall be free,
Let the blessed angel band shout the victory.

'' Victory, victory ! " shout the evil throng,
When a little heart gives room to purpose wrong ;
Then the holy angel bands do sadly turn away ;
" Victory, *our* victory ! " the evil spirits say.

'' Victory, victory ! " soon we all may sing,
" Glory be to Thee, O Lord, our heavenly King !
Thou hast overthrown the last, the dreaded enemy ;
Thine alone, the battle, Lord, be Thine the victory."

HELP.

Help me to sing,
Savior and King ;
Heart service only to Thee would I bring.

Help me to read,
Thy grace I need,
Lest I offend Thee in thought, word or deed.

Help me to pray ;
Guard lest I stray ;
Keep Thou my feet in the heavenward way.

Help I implore,
Thee to adore ;
Praise would I render to Thee evermore.

"ONLY A LITTLE CHILD.

"For whom is the bell tolling ?" I asked a man at the church door.
He replied, "Only a little child."

"Only a little child,"
Pause not here to weep ;
Scarcely on earth she smiled,
Ere she fell asleep,
Fell asleep.

"Only a little child,"
God to us had given ;
Pure and undefiled,
Only fit for heaven.
Fit for heaven.

"Only a little child,"
That our love possessed,
That our cares beguiled,
That is now at rest,
Now at rest.

"Only a little child,"
Such as Jesus blessed,
We were unreconciled,
Only He thought best,

WHERE HE LEADS WE WILL FOLLOW.

See the gentle Shepherd standing
  Where the quiet waters flow;
To the pastures green inviting,
  Hungry, thirsty, let us go.

CHORUS.—Where He leads we will follow,
    Where He leads we will follow,
    Where He leads we will follow,
    We will follow all the way.

Only by the door we enter,
  All who enter He will save;
Life abundantly bestowing,
  Though His life the Shepherd gave.

Safe within the fold He leads us,
  He the Shepherd, we His own;
And as Him the Father knoweth,
  Precious thought—of Him we're known.

WAITING AT THE WELL.

Little thought Samaria's daughter,
  On that ne'er forgotten day,
That the tender Shepherd sought her,
  As a sheep astray;
That from sin He longed to win her—
  Knowing more than she could tell,
Of the wretchedness within her,
  Wailing at the well.

CHORUS.—Hear, O hear! the wondrous story,
    Let the winds and waters tell—
    'Tis the Christ, the King of Glory,
    Waiting at the well.

'Neath the stately palm tree swaying,
  Listened she to words of truth,
While each thought was backward straying,
  O'er her wasted youth.

Hast'ning homeward with desire
  All His wondrous speech to tell,
Asked she, " Is not the Messiah
  Waiting at the well ?"

Yet salvation's well is flowing,
  And the Savior listens there—
Every want and care foreknowing—
  To our humble prayer.
By His gracious smile of favor,
  While our hearts with rapture swell,
Well we know it is the Savior,
  Waiting at the well.

WONDROUS LOVE.

Behold the love of God, wondrous love, **wondrous love,**
On sinful man bestowed, wondrous love.

CHORUS.—Herein, herein is **love** ;
        The Father from above
        His Son did give that **we might live !**
        Oh wondrous, wondrous love.

His love is full and free, wondrous love, wondrous love,
'Tis offered you and me ; wondrous love.

No merit of our own ; wondrous love, wondrous love,
He saves by grace alone ; wondrous love.

He offers life to-day ; wondrous love, wondrous love,
Accept it while ye may ; wondrous love.

ON WHAT FOUNDATION ?

On what foundation do you build, neighbor,
  Your hopes for the future fair ?
Do your walls reach down to the rock below,
  And **rest securely** there?
Sad wrecks lie 'round you on the sand, neighbor,
  The floods and the storms are near ;

Will the strong blast hurl to the earth **thy walls**,
  Or blanch thy cheek with fear?

CHORUS.—**On what foundation do you build, neighbor,**
    Your hopes for the future fair?
    Do your walls reach down to the rock below,
    And rest securely there?

On sure foundation would you build, neighbor?
  Take heed to the Lord's commands;
Ever fast and firm, while the storms go by,
  This Rock of Ages stands.
Alas! what folly 'tis to build, **neighbor,**
  A mansion so fair, so grand,
With its costly walls and its lofty **towers,**
  On Sin's delusive sand.

SAILING INTO PORT.

"Some ships cross the ocean with clear skies, smooth seas and fair winds, and come into port with streamers flying and bands of music making jubilee. Others come in storms, with the skies black as night, the wind like a hurricane, and the sea like mountains—and they come in all battered, yards gone, masts splintered, hardly enough left to hang together. But the difference amounts to nothing. The only important thing from first to last is, not what the log says about storm or calm, but that they all steer close to the compass, and do their best to make the harbor. So they only get there safely, what happened to them by the way is of no account. So as to God's children. There may, there will be vast variety of experience: to some, prosperity, success, joy—to others, adversity, defeat, grief. But what may be your lot or mine, is of no consequence. The one only thing of moment is, that we stick close to our chart and push for port with all our might. So we gain that, the pleasures or perils of the way do not matter."—*Extract from a sermon preached by Dr. E. P. Goodwin, First Congregational Church, Chicago.*

Sailor, though the darkness gathers,
  Though the cold waves surge and moan,
Trust thy bark to God's great mercy,
  Falter not, sail on, sail on.

CHORUS.—Sailing into port, what matter,
    Drooping sail or shattered mast?
    Glory, glory fills the harbor,
    There we'll anchor safe at last.

Sailor, though with streamers flying
  Yonder proud ship mounts the foam,
And with bands of music playing,
  Gains the port and welcome home.

Sailor, though the lightning flashes,
　　Though thy sails be rent and torn,
Peace shall come on Hope's bright pinions
　　And deliverance with the morn.

OVER YONDER.

Over yonder, over yonder,
　　Where the saints and angels dwell,
Over yonder, over yonder
　　Is the home I love so well.
There my loved ones wait to greet me,
　　Wait to clasp me by the hand,
There my Savior, too, will meet me,
　　Meet me in Immanuel's land.

Over yonder, over yonder,
　　Stands my mansion bright and fair;
All the glory, all the glory
　　Of the kingdom I shall share.
By the tree of life eternal,
　　Crystal streams forever flow;
While the leaves of healing mercy
　　On its waving branches grow.

Over yonder, over yonder,
　　Sin and sorrow are unknown:
Hallelujahs, Hallelujahs,
　　Evermore surround the throne.
Never will I fear the journey
　　Through the dark and shadowy vale;
For my Savior will be near me,
　　Never can His promise fail.

REMEMBER THE POOR.

'Tis winter, and ye by your fireside so warm
May feel not the blast of the pitiless storm;
But cold winds are sweeping o'er mountain and moor,
And lone ones are starving—Remember the poor.
　　Remember the poor,
　　Remember the poor.
And lone ones are starving—Remember the poor.

" To one of the least, in My name," saith the Lord,
" No visit of mercy shall lose its reward ; "
   But measure for measure shall earth-life restore,
   And treasure in heaven—Remember the poor.
      Remember the poor,
      Remember the poor.
   And treasure in heaven—Remember the poor.

Oh, give of thy bounty, thy gratitude show ;
So freely receiving, as freely bestow ;
   In mansions so fair on the evergreen shore,
   Would you be remembered ?   Remember the poor.
      Remember the poor,
      Remember the poor.
   Would you be remembered ?   Remember the poor.

PASSING AWAY.

Teacher.—What do the beautiful roses say ?
Scholars.—Sweet is our perfume, but short is our stay ;
Teacher.—What says the humming bird, do you know ?
Scholars.—Winter is coming and soon I must go.

   All.—Passing away, Passing away ;
      Second and minute and hour and day !
      Birdie and blossom, how brief is your stay ;
      Passing away, passing away.

Teacher.—What says the clock, with its tick-a-tick, tick ?
Scholars.—Time passes swiftly, be quick, oh, be quick !
Teacher.—What are the words of the rivulet's song ?
Scholars.—I cannot tarry, I must run along.

Teacher.—What does the sun in the morning say ?
Scholars.—Over I go for another bright day.
Teacher.—What does your heart by its beating tell ?
Scholars.—Earth-life is passing, then where will I dwell ?

GOD IS ALWAYS NEAR ME.

   God is always near me,
      Hearing what I say ;
   Knowing all my thoughts and deeds,
      All my work and play.

God is always near me,
  In the darkest night
He can see me just the same
  As by mid-day light.

God is always near me,
  Though so young and small;
Not a look or word or thought,
  But God knows it all.

----+ + +----

MAN THE LIFE BOAT.

Hark! I hear the captain calling,
  Earnestly and long:
"Rocks ahead! the breakers threaten!
  Bear a hand—Be strong!"

CHORUS.—Man the life-boat, blaze the signal!
      Never can we fail;
    No, the nation must be rescued,
      Temp'rance shall prevail!

Firm amid the storm and danger,
  Faithful, tried and true—
Though a mighty host opposes—
  Stand the Temp'rance crew.

Loud the billows dash around us,
  O'er the angry sea;
Night comes on and souls are dying,
  Will ye idle be?

----+ + +----

THE TEMPERANCE SHIP.

The temp'rance ship is sailing on;
      Sailing on,
      Sailing on,
The temp'rance ship is sailing on
  Though angry billows roar.
To bless the world she's sailing on,
      Sailing on,
      Sailing on.
To bless the world she's sailing on,
  To reach a fairer shore.

CHORUS.—Oh, rally, freemen, rally!
    Do you hear the fearful cry ?
  'Tis the solemn wail of warning
    From the drunkard doomed to die
  'Tis the prayer of wife and mother,
    'Tis the shriek of anguish wild ;
  " Will you help a falling brother—
    Will you save my darling child ? "

The mountain waves are rolling high,
    Rolling high,
    Rolling high,
The mountain waves are rolling high,
  The pirate fleet is strong.
We call for men to do or die,
    Do or die,
    Do or die,
We call for men to do or die
  To crush the mighty wrong.

Arise, young man, for you must fight,
    You must fight,
    You must fight,
Arise, young man, for you must fight,
  A foe that seems a friend.
The well worn way that seemeth right,
    Seemeth right,
    Seemeth right,
The well worn way that seemeth right,
  Alas ! in death doth end.

Ho, friends of temp'rance, firmly stand,
    Firmly stand,
    Firmly stand,
Ho, friends of temp'rance, firmly stand,
  To meet the daring foe.
For God, for Truth, for Native Land,
    Native Land,
    Native Land,
For God, for Truth, for Native Land
  We dare to strike the blow.

We see the blinded rush along,
    Rush along,
    Rush along,
We see the blinded rush along,

The broad and downward way.
Then raise at least a prayer or song,
Prayer or song,
Prayer or song,
Then raise at least a prayer or song
To save them while we may.

TURN TO THE RIGHT.

'Tis a rule in the land that when travelers meet,
Travelers meet,
In highway or byway, in alley or street,
Alley or street,
On foot or in wagon, by day or by night,
Each favors the other and turns to the right.

What a wonderful measure of trouble we'd shun,
Trouble we'd shun,
If all the humanity under the sun,
Under the sun,
While passing each other were truly polite,
And wishing " Good morrow," would turn to the right.

What a pity when selfishness stands in the way,
Stands in the way,
And hinders one's hearing what Wisdom would say,
Wisdom would say ;
There's joy on the journey, the end is delight,
To those in life's highway who turn to the right.

ONLY A STEP TO HEAVEN.

Day by day we saw her failing,
As the summer time went by ;
And the world grew dark and lonely
When we knew that she must die.
Still her heart seemed fondly clinging
To the blessed promise given :
" I am not afraid," she whispered,
" For 'tis but a step to heaven."

CHORUS.—Nearer, nearer come the angels,
    Till the earthworn bands are riven ;
    Nearer, nearer, seems the glory,
    Till 'tis but a step to heaven.

In the Savior's mercy trusting,
    Walking closely by His side ;
Scarcely did she hear the rippling
    Of the darkly flowing tide—
" Do not grieve "—sweet words of comfort
    To her weeping mother given :
" I am not afraid," she whispered,
    " For 'tis but a step to heaven."

" Do not sing to me of heaven
    As a home far, far away ;
'Tis a narrow stream divides us,
    We may cross it in a day.
Only let me cling to Jesus,
    To the blessed word He's given ;
Then my soul is filled with glory,
    Then 'tis but a step to heaven."

TO DEPART, WHICH IS BETTER?

TO THE MEMORY OF C. M. WYMAN.

And I heard a voice from heaven, saying unto me, Write, blessed are the dead which die in the Lord : Yea, saith the Spirit, that they may rest from their labors, and their works do follow them.

Hark, on the shore of " Immanuel's Land,"
Shout the " Triumphant " and glorified band ;
Singing as only the ransomed can sing—
Sweet hallelujah, to Jesus their King.
    Amen, Amen, Amen.

" Farewell," we sigh, as our friends leave the strand,
" Welcome," they sing in " Immanuel's Land."
Mourning below is rejoicing above ;
We tell of sorrow while they sing of love.

Lovingly called from his labors below ;
Suddenly summoned, but ready to go :
Laying the cross and the life burden down,
Gladly receiving the robe and the crown.

Not without hope are we mourning to-day ;
" Thy will be done," we are trying to say :
Here 'neath the " Shadowy Rock " we will rest—
God is " Our Father," and His ways are best.

PRAYING ALWAYS.

TEACHER.—Little eyes,
          Looking wise,
      Have you said your morning prayer?
          Have you thought,
          As you ought,
      Of our Heavenly Father's care?
          Tell me what our prayer should be
          When the morning light we see ?

ALL.—Pleasant light,
          Clear and bright,
      Shining on the world to-day.
          So may love
          From above
      Shine along our upward way ;
          So let every thing we see
          Turn our thoughts, O Lord, to Thee.

ALL.—Water clear,
          Standing near ;
      Wash our hands and faces clean.
          May the Lord,
          By his word,
      Wash our hearts from every sin.
          So let everything we see
          Turn our thoughts, O Lord, to Thee.

GIRLS.—Cloak and hood,
          New and good,
      Made to keep our bodies warm.
          Words of truth,
          Learned in youth,
      Keep our souls from every harm.

BOYS.—Boot or shoe,
          Old or new,
    Let us keep them clean and neat;
          Let us pray,
          That we may
    Some day walk the golden street;
          So let everything we see
          Turn our thoughts, O Lord, to Thee.

GIRLS.—Collar white,
          Ribbons bright;
    Apron, bonnet, shawl or dress;
          So may we
          Ever be
    Clad in Jesus' righteousness;
          So let everything we see
          Turn our thoughts, O Lord, to Thee.

BOYS.—Top or ball,
          Treasures all;
    Books and toys I dearly prize;
          Yet may I,
          When I die,
    To my heavenly treasures rise;
          So let everything we see
          Turn our thoughts, O Lord, to Thee.

ALL.—Night or day,
          Work or play;
    In our hearts may be a prayer;
          God can see,
          If there be—
    Well He knows what thoughts are there:
          So let everything we see
          Turn our thoughts, O Lord, to Thee.

SOON AND FOREVER.

    Only a few more years,
      Only a few more cares;
    Only a few more smiles and tears,
      Only a few more prayers:

> Only a few more wrongs,
>   Only a few more sighs:
> Only a few more earthly songs
>   Only a few good-byes:
>
> Then an eternal stay,
>   Then an eternal throng;
> Then an eternal glorious day,
>   Then an eternal song.

CHAPTER XIV.

"WHOSOEVER Will may Come," was written during the
winter of 1869 and '70, after hearing Henry Moorhouse,
of England, preach from the text, "God so loved the world that
He gave His only begotten Son, that *whosoever* believeth in Him
should not perish but have everlasting life," John iii, 16. Mr Moorhouse preached every night for a week from this same text, and the
new views of the freeness and fullness of the invitation of the Gospel
to sinners that many Christians in Chicago at that time received,
are well expressed in Mr. Bliss' hymn :

"WHOSOEVER WILL."

"Whosoever heareth," Shout, shout the sound !
Send the blessed tidings all the world around ;
Spread the joyful news wherever man is found,
"Whosoever will may come."

CHORUS.—"Whosoever will, whosoever will,"
Send the proclamation over vale and hill ;
'Tis a loving Father calls the wand'rer home ;
"Whosoever will may come."

Whosoever cometh need not delay ;
Now the door is open, enter while you may ;
Jesus is the true, the only living way ;
"Whosoever will may come."

> "Whosoever will," the promise secure ;
> "Whosoever will," forever must endure ;
> "Whosoever will," 'tis life forever more;
> "Whosoever will may come."

I think it was in June, 1870, that "Jesus Loves Me" was written. Mr. and Mrs. Bliss were at the time members of my family, at 43 South May street, Chicago. One morning, Mrs. Bliss came down to breakfast and said, as she entered the room : "Last evening, Mr. Bliss had a tune given him that I think is going to live and be one of the most used that he has written. I have been singing it all the morning to myself and cannot get it out of my mind." She then sang over to us the notes of "Jesus Loves Me." The idea of Mr. Bliss in writing it was that the peace and comfort of a Christian were not founded upon his loving Christ, but upon Christ's love to him, and that to occupy the mind with Christ's love, would produce love and consecration in keeping with Romans v, 5 : "The love of God (*to us*) is shed abroad in our hearts by the Holy Ghost, which is given to us." This view of Gospel truth was at this time being very preciously brought to the souls of believers in Chicago by the preaching of Moorhouse and Mr. Moody and by the Dublin tracts and English Commentaries upon Gospel Truth, which, through Mr. Moody, began to be circulated among Christians. How much God has used this little song to lead sinners and fearful timid Christians to "look away to Jesus" eternity alone can tell.

JESUS LOVES ME.

I am so glad that Our Father in Heaven
Tells of His love in the Book He has given ;
Wonderful things in the Bible I see,
This is the dearest, that Jesus loves me.

CHORUS.—I am so glad that Jesus loves me,
Jesus loves me, Jesus loves me,
I am so glad that Jesus loves me,
Jesus loves even me.

Though I forget Him and wander away,
Kindly He follows wherever I stray,
Back to His dear loving arms would I flee,
When I remember that Jesus loves me.

Oh, if there's **only** one song I can sing,
When in His **beauty** I see the great King;
This shall **my song** in eternity be,
O what a wonder **that** Jesus loves me.

"Blessed are They that Do His **Commandments.**" The verse in Rev. xxii, 14, suggested this hymn. The **tune was a** favorite with **Mr.** Bliss, but after he learned more fully the fullness of the Gospel, he was dissatisfied with the words on account of the impression they left that the right to the tree of life **was secured by** *our doing.* It seemed clear to **him that the** translation of the verse in question claimed by many of the commentators, "Blessed are **they** *that have washed their robes,* **that they may have right** to the **tree of life,"** etc., must be the **correct one, and it took away** all Scripture authority for the **teaching of his hymn in that direction.** The truth presented in the **Scriptures as to** *saved* ones walking in the path of obedience, **he could with a little change have** taught in the hymn, and **this he intended doing.** During his last week in Rome, he called the attention **of his brother-in-law, Mr.** Young, to the **above points** of objection to the words, **and said:** "I cannot use it **as it is.** I see so clearly its contradiction of the Gospel that I have **no liberty** in singing it, and must make a change in it before it goes **into another** book." This was the only hymn he has written, that **I am aware of, that is** liable to criticism in **this direction:**

BLESSED ARE THEY THAT DO.

Hear the words our Savior hath spoken,
Words of life unfailing **and true;**
Careless one, prayerless one, **hear and remember,**
Jesus says, "Blessed **are they that do."**

CHORUS.—Blessed **are they that do His** commandments,
Blessed, blessed, **blessed are they.**

All in vain **we** hear His commandments.
All in vain His promises too;
Hearing them, fearing them never can **save us,**
Blessed, oh, blessed are they that do.

> They with joy may enter the city,
>   Free from sin, from sorrow and strife;
> Sanctified, glorified, now and forever,
>   They may have right to the Tree of Life."

"Free from the Law." Just before Christmas, 1871, Mrs. Bliss asked a friend, "What shall I get for my husband as a Christmas present?" and, at the suggestion of this friend, purchased and presented him with the bound volume of a monthly English periodical called *Things New and Old*. Many things in these books of interpretation of Scripture and illustrations of Gospel truth were blessed to him, and from the reading of something in one of these books, in connection with Romans viii, and Hebrews x, 10, suggested this glorious Gospel song:

ONCE FOR ALL.

> Free from the law, oh, happy condition!
> Jesus hath bled and *there* is remission;
> Cursed by the law and bruised by the fall,
> Grace hath redeemed us once for all.

> CHORUS.—Once for all, oh, sinner, receive it,
>   Once for all, oh, brother, believe it:
>   Cling to the Cross, the burden will fall;
>   Christ hath redeemed us, once for all.

> Now are we free—there's no condemnation;
> Jesus provides a perfect salvation,
> "Come unto *Me*," oh hear His sweet call,
> Come and He saves us, once for all.

> "Children of God!" oh, glorious calling!
> Surely His grace will keep us from falling,
> Passing from death to life at His calling,
> Blessed salvation, once for all.

"Only an Armor-Bearer" was suggested by the account of Jonathan's going up against Michmash, as given in I Samuel, xiv:

ONLY AN ARMOR-BEARER.

Only an armor-bearer, proudly I stand,
Waiting to follow at the King's command ;
Marching, if Onward shall the order be,
Standing by my Captain, serving faithfully.

Chorus.—Hear ye the battle cry, "Forward," the call !
    See ! see the faltering ones, backward they fall.
    Surely the Captain may depend on me,
    Though but an armor-bearer I may be.

Only an armor-bearer, now in the field,
Guarding a shining helmet, sword and shield,
Waiting to hear the thrilling battle-cry,
Ready then to answer, " Master, here am I."

Only an armor-bearer, yet may I share
Glory immortal, and a bright crown wear :
If, in the battle, to my trust I'm true,
Mine shall be the honors in the Grand Review.

PULL FOR THE SHORE.

" We watched the wreck with great anxiety. The life-boat had been out some hours, but could not reach the vessel through the great breakers that raged and foamed on the sand-bank. The boat appeared to be leaving the crew to perish. But in a few minutes the Captain and sixteen sailors were taken off, and the vessel went down.

" ' When the life-boat came to you, did you expect it had brought some tools to repair your old ship ? ' I said.

" ' Oh, no, she was a total wreck. Two of her masts were gone, and if we had stayed mending her only a few minutes, we must have gone down, sir.'

" ' When once off the old wreck and safe in the life-boat, what remained for you to do ?'

" ' Nothing, sir, but just to pull for the shore.' "

" Therefore, if any man be in Christ, he is a new creature : old things are passed away ; behold, all things are become new."

"Wherefore, my beloved,   *   *   *   work out your own salvation with fear and trembling."—*Things New and Old.*

> Light in the darkness, sailor, day is at hand !
> See o'er the foaming billows fair Haven's land.
> **Drear was** the voyage, sailor, now almost o'er ;
> **Safe within** the life-boat, sailor, pull for the shore.

> CHORUS.—Pull **for** the **shore, sailor, pull for the shore !**
> Heed not the rolling **wave, but bend to** the oar ;
> Safe in the life-boat, sailor, **cling to self** no more !
> Leave the **poor** old stranded wreck **and** pull for the shore.

> Trust in the life-boat, sailor, all else will fail,
> Stronger the surges dash and fiercer the galo ;
> Heed not the stormy winds, though loudly they roar ;
> Watch the "bright and morning star," and pull for the shore.

> Bright gleams the morning, sailor, uplift the eye ;
> Clouds and darkness disappearing, glory is nigh ;
> Safe in the life-boat, sailor, sing evermore ;
> "Glory, glory, hallelujah !" pull for the shore.

"I Know not the Hour when my Lord will Come." These
words, Mr. Bliss has told me, were suggested to him in reading the
book "Gates Ajar" and criticisms upon it. His idea was that what
we may know from the Scripture, that we shall be with the Lord,
is sufficient, and that we may be happily content in saying of all
that is mere speculation, "*I know not,*" offsetting it by what we
are permitted to say "*I know.*" The music for the words was composed by his friend, James McGranahan, while visiting Mr. Bliss.
Both **Mr.** and Mrs. Bliss loved the song very much and often sang
it together, and have both told me of how the tune came to Mr.
McGranahan. Mr. Bliss had handed him the words and asked him
to see what he could get for a tune. He worked upon it a long
time, making harmonies and trying to satisfy himself with something that would properly express the words, but without success.
When supper time came he did not care for supper, and when bed
time came they all went to their rooms leaving him in the parlor at
the piano. He worked away for some time, but, dissatisfied with the

result, lay down upon the floor and fell into a doze. After a little time he woke up, and the tune, chorus and all had come—different from the harmonies he had worked upon, but just the thing. In the morning he sang it to Bliss, who was delighted with it and immediately adopted it for use.

THAT WILL BE HEAVEN FOR ME.

I know not the hour when my Lord will come
To take me away to His own dear home ;
But I know that His presence will lighten the gloom,
    And that will be glory for me.
Yes, that will be glory, oh, that will be glory, be glory for me ;
    And that will be glory for me,
    Oh, that will be glory for me ;
Yes, that will be glory, oh, that will be glory for me ;
But I know that His presence will lighten the gloom,
    And that will be glory for me.

I know not the song that the angels sing,
I know not the sound of the harp's glad ring :
But I know there'll be mention of Jesus our King,
    And that will be music for me.
Yes, that will be music, oh, that will be music, be music for me ;
    And that will be music for me,
    Oh, that will be music for me ;
Yes, that will be music, oh, that will be music for me ;
But I know there'll be mention of Jesus our King,
    And that will be music for me.

I know not the form of my mansion fair,
I know not the name that I then shall bear ;
But I know that my Savior will welcome me there,
    And that will be heaven for me.
Yes, that will be heaven, oh, that will be heaven, be heaven for me ;
    And that will be heaven for me,
    Oh, that will be heaven for me ;
Yes, that will be heaven, oh, that will be heaven for me ;
But I know that my Savior will welcome me there,
    And that will be heaven for me.

"Down Life's dark Vale We Wander" was written in Peoria, Illinois—I think in 1872. It was suggested by a conversation with

Mrs. Wm. Reynolds and Mrs. Tyng upon the subject of our Lord's personal return. One of the ladies quoted a sentence from a work of Anna Shipton's as to the joy and comfort it gave her, day by day, to think each morning at sunrise, "This may be the day of His coming." Mr. Bliss was much impressed—more deeply so than ever before—by the reality of the subject, and a few days after, as he was coming down stairs from his room with the thought of looking for the Lord upon his mind, he commenced singing "Down life's dark vale we wander," the words coming to him as easily as the steps he took down the stairs. He at once wrote it out with the music as now sung.

WHEN JESUS COMES.

Down life's dark vale we wander,
　Till Jesus comes;
We watch and wait and wonder,
　Till Jesus comes.
Oh, let my lamp be burning,
　When Jesus comes;
For Him my soul be yearning,
　When Jesus comes.

CHORUS.—All joy His lov'd ones bringing,
　　When Jesus comes:
　All praise through heaven ringing,
　　When Jesus comes.
　All beauty bright and vernal,
　　When Jesus comes,
　All glory, grand, eternal,
　　When Jesus comes.

No more heart-pangs nor sadness,
　When Jesus comes;
All peace and joy and gladness,
　When Jesus comes.
All doubts and fears will vanish,
　When Jesus comes;
All gloom His face will banish,
　When Jesus comes.

He'll know the way was dreary,
　When Jesus comes;
He'll know the feet grew weary,
　When Jesus comes.

He'll know what griefs oppressed **me**,
  When Jesus comes ;
Oh, how His arms will rest me !
  When Jesus comes.

"The Light of the World is Jesus" was written in the summer of 1875, at his home, No. 664 West Monroe street, Chicago. It came to him all together, words and music, one morning while passing through the hall to his room, and was at once written out.

THE LIGHT OF THE WORLD IS JESUS.

"I am the light of the world."—JOHN ix, 5.

The whole world was lost in the darkness of sin ;
  The Light of the World is Jesus.
Like sunshine at noonday His glory shone in ;
  The Light of the World is Jesus.

CHORUS.—Come to the Light, 'tis shining for thee ;
  Sweetly the Light has dawned on me.
  Once I was blind, but now I can see ;
  The Light of the World is Jesus.

No darkness have we who in Jesus abide ;
  The Light of the World is Jesus.
We walk in the Light when we follow our Guide ;
  The Light of the World is Jesus.

Ye dwellers in darkness with sin-blinded eyes,
  The Light of the World is Jesus.
Go wash at His bidding, and light will arise,
  The Light of the World is Jesus.

No need of the sunlight in heaven, we're told,
  The Light of the World is Jesus.
The Lamb is the light in the City of Gold,
  The Light of the World is Jesus.

"The Holy Spirit, Resist not, Grieve not, Quench not," was
suggested to him by B. F. Jacobs.   He loved the song himself, and
the words are among the most beautiful he has written.   He felt
that more should be sung of the Holy Spirit, and wrote this after
being in the work.

THE HOLY SPIRIT.

" Three warnings ; Resist not, Grieve not, Quench not."

The Spirit, oh, sinner,
  In mercy doth move,
Thy heart, so long hardened,
  Of sin to reprove.
Resist not the Spirit,
  Nor longer delay ;
God's gracious entreaties
  May end with to-day.

Oh, child of the kingdom,
  From sin service cease ;
Be filled with the Spirit,
  With comfort and peace.
Oh, *grieve* not the Spirit,
  Thy Teacher is He,
That Jesus, thy Savior,
  May glorified be.

Defiled is the temple,
  Its beauty laid low,
On God's holy altar
  The embers faint glow,
By love yet rekindled,
  A flame may be fanned ;
Oh, *quench* not the Spirit,
  The Lord is at hand.

"Wishing, Hoping, Knowing," he wrote to bring Christians
into a more full assurance of salvation, in connection with his experience in Gospel meetings with doubting Christians who were looking to their feelings instead of the word of God.

WISHING, HOPING, KNOWING.

A long time I wandered in darkness and sin,
And wondered if ever the light would shine in;
I heard Christian friends tell of raptures divine,
And wish'd, how I wish'd that their Savior were mine.

CHORUS.—I wish'd He were mine, yes, I wish'd He were mine;
      I wish'd, how I wish'd that their Savior were mine.

I heard the glad gospel of "good will to men";
I read whosoever again and again;
I said to my soul, "Can that promise be thine?"
And then began hoping that Jesus were mine.

CHORUS.—I hoped He was mine, yes, I hoped He was mine:
      I then began hoping that Jesus was mine.

Oh, mercy surprising, He saves even me;
"Thy portion forever," He says, "will I be."
On His word I'm resting—assurance divine,
I'm "hoping" no longer—I know He is mine.

CHORUS.—I know He is mine, yes, I know He is mine;
      I'm "hoping" no longer— I know He is mine.

Rev. Mr. Brundage tells of the origin of "Almost Persuaded," in a sermon preached by him many years ago. The closing words of the sermon were—"He who is almost persuaded is almost saved, but to be almost saved is to be entirely lost." Mr. Bliss being in the audience, was impressed with the thought, and immediately set about the composition of what proved one of his most popular songs, deriving his inspiration from the sermon of his friend, Mr. Brundage.

ALMOST PERSUADED.

"Almost persuaded" now to believe;
"Almost persuaded" Christ to receive.
  Seems now some soul to say,
"Go, Spirit, go Thy way,
  Some more convenient day
  On Thee I'll call."

> " Almost **persuaded**," come, come, to-day ;
> " Almost persuaded," **turn not away.**
>   Jesus invites you here,
>   Angels are ling'ring near,
>   Prayers rise from hearts so dear ;
>   O wand'rer, come !
>
> " Almost persuaded," harvest is past !
> " Almost persuaded," doom comes at last !
> " Almost " cannot avail ;
> " Almost " is but to fail !
>   **Sad,** sad that bitter **wail—**
> " Almost, *but lost !* "

" Hallelujah ! 'tis Done."   In compiling **Gospel** Songs, in **1874**, Mr. Bliss desired to publish in it the well-known hymn, " Hallelujah ! Thine the Glory," then much used in religious services.   The owners of the copyright of the hymn declined his application **for its** use, and he wrote " Hallelujah ! 'tis Done," to supply the **want.** Hundreds of souls have been led to decide for Christ by **this hymn,** and the church has reason to rejoice at **that refusal.**

HALLELUJAH! 'TIS DONE.

'Tis the promise of God, full salvation to give
Unto him who on Jesus His Son will believe.

CHORUS.—Hallelujah ! **'tis done,** I believe on the Son ;
    I am saved by **the blood** of the Crucified One ; **Crucified One.**

Though the pathway be lonely, **and** dangerous, too,
Surely Jesus is able to carry us through.

Many loved ones have I in yonder heavenly **throng ;**
They are safe now in glory, and this is their song,

Little children I see standing close by their King,
And He smiles as their song of salvation they sing :

There are prophets and kings in that throng I behold,
And they sing as they march through the streets of pure gold :

There's a part in that chorus for you and for me,
And the theme of our praises forever will be:

CHORUS.—Hallelujah! 'tis done, I believe on the Son;
        I am saved by the blood of the Crucified One, Crucified One.

"Good News" was written in March, 1874, about the time Mr. Bliss went to Waukegan for his first Gospel meetings, and was first sung there:

GOOD NEWS.

Hear ye the glad good news from heaven?
Life to a death-doomed race is given;
Christ on the cross for you and me
Purchased a pardon full and free.

CHORUS.—He that believeth, he that believeth,
        He that believeth hath everlasting life;
        He that believeth hath everlasting life.

When we were lost, the Son of God
Made an atonement by His blood;
When we the glad good news believe,
Then the atonement we receive.

Why not believe the glad good news?
Why still the voice of God refuse?
Why not believe, when God hath said,
All, all our "guilt on Him" was laid.

"Will You Meet Me at the Fountain?" was suggested by a remark of a friend at the Chicago Exposition, in 1873, as they parted to make the tour of the building. The remark was, "Meet Me at the fountain." It made a melody in his heart in the suggestion of another meeting, and blossomed out into the song:

WILL YOU MEET ME AT THE FOUNTAIN?

Will you meet me at the fountain,
    When I reach the glory-land?
Will you meet me at the fountain?
    Shall I clasp your friendly hand?

Other friends will give me welcome,
　Other loving voices cheer;
There'll be music at the fountain;
　Will you, will you meet me there?

CHORUS.—Yes, I'll meet you at the fountain,
　　At the fountain bright and fair;
　Oh, I'll meet you at the fountain,
　　Yes, I'll meet you, meet you **there**.

Will you meet me at **the fountain**?
　For I'm **sure that** I shall know
Kindred souls and sweet communion
　More than **I have known below**,
And the chorus will be sweeter,
　When it bursts upon my ear,
And my heaven seem completer,
　If your happy voice I hear.

Will you meet me at the fountain?
　I shall long **to** have you near,
When I meet my loving Savior,
　When His welcome words I hear.
He will meet me at the fountain,
　His embraces I shall share;
There'll be glory at the fountain;
　Will **you**, will you meet me there?

———————————◆◆◆———————————

"Hallelujah! He is Risen," was written in the South, in the spring of 1876, and was first sung by him on Easter afternoon, 1876, in the Court House Square of Augusta, Georgia, to an audience of five thousand people gathered to hear the Gospel. None who were there will ever forget the radiant face, or the triumphant, ringing tones with which he sang—

He is risen, He is risen,
Living Lord and coming King.

HALLELUJAH! HE IS RISEN!

Hallelujah! He is risen!
　Jesus is gone up on high!
Burst the bars of death asunder,
　Angels shout and men reply:

He is risen, He is risen,
  Living now no more to die.

Hallelujah, He is risen!
  Our exalted Head to be ;
Sends the witness of the spirit
  That our Advocate is He ;
He is risen, He is risen,
  Justified to Him are we.

Hallelujah, He is risen!
  Death for aye hath lost its sting,
Christ, Himself the Resurrection,
  From the grave His own will bring
He is risen, He is risen,
  Living Lord and coming King.

"Seeking to Save" was suggested by some remarks made in conversation with Mr. Bliss, by Dr. Wadsworth, of the Methodist Episcopal Church of Mobile, Alabama, upon the unity of the three parables in the fifteenth chapter of Luke.

SEEKING TO SAVE.

Tenderly the Shepherd,
  O'er the mountains cold,
Goes to bring his lost one
  Back to the fold.

CHORUS.—Seeking to save, seeking to save,
    Lost one, 'tis Jesus seeking to save.
    Seeking to save, seeking to save,
    Lost one, 'tis Jesus seeking to save.

Patiently the owner
  Seeks with earnest care,
In the dust and darkness
  Her treasure rare.

Lovingly the Father
  Sends the news around :
" He once dead now liveth—
  Once lost is found."

"At the Feet of Jesus " came from the Scripture suggestions of passages containing that phrase.

AT THE FEET OF JESUS.

At the feet of Jesus,
  List'ning to His word,
Learning wisdom's lesson
  From her loving Lord,
Mary, led by heavenly grace,
Chose the meek disciple's place.
At the feet of Jesus is the place for me,
There a humble *learner* would I choose to be.

At the feet of Jesus,
  Pouring perfume rare,
Mary did her Savior
  For the grave prepare;
And, from love the "good work" done,
She her Lord's approval won.
At the feet of Jesus is the place for me,
There in sweetest *service* would I ever be.

At the feet of Jesus,
  In that morning hour,
Loving hearts receiving
  Resurrection power,
Haste with joy to preach the word:
"Christ is risen, Praise the Lord!"
At the feet of Jesus, risen now for me,
I shall sing His *praises* through eternity.

"The Half was Never Told " was suggested by reading notes by his dear friend and sometimes fellow laborer in Gospel work, James M. Brookes, of St. Louis, upon the Queen of Sheba's visit to Solomon.

THE HALF WAS NEVER TOLD.

Repeat the story o'er and o'er,
  Of *grace* so full and free;
I love to hear it more and more,
  Since grace has rescued me.

Chorus.—The half was never **told**,
The half was never told,
Of grace divine, so wonderful,
The half was never told.

Of *peace* I only knew the name,
Nor found my soul its **rest**
Until the sweet-voiced angel **came**
To soothe **my weary** breast.

My highest place is lying low
At my Redeemer's feet ;
No real *joy* in life I know,
But in His service sweet.

And oh, what rapture will it be
With all the host above,
To sing through all eternity
The wonders of His *love.*

The Columbus Glee Club lately paid a visit to the President and Mrs. Hayes **at the White House.** They sang a number of ditties in the corridor. **At the close of the second song Mrs. Hayes** made a special request for **her favorite tunes. Among them was,** " Let the Lower Lights **be Burning."**

The last time **Mr.** Bliss sang for Mr. Moody was on Thursday, **November 23,** at Farwell Hall. Mr. Moody conducted, at ten o'clock **that morning, a** prayer meeting of ministers. Nearly **one** thousand **pastors from all parts** of the Northwest were **present. It was a very earnest, very solemn, and impressive gathering. The Spirit of God was present, and many hearts were brought to a new and more en-tire consecration to Christ. Mr. Moody at this meeting suggested** the **Alliance for Prayer, and a list was there made of over four hun-**dred **churches who covenanted to pray for each other until God re-**vived His **work in their midst.**

Rev. **W. A. Spencer was** appointed **as the** Secretary **of** the Alli-ance, and **very blessed and encouraging to the** faith of God's people have been the reports **that have come to him** as the result of this **united** prayer.

Mr. Bliss was seated **at the organ and** led in the singing. His **own heart** was full of Christ, and **he was** melted by the scene before **him of these** hundreds of dear ministers re-consecrating themselves so humbly and tearfully to the work of saving souls. His singing came with mighty power from a full heart, and with the conscious power of the Spirit of God. At the height of interest in the meeting, at Mr. Moody's request he sang, "Are your windows open toward Jerusalem?" His face fairly shone as he sang, and half of those present were in tears under the influence of the song. Mr. Moody leaned his head forward upon the desk, filled with emotion, and as the words, so gloriously sung, "For the coming of the King in His beauty are you watching day by day?" died away, the feeling of every heart, I believed, was expressed by a dear minister who exclaimed "God bless Mr. Bliss for that song." "*Amen*" came from many a voice and from all hearts.

It was the last song he sung in Farwell Hall. It was the last time that his loved friend and brother Mr. Moody heard his voice in song. A fitting scene and a fitting theme to close the record of their work together on the earth.

CHAPTER XV.

THE second collection of hymns bearing Mr. Bliss' name on the title page is "Sunshine for Sunday Schools," published by Messrs. John Church & Co., in 1873. The following hymns were included in that work, and are given here by permission of the publishers.

MY PRAYER.

More holiness give me,
  More strivings within,
More patience in suff'ring,
  More sorrow for sin,
More faith in my Savior,
  More sense of His care,
More joy in His service,
  More purpose in prayer.

More gratitude give me,
  More trust in the Lord,
More pride in His glory,
  More hope in His word,
More tears for His sorrows,
  More pain at His grief,
More meekness in trial,
  More praise for relief.

More purity give me,
  More strength to o'ercome,
More freedom from earth-stains,
  More longings for home.

More fit for the kingdom,
  More used would I be,
More blessed and holy,
  More, Savior, *like Thee*.

MORE TO FOLLOW.

"A vast fortune was left in the hands of a minister for one of his poor parishioners. Fearing that it might be squandered if suddenly bestowed upon him, the wise minister sent him a little at a time, with a note, saying : ' *This is thine ; use it wisely ; there is more to follow.* Brethren, that's just the way God deals with us."—D. L. MOODY

Have you on the Lord believed ?
  Still there's more to follow ;
Of His grace have you received ?
  Still there's more to follow.
Oh, the grace the Father shows !
  Still there's more to follow ;
Freely He His grace bestows,
  Still there's more to follow.

CHORUS.—More and more, more and more,
  Always more to follow,
Oh, His matchless, boundless love !
  Still there's more to follow.

Have you felt the Savior **near ?**
  Still **there's** more to follow ;
Does His **blessed** presence cheer ?
  Still there's more to follow.
Oh, the love that Jesus **shows !**
  Still there's more to **follow ;**
Freely He His **love** bestows,
  Still there's more to follow.

Have you felt **the** Spirit's power ?
  Still there's more to follow ;
Falling like the gentle shower ?
  Still there's more to follow.
Oh, the power the Spirit shows !
  Still there's more to follow ;
Freely He His power bestows,
  Still there's more **to follow.**

CALLING NOW.

" Behold, I stand at the door and knock."
" They that are whole have no need of the physician, but they that are sick . I came not to
call the righteous, but sinners to repentance."
" I have redeemed thee—I have called thee by thy name."
" To-day, if ye will hear his voice, harden not your hearts."

This loving Savior
   Stands patiently ;
Though oft rejected,
   Calls again for thee.

CHORUS.—Calling now for thee, prodigal,
      Calling now for thee ;
      Thou hast wandered far away,
         But He's calling now for thee.

Oh, boundless mercy,
   Free, free to all !
Stay, child of error,
   Heed the tender call.

Though all unworthy,
   Come, now, come home—
Say, while He's waiting,
   " Jesus, dear, I come."

SPIRIT DIVINE.

Spirit Divine, Spirit Divine.
Be Thou the Day-star in my darkness **to shine**

Spirit of Truth, Spirit of Truth,
Be Thou the Teacher and the Guide **of my youth.**

Spirit of Love, **Spirit of Love,**
Be Thou **the Leader to my** mansion above.

Spirit of Power, Spirit of Power,
Be Thine the praises of my song evermore.

BEAUTIFUL SONG OF LOVE.

I may not know all the melodies of heaven,
  Sounding afar o'er the golden streets aglow,
Yet to my soul let the sweet refrain be given,
  Come, blessed angels, your chorus I would know.

CHORUS.—Teach me, teach me,
    Teach me the song of the beautiful and holy ones,
      Teach me the song of the pure ones above;
    Oh, teach me the song of the beautiful and holy ones,
      Teach me the beautiful song of love.

I may not know all the glorified immortals
  Standing before Him, the holy, holy King,
Yet would I join, as I near the shining portals,
  Loud hallelujahs, your chorus sweet to sing.

Soon shall I hear them, the melodies of heaven,
  Sounding afar through the golden streets aglow.
Soon to my soul shall the sweet refrain be given,
  Soon, blessed angels, your chorus I shall know.

DANIEL'S BAND.

Dedicated to " Daniel's Band " of the First Congregational Church, Chicago.

Standing by a purpose true,
  Heeding God's command,
Honor them, the faithful few,
  All hail to Daniel's Band !

CHORUS.—Dare to be a Daniel !
    Dare to stand alone !
    Dare to have a purpose firm,
    Dare to make it known.

Many mighty men are lost
  Daring not to stand,
Who for God had been a host,
  By joining Daniel's Band.

Many giants great and tall,
  Stalking through the land,
Headlong to the earth would fall,
  If met by Daniel's Band.

Hold the Gospel banner high,
  On to victory grand!
Satan and his host defy,
  And shout for Daniel's Band.

ASK, SEEK, KNOCK.

" Ask, and it shall be given; Seek, and ye shall find."
  Precious promise! Lord, I wonder Thou art still so kind!
" Knock, it shall be opened," if we only could believe.
  Ask, seek, knock—Savior, help us to receive.
CHORUS.—Ask, seek, knock, hear the loving Savior say:
  Ask, seek, knock—Savior, help me to obey.

Jesus, I ask Thee now, for Thine is all the power,
Give me grace to look to Thee in dark temptation's hour.
Help me to remember 'tis Thy gentle voice I hear.
Ask, seek, knock—Savior, wherefore should I fear?

Lord, I am waiting now Thy blessed face to see;
Earnestly I'm knocking, knocking; open, Lord, to me.
To Thy cross I'll cling till Thou a blessing dost bestow.
Ask, seek, knock—Lord, I will not let Thee go.

LOVE ONE ANOTHER.

This is My commandment,
That ye love one another,
That ye love one another,
As I have loved you.

Blessed words of Jesus
  We have heard to-day—
Savior, by Thy spirit,
  Help us to obey.
May Thy love unite us
  To the living Vine!
May our hearts, enlightened,
  Glow with love divine!

May we seek Thy glory,
  Strife and envy flee ;
By our love to others,
  Prove our love to Thee.
Ever more as brethren,
  In sweet union live.
As we wish forgiveness,
  May we each forgive.

Grant us Thy salvation,
  Fill us with Thy love ;
Give us each a foretaste
  Of the joys above.
Ever meek and lowly,
  Ever kind and true,
Ever pure and holy,
  Paths of peace pursue.

This is My commandment,
That ye love one another,
That ye love one another,
As I have loved you.

------------+ • +------------

FEAR NOT.

What did the angel to the shepherds say ?
  Fear not, fear not,
On that bright morning of our Lord's birth-day ?

Chorus.—Fear not, fear not,
  Fear not, fear not, let the Gospel sound,
Fear not, fear not,
  Roll the world around ;
  Trembling souls, dismiss your fear,
  To the mercy seat draw near,
  To the mercy seat draw near.

What said the Master when the waves ran high ?
  Fear not, fear not,
To His disciples said He, " It is I."

What to the ruler did the Savior say ?
  Fear not, fear not,
When cold and lifeless His dear daughter lay ?

What to the Marys was the cheering word?
   Fear not, fear not,
When they with joy beheld the risen Lord?

What saith the Son of Man, the First and Last?
   Fear not, fear not,
He whose eternal word abideth fast?

GOING HOME.

  Though the way seems lone,
  And the sunlight gone ;
Though the blinding tears will fall,
  Let us look away,
  And be glad to-day,
At the thought of going home.

CHORUS.—Going home,
   Going home,
To our Father's house on high, going home
  Where there's no more night,
  And the Lamb is the light,
   We are going by and by.

  Though the world is drear,
  And the tempter near,
And his arrows pierce the soul ;
  Yonder beams the strand
  Of the Promised Land,
'Tis the long-sought final goal.

  Though in hostile lands,
  Over burning sands
Now with weary feet we roam,
  But a few years more,
  And 'twill all be o'er,
He *will come* to take us home.

MOURN, PRAY, PRAISE.

Mourn, yes mourn,
But not for her at rest,
And happy with the blest ;

Her toils and trials cease,
Her soul may rest in peace,
    In perfect peace.

Pray, yes pray,
But not for her in heaven;
Pray we may be forgiven,
And at the last may stand,
With her in Glory Land,
    A happy band.

Praise, yes, praise,
That in the Crucified
She lived, and loved, and died.
May grace our souls refine,
And may her hope divine
    Be thine and mine.   Amen.

SONG IN SCRIPTURE.

A song bursts from the starry sky,
    Starry sky, starry sky,
And angels from their throne on high
    Shout aloud their holy joy.

JOB xxxvii, 4, 5, 6, 7.

But oh, earth's first and warlike song,
    Warlike song, warlike song,
Of vengeance, murder, guilt and wrong!
    Evermore it rolls along.

GENESIS iv, 23, 24.

A song rings o'er the sounding sea,
    Sounding sea, sounding sea,
"The Lord hath triumphed gloriously"—
    Praise Him for the victory.

EXODUS xv, 1, 2.

O, list the welcome Christmas song,
    Christmas song, Christmas song!
Of heaven's bright and shining throng—
    We the Gospel strain prolong.

LUKE ii, 8, 9, 10, 11.

A psalm floats on the evening air,
  Evening air, evening air,
And Jesus' gentle voice is there—
  Oh, may we His worship share!
MARK xiv, 22, 23, 24, 26.

There'll be a song of glad accord,
  Glad accord, glad accord,
Through heaven's eternal anthems heard,
  "Alleluia, praise the Lord!"
REVELATION xix, 6.

GOOD CHEER!

Good cheer, good cheer!
For a happy New Year
Is brightly smiling before us;
  Let merry bells ring,
  Let happy hearts sing,
Good cheer, good cheer is the chorus.
  Adown the past,
  One look we cast,
For friends and fancies olden;
  Then forward glance,
  And dream perchance,
Of future days more golden.

CHORUS.—Good cheer, good cheer!
    For a happy New Year
  Is brightly smiling before us,
    Let merry bells ring,
    Let happy hearts sing,
  Good cheer, good cheer is the chorus.
    Good cheer, good cheer!
  For the glad and happy New Year!
    Good cheer, good cheer!
  For the glad and happy New Year!

Good cheer, good cheer!
For a happy New Year
Is brightly smiling before us,
  Let merry bells ring,
  Let happy hearts sing,
Good cheer, good cheer is the chorus.

In future years,
From smiles and tears,
Our lives shall luster gather;
And come what may,
We'll always say,
"Thy will be done, our Father."

INNOCENT CHILDHOOD.

Sweet little violets,
Born in the wild-wood;
Purest of loveliness,
Innocent childhood;
Shy as the antelope,
Brown as a berry,
Free as the mountain air,
Romping and merry.

CHORUS.—Tra la, la, la, la, la, &c.

Blue eyes and hazel eyes
Peep from the hedges,
Shaded by sun-bonnets
Fray'd at the edges;
Up in the apple-trees,
Heedless of danger,
Manhood in embryo
Stares at the stranger.

Out in the hilly patch,
Seeking the berries—
Under the orchard trees,
Feasting on cherries—
Trampling the clover blooms
Down 'mong the grasses,
No voice to hinder them,
Dear lads and lasses.

Dear little innocents!
Born in the wild-wood;
Oh, that all little ones
Had such a childhood!
Heaven's blue over them,
Earth's green beneath them,
No sweeter heritage
Could we bequeath them.

LORD JESUS, COME.

Lord Jesus, come !
Nor let us longer roam
Afar from Thee and that bright place
Where we shall see Thee face to face.

CHORUS.—Lord Jesus, come !
Lord Jesus, come !

Lord Jesus, come !
Thine absence here we mourn :
No joy we know apart from Thee,
No sorrow in Thy presence see.

Lord Jesus, come !
And take Thy people home,
That all Thy flock, so scattered here,
With Thee in glory may appear.

GOOD NIGHT TILL THEN.

I journey forth, rejoicing,
From this dark vale of tears,
To heavenly joy and freedom
From earthly bonds and fears,
Where Christ our Lord shall gather
All His redeemed again,
His kingdom to inherit;
Good-night, good-night till then.

Why thus so sadly weeping,
Beloved ones of my heart ?
The Lord is good and gracious,
Though now He bids us part
We oft have met in gladness,
And we shall meet again.
All sorrow left behind us;
Good-night, good-night till then.

I go to see His glory,
   Whom we have loved below ;
I go, the blessed angels
   And holy saints to know ;
Our lovely ones departed,
   I go to find again,
And wait for you to join us :
   Good-night, good-night till then.

The two hymns following are taken from " The Joy," issued by Messrs. Church & Co., in 1873 :

THE FOUR RULERS.

" Is it safe ? is it safe ? " hear the timid cry !
   " Who will tell me what to do ?
Is it safe to wait ? is it safe to try ?
   Ah me, if I only knew ! "
Alas, said I, come tell me, pray,
   What foolish man is this ?
The laughing echoes seemed to say,
   " His name is COWARDICE."

' Will it pay ? will it pay ? " came a frenzied yell
   From a surging, scowling crowd ;
From the men of State and of Church as well—
   In sorrow my head I bowed.
Can man, immortal man, thought I,
   So low and selfish be ?
Their gilded motto streamed on high,
   I read it POLICY.

" Will it please ? will it please ? " 'twas a soulless sound,
   Floating on the perfumed air,
And again I sighed as I looked around
   On the captives of fashion there.
' What ho," I cried, " and whither now ?
   Whose worshipers are ye ? "
Before their queen I saw them bow ;
   'Twas cruel VANITY.

"Is it right? is it right?" 'twas a ringing tone,
    And the jostling crowd stood still,
For the voice was clear though it rose alone,
    And spake with a heavenly thrill.
"Joy, joy, sweet angel voice," I cried,
    "Dwell, ever dwell with me,"
"This thine to choose," the voice replied,
    "My name is HONESTY"

TO DIE IS GAIN.

"To die is gain,"
All earthly cares forsaking,
  From toil and pain,
To endless joy awaking,
  To die is gain.

To die is gain,
My weary soul home bringing;
  O'er heavenly plain,
Sweet angel voices singing,
  To die is gain.

To die is gain,
From strife and sin to sever,
  With Christ to reign,
Forever, oh, forever,
  To die is gain.

CHAPTER XVI.

IN 1874, Messrs. Church & Co. published " Gospel Songs, a Choice Collection of Hymns and Tunes, New and Old, for Gospel Meetings, Sunday Schools, etc., by P. P. Bliss." In addition to compositions formerly published, the following were contained in that work :

NEARER TO ME.

Be near, O God, to me,
  Nearer to me ;
So shall I truly be
  " Nearer to Thee."
Thy face I cannot see,
Still be Thou near to me,
Nearer, O God, to me,
  Nearer to me.

Fold me beneath Thy wing,
  O Savior divine :
There may I sweetly sing,
  " Jesus is mine."
O'er all life's stormy sea,
Still be Thou near to me,
Nearer, O God, to me,
  Nearer to me.

Thy hand, in youth's wild way,
  Did me uphold ;
Forsake me not, I pray,
  When I am old ;

I put my trust in Thee,
Now and eternally,
Be near, O God, to me,
    Nearer to me.

WE GLORY IN THE LORD.

Written for K. A. Burnell upon his fiftieth birthday, July, 1874.

Come, brethren, as we march along,
    Come glory in the Lord :
Bring each a psalm, a sacred song,
    And glory in the Lord :
His hand hath led us hitherto,
    Come glory in the Lord ;
We've proved His precious promise true ;
    Oh, glory in the Lord.

CHORUS.—Forget the trials by the way,
        Press toward the great reward ;
        Exalt the cross of Christ to-day,
        And glory in the Lord.

Though we in danger dread may be,
    We glory in the Lord ;
In perils oft, by land and sea,
    We glory in the Lord ;
In weary watchings night and day
    We glory in the Lord ;
He says, " With you I am alway "—
    We glory in the Lord.

Fight on, O soldier of the cross ;
    We glory in the Lord ;
For Jesus' sake count all things loss,
    And glory in the Lord ;
In life or death, in ease or pain
    We glory in the Lord ;
" To live is Christ, to die is gain "—
    We glory in the Lord.

HOW MUCH OWEST THOU?

How much owest thou?
How much owest thou?
For years of tender watchful care,
A father's faith, a mother's prayer,
How much owest thou?

How much owest thou?
How much owest thou?
For calls and warnings loud and plain,
For songs and sermons heard in vain,
How much owest thou?

How much owest thou?
How much owest thou?
Thy day of grace is almost o'er,
The judgment time is just before,
How much owest thou?

How much owest thou?
How much owest thou?
O child of God and heir of Heaven,
Thy soul redeemed, thy sins forgiven,
How much owest thou?

THE THREE MOUNTAINS.

Between me and my Savior
  Three mighty mountains rose,
That all the way and ever
  My coming did oppose;
And darkness gathered round me,
  The light was growing dim,
Until my Savior found me,
  And now I rest in Him.

I waited for a feeling,
  Some new, mysterious power,
A heavenly light revealing
  My heart as ne'er before;

This mountain dark and gloomy
      Concealed a loving Lord,
Until His voice came to me—
      "My child, believe My word."

I waited for a fitness ;
      To pray would be a sin ;
My past life bore the witness
      How vile my heart had been ;
This mountain crushed my spirit
      Till God deliverance gave—
'Twas sinners without merit
      That Jesus came to save.

And then my fear of failing,
      Of hopes indulged in vain,
Of efforts unavailing
      Eternal life to gain—
This mountain rose before me ;
      I called for help divine ;
Said Jesus, " Dost thou love Me ?
      Then rest thy life in Mine."

"Gospel Hymns and Sacred Songs" was the joint production of
Messrs. Bliss and Sankey, and the preface to it bears fac-similes of
their autograph signatures. The work was published in 1875, by
Biglow & Main, New York and Chicago, and John Church & Co.,
Cincinnati. The following hymns were published in it :

WHERE ARE THE NINE?

Wand'ring afar from the dwellings of men,
Hear the sad cry of the lepers—the ten.
" Jesus have mercy !" brings healing divine ;
One came to worship, but where are the nine?

CHORUS.—Where are the nine ?
            Where are the nine ?
                Were there not ten cleansed ?
            Where are the nine ?

Loudly the stranger sang praise to the Lord,
Knowing the cure had been wrought by His word,
Gratefully owning the Healer Divine ;
Jesus says tenderly, " Where are the nine ? "

" Who is this Nazarene ? "　Pharisees say ;
" Is He the Christ ? tell us plainly, we pray."
Multitudes follow Him seeking a sign,
Show them His mighty works—Where are the nine ?

Jesus on trial to-day we can see,
Thousands deridingly ask, " Who is He ? "
How they're rejecting Him, your Lord and mine !
Bring in the witnesses—Where are the nine ?

WHERE HAST THOU GLEANED TO-DAY ?

Weary gleaner, whence comest thou,
With empty hands and clouded brow ?
Plodding along thy lonely way,
Tell me, where hast thou gleaned to-day ?
Late I found a barren field,
The harvest past my search revealed,
Others golden sheaves had gained,
Only stubble for me remained.

CHORUS.—**Forth to** the harvest field, away !
　　　　Gather your handfuls while you may ;
　　　　All day long in the field abide,
　　　　Gleaning close by the reaper's side.

Careless gleaner, what **hast thou here,**
These faded **flow'rs and leaflets sere ?**
Hungry and **thirsty, tell me, pray,**
Where, oh, **where hast thou glean'd to-day ?**
All day long in **shady** bow'rs,
I've gaily sought earth's fairest flow'rs ;
Now, alas ! too late I see
All I've gathered is **vanity.**

Burden'd gleaner, **thy sheaves I see ;**
Indeed thou must **a-weary be !**
Singing along the homeward way,
Glad one, where hast thou glean'd to-day ?

Stay me not, till day is done,
I've gathered handfuls one by one;
Here and there for me they fall,
Close by the reapers I've found them all.

NO OTHER NAME.

One offer of salvation,
  To all the world make known;
The only sure foundation
  Is Christ the Corner Stone.

CHORUS.—No other name is given,
    No other way is known,
    'Tis Jesus Christ, the First and Last,
    He saves, and He alone.

One only door of heaven
  Stands open wide to-day,
One sacrifice is given,
  'Tis Christ, the living way.

My only song and story
  Is—Jesus died for me;
My only hope for glory,
  The Cross of Calvary.

In 1876, " Gospel Hymns No. 2 " made its appearance, containing the following of Mr. Bliss' compositions :

IN ZION'S ROCK ABIDING.

In Zion's Rock abiding,
  My soul her triumph sings;
In His pavilion hiding,
  I praise the King of kings.

CHORUS.—My High Tower is He!
    To Him will I flee;
    In Him confide, in Him abide;
    My High Tower is He!

Wild waves are round me swelling,
  Dark clouds above I see;
Yet, in my Fortress dwelling,
  More safe I cannot be.

My Tower of strength can never
  In time of trouble fail;
No power of hell, forever,
  Against it shall prevail.

————— ◆ ◆ ◆ —————

I'M ON THE LORD'S SIDE.

We're marching to Canaan with banner and song,
We're soldiers enlisted to fight 'gainst the wrong;
But, lest in the conflict our strength should divide,
We ask, who among us is on the Lord's side?

CHORUS.—Oh, who is there among us, the true and the tried,
    Who'll stand by his colors—who's on the Lord's side?
    Oh, who is there among us, the true and the tried,
    Who'll stand by his colors—who's on the Lord's side?

The sword may be burnished, the armor be bright,
For Satan appears as an angel of light;
Yet darkly the bosom may treachery hide,
While lips are professing, " I'm on the Lord's side."

Who is there among us yet under the rod,
Who knows not the pardoning mercy of God?
Oh, bring to Him humbly the heart in its pride;
Oh, haste while He's waiting and seek the Lord's side.

Oh, heed not the sorrow, the pain and the wrong
For soon shall our sighing be changed into song;
So, bearing the cross of our covenant Guide,
We'll shout, as we triumph, " *I'm on the Lord's side.*"

————— ◆ ◆ ◆ —————

HALLELUJAH! WHAT A SAVIOR!

" Man of sorrow " what a name
  For the Son of God, who came
Ruined sinners to reclaim—
  Hallelujah! what a Savior!

Bearing shame and scoffing rude,
In my place condemned He stood,
Sealing my pardon with His blood—
   Hallelujah! what a Savior!

Guilty, vile and helpless we;
Spotless Lamb of God was He,
"Full atonement"—can it be?
   Hallelujah, what a Savior!

Lifted up was He to die,
"It is finished" was His cry,
   Now in heaven exalted high.
   Hallelujah, what a Savior!

CHAPTER XVII.

THE following letter from Mr. Bliss' friend and co-worker, Mr. Sankey, will be read with peculiar interest at this time :

It was in the autumn of 1870 that I for the first time met P. P. Bliss. I had just arrived in Chicago to join Mr Moody in his work in that city, and had gone with him to attend the noon-day prayer meeting in Lower Farwell Hall. Mr. Bliss was leading the singing, and at the close of the meeting Mr. Moody demanded of us a song. Seating himself at the piano which was in the room, we sang from " Hallowed Songs : "

> Oh, think of the home over there,
> By the side of the River of Light,
> Where the saints, all immortal and fair,
> Are robed in their garments of white,
> Over there, over there.

This was our first song together, and the last one we sang, a few days before he passed " Over There," was " Hallelujah ! what a Savior ! " It was my pleasure to have met Mr. Bliss very often afterward, in the Saturday noon meetings, for the study of the International Sunday School Lessons. In these meetings, as well as in the usual daily prayer meetings, he was always a blessing and an inspiration.

During the time I was in Chicago, prior to our going to England, I became familiar with many of Mr. Bliss' songs, and they struck me as being specially adapted for reaching the masses, and, that I might have them in convenient shape for use in evangelistic work, I gathered a number of them from his " Charm " and " Sunshine," and, with other sacred songs, arranged them into a " Musical Scrap Book," which, with my Bible, was the only book I took with me across the sea.

It was while singing from this scrap book, " Jesus of Nazareth Passeth By," " Come Home, Prodigal Child," and Mr. Bliss' " Hold the Fort," " Jesus Loves Me," and " Free from the Law," in the old Cathedral city of York, and in Sunderland, England, that we began to fully realize the wonderful power there was in these Gospel songs. The demand for them soon became so great that we were compelled to have them published in a cheap form, which we did, under the title of "Sacred Songs and Solos." This collection contained a number of Mr. Bliss' best songs, which, together with a companion book of "Words Only" (the latter being sold for a penny) is believed to have attained a larger circulation than any collection of hymns and tunes ever published.

The first of Mr. Bliss' hymns that became popular in Great Britain was "Jesus Loves Even Me," and, more than any other hymn, it became the key note of our meetings there. The next song which became immensely popular was "Hold the Fort," and it is to-day, perhaps, the most popular sacred song in England or America.

I should think Mr. Bliss' "Almost Persuaded" has won more souls to the Savior than any other hymn written by him.

It has been no unusual thing, in our special meetings for young converts, to have them testify that it was the singing of "Almost Persuaded," or "What shall the Harvest Be?" that led them to decide for Christ. During the last year, the hymn "Waiting and Watching" has been specially blessed, and we believe that through the singing of this little hymn, thousands have been led to desire to live a better and a holier life. This song, with many of his new ones, will ever have a deeper and a tenderer meaning to us, now that he has entered within the gates into the city of the great King, where he may be "Waiting and Watching" for us ; and with what new joy and rejoicing shall we now sing his sweet words :

> Many loved ones have I in yon heavenly throng ;
> They are safe now in glory, and this is their song
> Hallelujah ! 'tis done ! I believe on the Son ;
> I am saved by the blood of the crucified One."

"He was not, for God took him." Gen. v, 24.

IRA D. SANKEY.

BOSTON, Feb. 1877.

The following letters from Japan and China are given in full to show the far-reaching influence of the Gospel Hymns and the sympathy of Mr. Bliss in work for Christ all over the earth. He loved and prayed for all who named the name of Christ, and especially prayed for those engaged in missionary labor in foreign lands. The writer of these letters he became interested in through his wife, who was a cousin of Mrs. True. She had accompanied her husband, who was a missionary in Japan, and after his death remained in that country with her little girl, to carry on the work of winning souls for Christ. The letter of October 11th Mr. Bliss received at Jackson, Michigan, in the latter part of November. He read it over to me, with his heart full of sympathy for the lonely one in the Lord's work in the far off land, and with much emotion said : "Whittle, we should be ashamed of ourselves if we ever speak of sacrificing anything in being in the work as we are, compared with such devotion." Very fervent and tender was the prayer that followed for this sister and for all missionary laborers. The same day he ordered a hundred books forwarded by his publishers to Japan. The happy letter of January 1st he, of course, never saw. Two days before it was written he had passed into the presence of the King to receive the "*well done*" of the Master, in answer to the prayers in the far away mission home in Japan, and from many and many another home and heart made glad by his Christian sympathy and Christian song. May many a Christian who reads these letters be stimulated to remember in prayer this dear sister in Christ, for whom Mr. and Mrs. Bliss prayed, and the cause of Christ in Japan, and all over the earth. These dear servants of Jesus who have gone out from us are our brethren in the Lord. Let us bear them often before the Throne. Let us have a place in our hearts for them always, for "their work's sake," and let us encourage them by our sympathy and by our aid in every way we can, for Jesus' sake.

"There is one body, and one spirit, even as ye are called in one hope of your calling ; One Lord, one faith, one baptism, One God and Father of all, who is above all, and through all, and in you all." Eph. iv, 4–6.

It was clear to Mr. Bliss, from the Scriptures, that the coming of the Lord was delayed by the lukewarmness of the Church in spreading the Gospel, and may his frequent and oft-repeated prayer be speedily answered, that the baptism of the Spirit may come upon the Church, that she may complete the number of such as shall be saved, and the Lord may return.

Tokio, Japan, October 11, 1876.

Prof. P. P. Bliss:

Dear Brother,—Your kind note of July 8th lies before me. I had it in my heart to reply by the first mail after its reception, but an unusual pressure of care and labor, incident to a change of residence and work, made it impossible.

You know somewhat of our work in Yokohama, by way of Sister Sarah, I presume. Perhaps you will not take less interest in my present field of labor. Last August, I was applied to, by a Japanese Christian, to take charge of a school for girls, in one of the principal streets of this immense city. He proposed to furnish the building and be responsible for all of the expenses of the school except the salary of myself and assistant.

The fact that such an opening occurred in the native city, where all of the missionaries wished to go, but were not able, because of government restrictions, made it seem to me, and to all with whom I spoke of the matter, sufficiently important to warrant me in leaving the work in which I had been engaged to occupy a field so hopeful. Now I am here in the midst of heathendom with my little girl, and no other person in the house except natives. The school is opening well, I think, and I hope to be used of God in preparing many of these dear girls for usefulness in this land, where Satan has so long reigned. I do indeed find that, were it not for the very precious promises of God, my lot would be one of special trial. I am not alone, but even the presence of a Heavenly Friend does not still the heart-cries for earthly love and sympathy.

The harvest is great and the laborers few; so I will not be impatient, but when the Master has finished the plan for me here, I shall be glad, I think, to join my dear one on the other shore. I hope you will not understand me to complain of my lot. Far from it. I know that I am entirely unworthy of this blessed work ; my heart will sometimes ask why my dear husband, who was so much better fitted for it, and who so wished to engage in it, was taken home, and I sent alone. God does not make mistakes.

You very kindly offer to furnish some singing books for our use. I am very *glad* to accept, as we teach English (that is the attraction to bring in pupils), and singing is a very important help. I have one copy of Gospel Hymns and Sacred Songs, and we have already learned a few pieces, but, of course, find it very difficult to do so without books.

I do not wish to make too large a request, but if you can send fifty copies, I will sell as many as I can to the girls, and pay you for as many as you wish, or use the money for other mission purposes. You see I take you at your word, and believe in accepting all the aid offered us by Christian friends.

I wish I could tell you how much we need your prayers. I can not, but I pray God to teach all Christians at home to pray as never before for this land in this time of special interest in her history.

With the prayer that God will make you the instrument for leading many more souls into the Kingdom, I am your sister in Christ,

MARIA T. TRUE.

No. 12 GINZA SANCHOME, TOKIO, JAPAN.

I meant to have said if you prefer to send any other book, do so, of course. I spoke of that because I have enjoyed the music much.

No. 12 GINZA SANCHOME, TOKIO, Jan. 1st, 1877.

PROF. P. P. BLISS :

DEAR BROTHER,—Surely it is a pleasant thing to be able to begin this new year by writing a letter of thanks.

We had our Christmas festivities on the 26th, as we could not prepare in one day, and our school-rooms are also our church, and so we did not wish to decorate on Saturday. There were more than three hundred persons present, and nearly all were Japanese. For this I was very thankful, as it furnished the opportunity to tell many for the first time of our Savior's wondrous love.

I retired exceedingly weary, but glad in heart, because I believed the Master was pleased with our efforts to spread the news of His love. Before I arose next morning, a servant announced at my door, "Americano yubin" (American mail)! He knew full well that, notwithstanding my fatigue, I would wish to know at once the glad tidings. I hastened to see what was in store for me and to my *surprise* and *joy*, there were the "hymn books." I cannot tell you how glad I was, but I told our Father, and I am sure He will return a hundred fold. At morning worship we had a thanksgiving service, and afterward the girls and I had a "sing." I wish you could have seen their happy faces, as they saw the nice new books, and turned at once to find "Whosoever Will." They had learned that from my one copy, and sang it the evening before. But there were *so many!* What was intended? There was no letter to explain, and I could not wait a whole month to know, and so I just said we will share our joy with the other three schools in our mission. I gave a part to Miss Youngman, who has a girls' school, and some to Mr. Ballagh, who has a boys' school in Yokohama, and sent some to Miss Marsh for her school, also in Yokohama. That leaves a nice supply for us, and we sing and sing until we are hoarse! I hope I have not done wrong with them. The others were delighted, and you may be sure that your name and songs will be well known in our mission in Japan at least.

I wonder whether you would not be interested in a sketch prepared by one of the girls in my school for our Christmas entertainment. I have a class of three, in English composition, and a few days before Christmas I told them that for their own profit and the pleasure of their friends, I wished them to prepare something on the life of Daniel. There is no translation of the Old Testament, and they must do it from what they could get from their English Bibles without help, and read without correction. I think I will send you one of them ; not because it is so good, but to show you a little the ability, and turn of mind of a girl fifteen years old.

This is, as you see, "New Year's," and the custom of calling prevails even in Japan. I have written in odd minutes between calls.

With many thanks, and ready to refund whatever part of price you say, and with love to Mrs. B., I am yours truly,

M. T. TRUE.

Mrs. True sends the sketch spoken of, which we omit here, as foreign to the purpose of this work. She adds a postscript, concluding as follows :

I will send by this mail a Japanese hymn book. If you have not seen one, you may be interested in it. There is great difficulty in getting hymns to fit any meter which pleases the Japanese ear. I wish we had some musicians to compose music according to their ideas—that is, in a meter which they like—

and we could get translations to fit, I think music is such a power here as everywhere.

The following letter from a missionary lady in China testifies to the appreciation there of Mr. Bliss' hymns :

Soochow, China, Dec. 11, 1876.

Mr. P. P. Bliss:

Dear Sir,—I am sure from the spirit of your songs—which many of us in this far land love to sing—that you are interested in all missionary operations and will be interested in hearing that some of your hymns are being given to this people. I know a number of the missionaries have translated your hymns into Chinese, and, as they are favorites with me, I translate them oftener than those of any other writer, to use in a little paper I edit, called the *Glad Tidings Messenger*. Thinking you may like to see one of your songs in Chinese, I send you my last little paper, in which you can perhaps recognize, " Blessed are They that Do," though I changed it somewhat for convenience in rhythm.

May God use your service of song, and bless you richly in all its effects.

Yours truly,

Mrs. Geo. F. Fitch.

A St. Louis friend writes :

St. Louis, Missouri, February 5, 1877.

Major D. W. Whittle

On one of those Sunday afternoons when a Gospel meeting was being held by yourself and Mr. Bliss, in the skating rink, there came as fearful a storm of wind and rain as I ever witnessed. The old timbers quivered ominously. You were speaking, but the noise was so great as to cause you to stop. The storm continuing, plain symptoms of alarm were becoming visible in the audience. Mr. Bliss, noticing this; by an inspiration from God, struck up a verse of the grand old hymn, " God moves in a mysterious Way." The storm was at its fiercest. Just as he sang the words, " He rides upon the storm," there was an instantaneous cessation of the storm ; a little break occurred in the cloud, and a bright ray of brilliant light flashed directly and fully for a moment upon his face. Mrs. B. had been uneasy, and asked me—I was right at her side— if there was any danger. I reassured her, and when the incident occurred, she looked at me with one of the pleasantest and sweetest smiles and nodded her head ; her look and manner being as much as to say, all is perfectly safe, for He who rides upon the storm has sent the brightness of His sunshine upon us at this moment, as He sent the rainbow.

W. H. W.

Rev. Arthur T. Pierson, of Detroit, speaks from the fullness of his heart respecting the dead singer :

DETROIT, February 13, 1877.

MY DEAR BROTHER WHITTLE:

I have but a few moments in which to give you my estimate of our dear departed Brother Bliss. You know what rare opportunity that four weeks' stay at my house afforded me for knowing you both. When I think of him, I think of *Anointed Song.* You remember when, to fit your sermon, I wrote those words, "With harps and with viols," that he went away to his room for a season of prayer, before he was willing to attempt to compose the music for those verses. Is it any marvel that dear Bliss' songs have been made so conspicuously the channels for the conveyance of spiritual impressions, when we know that not only the words, but the music, too, are "sanctified by the word of God and prayer?" Has not Mr. Bliss been God's instrument, in these days of perverted church music and operatic quartettes, to teach us how the Gospel may be sung, as well as preached?

He was well named "*Bliss.*" What a happy man he was! What a ray of sunshine, what a spring of joy in the household! My children will never forget him; and will always think of him as an illustration of the blessed peace and radiant cheerfulness of a Christian life. Ah, dear Whittle, what Cowper calls that "poor, lisping, stammering tongue" lies silent now, but "in a nobler, sweeter song," he sings the power of Christ to save.

Affectionately thine,

ARTHUR T. PIERSON.

Extract from a letter dated

MOBILE, ALABAMA, February 6, 1877.

The night of that fearful disaster we were holding a church sociable at our house. It was bitter cold, but a good many had assembled, and near the close of the evening my brother sat down to the piano and with a group of voices commenced singing some of those now household hymns of the Bliss and Sankey collection—among others, "We're going Home To-morrow." How little we thought then of the terrible tragedy that was being enacted in another part of our land, and was even then taking home the two who first sang it to us here in Mobile, and in the singing led so many to long for the home beyond. To me it will ever be sacred to their memory.

How vividly are the incidents of his short stay here with us recalled. Our acquaintance makes us feel a part ownership in him as a friend; and is he not the dear noble brother of us all who name the name of Christ?

The church has lost in him and his dear wife two members of its very own family circle. Eternity alone can tell the deep impression made upon all by his song sermons in the pulpit, where his beautiful voice told so pleadingly the "old, old story" to poor dying sinners, or spoke the praises of his God in hallelujahs for the finished work of the Son. A chord of universal sympathy has been touched in our city, and we would fain join our voices with those of his many friends everywhere, in chanting his last sad requiem. May we be as ready when our summons comes.   H. H. D.

APPLETON, WIS., March 6, 1877.

In the spring of 1875, it was my privilege to hear the vocalist, Mr. P. P. Bliss, in Chicago. With the earnest preaching and exhortation of Mr. Whittle, some of the sweet melodies of Mr. Bliss were intermingled. Never before did I so understand the power of sacred song to touch the heart, leading Christians to clasp closer and closer their birthright, and calling the wanderer home. It was a mixed multitude that evening, of high and low, rich and poor. Near me sat a group of young men, looking torn and "bruised by the fall." As Mr. Bliss sang the appeal embodied in the song, "Oh, brother, believe it, Christ has redeemed us once for all," I observed tears coursing down those hard cheeks. The wanderers were touched,—perhaps saved.

Eternity alone can estimate the value of these consecrated gifts of song, and the part they bear in the rescue of fallen humanity. Humanly speaking, great multitudes have heard and obeyed the call sent to them, through the "Gospel Hymns" of our departed friend. His voice will be heard on earth no more, but his work still lives. And *he* lives. Ashtabula was but the dark river, or the "chariot of fire" to bear him away to the home of which he had so often sung. It was the new life, and the "new song" begun; 'twas Immortality. L. A. B.

One Sunday a man came into the Sunday School at the Boston North End Mission, drawn by the sweetness of the children's singing. He remained until the close, and came again that evening to the prayer-meeting. When the customary invitation to seek the Savior was given, he came forward and found "peace in believing." To a few who had remained to pray with the penitent seekers he said, "My friends, I feel that I'm a saved man, and *I owe it to your children's singing 'Jesus loves me,' this afternoon.* I couldn't realize it, I've been such a miserable sinner; but after I went away I thought it over, 'Jesus loves me;' and then I thought of the next line, 'For the Bible tells me so,' and I tried to *believe* it, and I came here this evening to get you to pray for me." He became a regular attendant at the Mission, and gave the clearest evidence of a genuine change of heart.

At one of the revival meetings at Edinburgh a gay, giddy girl attended. She went late and was unable to get a seat, so she wandered about in the hall outside. Inside the church they were singing, led by Mr. Sankey,—

> Oh, I am so glad
> That Jesus loves me,
> Jesus loves me,
> Jesus loves me.

The words went to her heart and her conscience, and she said, "I cannot sing that." When that meeting broke up she went to the meeting for anxious inquirers, and is now a rejoicing Christian.

A missionary of the American Sunday School Union in Missouri, after he had organized a Sunday School recently, sang to them Mr. Bliss' delightful song,—

> I am so glad that Jesus loves me,

and followed it with the question, "Are you glad? If not, why?" He had hardly finished when a young man rose, and rushing up to him, threw his arms around his neck, sobbing, "Oh, sir, you must not leave here till I'm a Christian!" Prayer was offered for him, and he was saved. Then he exclaimed, "Oh, that song! I could not get away from it and it has saved me."

A young woman in England went to a meeting where she heard Mr. Sankey singing this same hymn,—

> I am so glad that Jesus loves me,

and while the hymn was being sung, began to feel for the first time in her life that she was a sinner. All her sins came up in array before her; and so numerous and aggravated did her sins appear, that she imagined she never could be saved. She said in her heart, "Jesus cannot love me. He could not love such a sinner as I." She went home in a state of extreme mental anguish, and did not sleep that night. Every opportunity of obtaining more light was eagerly seized. She took her place in the "Inquiry Room." There she found to her astonishment and joy that Jesus *could*, DID, DOES love sinners. She saw in God's opened Word that it was for sinners Jesus died, and for none others. When she realized this she too began to sing:

> I am so glad that Jesus loves me,
> Jesus loves me, Jesus loves me, even me.

In a praise meeting, during the revival services in Chicago, Mr. Sankey spoke as follows in regard to the power of this and other hymns:

What I have to thank God especially for is the wonderful way He has used the power of song. I remember about five years ago coming to yonder depot one morning early. It was my first visit to this great city, and I knew none here save one man. I went along Madison street, up State street, to the North Side, and met my dear brother Moody. I had met him one year before in a distant State, while he was engaged in the work of the Master. As I went along those streets, I recollect how I wondered if God had a work here for me in my coming to this city, or whether I had come on my own volition, and how while thinking in this way I sent up a prayer to God to bless me in the service in which I was about to engage. With thankfulness I remember the very first day I spent in this city. Somewhere down here we came among the sick and lowly, and went from one house to another singing and praying with the people; and what a blessing we received!

God led us into other fields. I remember when the Tabernacle was rebuilt how I used to enjoy gathering the little people in, and teaching them those sweet songs that are already encircling the globe. Yes, encircling the globe, for but a few days ago I received a copy of these Gospel Hymns printed in the Chinese language. They are sung in Africa and Asia, and are heard in France and Germany, England and America. I remember what peace and pleasure I had as I first taught these little hymns on the North Side. One day a lady called on me when I first had those classes, and said, "There is a little singing girl belonging to one of your classes who is dying. She wants you to go and see her." I went to her home—a little frame cottage—and there I found a little maid dying—one whom I had known so well in the Thursday evening meetings. I said, "My dear child, how is it with you?" "Will you pray for my father and mother as you pray for us?" was the reply. "But how is it with yourself?" I again asked. "Oh, sir," she answered, "they tell me I am about to die, but I have found the Lord Jesus Christ." "When did you become a Christian?" I inquired. "Don't you remember one Thursday when you were teaching me to sing—

> I am so glad that Jesus loves me,
> Jesus loves me, Jesus loves me;

and don't you remember how you told us that if we only gave our hearts to Him, He would love us?—and I gave it to Him."

What that little dying girl said to me helped to cheer me on more than anything I had heard before, because she was my first convert. Thank God, there have been many since.

During a Western Sunday School Convention, there arose a cry of dissatisfaction, "A ring!" "A ring!" The strange and false charge was made that the managers were conducting the convention according to some recent scheme.   Quite a discordant excitement ensued, during which a distinguished singer who was present, was called on to sing.   He sang,—

> All this I did for thee,
> My precious blood I shed
> That thou mightst ransomed be,
> And rescued from the dead ;
> All this I did for thee—
> What hast thou done for me ?

Through the song Christ seemed to whisper to the discordant convention, " Peace, be still," and when the song had ceased, a calm, Christ-like spirit had filled the convention and continued with it to the end.

A gentleman in Edinburgh was in distress of soul, and happened to linger in a pew after the noon meeting.   The choir had remained to practice, and began

> Free from the law, oh, happy condition, etc.

Quickly the Spirit of God carried that truth home to the awakened conscience, and he was at rest in the finished work of Jesus.

Mr. Sankey was with Mr. Moody in Philadelphia, years since, during the progress of a very interesting meeting at Dr. Reed's church, when many were being awakened, and sang the beautiful Gospel hymn, "Almost Persuaded."   After the close of the meeting, an attorney, who had been very much interested, came forward and said that he was not only "almost" but "altogether persuaded" to put his trust in the Lord Jesus.   This sweet song was used of the Holy Ghost in carrying the blessed Gospel of God's Son to his heart.

CHAPTER XVIII.

THE following letter from Rev. Henry Burton bears testimony
to the influence of Mr. Bliss' hymns upon the people of
England.

15 APSLEY CRESCENT, BRADFORD, Eng. Feb. 19, 1877.

MY DEAR BROTHER :

I am much obliged for your letter received yesterday, with its deeply interesting notices of our beloved friend. His death has been quite a shock to us
all on this side the water, for though not personally known to us, his name has
become a household word in all the Christian churches of Great Britain.
We seemed to love him as a brother. There was such a sweet and winning
power about his simple songs that they carried us captive before we knew it.
No one can estimate the influence his melodies have exerted upon the spiritual
life of England. We praise God for His precious gift of song, and now that
He has called our dear brother up to the hallelujahs of the sky, we are dumb
because *He* has done it.

I had a letter from Brother Bliss, dated, " Rome, Pa., 25th May, 1876." It
was mainly in reference to the hymns I sent him, but there is one sentence in
it that is so characteristic of the humble follower of Jesus, I will transcribe
it for you :

Thanks for your complimentary mention of the songs I have had the pleasure of writing.
You need not call them mine. If there is any good in any of them, it came from Him, the
Source of all good. To Him be all the praise.

As to the hymns I sent, you are quite at liberty to make any use of them
you may see fit.

Praying that the rich blessings of the All-Mighty, the All-Loving One may
rest evermore abundantly upon your labors, I am

Yours in Christian Fellowship and Love,

HENRY BURTON.

The following, from an unknown writer, is clipped from the
Youth's Companion :

On the stage at one of the Liverpool theaters, a comic singer came out before the footlights to sing. Just as he was about to commence his waggish melody, the tune of a sweet Sunday School hymn, learned before, came suddenly to mind, and so confused him that he completely forgot his part. He stood a moment trying to recall it, and then retired, covered with shame. The manager, enraged at his failure, and still more enraged at his apparently foolish explanation, paid him the remainder of his wages and ordered him at once to quit his service. Out of employment, he wandered about the city like the unclean spirit, seeking rest and finding none. His heart was full of curses, and to drown his mortification he drank deep and desperately, till his days and nights were one continual debauch.

In the meantime, Mr. Moody and Mr. Sankey began their meetings in Liverpool. The fame of the evangelists was in every mouth, and the young actor, hearing them discussed and ridiculed among his low associates, conceived the idea of writing a burlesque about them, to be put upon the stage. He sobered himself sufficiently to begin. But he felt he could not make his work complete without more " points " or " hits " to give it zest. So he determined to attend a meeting himself, and hear the men whom he intended to lampoon. He went, and the same power that in the sudden memory of that early hymn had driven him once from the stage arrested him and held him a reverent listener. At the close he remained among the penitent inquirers, and was soon led to accept the Lord Jesus as his Master. The young man is now in London, preparing himself to be a missionary.

Often a remembered hymn will keep sacred hold of a wicked heart when nothing else can. That simple Sunday School song, to the poor comedian, was a voice come back from his by-gone and better days. In spite of himself it changed his fate, and led the way to the still better days beyond.

Our meetings in Nashville, Tennessee, were advertised to commence April 15. When the time drew near, the writer was detained in Chicago by sickness in his family, and Mr. Bliss started alone. Before starting, application was made by telegraph and letter to different brethren to accompany him and preach at the opening services, but without success. Bliss prayed over the matter, and left Chicago very happy and peaceful in mind, saying, " Don't you worry a bit, W. The Lord has some one to be with me, I know." We had both thought of telegraphing Dr. Brookes, of St. Lonis, to go, thinking of him as just the one needed, but deciding that it would be of no use to send to him, as he was too busy in his work at St. Louis to go so far from home. The morning after leaving Chicago, before the train reached Louisville, Bliss went through the cars, distributing Scripture texts. As he entered the St. Louis sleeping car, there sat Dr. Brookes. With a joyous greeting Bliss exclaimed, "This is the answer to my prayer. You are to go to Nashville to-night with me, to take W.'s place." The Doctor looked rather puzzled at his assurance, and replied, "I am sorry to disappoint you, but I am on my way to deliver a lecture to the students at Danville College, at their commencement to-morrow; and as I can't possibly reach Danville in time by going on to Nashville, I am afraid your prayer is not answered." Bliss said, "Well, wait until we get to Louisville and see. I am sure that you are going to Nashville with me." On their arrival at Louisville, Dr. Brookes was amazed to find that he had made a mistake of seven days in the date of his appointment, and that his lecture could not be delivered until the week following. He went on with Bliss and conducted the meetings for a week. The evening services were held in the Exposition Building, and from four to five thousand people gathered nightly to hear the Gospel preached by Brookes and sung by Bliss, and very blessed results were secured. Bliss has told me that the first evening he was with the Doctor at the Exposition service, he sang, "When Jesus Comes." He was troubled at noticing that the Doctor leaned forward and covered his face with his hands. He thought something in the hymn must have met with his disapproval; but before he closed the song he saw that it was sympathy with the song and emotions in glad accord with it, that possessed him. Many, many times afterward did he have to sing to the Doctor "When Jesus Comes."

I believe it was at Nashville that Mr. Bliss called upon an invalid lady who had been speechless for some years. She had once been a singer, and after he had sung to her, she whispered to him, "My great regret now is that when I had my voice I did not use it more to sound His praises." The incident made a deep impression upon him, and led him to write the words of the song, "Work for your Master," found in an incomplete condition among his papers and finished by "Paulina."

The following letters need no introduction or explanation:

Boston, February 19, 1877.

MAJOR D. W. WHITTLE:

A young lady came into the inquiry room at the Tabernacle, on Wednesday evening in great distress, saying she had been seeking for years for forgiveness of her sins, but had kept the matter very secret and never intended to "confess Christ" till He had given her abundant light and assurance. She would not promise to make known her seeking to her companions, and went away as dark as she came, carrying with her, however, the verse, "He that believeth not God maketh Him a liar." She returned on Friday night, and while Mr Sankey was singing "There's a Light in the Valley," she said, "I will do anything for such a Savior," and peace came at once. In the inquiry room she arose and said, "I will take Jesus." She is now rejoicing.

I am truly yours,

W. G. CORTHELL.

---

209 BROADWAY, INDIANAPOLIS, January 27, 1877.

DEAR BROTHER WHITTLE:

I notice in one of my religious papers a call on all who may have any facts to communicate respecting the influence of the compositions of the lamented Bliss to communicate them to you. It is certainly due to his memory and eminent services that I acknowledge the very large use my family, (who have labored widely for years as Gospel singers, and are known as the "Carman Family") have made of his songs. I may particularly instance his "Ninety and Nine," "If Papa were only Ready," "Jesus of Nazareth," "Almost Persuaded," "How Much Owest Thou?" and "Calling Now." They have sung these in revival meetings in Syracuse, Rochester, Erie, Cleveland, Norwalk, Dayton, Richmond, Indianapolis, Evansville, and many other places, deeply impressing thousands.

An aged and skeptical gentleman in Norwalk, Ohio, dated his convictions, which led him to Christ, to hearing Mrs. Carman sing "If Papa were only Ready." Quite a list of persons in Cleveland were reported to her as converted through her singing in that city, where she and our three boys made much use of Mr. B.'s pieces. Both in direct Gospel work, and also in their "Evenings of Song," his compositions have been found by them invaluable. And beyond any of these, Mrs. B.'s "Rock of Ages" has been their great standard quartette.

Yours fraternally,

J. N. CARMAN,
Pastor North Baptist Church, Indianapolis

GENEVA LAKE, WIS., February 8, 1877.

MAJOR WHITTLE:

In compliance with your request, made through the columns of the *Standard*, permit me to tell you of the great blessing which has come to me through the hymns of "dear brother Bliss." That one commencing, "Down life's dark vale we wander," has been *such* a comfort. His hymns are so full of the Gospel of Christ, I shall ever remember with pleasure those days when I was permitted to listen to that voice, which is now hushed to human ears, but which is continually praising "Him who loved us and washed us from sin and unto Him be the glory forever, Amen," and with whom we hope to join in singing praises forever, "when Jesus comes."   ******** *****.

LEAVENWORTH, Feb. 7. 1877.

MAJOR D. W. WHITTLE:

DEAR BROTHER —Having seen a notice of your request published in the *Sunday School Times,* I take pleasure in responding and giving my testimony in favor of the music written by your late friend and colleague. I have been singing and teaching for twenty-five years, and in all that time have never been more impressed for good, or so thoroughly awakened and revived spiritually, by any music, as by that of Mr. Bliss. Last Sabbath, I sang selections from it (including Mrs. Bliss') for the convicts in the Military Prison at Fort Leavenworth, and all seemed deeply interested and affected.

The songs call commendations from many wherever heard, and the fate of their author is felt and sincerely lamented here as elsewhere. I am heartily in love with his sweet melodies and recommend the use of the book wherever I go. Respectfully,

L. J. EARLY.

DARLINGTON, WIS., Jan. 27, 1877.

MAJOR WHITTLE:

DEAR SIR —I can truly say that I have been blessed, in listening to many of the songs of the late P. P. Bliss. The song, "What hast Thou done for Me?" has been more impressive to me than many a sermon that I have heard. I had a little brother about three years and a half old, who died on the 23d of March, 1876, who, a few hours before his death, told his papa to sing. "I should like to die, said Wilie, if my Papa could die too," and his papa sung that beautiful song composed by Mr. Bliss, "If Papa were Only Ready," and before night his soul had taken its flight to the Spirit Land. Often, when he was with us, he used to sing, in his childish way, "I am so glad that Jesus loves Me."

Eternity alone can reveal the good that has been and will be accomplished by the beautiful songs of P. P. Bliss. Yours truly,

EUGENE HALSTEAD.

HUNTINGTON, INDIANA, February 4, 1877.

D. W. WHITTLE:

DEAR CHRISTIAN BROTHER IN CHRIST —I can see that I have been greatly blessed by the hymns of the late P. P. Bliss—especially with the one called "Jesus Loves Me." It was daily food to my soul. I greatly regret that so fine a musician and useful man was so suddenly called away in the prime of life. I pray to our Father in Heaven that his music may be a blessing to all generations. Yours in Christian love,

SOLOMON DILL.

New York, February 8, 1877.

MAJOR D. W. WHITTLE:

DEAR SIR —I was converted at Louisville, Kentucky, while your meetings were being held there, about two years ago, and I can say that I was greatly blessed through the sweet singing of Mr. P. P. Bliss.

Yours respectfully,

E. P. BRIGGS.

Chicago, March 8, 1877.

DEAR BROTHER WHITTLE:

In response to your request, I take pleasure in communicating the following facts in regard to my life, and conversion through the instrumentality of that song by Mr. Bliss, "What shall the Harvest Be?"

At the breaking out of the war, in 1861, I hastened to take service in the army, and soon after—in August of that year—I was appointed a First Lieutenant in the regular army. At that time, I was not yet eighteen years of age, and never had been away from home influences. I had never tasted any kind of intoxicating liquor, and did not know one card from another. The regiment to which I was assigned was principally officered by young men, many of whom were old in dissipation. The new life was an attractive one, and I entered upon it with avidity. In a very few months, I became a steady drinker and a constant card player. I do not remember to have made any attempt to resist the encroachments of vice; on the contrary, I took a mad delight in all forms of dissipation. I laughed at the caution of older heads, and asserted, with all the egotism of a boy, that I could abandon my bad habits at any time. But the time speedily came when I recognized the fact that my evil desires had obtained the complete mastery of my will, and that I was no longer able to exercise any control over myself. From that hour I knew no peace. The years that followed were but a succession of struggles against the dominion of my appetite, and a repetition of failures. With each failure, I lost something of my power of resistance and gained something of evil. In 1870, I resigned my commission and returned to civil life, determined to make one last stand against my passions by breaking away from my old associations and beginning a new life. The result was attained in my condition of a few months ago. I do not like to recall the past six years. They are as a frightful dream, from which, thank God! I was at last awakened; but the recollection of which will always bring sorrow and remorse.

When the Tabernacle was opened, last fall, I was in Chicago, presumably on my way to Minnesota. Only a few weeks before, I had left my family, promising with my last words that I would stop drinking, and try once more to be a sober man. I did not keep the promise five minutes; I *could* not. I stopped here, actuated by a desire to indulge, unrestrained, my appetite for liquor and cards, and in those few weeks I had taken a fearful plunge downward. At last I had made up my mind that there was absolutely no hope for me, and I wanted the end to come quickly. I gave myself up to the wildest debauchery, and speculated, with a reckless indifference on how much longer my body could endure the fearful strain. In anticipation of sudden death, I carefully destroyed all evidences of my identity, so that my friends might never know the dog's death I had died. It was while in this condition that I one day wandered into the Tabernacle and found a seat in the gallery. I looked at the happy faces about me and I hated them. I had all the vindictive feeling of a wild animal hunted to his last covert and waiting in impotent rage the final blow that is to end his miserable life. I did not pay much attention to the service. I was drowsy and stupefied with liquor. But after a while there was a perfect stillness, out of which presently rose the voice of Mr. Sankey (may God forever bless him!) in the song, "What shall the Harvest Be?" The words and music attracted my attention, and I straightened up to listen. They stirred me with a strange sensation, and when presently he sang—

> Sowing the seed of a lingering pain,
> Sowing the seed of a maddened brain,
> Sowing the seed of a tarnished name,
> Sowing the seed of eternal shame,
> Oh, what shall the harvest be?

the words pierced me like an arrow. My deadened conscience was aroused, and with one swift glance memory recalled my bright boyhood, my wasted manhood, and showed me my lost opportunities. Every word of the song was true of my own case, and in bitter agony I was reaping the harvest my misdeeds had brought me. I thought of my old mother, my loving, faithful wife and children, and of how they, too, were compelled to reap of my harvest of dishonor. My awakened conscience lashed me as with a whip of scorpions, and I rushed from the Tabernacle and sought to drown its voice in more whisky. But it was of no use. Wherever I went, whether to the bar of the saloon, or to the gaming table, or to the solitude of my own room, before my eyes in letters of fire were always the words, "What shall the harvest be?" For two weeks I endured this torture, having no rest, until at last on my knees I cried to God for mercy, and He heard my prayer. Broken, weak, and vile and helpless, I came to Him, believing that "the blood of Jesus Christ His Son cleanseth us from *all* sin," and trusting that His love and compassion would regard even me. And, Major, I have not trusted in vain. He has removed from me my old desires and appetites, and made me a new creature in Christ Jesus. He has guided me, shielded me, and fought my battles for me, and day by day my faith grows brighter, and my love stronger.

"The Lord is my rock, and my fortress, and my deliverer; my God, my strength, in whom I will trust; my buckler, and the horn of my salvation, and my high tower."

Very truly, your friend and brother in Christ,

W. O. LATTIMORE.

UPPER ALTON, Illinois, February 30, 1877.

BROTHER WHITTLE:

During Mr. Bliss' tour with Dr. John Hall, in 1874, I met him in Springfield, Illinois. The services were held in the interests of the Sunday School

Union, in the First Presbyterian Church. Governor Beveridge, in a few re
marks, introduced the speaker (Dr. Hall) and the singer (P. P. Bliss). At the
close of the services, while conversing with Brother Bliss, when I inquired of
his welfare, he said, "I am happy as a king to-night. This has been one of
the most joyful days of my life." "Why so?" I asked. "I am just thirty-
five years old to-day," he replied. "Indeed; then I congratulate you on your
present; and pray tell me how does the review of the past appear? Has not
God helped you?" A glow of gratitude and meekness lightened up his face
as he said, "Yes, wonderfully; I am amazed. Oh, how God has helped me."
Then, grasping my hand, while great tears welled up in his eyes, with all the
pathos of his soul he said: "Pray for me, that success may not be a temptation to me." Evidently the great desire of his heart was—

Oh, to be nothing—nothing
Only to lie at His feet.

Yours in the word and work of the Gospel till Jesus comes,

W. S. SLY.
Pastor M. E. Church.

St. Louis, Mo., February 10, 1877.

To Brother Whittle:

Dear Sir— *　*　*　*　*　*　* You will,
recollect that whilst engaged at St. Louis, I was a constant attendant at all the
meetings you two held at the Rink, the First Presbyterian Church (Dr. Gantz's)
and also at the First Methodist Episcopal Church. I've never forgotten you in
my daily and evening prayers, and would love to see you once more. Bro. Bliss
seemed to take deep interest in my spiritual welfare, and he told me that God
had a work for me to do in a singing capacity, as he had, and he gave me great
encouragement in that direction. I do not regret his sudden departure from
earth at all, because God was satisfied with what he had striven hard to do
while in the body, in saving souls for the Master's use. The harvest is great,
I know, but then new laborers will spring up, and finish the work left unfinished by those our Heavenly Father deemed proper to take unto Himself

From your Brother in Christ Jesus our Lord,

JAS. W. SPARKLIN.

Owego, Feb. 9, 1877.

Mr. Whittle:

Dear Sir —In looking over the letters I have received from Mr. Bliss, I find
one written to me January 28, 1873, in reply to one I wrote, informing him of
the death of one of the members of our church whom he was acquainted with,
she being the leading soprano singer in our choir and a very active and useful
member of our Sabbath School, and in the prime of life.

He writes: "It has always seemed desirable to me to be permitted to go
directly from the full activities of Christian life here, to the beautiful mansions

yonder; no interim of old age, second childhood, or idle waiting." It seemed to me that this had been so literally fulfilled in his case that it might add interest to his biography. You will notice that the word directly is underscored, which is the same as it is in his letter to me. His whole letter is full of good cheer. It was written just after the church in Chicago was burned, of which he speaks, and finally ends up by saying: "But know the living Lord has something better for us; shall rebuild immediately."

We are glad to see that you have found a man to take Mr. Bliss' place, and that you are laboring on in the Master's cause.

We pray that you may have great success in the work.

Yours truly,
D. M. PITCHER.

DETROIT, MICH., Feb. 3, 1877.

MAJOR WHITTLE:

DEAR BROTHER:—Though we are comparatively strangers, I trust we are trying *now* to serve the same Master. I say *now*. As you may remember, in the business men's meeting at Kalamazoo, election morning, I spoke to you and told you I could not make a start, though I was a church member, I felt so guilty on account of my past life. You told me to just take God at His word and trust the results with Jesus. I went home and resolved, God being my helper, I would. I told my wife (whom you will probably remember as the invalid who came to the four o'clock meeting and requested Brother Bliss to sing the Ninety and Nine) of my resolve, and we started there and then, *but very weak*. The next afternoon, Brother Bliss called on us at our house and spent about half an hour in singing those sweet songs, in which myself and wife joined by special request from that dear brother. He sang "Rock of Ages," and related the circumstances under which Mrs. B. composed the tune. He then sang "Sowing the Seed." I gave him a little bouquet of violets for Mrs. Bliss, and we parted to meet no more on earth. I mention these little things as I date all my true Christian experiences to those two meetings—one with you, the other with him; and, dear brother, I truly thank God to-night that His servants pointed me to God and not to any explanation of their own. I did, I trust, take God at His word.

I soon moved to Detroit and here I have joined the Y. M. C. A. and am trying to work for the Master. My prayer to God is to be such an one as the blessed Savior will be willing to work through for His name's honor. I have several missions to superintend in connection with the Y. M. C. A., and feel that I want Brother Whittle to remember me at the Throne of Grace. May our blessed Jesus prosper His work in your hands, is my prayer.

I remain very truly your friend in Christ,
GEORGE H. EVENS.

LINDLEY, Steuben Co., N. Y., Feby. 12, 1877.

MR. D. W. WHITTLE:

DEAR BROTHER:—During the summer of 1874, I met a person who heard Mr. Bliss sing "Almost Persuaded;" he said he never heard anything like it.

I shortly saw an advertisement of the Gospel Songs by P. P. Bliss, for sale by Church & Co. in Cincinnati, and thought this particular piece must be in it; so, in November, 1874, I sent for the Gospel Songs. Lo and behold, I then had "Almost Persuaded "—my wife being a splendid soprano singer, myself only an ordinary bass—and we commenced learning them. Every new one we commenced was always better than the last one; so in the course of six months we could handle every piece in the book. After these came along the Gospel Hymns, and of course we could not do without it.

In February, 1875, a stranger (by name L. D. Ayers) came in our midst and got permission to preach in the Free Methodist Church, the only one here, it being a mile from my house. He had been preaching about a week before I thought it worth while to go and hear him; and when I did go, I was satisfied that he was no fanatic. He could not sing, and the singing was very poor. I then took hold to help him with the four others, so that the singing was put on me. After going a week, I told my wife I could not get along any longer with the singing without her help, and that she must go and do the singing, which she did. After going a few nights, singing from our old hymn books, we then commenced singing one and two pieces of Bliss' on an evening and it was just like magic on the preacher and audience, and the house began to fill with people from a distance to hear the singing and preaching. About seventy were converted, nearly all heads of families; backsliders were reclaimed. It was indeed a great feast of good things. The preacher admitted, as did nearly all, that these Gospel Songs of P. P. Bliss did more than the preaching. The result was that a couple of hundred of Gospel Songs are now distributed in Tioga valley, including a large number of Gospel Hymns.

Yours in Christ,

ISAAC SANDT.

KALAMAZOO, MICHIGAN, Feb. 16, 1877.

MY DEAR BROTHER WHITTLE :

We were holding our watch-night service when the news of the death of Brother Bliss and wife came. The 10.30 train of Sunday evening brought us a paper at 11, and just before the hour of 12 I made the announcement. I never saw anything like it. There were four hundred people in the chapel, and all were in deepest sorrow in an instant—many in sobs and tears, others in silent and solemn meditations and prayer for God to help and comfort the poor mother—for we then supposed the whole family had gone together.

With reference to Brother Bliss' labors, I would say that last Thursday evening, at our prayer service, Miss Jessie Ainsworth, who has united with our church, came to me and said that she was led to the Savior through the singing of Brother Bliss. I asked her if she could name any particular piece that led to her awakening. She said he sang the piece with the words "Cut it down," referring to the fig tree, and she felt it meant her. She told me this with rejoicing that she ever heard Brother Bliss.

There are other individuals, and many of them, I dare say, who have attributed their conversion to his singing. I am quite sure Brother E. C. C. was
first awakened by his singing.

And now a word about our religious state. I may say our condition as a
society has never been better in the history of the church. There have been
to date one hundred and seventeen accessions to the Methodist E. Church, and
scarcely a week that does not bring some new heart to the Blessed Christ. To
Him be all the glory.

When we have given the silver trumpets the right sound, till the dear
Savior says, as in Brother Bliss' case, it is enough, then we will meet Brother
B. again and the throng of the blood-washed.

I think of Brother B.'s words and song daily, and endeavor to respond, Yes!
Yes! My Savior, Yes!

> Are your windows open toward Jerusalem ?
> Though as captives here a little while we stay ;
> For the coming of the King in His glory,
> Are you watching day by day ?

Your Brother, H. F. Spencer,
Pastor Methodist Church.

Kalamazoo, March, 1877.

Dear Mr. Whittle :

The Gospel in Mr. Bliss' sweet hymns and the Gospel in his own and Mrs.
Bliss' personal pleading with me led me to Christ. What this interest was in
Christ-like spirit and faithfulness can be judged by the following incident and
the two extracts from Mr. Bliss' letters that I enclose: A lady came to me
since Mr. Bliss' death, and said she had something to say to me, and it was
this : The evening before Mr. B. left Kalamazoo, Mrs. Bliss came to her after
the evening meeting and spoke to her about me, asking her to keep her eye
on me and after she had left to talk to me on the subject of religion, " For,"
said she, " I may never see him again, and I have taken a deep interest in
him." Oh, Mr. Whittle, how this message comes to me now as from the dead.
Now I have at least two less to pray for me on earth, but two more in heaven.
I trust that I may ever hold up the cross of Christ wherever I may be, and at
last, when God will call on me, that I may be able to say, *understandingly,* " It
is well, I am ready." Pray for me, Mr. Whittle, for I have a great many things
to contend with, and above all pray that I may be able to fully overcome my
greatest enemy, smoking. John xiv, 14.

Every day I see or hear something about Mr. Bliss. My greatest hope is
to meet him in heaven.   Yours,

R. H. D.

I remember once hearing Mr. Bliss talking to old Father Denary, of this place,
who has but one arm. He said, " Well, Father Denary, when we meet in
Heaven, I shall not know you by your one arm, shall I ? Remember, we're

going home to-morrow." And the tears streamed down the old man's cheeks as he answered, " No, thank God, thank God!"

The following are Mr. Bliss' letters above referred to :

JACKSON, MICH., November, 1876.

DEAR SIR :

Remember still there's more to follow. Do not depend on yourself, but look *ever* to Jesus. He'll carry you through. * * * * Oh, how my heart goes out toward you and my dear friends in Kalamazoo. May God bless you all.   Yours for His sake,

P. P. BLISS.

MY DEAR BROTHER :

Your letter gives us much pleasure. May you ever take Jesus as your leader, and be an armor-bearer, working for the Lord. When you are sure that you are free from everything (you know the old enemy I make this fling at), please write to me again. * * * I shall always feel that I have an interest in you and your welfare. * * * May God ever bless you and have you in His keeping. Mrs. B. and the rest send regards to yourself and friends.   Yours for His sake,

BLISS & CO.

JACKSON, Mich., January 3, 1877.

MR. D. W. WHITTLE :

BELOVED BROTHER —In Jackson, as elsewhere, many hearts are mourning for the loved ones in Israel that have fallen. How dear and precious is their memory to us.

You will remember that on the evening of your first Sabbath in Jackson, Mr. Bliss came over to the Second Congregational Church. His singing and speaking were blessed of God, and on that evening our chorister and wife were converted through Mr. Bliss, and joined the church last Sunday. The entire congregation were deeply impressed.

Affectionately your brother in affliction,

J. L. MAILE.

Pastor 2d Cong. Church, Jackson, Mich.

From Charlie, a little lad in Nashville, who trusts he became a Christian in Mr. Bliss' meetings there in April, 1875 :

NASHVILLE, February 25, 1877.

MY DEAR FRIEND, MR. WHITTLE :

I received your kind letter a few weeks ago ; also Mr. Bliss' picture and song, for which Ma, my little sister and brother, join me in returning many thanks.   I wish you to remember me in your prayers.   I would be so glad to see you.   Below I send a copy of Mr. Bliss' letter to me:

MASTER CHARLES:

MY LITTLE FRIEND —Your kind letter was received in due time. We have been flying about so that this is the first good chance I have had to reply. Mr. Whittle and I both thank you very much for your token of good will to our little boys. They are not old enough to answer, but we will keep your gifts for them. We will pray for you. I was, as your mother says, full of fun when I was a boy. Mrs. Bliss says I have not gotten over it yet. I do love fun, and love to romp and play with my little boys. We have a little baby boy ten months old. Paul Bliss is nearly three years old, and I love my friends and music very much; but that does not prevent my loving Jesus. No, I think I love Him all the more for giving me so many pleasant things and a cheerful, happy heart. I hope you pray to God every day. Pray for me. My love to Sister Annie, for Jesus' sake.   Yours in Him,

P. P. BLISS.

P. P. BLISS—IN MEMORIAM.

[From the St. Paul (Minnesota) Dispatch.]

In a burst as of heavenly music, he came,
    And heart spoke to heart with each tone!
'Twas Christ and His cross was the glorified theme
    Which gathered all hearts into one!

We heard him! it seemed that a seraph had sung
    Enwrapped in a mortal's disguise!
But while the deep cadence around us still hung,
    The seraph had pass'd to the skies.

Oh mourn not for him, or the dear ones he loved,
    For soon was the agony o'er,
And the jewels God gave him to gladden his life
    Will be his on the evergreen shore!

Dear Brother, farewell!   What wonders desired
    Shall now to thy vision unfold!
What chords thou didst touch in thy moments inspired,
    Whose vibrations may never be told!

R. M.

ST. PAUL, January 2, 1877.

CHAPTER XIX.

NEARLY all of the following have been published in sheet music form by Messrs. Church & Co. The others appeared in the *Song Messenger*, by the same publishers. The words are here given by their permission.

FORTUNE'S BEST GIFT.

Dame Fortune smiled upon my youth,
  Gave me kind friends and parents dear,
Who taught me virtue, love and truth,
  The right to love, the wrong to fear.

Gave me of learning my small share—
  My verse exhibits that is small—
Gave my heart strength its ills to bear,
  Gave health, strength, voice, friends, learning, all.

Through childhood's days she led me on,
  And smiled upon my boyhood years;
Her favors all, save wealth, I've won,
  But wealth brings cares and toils and tears.

She's given me all I'd have her given,
  She's given me cause to hope through life,
And after life to hope for heaven,
  And next to heaven she's given MY WIFE.

ARCADE N. Y., Last day of October, 1874.

FAREWELL, OLD YEAR.

Farewell, old year, farewell;
  We can no longer stay;
Our spreading sails the breezes swell
  To speed our onward way:
With song of wave and splash of oar
We leave thy fond, familiar shore.

Farewell, old year, farewell;
  We leave thy sacred shore;
Yet oft on thee will mem'ry dwell,
  And count thy treasures o'er,
While future years will brighter shine
Reflecting joys as pure as thine.

Farewell, old year, farewell,
  'Tis late—we must be gone;
One day, again, thy scenes will tell
  When earthly life is done;
One day again thy joys we'll see,
From earthly ills and sorrows free.

December, 1869.

THE WOOD BIRD'S SONG.

Hear ye not the wood bird's song,
As it gaily floats along,
On the breeze so sweet and clear,
Telling that the spring is near?
Cold the winter winds have blown,
Sad the leafless moan,
Silent now those perfumed bowers,
Gone the fragrant, blooming flowers.

Over prairie, grove and hill,
Hear that song, so loud and shrill.
Blessed harbinger of spring,
Welcome tidings dost thou bring—
Tidings of a brighter clime,
Tidings of a sweet spring time,
Blooming flow'ret, bush and tree—
Songster sweet, we welcome thee.

April, 1869.

LET US HAVE PEACE.

Over the land of our weal,
　Freedom and union increase ;
List to the earnest appeal,
　"Let us, oh, let us have peace."

Members of church and of state,
　Let your iniquities cease ;
Only the good are the great—
　"Let us, oh, let us have peace."

What though our neighbors do wrong,
　Slander and envy increase ?
Cheerily join in our song,
　"Let us, oh, let us have peace."

Fortune to freedom shall yet
　Grant a perpetual release :
Let us forgive and forget ;
　"Let us, oh, let us have peace."

August, 1869.

AUNT TABITHA'S TRIALS.

Pots, kettles and pans, pans, kettles and pots !
I'm sick of their sight, and I'd give them all for a bunch of " forget-me-nots ; "
But my children cannot live on the scent of a nosegay fair ;
They would much prefer a chicken pie to flow'rets rich and rare,
　　　But I never complain.

Tub, boiler and suds, suds, boiler and tub !
My arms are red and my fingers are spread, with terrible, terrible rub.
You may talk of your babbling brooks, you may sing of the streamlets bright ;
It would take waters of both, I know, to make these clothes white,
　　　But I never complain.

Wood, shavings and coal, coal, shavings and wood !
My fire has gone out, though I coaxed it as long and patient as any one could
You may sing of the " Brave Old Oak," you may praise " Mountain Pine,"
I'd rather have some splinters now, to kindle this fire of mine,
　　　But I never complain.

Pan, duster and broom, broom, duster and pan !
I'm worried to death, and I'd give all the world if I'd only been born a man.
Oh, pity me, ye who dwell in cabins with one small room ;
Oh, pity me, ye who never know what 'tis to handle a broom.
> But I never complain.

January, 1870.

THE LAST BUGLE.

The sad muffled drum sounds the last march of the brave,
The soldier retreats to his quarters, the grave,
Under death, whom he owns his Commander-in-chief.
No more he'll "turn out with the ready relief,"
But in spite of death's terrors and hostile alarms,
When he hears the last bugle, he'll stand to his arms.

Farewell, brother soldier, in peace may you rest,
And light lie the turf on each mouldering breast,
Until that review when the souls of the brave
Shall behold their chief ensign, fair mercy's flag wave ·
Then, freed from death's terrors and hostile alarms,
When we hear the last bugle, we'll stand to our arms.

BOYS WANTED.

Written for Daniel's Band, Louisville, Kentucky.

Boys are wanted, so they say,
Boys are wanted every day,
Boys are wanted ; we will pay
> Cash for boys.

Chorus.—Boys are wanted, brave and true,
> Boys of mind and muscle, too,
> Boys who dare the right to do,
> Faithful boys.

Boys are wanted, here and there,
Boys who will for work prepare,
Boys are wanted everywhere,
> Willing boys.

Boys to handle hoe and spade,
Boys to bend who're not afraid,
Boys to follow any trade,
> Business boys.

> Boys of speech and boys of song,
> Boys to righten many a wrong,
> Boys to help the world along,
>   Noble boys.
>
> Boys the busy world employ,
> Boys, and not self-acting toys,
> Boys are wanted—real boys—
>   Boys, Boys, Boys.

WORK AND PRAY,

OR, THE TEMPERANCE WOMAN'S WATCHWORD.

Do you hear the thrilling sound, floating out upon the air,
  That stills at once the noisy throng?
'Tis the tender, pleading tone of a mother's voice in prayer,
  'Tis followed by a burst of song.

CHORUS.—Rise, oh rise, the day begins to dawn,
          The shadows flee away, away;
          We're a faithful praying band, bound to purify the land—
          Our watchword "work and pray."

In the sweet and holy name of humanity we plead,
  For temperance we sing and pray;
For our fathers and our sons and our brothers intercede,
  To drive the demon drink away.

'Tis the old familiar shout of the army of the Lord,
  The Ruler of the earth and heaven.
He alone can give the power, He alone can speak the word,
  To Him alone the praise be given.

THERE'S MONNY A SHLIP.

> Och, list to my sorryfull song,
> For matthers is all goin' wrong :
> And shure I must shpake,
> Or me heart it will break,
> An' I'll not be detainin' ye long.

Bad luck to Miss Kittie McKay,
She's taken me sinses away,
Sayin' " Monny a shlip twixt
The cup and the lip."
Ah, there's monny a shlip now, they say.

Ah, Kittie was nate as ye plaze,
Faith, she could make butther and chaze,
She minded the pig,
And the praties she'd dig
In sich illegant, lady-like ways.
I bought me a rake and a shpade,
A gim of a gairden I made,
' Coom tind it," I said,
But she shook her swate head,
And I'm wonderfull sorry indade.

My shanty I plashtered wid mud,
And I shtop't all the howels that I could ;
Thin my blankets I shpread
Wid new shtraw in my bed,
And the matther so pleasantly shtood.
Then I towld her my love and intint,
But she said she wad niver consint,
And from my poor lip, thin,
The cup she let shlip, thin,
And off wid Mike Rooney she wint.

And shure, I'll be niver supplied
While her shweetness to me is denied.
Me heart is so lone,
In me bosom, och, hone!
I'd as soon we'd a both of us died.
Me sorrows to shmodder I'll try,
Though monny a time will I sigh,
To think that the cup
Which others may sup
Has no dhrop for my two lips so dry.

———— ✦✦ ————

SIRE AND SON.

Farewell, my son, if thee must go
  To find a western home,
Thy father's blessings follow thee,
  Though far thy feet may roam.

MEMOIR OF P. P. BLISS.

Thee was a frail and feeble lad—
　How soon to man has grown ;
Now I am feeble, failing, too—
　'Tis hard to stay alone.

Good cheer, my sire, a year or two,
　And you my home will share,
In peace and comfort spend your days
　Without a want or care.
Old neighbor Williams' letter says
　That he is well to do,
And gives consent to my request
　About his daughter Sue.

'Tis well, my son.　Long since I mind
　Another bright-eyed maid—
How like thy mother is that smile—
　But now I'm sore afraid
Thee'll hardly find a place for me.
　A year—how long 'twill be ;
My son, I may not need thy care ;
　God bless thy home and thee.

Farewell, my son, though miles away,
　For thee my prayers shall rise
That heaven may cheer life's fleeting hours
　And peace illume thy skies ;
My heart to thee will fondly turn
　Where'er my feet may roam ;
And by and by we'll meet again,
　My son, we'll meet at home.

FOR ME.

There's not a flower that decks the field,
Nor bud by wayside bower concealed ;
Whose life a perfume rich doth yield,
　But blooms for me, but blooms for me ;
There's not a star in yon deep blue,
That shines with radiance calm and true,
Nor mirrored in the morning dew,
　But shines for me, but shines for me.

There's not a heart whose beating thrills
In sympathy with human ills,

Whose longing loving only fills,
  But beats for me, but beats for me.
There's not a joy the heart can move,
No pleasure here, no bliss above,
No earthly weal, no heavenly love,
  But waits for me, but waits for me.

The ten songs that follow are published in sheet music form by
S. Brainard's Sons, Cleveland, Ohio, by whose permission the words
are here inserted:

'TIS THE HEART MAKES THE HOME.*

'Tis the heart makes the home, ever brightly to bloom :
'Tis the heart, 'tis the heart makes the home.
Through the dark, weary day or in joy's milder ray,
'Tis the heart, 'tis the heart makes the home.
Though humble and poor is my cot on the moor,
The love-light brightly beams through the gloom ;
Though storms gather round, purest joys here are found,
And I turn, fondly turn to my home.

'Tis the heart makes the home, though afar we may roam ;
'Tis the heart, 'tis the heart makes the home.
How we turn from the new to the old, tried and true ;
'Tis the heart, 'tis the heart makes the home.
No halls of the gay, let them lure as they may,
Ever charm while the heart longs for home ;
We laugh o'er our fears, and we smile through our tears,
Still the home of the heart whispers come.

LOVING LITTLE LOU.*

With a bright winning smile I remember,
  And a glance of her witching eye so blue,
Like a soft sunny day in December,
  To my life came my loving little Lou.
And the dim future way seemed to brighten,
  And life's daily duties dearer, dearer grew,
And my lone, weary heart seemed to lighten,
  At the thought of my loving little Lou.

CHORUS.—And to-day with my darling here beside me,
  With her loving heart, so noble, kind and true,
I can battle with the sorrows that betide me,
  For the sake of my loving little Lou.

* By permission of S. BRAINARD'S SONS, Cleveland, owners of Copyright of words and music.

Softly down on a calm summer even,
  Shone the stars from the distant dome of blue;
But a light brighter far had been given
  To the eye of my loving little Lou.
As I told her the old simple story,
  To my heart her form I nearer, nearer drew ;
Just a tear and a smile bright with glory,
  Then I called her my darling little Lou.

Many years, happy years have departed ;
  Many friends, faithful friends, are lost to view,
But can I ever bow broken-hearted,
  While I'm blessed with my loving little Lou ?
No, the dream of the past stealing o'er me
  Gives the present all the fairer, fairer hue,
While the bright future smiles aye before me,
  With the life of my loving little Lou.

THE PHOTOGRAPH.*

Oh, what a pretty picture, dear,
  Your likeness, darling Lou,
'Twill make you jealous yet, I fear,
  It is so much like you.
A pretty picture, really ;
  I'd know if I shall see,
But if 'tis very pretty, why,
  It can't look much like me :

DUET.—Not at all like me, not at all like me?
      Oh, the likeness I don't see,
        Tho' 'tis true, tho' 'tis bright, tho' 'tis beautiful,
        Tho' 'tis true, tho' 'tis bright, tho' 'tis beautiful.
      Oh, 'tis not at all like me.

Oh, yes, my dear, 'tis true as life,
  And art can do no more.
It is so very much like you,
  I've kissed it o'er and o'er.
Ha, ha, 'tis poor, the likeness, sir,
  I do not quite discern,
But tell me, pray, can you e'er say
  It kissed you in return ?

The picture kissed me? now, my dear,
  You surely are in fun,
For though I kiss it o'er and o'er
  It never pays me one.
Ha, then you're wrong, I've caught you now,
  And you will quite agree,
That if it never kisses back,
  'Tis not at all like me.

DUET.—'Tis like you, as all can see,
          'Tis like you, as all can see,
          Oh, the likeness you must see,
          So true, so bright, so bright, so beautiful,
          So true, so bright, so beautiful,
          'Tis like you, as all can see.

ROOM FOR ONE MORE.*

All aboard for the depot; hurrah, we can't wait;
Ten minutes to train time, hurry up, you'll be late!
Oh, yes, here is room, find a seat near the door;
For we're never so full but there's room for one more.

CHORUS.—Room for one more.   Room for one more,
          Never so full but there's room for one more.
          Room for one more, Room for one more;
          So we're never so full but there's room for one more.

There is "room for one more," in the world's omnibus;
What need of complaining, or making a fuss?
We can bear being crowded, the ride is soon o'er,
So we'll just move along and make "room for one more."'

There is "room for one more," in the cause that is just,
Stand firm to your purpose, be patient and trust;
• Though the basement be crowded, the hall running o'er,
In the broad upper story "there's room for one more."

There is "room for one more" in the heart that is true;
Always room for the worthy, it may be for you;
Love's realm is unbounded, its sea has no shore,
And there's never a heart but has "room for one more."

* By permission of S. BRAINARD'S SONS, Cleveland, owners of Copyright of words and music.

MR. LORDLY AND I.*

Mister Lordly keeps a wallet, so do I,
He has piles of greenbacks in it, none have I,
He's no happier with his coupons than am I
With my little empty wallet light and dry.
I hide my purse, lest he should see
The empty thing and pity me.

His fine wife has dainty fingers, mine has not ;
But she gives him curtain lectures, mine does not.
He goes home and gets a scolding, I a kiss ;
She a frown, but mine a smile and perfect bliss.
She rules his house, her rights demands
And holds possession in her hands.

Mister Lordly has his failings, so have I,
But he wears his in his bosom, outside I.
He will leave the world his money by and by,
I shall leave my friends my mem'ry when I die.
He's worlds of wealth his own to call,
I've love and hope, and that is all.

He has those that court his favor, none have I ;
But I've wondrous satisfaction, glad am I.
I'd not change it for his millions, no, not I.
We must both return our income by-and-by,
Then pray what difference will there be
Twixt Mister Lordly's self and me ?

THE TIN WEDDING.*

Ten years ago to-day two hearts did fain begin
To walk in wedlock's winding way, and share their mutual tin ;
Ten years ago to-day, it seems but yester morn,
And now they come around and say 'tis time to blow the horn. ·

CHORUS.— We come with a clatter and din, we come with a trumpet and tray,
We come with a tinkle of tin, to welcome our friends to-day ;
Hear the tinkle, tinkle, tinkle of the tin
In the dining-room, the kitchen and the hall ;
With a culinary chorus we'll perpetuate the din
And our wishes for the weal of all.

* By permission of S. BRAINARD's SONS, Cleveland, owners of Copyright of words and music.

Ten years ago—'tis strange, how swift the years have flown—
But you and I don't seem to change, like some that we have known ;
We love our kith and kin, our friends are kind and true,
And all our hopes, and loves and tin are just as good as new.

Then fill the cup to-day, and raise Britannia high,
Enjoy their luster while we may, 'twill tarnish by and by ;
The present let us prize, the future welcome in,
With " crystal," " silver," " golden" joys, we'll never want for tin.

WILLIE'S WOOING.*

When the snowy daisies decked the meadows fair,
And the apple blossoms filled the balmy air ;
When the verdant woodlands smil'd in beauty rare,
 My Willie came to me a-wooing.

CHORUS.—Darling Willie came across the lea,
 Bright-eyed Willie came a-wooing me ;
 Oh, skip, ye little lambkins, sing, ye birds, in glee,
 For Willie came to me a-wooing.

Violets he brought me from the shady dell,
And his loving glances told he loved me well ;
But the half he said I'll never, never tell,
 When Willie came to me a-wooing.

Now the flow'rs have faded with the blooming spring,
Soon the fruitful autumn brighter joys will bring ;
Here upon my finger shines a golden ring,
 Since Willie came to me a-wooing.

JOHN CHINAMAN.*

John Chinaman, dear sir, since you're making such a stir
 In the waves that wash along our western strand ;
Stop the jingle of your gong, while we sing our greeting song,
 As you gaze upon our broad and happy land.

CHORUS.—Ho, John Chinaman, now, John Chinaman,
 Leap o'er the crumbling wall,
 Bring along your tea, for don't you see
 We've room enough to welcome all?

* By permission of S. BRAINARD'S SONS, Cleveland, owners of Copyright of words and music.

John Chinaman, Esquire, though we really don't admire
All the Oriental notions you may bring,
We have room enough for you, and we've work enough to do,
And our nation's song of welcome now we sing.

John Chinaman, they say you have loitered by the way,
While the nations of the world were marching on,
So we're waiting now to see what a " forward march " there'll be
In the future of our distant neighbor, John.

A TRAGICAL TAIL.*

Oh, listen a while to my tragical tale,
  Be still as you ever can be,
For I will be heard while I wildly bewail
  The fate of poor Thomas Maltese.

Chorus.—Ah, pity poor kitty Thomas Maltese ;
    Ah me, ah me, ah me ; ah, pity poor kitty, ah me, ah me.

Old Thomas was one of the nicest of cats ;
  So kind, and so clean, and so quick ;
We s'pose that he used to kill mices and rats,
  But we know that he killed the poor chick.

Well, what if he did ? must the poor fellow die ?
  You've enough ; do you grudge him a crumb ?
We're all fond of chicken, though may be more sly,
  We're none of us better than " Tom."

Old Thomas has been a faithful old friend,
  But now they declare he must die ;
I'm sorry to think of his terrible end ;
  If I only had time, I would cry.

Don't kill the poor Thomas ; I think it a sin,
  Because he has seen his " best day ;
But they'll dig him a grave and they'll tumble him in,
  And that's what he'll get for his pay.

* By permission of S. Brainard's Sons, Cleveland, owners of Copyright of words and music.

WHEN GRANDMOTHER IS GONE.*

In her old arm chair she's sitting,
  As in the days of long ago,
While she's knitting, knitting, knitting,
  Gently rocking to and fro;
And a dark'ning thought steals o'er me,
  Like a shadow o'er the lawn,
Of the lonely days before me
  After grandmother is gone.

CHORUS.—Oh, when grandmamma is gone, when grandmamma is gone,
  And her prayers, and tears and toils for us are o'er,
Who will cheer us day by day all along our weary way
  To the beautiful, the ever shining shore?

Silvered locks beneath the border
  Of her snow-white cap I see,
" Through a glass," though dimly, fondly,
  Falls her loving gaze on me ;
On the high, old-fashioned bureau,
  Lies the choicest book she's known ;
Who will turn its sacred pages
  After grandmamma is gone?

Years ago, a dear companion
  Promised her, a blushing bride,
" To protect, to love, to cherish "
  " E'en till death should them divide."
O'er a low mound 'neath the willow,
  Summer roses long have blown;
They will bloom above another
  After grandmamma is gone.

O'er the hills the sun is setting,
  And the twilight shadows come —
Still she's waiting, waiting, waiting,
  Till the Master calls her home.
Though I weep for friends departed,
  While they're going one by one,
I shall have one more in heaven
  After grandmamma is gone.

* By permission of S. BRAINARD's SONS, Cleveland, owners of Copyright of words and music.

RESOLUTION.

If you've any task to do, task to do,
Let me whisper, friend, to you, do it, do it, do it.

If you've anything to say, thing to say,
True and needed, yea or nay, say it, say it, say it.

If you've anything to give, thing to give,
That another's joy may live, give it, give it, give it.

If some hollow creed you doubt, creed you doubt,
Though the whole world hoot and shout, doubt it, doubt it, doubt it.

If you've any debt to pay, debt to pay,
Rest you neither night nor day, pay it, pay it, pay it.

———————————

The two compositions following appeared in "The Joy," published by Church & Co. in 1873 :

BUSHNELL.

" In me ye may have peace ;
    My peace I give to you.
Rest, troubled soul, rest in the Lord,
    His love will bear thee through.

" In me ye may have peace ;
    Though wars against thee rise,
Hope thou in God, be not dismayed,
    Lift up thy weeping eyes.

" In me ye may have peace ;
    Dear Lord, our refuge be,
In weal or woe, in life or death,
    We would abide in Thee."

———————————

WELCOME.

Welcome, welcome, welcome,
    Messengers of love !
Kindred souls with joy are swelling,
    Like the blest above.

Welcome, welcome, welcome,
  Joy illumes our way ;
Love shall reign in every bosom
  With unbounded sway.

Praises, praises, praises,
  For the sacred past,
For the mercies, rich, abundant,
  Freely o'er us cast ;
Praises, praises, praises,
  For the glad to-day,
For the future, grand and glorious,
  Praise, oh, praise for aye.

CHAPTER XX.

THE following composition was written by Mr. Bliss when at
school, in 1859:

You are aware, my old friends, that you live in an age of darkness and
ignorance —an age in which temptation and depravities are becoming more
and more numerous. You, too, live in a land of slavery—a land on which the
frowns of a just condemnation shade with an uncommon darkness. The cry
of the oppressed and howl of the drunkard are ever to be heard on our mountains and in our valleys ; deeds of sin are ever before us ; the wicked struggle that sin may ever be predominant ; and we live to endure the deep curse
of slavery and poverty which was brought on by the sins of our fathers. These
considerations seem to forbid that we should ever attempt to elevate ourselves,
our country, or succeeding generations by the acquirement of knowledge.

We cannot but remember that ignorance is weakness ; that an ignorant and
depraved people will ever be slaves ; and that on the ignorance of our youth
depends the future slavery, the poverty, the misery, the contempt, and the
disgrace of our despised country. Go on, then, with a contemptible ambition
and dogged perseverance in the gully which leads to disgrace and dishonor.
Press downward. Go and gather thorns from the marshes of ignorance ; inhale
of the foulness therein ; drink deep of their stagnant pools and then join in
the march of retrogradation. Become ignorant and depraved and you will be
contemptible. Hate God and disobey Him, and continual unhappiness will be
yours.

In the bound volumes of the *Song Messenger*, a monthly musical
publication formerly issued by Root & Cady, now published by John
Church & Co., are found several contributions from Mr. Bliss, written over the pseudonym of Pro Phundo Basso. Mr. Bliss was, at
the time they were written, connected in a musical way with Root
& Cady, and at their request contributed these pieces to make
the paper more spicy and attractive by the vein of fun and good-

natured satire that runs through these compositions. A few speci-
mens are given, that Mr. Bliss' fun-loving and wit-creating char-
acteristics may be appreciated.

A RETROSPECTIGRAPH.

At ye close of ye Normal Academie of Musick, at Janesville, 12th daye of 8th month, 1869.

I must confess almost of you,
    And take ourselves to thee,
And then I want to be a while,
    And then—well, let us see.

Gone is our Normal, past, expired—
    The hand of mem'ry sweeps
Backward, still backward, there, I'm wired ;
    Hush, booby, "why these weeps?"

We've had a good time, haven't we?
    And every one supposes
Of all the chorus, psalm or glee,
    The biggest thing was " Moses."

As King of Egypt, I confess,
    He's taken some attention,
But as a Pennamite, I guess
    That from this ere convention,

About the sweetest influence shed,
" Still gently o'er me stealin',"
As once a brother poet said,
    Is this kind, social feelin'.

And let's not choke it down with care,
    Nor let the sweet flower perish,
But keep it blooming fresh and fair,
    And friendly feelings cherish.

And when life's croquet game is o'er
    And all our arches past,
May we wild rovers rove no more,
    But hit the port at last.

Ah, beg your pardon ; by your grace,
    'Twas also my intention,
If you would grant me time and space,
    Some local points to mention.

14

Three cheers for Janesville I propose,
  Hip, hip—ah, that don't bring it ;
If I'd count, one, **two**, three, I s'pose.
  You'd all jump up and sing it.

Such lovely ladies, model men,
  What verse shall sound your praises ?
Such soothing sidewalks (!), then again
  Such beautiful bouquetses.

Joy be with Janesville, so say I,
  And so say all of us,
May thine aquatic fowls hang high,
  Thy singers sing no wuss.

And now, good bye, Janesvillians, all,
  We take our leave informal ;
May no sad tho'ts your hearts appal
  At mem'ry of our Normal.

I cannot stop till I declare
  That no field hand or farmer
In music's realm can we compare
  With our Prof. H. R. Palmer.

And though the singers bloom at morn,
  At noon his larynx withers,
While here for weeks, fatigue we scorn,
  And *scale* him all to slithers.

In every heart some seeds of truth
  Strong root have daily taken,
And oft the sweetest songs of youth
  Will thoughts of Root awaken.

We came to learn the laws of song,
  And now we go as sudden,
And won't we keep, thro' all life long,
  Kind thoughts of W. Ludden ?

And yet around the faculty
  My muse immured still lingers,
To celebrate the praise of he
  Who teacheth " wiggling fingers."

A model teacher, too, is he,
  Nor doth waste words nor wrath use,
A man and a musician see
  In W. S. B. Mathews.

Then my friend Titcomb—friend ? Yes, sir,
  Because of *genus homo,*
He's more than *homo,* he is *vir,*
  They say he's found a chromo.

All sorts of dispositions here
  We've had, though now dispersing,
And as we go, I think 'tis clear,
  We've all had first rate Nourse-ing.

And now I'm done, you think 'tis time ;
  Good bye—we're off to-morrow ;
May life be smoother than my rhyme,
  And more of heaven's light borrow.

A LAYE.

Wouldst have renown, dost thirst for fame
  High honors wouldst thou see ?
Seekst wealthe, withal, and for thy name
  Large popularitie ?

Harkee.   I know a handiwaye
  Of which I'll blaze to thee ;
My charges ?   Naught !   I'll sing my laye
  Gratuitouslie.

" Highwaye to honor," is ye name
  " And immortalitie,"
But of ye plan I dare not claime
  Originalitie.

While he his conscience sore must hurt,
  Whate'er his calling be,
Who doth to wealthe and fame assert
  Insensibilitie.

Do this, and thus thy aims conceal,
  So noted thou shalt be,
Nor word nor look shall e'er reveal
  Thine ingenuitie.

First : Love thyself all things above,
    So loved thou shalt be,
And joy at finding in thy love
    Compatibilitie.

Next . Praise thyself, thyself may bless,
    Thyself continuallie ;
So shall thy sweet self-praise possess
    Immutabilitie.

And yet two simple souls, I praye,
    Might 'scape ye rules scot free—
Ye mindeful list'ner to my laye,
    And eke   PRO PHUNDO B.

December, 1869.

HIS COURTSHIPPE.

Written by himself with ye full and willinge consent of his lawful and beloved Miranda.
(In ye tone of A.)

'Twas on a sunfull morning,
    All in ye month of May,
When all ye birds and lambkins
    Did skippe and eke did playe ;
A songfull youth did saunter
    With hearte so glad and gaye,
Adown a trodden cow-path,
    Yclept ye " Milkey Waye "
(Which youth itt was Pro Phundo
    Maybe 'twere good to saye),
His tunefull voice lamenting
    Of " faithfull ole dogg Traye,"
Whose gentle, kinde attentions
    Nor age nor grieffe could swaye.

Bewhiles ye kine bereaved
    Most mournfully did braye,
All for ye youthfull callings
    Ye butcherman did slaye
Full many a cock a-crowing
    With many a piping jay,
To greete ye gladsome morning
    Did cheerfully essaye,

Likewise to joine Pro Phundo,
  And swell his roundelaye ;
Ye gorgeous sun aslantwise
  Did send his kindest raye ;
Beglimmering on ye milk paile
  Of Miss Miranda Gray.

Pro Phundo's hearte did kindle
  As it were kiln-dried haye
Upon a bar post leaning
  (Long since gone to decaye),
Ye question there he popped,
  Nor risked to delay,
Whiles Miss Miranda blithely
  Drew forth ye foaming spraye ;
Nor fright nor fitt of fainting
  Did she at this betraye,
But gentlemaidly courage
  And valour did displaye.
Consented ♥ hence Pro Phundo
  Pro Phundo is to-daye

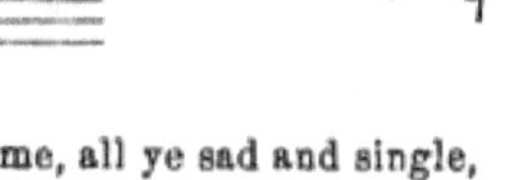

Come, all ye sad and single,
  Who listen to my laye,
Attende unto my counsell
  And eke ye same obeye.
From sweete and solid comforte
  Prythee no longer straye ;
From foolish affectation
  Turn heartily awaye.
Be honest in your courtshippe,
  And frank also, I praye.

When to an honest damsell
  An honest youth doth paye
His honest hearte's affection,
  Why should she answer " Naye ? "
" Begone ! " her tonge a telling,
  Whiles all her hearte says " staye ! "
Pro Phundo and Miranda,

  May all be blest as they. 

HOW INTO MUSIC.

Miranda says —whitch makes itt so—
  I'd better write and tell
Why into musick I did go,
  And *where* and *how*, as well.

No doubt to me you've noticed oft
  His is ye longest life,
And eke his head doth lie most soft
  Who most doth please his wyfe.

So list, give ear, attende while I
  My narrative unfold ;
So shall my head reposefull lie
  For doing as I'm tolde.

" *Why* I'm in musick ?" oh, my eye
  I can no clearlier see,
Than I could guess ye reason why
  Miranda married me !

Where ? 'neath ye tunefull hemlocks dear
  That roll their anthems grand
O'er Pennsylvania's northern tier —
  Miranda's native land.

Elk Run first taught me melodie,
  While angling through its dales,
Its saw-mills gave my *rhythm* to me,
  Its sun-fish gave me *scales*.

Ye friskie fox *staccato* taught,
  Ye screech owl *tremolo ;*
Ye mill wheels *mezzo forte* brought,
  Ye dam *fortissimo*.

Ye scythe whet and ye cross cut's ring,
  Ye ox cart's *tenore* creake
Did to my hearte a musick sing
  That words can never speake.

Thus all things musick brought to me,
  Whitch still to me doth cling,
Whitch same, I argue, easilie
  Did me to musick bring.

How into musick I did go
  I'll lastlie saye to thee,
And of my scantie ways I know
  Thou'lt laugh right merrilie.

In '59 resolved I
  Tu " go itt " though so young,
So started out with—purpose high—
" Old Fannie " and ye " pung."

O'er Bumptown hills and Litchfield's heights,
  By Susquehanna's shore,
I taught, by tallow candle's light,
  Myself, if no one more.

In schoolhouse, church and tavern halle
  Ye "singin' skule" was founde ;
But once a week on each I'd call,
  And so I " boarded 'round."

Two dollars by a night received
  My every waunt supplied,
Miranda (may I be believed)
  Was also satisfied.

Through snowdrift, mud and rain I'd ride,
  By turnpike, gulfé or ferrie,
Miranda moastlie by my side,
  And we were happy—verrie.

Such lots of friends and worlds of funn
  Would more than fill this letter,
I'll stop and write another one,
  Miranda says I'd better.

February, 1870.

WHAT FOR ?

Why do you sing? Say? can you tell?
  Speak, Tenor, Base, Soprano !
Why all this fuss of " scale " and " swell "—
  This " mezzo " and "piano?"

Why waste at " Normals " time and strength—
  Say nothing of the money —
To talk of " power, pitch and length ? "
  It seems to me so funny.

Just here I want to stop and laugh
  To see Don Quix dismounted,
When asked the spaces of the **staff**—
  Don't answer till you've counted.

Then think of taking lessons, too—
  A notion universal—
And some, with nothing else to do,
  Frequent the choir rehearsal!

Alas, this **wanton waste** of breath
  Doth rouse my indignation,
And loudly—so my judgment saith—
  Demands investigation.

" Why do you sing?" Here comes Lo Dee
  With voice of mimic thunder ;
He always flats on fourth space G,
  But that's a *minor* blunder.

" Haw, haw! old boy, who wouldn't **sing?**
  My treat ; come on," he thundered ;
" Two thousand from the minstrel ring,
  For chorister twelve hundred."

" Why do you," ah, who comes ?—let's see—
  Walk in, Professor Blowhardt ;
They say you sing the tenor B.
  Be seated ; you need no card.

You say you've left the St. Paul choir.
  I've heard the tale completer ;
They couldn't raise your sal'ry higher
  Unless they robbed poor Peter.

" Why do "—Miss Hisee is it you ?—
  You want a what ? position ?
But fifteen hundred won't quite do
  For such a fine musician ?

O, yes you'll advertise, I see,
  With lengthy explanation—
No odds, you say, what liturgy
  Or what denomination.

Why! Bless my soul, here's Prima Don
  Signora Al To Etta!
With diamond brooch and broad chignon,
  And says " Write me a letter

" To introduce me in St. L——
  To Mr. Blank's committee;
They say they'll pay their quartet well;
  I'm tired of this dull city."

    *   *   *   *

" Jesus loves me, loves me well—
  'Twas my little daughter, Nell,
Out beneath the cherry tree
  Singing quite extempore.

" Darling, come."   I call her twice,
  But the bird-like, childish voice
Caroled still the sweet refrain,
  So my calling was in vain.

Then I went and joined her there,
  Kissed her cheeks and stroked her hair,
" Darling," said I, " Can you tell
  Why you sing ?"   Then little Nell

Raised her witching hazel eyes
  With a look of sweet surprise,
" Cause I love to," answered she;
  " Papa, come and sing with me."

August, 1870.

THE REVERIE.

'Twas night.   Above South Bend the silvery stars
Shone softly ; and the dust that all day long
Kept drifting heap on heap, until the streets
Like turbid rivers rapid rolling seemed
And on the sidewalk gathered ankle deep ;
And in the parlor, dining-room and hall
Flew freely, penetrating everywhere
In copious showers, begriming hands and face
In rich abundance, and in clouds profuse
Eyes, ears, hair, teeth beclouding, was at rest.

On the veranda, where the cooling breeze,
Sweet-scented as by water lilies, rose,
Alone in somber silence, thus I mused:

"The Normal's ended; and how brief it seems;
Begun—half done—and, ere we knew it—gone,
And with it what? * * * * * *
     (Some 'skeeters,' I am sure.)

How rich and wise we came; and though our friends,
The teachers and the dear South Benders say
All right—good bye!—we leave, alas! how poor,
And so lament—(oh, bother, dogs, be still :)

Down in the country we were first—here last;
There king of toadies; here a toad 'mong kings.
And what a fall was there, my countrymen,
When all our princely ornaments did turn
To warts unseemly.

   Ah, what sickening grief,
When Maestro Bassini said, Not so;
And down to 'Zca, i-a' with saddened heart
Ingloriously we tumbled;
     or when he
Who touched the keys, and at his bidding gushed
With limpid, liquid sound the ' silver spring,'
Our fort(e) demolished with his magic 'touch,'
And then, like Master Mason as he was,
On firm foundation taught us how to build
More lasting structure;
     or when G. F. R.
Urbanely smiled and drew with cruel skill
The lever of our teaching safety valve,
And all the gas of self-esteem escaped,
And with a chill of disappointment sore
We saw the bubble of our fame collapse;
Or when a voice from Boston said ' lum tum!'
And we were silent, or 'achieved' cried,
' A new created world,' right on the tick.'"

What wonder we go home disconsolate,
And fail to see wherein the 'vantage lies
Of tending Normals thus?   But there's the bell
Notre Dame—'tis midnight—I retire,

Miranda long in sleep serene hath lain,
Sweetly unconscious of my whereabouts ;
Softly my downy couch I seek and so
To wonted labor, teachers hence repair,
Though humbled, earnest ; though in weakness strong,
Boast not, but labor patiently ; anon
The glory cometh.

           Bear in mind,
The empty hogshead makes the louder noise ;
And brass may glimmer e'en where gold is dim,
The shallow brook may down the rivers roll,
And you—Whist, Hush !

           Miranda waketh ;

I may 'quit.'

September, 1870.

CANST THOU IMAGINE?

    Well, there,
    I declare !
I can't sing or write a pæan
Fit to sound the praise of Leon,
    Mid this humming,
    Fiddling, drumming,
Though a pleasant street to be on.

    There, hark !
    Yes, it's Clark—
Fife, guitar, triangle, flute,
Organ,—anything to suit,—
    Pipe and horn,
    Night and morn,
Rumpty tumpty, hootty toot.

    Hey, boys,
    What a noise !
Ah, I wonder what that air is,
Wonder if they know what care is !
    Ho, ho, ho !
    See the show—
" Who can beat that ? "   Rome or Paris ?

*   *   *   *   *

Canst thou imagine a beautiful day
And a long wagon-box half full o' hay
A-rolling afar o'er the mountains away,
Containing a dozen of singers so gay ?

Canst thou imagine a beautiful tree,
A-spreading its branches so fair and so free,
A-saying to you and a-singing to me—
" Evergreen, evergreen mayst thou be ?"

Canst thou imagine a beautiful bird,
A-singing the sweetest song you ever heard ?
Listen thou, listen thou, catch every word,
So should this bosom by this song be stirred.

Canst thou imagine a beautiful stream,
A-babbling, a-babbling along like a dream,
Like life's low lullaby doth it not seem ?
Here we uncheck, thus, and water our team.

(A large snake is seen in the water ; the off horse starts up suddenly, a
carpet bag falls out behind, etc, etc.)

*   *   *   *   *   *

'Twas night—
Clad in white,
I was sleeping—sleeping some ;
For Miranda was—yes—dumb ;
But she woke
Me and spoke—
" The Turks ! The Turks ! They com(b) ! they com(b) !"

" Then there was hurrying to and fro,"
And I am very much afraid
I ne'er again on earth shall know
Another just such serenade !

*   *   *   *   *   *

The Leon farmers and their farms—
The floral beauties of the vales,
Its daughters, daisies—matchless charms—
I can't describe—my pencil fails.

Sing ? Yes,
More or less,
But it isn't my intention

> To describe our Grand Convention
> In this letter,
> Though a better
> Is beyond my comprehension.

No. 2 Clark street, Leon, New York, October, 1870.

ROME, PA., May 23, 1870.

MR. EDITOR:

Is it pretty to sing in the cars?

We drew out a thousand miles of music from the " Prize " last week, coming from Chicago. There was also an opposition quartet, led by a Buffalo editor, accompanied by spotted pasteboards and a wicker demijohn. Supported by some ministerial and musical friends, we opened on them such batteries as " The Armor of Light," " Immanuel's Land," " There's a Light in the Valley," etc., which soon compelled them to beat an ignominious retreat, taking their demijohn, but leaving a visible odor of poor tobacco and worse whisky.

But didn't we have a pleasant children's meeting last night, introducing the " Prize " as a prize to the delighted Sunday School ? and didn't we enjoy their hearty hand-shakings and their boisterous " Thank you, sirs ?" And didn't we pick up the bouquets that were thrown for " Remembered," etc., if it was Sunday night?

> " New life I breathe while on the sea,"
> Or in " my country home ; "
> And " a farmer's life is the life for me,"
> But " there's no place like "—Rome.

> And if I had time,
> I'd tell you in rhyme
> The farmer's dolce joys ;
> But such a song
> Would be so long
> That—ho, here come the boys
> With an extra hoe,
> And away we go
> To the field to plant the corn ;
> How I love the flowers,
> And the blast of the dinner horn.

HOW SHOULD CHILDREN SING ?

All agree that children *should* sing. The time for discussing that question ceased when music, as a science, began to be taught in our common schools ; when piano and organ became as common in household furniture as book-case and bureau, and when instruction book and sheet music came to be as familiar to our boys and girls as spelling-book and newspaper.

All know that children *love* to sing. Next after the adoption of a resolution that the birds " can and are hereby authorized to warble," may come the question of granting the children—God's own bright birds of Paradise—permission to express *their* delights in song. All thoughtful, observing people admit the power of children's songs. We may question the introduction into Sunday Schools of object-teaching, of blackboard exercises, or of the library books; but we must have singing books. A Sunday School may prosper in a dark basement room, with low walls and poor ventilation, but music is indispensable. You may have a flower garden without a fountain, a parlor without pictures, or a summer day without the sunshine; but do not expect a wide-awake, stirring, effective Sunday School—a school that shall enjoy a healthful popularity, and be in the highest sense successful, without Sunday School sing-ing—the "Sunshine of Songs."

Therefore, we are not here to meet the question, "Shall the children sing?" but to suggest WHAT, and HOW. Singing is emotional utterance. Singing "earnestly," "heartily," "lustily," as Wesley directs, is one thing, and a good one; making a loud, harsh, discordant sound is quite another and different exercise.

While all that really deserves the name of music is usually regulated by the law of musical form, it does not follow that all emotional utterance is singing. All music is sound; but all sounds are not music.

What shall the children sing? Unquestionably we cannot be too careful to guard against putting a cup of poisoned song to their youthful lips, and yet I cannot sympathize with those who would have only doctrinal, didactic, dog-matic songs, or rather sermons. If a child really sings, he must not only fully understand, but love the meaning of the words employed.

We must not expect the infant class or ten-year-olds to appreciate and enjoy as we do that which we call the best, in sentiment or in song. Remem-ber, " milk for babes, strong meat for men." Make the difference apparent; strive to lead them to a higher musical taste and nobler spiritual enjoyments, but do let the children sing of birds as well as of burdens; of beauty as well as of duty; of earth pleasures as well as of heavenly treasures; of temporal employments as well as of spiritual enjoyments. Let song develop feeling, while it never fails to direct and purify the affections.

I well remember a loving, large-eyed lad who in the day-school could scarcely sing the old song of A B C D E F G, but that the tears would fall and mark the time. The lad knew not why he wept, but the faithful Christian teacher turned this mighty motive power to heavenly purposes, and gave these outflowing sympathies wholesome food. So the love of song grew and pre-vailed; so the channel of the affections widened, and so the lad, though taller grown, stands here to plead for song.

> Thank God for simple school-day song,
> Scorn not the childish lay;
> The feeble spark of love-light fanned
> May end in heavenly day.

In order to sing properly and profitably, the time must be entirely given to and the attention wholly fixed upon the exercise. No slamming of doors, no communication among officers, no walking, talking nor parade of visitors should be allowed to disturb. We might as well walk or talk during a prose prayer (I did not say prosy) as to thus disturb a prayer in verse. I would as soon think of speaking to a brother while praying as while singing.

Then it seems to me the leader of children's singing needs often to say. "Not too loud." Earnestness is not always best manifested by loudness. Noise is not always power. Besides, more voices are injured by forced, screamy sounds than, perhaps, by all other evil means combined. "Like pastor, like people;" so, like choristers, like choir. If the leader be careless in style, intonation, pronunciation, etc., those led will very likely be even more so. "Good singing" means, first, sweet, pleasant tones, true intonation, distinct articulation, etc. Earnestness, vigor, life, spirit, etc., come afterwards, and depend upon the first. Mr. O. Blackman, teacher of music in the high and primary schools of Chicago, and author of "Graded Singers," for juvenile instruction, says that the Sunday hour in some of the mission schools nearly counteracts all the week's work, by this terrible practice of screaming.

In teaching children new songs, is, perhaps, the greatest care necessary. Let the chorister sing over two or three times, in easy, pleasant, correct manner, lines and stanzas of the hymn, thus giving good examples, which in music as in morals, are much more powerful than precepts; especially if precept and example differ.

May not the Sunday School meet once a week, say on Thursday or Friday evening, and practice their music? Now, don't frown and say, "impracticable," unless you have tried and found it so. Usually young people are glad enough to be called together; and cannot a "singing meeting" be made interesting and profitable? Engage some earnest lady or gentleman leader at a *fair salary;* if convenient, have a piano or organ to accompany; invite the choir of the church to assist, and singing meetings will "pay." Invariably question the children as to the meaning of the difficult and unusual words of the song, so that first of all they may be able to sing with the *head*—that is, "with the understanding." I have a painful recollection of some ridiculous misconceptions of such words as "Prone to wander," which I thought meant a long-legged fowl wandering in a swamp! "Fearless I'll launch away," was simply a mispronunciation of lunch away. Nor do I like to admit that my comprehension was unusually dull; in proof of which, let me mention the case of a little imaginative listener—he sings among the angels now, and can understand their song better, I am sure—who came home from Sunday School one day praising the song, but wondering at the request, "Let me die in a harness-shop!" You smile at the mistake; but is it not a serious neglect not to give the dear children more light? One of the greatest evils of fashionable singing is the inarticulate delivery of words.   •

Adaptation of songs to the lesson, especially that of the closing piece, is very important, though often disregarded by superintendents and choristers. How much more effective a lesson when "harrowed in" by an appropriate song ; and, on the other hand, how often have we seen the impression of a lesson almost completely removed by the unfortunate introduction of some inappropriate rattle-te-bang song, because the children could "make it go" well, or visitors were present, and the school must be made to "show off."

A great need in all Sunday-school work is *sincerity*. Nowhere is hypocrisy so wofully apparent, so generally tolerated, and so powerfully taught, as in singing. What else can we expect when children see the church members turning leaves or idly gazing about the room while singing "Nearer, my God, to Thee," or witness a solo or quartet display the words, "Jesus, Lover of my Soul," to the tune "When the Swallows Homeward Fly?" Not to speak of a singing master who, if he be not otherwise intemperate, stands before them with tobacco-stained teeth, or with smoke-tainted breath, singing the sweet, pure songs of Zion.

Above all things, then, sing and thereby teach others to sing *feelingly*, with the spirit. Show your sincerity in song worship, and the children will learn to be sincere. In a word, if you would have them sing sweetly, earnestly and devotionally, sing thus before them ; for in nothing are children more apt at imitation than in singing.

> Sing not alone with lip and voice,
> But with the heart and soul rejoice ;
> Then they that hear will join thy praise,
> And real, heartfelt songs shall raise.

April, 1873.

THE POWER OF SONG.

Sunday School worker, do you appreciate the power of song ?

Think how readily children catch the meaning of a hymn, and how lasting may be its influence. Remember how many have been led to the cleansing Fountain through the instrumentality of song, when argument and entreaty have failed. Cannot you, yourself, remember now songs that you heard in childhood ? More, can you not recall the very voice and manner in which they were sung ? While the sermons—ably written, well delivered sermons, with their flights of oratory and tender appeal—where are they ? Their very texts forgotten ! Their flashing brilliancy lost in the dark sea of forgetfulness, at least so far as you are concerned. Not so the song. Many of us can remember the tunes and hymns sung in church last Sunday. How many can repeat the text from which the sermon was published ?

Fellow-singer, are you not guilty of under-estimating our talents, while we may be over-estimating our rights ? Bury not the God-given talent, but with *all* thy powers serve the Master. "Sing unto the Lord, then, *all* ye people, both young men and maidens, old men, and children ;" and let us remember, when we stand up in the congregation to sing, that we are either singing to the Lord.

or (is it possible?) taking His name in vain! Praising, or playing the hypo-crite! Worshiping or mocking!

Sing on, then, oh children, teachers, Christians! and may there be not a few who hear, and learn to love the story of the cross, by singing it. Sing on, fellow traveler, and may there meet you in the "Better Land" many a redeemed soul washed and made white, to whose mortal ear *your* voice is familiar, and who will give thanks eternally for being led thither by the sanctified influence of your song.

June, 1873.

TO YOUNG WRITERS OF MUSIC.

EASY DIRECTIONS.

1. *Write much.* All old masters wrote much; otherwise they would never have obtained what you and I so much desire—immortality. For instance, what would one page of Shakespeare's "Paradise as you like it," have amounted to? Or, read a single paragraph of Mark Twain's "Impudence Abroad," and stop! No, my dear young friend, with the voluminous Beethoven, the pro-digious Mozart and the everlasting Wagner for your illustrious examples—*write, write, write! !*

2. *Think well of your own.* Nothing can be more unnatural in a young author, writer, poet, etc., than lack of appreciation. I speak with much earnestness on this point; for, depend upon it, your reputation at home and abroad, nine times out of ten, will be no "freak of fortune" bestowed by fairy hands, or thrown gratuitously at your feet by an indulgent public, but will begin and end with yourself.

Think of the youthful Mendelssohn rehearsing snatches of his "Creation" before the crowned heads of England and the Sandwich Islands! Think of the immortal Nero playfully stabbing his youthful associates, so that he might gain the first prize in thorough bass and madrigal! Think of Mephistopheles, etc., ad lib.

3. *Live and die poor.* Here a great many fail. 'Tis so hard to continually and effectually turn a deaf ear to the seductive wiles of earthly riches. Alas! how many buds of poesy are choked by sordid thoughts of filthy lucre! How many sweet singers have been gagged by Mammon's golden chain! How many Fra Diavolos have been lured from zenith of the lofty art by the *ignis fatuus* of earth's glittering gems! How many a poor singing-master do you know, who is likely soon to retire and die in affluence!

Remember Edgar A. Poe, who, in spite of "marble bust," his "velvet sofa" and "purple lining," was poor as a raven. Remember poor John Howard Paine who wrote some sweet verses about home and birds, etc., and then died with-out one. Remember Rossini, Parepa, etc.; be careful to live poor and die poor.

4. *Go West!* Doubtless upon this, more than anything else, depends your future greatness. By all means follow the star of empire! What would Christopher Columbus have known of fame to-day if he had sailed North from

Genoa (or even East), instead of West? Where would the May Flower have landed, had she pointed otherwise than West? Remember, oh, my young Verdis, Handels, Goethes, Chaucers, Coopers, etc.—remember the great Yo Semite. Remember the great undeveloped future. Remember Brigham Young. Remember the Modocs, and go West.

June, 1873.

IT PAID.

I refer to our vacation. Spiritually, physically and financially, it was a success. Here is the record .

One week visiting at Portage, New York, amid scores of relatives and the scenery of the Genesee River, the wildest in creation (the scenery, not the relatives). One week working on the farm, "the dear old farm," in Rome, Pennsylvania, and my arm is lame yet. One week convention in Rome, and it was joyous (new). One week in Towanda, Pennsylvania, likewise joyful (first time). One week in Chester, Vermont, at State Sunday School Convention, "Brilliant with Bliss and Sunshine !" (Original.)

Firstly, then, it paid spiritually. Any man's heart will be rested by going home and looking again into the loving faces of his mother and sisters. A singing man will be much cheered by taking his own new book and going back to his "own native land " for a convention. But how my soul feasted on the Sunday School praise meetings, Bible readings, etc., and the wonderful sympathy of the Vermont State Convention. C. M. Wyman, whose name is so precious to many who will read this, used to teach music in Chester, and his brother, remarkably like him, was in the Convention. Do you wonder that I enjoyed making mention of his intense Christian character and musical fervor? Do you blame me for asking Vermont to send us more such men? Do you suppose I could then and there sing his own "Immanuel's Land" unmoved ? Surely, voice and skill are much, but soul and character more.

Secondly, it paid physically. All singing men are not constitutionally lifters. Therefore the variety of digging potatoes for one's own breakfast, of splitting kindlings, shaking apple trees, engineering wheelbarrows, etc., to say nothing of moving pianos, transferring baggage and carrying valises, babies, etc., has been found useful. Depend upon it, my dear fellow-sitter, the thinking machine will not "produce" unless some attention be paid to the furnace, boiler, pipes, etc. Don't crowd. You're on time ! What's the hurry?

Lastly, (and leastly, if we only could see it), it paid financially. Of course the expense was, like many a musical man's expense, greatly in excess of receipts, but money is worth only what it will bring, and we doubt if ever the money expended would have brought us more satisfaction. Somehow the "panic" didn't seem to reach Vermont, as they paid and over-paid us, and *no collection !* I go to Clinton, Missouri, next week, and I hope it will pay.

Musically and truly,

P. P. B.

PRAISE MEETINGS.

The terms "praise meeting," "service of song," "praise service," etc., have of late become quite common in connection with religious gatherings. What is the best manner of conducting a praise meeting?

First: Every meeting for God's worship should be a praise meeting. We always have much for which we should offer praise. "In everything by prayer and supplication with thanksgiving let your requests be made known unto God." "The joy of the Lord is your strength," and "whoso offereth praise glorifieth Me."

Many a good sermon has been blown away for want of a hearty hymn to harrow it in. Many and many a poor prayer-meeting has dragged its slow length along for want of the lubrication of a cheerful praise-spirit manifested in some soulful song.

A special "praise meeting," like any other, can't be worth anything and cost nothing. Preparation and percussion are the two p's requisite. Give, a meeting-house, with a common-sense platform, a cabinet organ, and one book of hymns and tunes to each individual present, good light and perfect ventilation, and he is indeed a heavy minister who can manage to have a dull, uninteresting, unprofitable service. Preparation may extend to arrangement of hymns selected beforehand, as didactic, descriptive, devotional, etc., and tunes as chanting, cantabile, choral, etc., authorship and incidents of hymns and tunes, date of composition, etc.; Bible texts volunteered from the audience, on praise, containing the word "praise," or, whom should we praise? why? when? where? how? etc., with prayers full of purpose, are among the necessary preparations. Percussion in my next.

DETROIT, October 22, 1874.

"How did it go off?" is as frequently and as properly asked of a praise meeting or any other religious or musical meeting, as of a cannon.

One very important thing is promptness. Don't wait for anybody, or anything. First, ask a blessing. "My soul, wait thou only upon God; for my expectation is from Him;" then a familiar hymn and tune which all can sing. "Ariel," "Shining Shore," "Rock of Ages," or "Sweet Hour of Prayer," will be a good "send off." Urge every one to sing as well as may be, but be very careful that no one or two or four sing so well as to separate themselves from the rest. When the sun rises, stars disappear. One who sings a little too well may discourage a dozen. Stimulate the desire to sing rather than urge singing as a duty.

"Why is ye always a whistlin', Jem?" asked a laboring man of his fellow. "I whistles to make myself happy," said he; "What for do you?" "I has to whistle 'cause I is happy," was the reply. How many poor Christians we've seen singing to make themselves happy; how few have to sing because they are happy. Good singing may produce good feeling, but better have the heart right, then good singing, true praise, will be

The Christian's vital breath
The Christian's native air.

Don't criticise too severely. Many matters of time, tune, etc., will regulate themselves, or, at least, be most improved by being well let alone. And generally, those who sing at all think they sing pretty well ; so don't waste time and breath by scolding. If your congregation had a chance to sing oftener, they would sing better.

The best way to learn to sing is to sing. Make due allowance for the modesty of such singers as that good old deacon who said he knew his voice was rough and heavy, so in order to not make any discord he always tried to keep a little behind the rest !

Occasional Scripture texts, illustrations, prayers, etc., will add greatly to the interest of a praise meeting. Finally, adjourn just before the meeting is out. The best time to stop is just when you feel most like going on. So I stop.

December, 1874.

I. E. THAT IS MIRANDA.

[Of course I write it ; but it's about her.]

On reading something like this from a letter received from her old fellow in New York. She don't know that I read it ; but while she was getting the baby to sleep, I peeped into her desk, and as the letter lay there in the further corner, in plain sight, under some old scrap-books and things, my eye very naturally fell on the following sweet and touching extract :

" And now my own dear Mirandy, i sympathize for you. If you can't stand it any longer fly—i will meat you. How can you indure that base one ? i pity you i pity you. M.K. t., esq."

After reading that and some more, I felt inspired, and sat right down on the spur of the occasion, and wrote the following beautiful philippic :

Pity that blackbird singing on that thorn bush,
Pity that thorn bush that that blackbird sings on,
Pity Pro Phundo and the tears he would shed—
Don't pity me, sir.

Pity that terrier that has a wharf rat caught,
Pity that wharf rat that a terrier has caught,
Pity yourself and your own poor wife, but
Don't pity me, sir.

We're awful poor, but still we're middling happy,
We're not to blame for living in Chicago ;
Some folks may think Pro Phundo is a bore, but
Don't pity me, sir.

I am content to board and wash and darn him,
I am not growing poor by living with him,
I am not, by a long shot, "Mirandy"—
  Don't pity me, sir.

And ten more similar stanzas, when my feelings overwent me, and I laid my head down on my penwiper, and, in the ecstasy so familiar to all poets, soon fell asleep.

YOURS AND OTHERS.

March, 1874.

CHAPTER XXI.

THE greater part of the following letters were written by Mr.
Bliss to his relatives ; the others, to those who were so near
and dear to him as to seem to be of his own kin. The first one contains the first poetry he is known to have written :

EAST TROY, July 29, 1855.

EVER DEAR BROTHER AND SISTER:

* * * * * * * * *

My mind is established, with full purpose of heart, to serve God, to live
acceptably and be prepared to meet my Judge in peace. Let us be careful to
love God supremely, and keep His commandments, that He will be willing to
own us, and that we may all meet around His throne to part no more.

P. P. B.

This world is all a fleeting show,
  With trouble, toil and care ;
Its joys are trivial and we know
  Its pleasures can't endure.

The best of friends and neighbors part,
  And as we say farewell,
How often does the tender heart
  With thoughts of friendship swell.

But if no more on earth we meet,
  Our friendship can't be riven,
And let us live prepared to greet
  With raptured joy in heaven.

Written and composed by
PHILIP P. BLISS.

SPRINGFIELD, March 2, 1856.

DEAR FRIENDS:

With much pleasure I take up my pen to inform you of my condition. At present, I am in the enjoyment of good health; my cough is nearly cured by taking—*good care*, and as to my having been hurt, I am sorry you have heard of it, for it is entirely well now. The circumstances are thus: Last Friday as I was drawing logs with a pair of young oxen, belonging to Mr. Campbell, they started while I was astride of the log, hooking the chain, and rolled the log on to my left foot, and drew it about twelve feet before I could stop them; then you see I was in a predicament noways desirable; being entirely alone, and some ways from the house. I was obliged to dig away the snow from under my foot (a process somewhat tedious) before I could get loose. My boot was considerably mangled, but, happy to say, my foot escaped injury, or nearly so, although it was quite painful for a day or two. I was able to go to school the next Monday.

I am sorry to say that yesterday was the last day of our school. Oh, how I wish you could have been here. We had a grand exhibition in the Baptist Church, before about 200,000,000,000,000,000—no! no! 200 spectators; and it was a show indeed. Such times we had with the gal-gal-galvanic battery and slippers, which made us dance whether we felt disposed to or not; and such good dialogues, and everything passed off so interestingly and agreeably that all enjoyed themselves very well. But when we had finished our performances, and had to take the farewell hand and to say good-bye in earnest, I tell you it seemed like parting with friends, and indeed it was; for many an eye was filled with tears, and all expressed their wishes that we might meet again, on earth; but I have reason to believe that if we are not granted this privilege, the greater part of us will meet in heaven, to enjoy each other's friendship forever.

I have formed a great many acquaintances in my life, but never did I associate with those that were so dear to my heart, as since I have been here. All are so friendly, so charitably disposed, that one cannot but love their society. I shall prefer staying in Springfield this summer to any other part of the world excepting home. Mr. Campbell wishes me to remain with him this summer, but I have made no agreement with him to that effect, nor shall I until I hear your minds expressed on the subject.

For myself I feel as strong in the Lord as ever and have nothing discouraging to say to any one, and I thank God I am what I am, and am determined that nothing shall separate me from the love of Christ. Pray for me that I may make Heaven my home when done with the things of this world. I wish I could be at home to enjoy the good of the meetings with you, but you must remember me. Give my love to all who take the trouble to inquire after my welfare.

Write often and give me all the news. When you have made any maple sugar, just send me word, and I will start for home, I reckon!

It is still good sleighing here and pretty cold weather too. No news, I believe, so good bye.

In a hurry,
P. P. BLISS.

TOWANDA, SUSQUEHANNA COLLEGIATE INSTITUTE, August 26, 1857.

DEAR FRIENDS:

You will see by the date of this, that I am here, and I can tell you I am well, and well satisfied, too, with my situation, being now comfortably located in the institution and commenced my collegiate course to-day. I put right down to Towanda, Monday afternoon, after I came back from home a-foot; stayed over night; came up here Tuesday morn and did chores all day; got my board, and was allowed $1.00 to apply on tuition; since that time have earned 50 cts. There is a chance of my getting all the jobs of work I want to do, which will pay my way. Board, lodging, washing, lights and fuel, room rent included, cost me just $2.00 per week. Have a nice spacious room on the fourth floor, facing Front St., where I have a full view of the whole city and suburbs. A very pleasant place this is, and the people are very hospitable, especially the steward and his wife, which will be of great benefit if I can retain their good will and friendship, which, of course, I shall strive to do. I am a kind of chore-boy, but I am not ashamed of it. I saw wood, bring water, sweep rooms at so much apiece, and am resolved to earn every penny I possibly can honorably.

To-day we commenced; just organized; classed off a few classes. Don't expect to have much of a school this week; just got arranged into classes. I intended to go to some other school than this, but I guess I could not have been better situated. Hear what Mr. Dayton, the steward, says:" Come along to school one, two or three terms, and if you can't pay me now, pay me after you have earned it; for if you teach this winter, you can then pay me; so come along." So I've come, and oh, how I wish I could afford to stay about four years; but it is as it is, and I won't complain, but " *do the very best I can*," you may be sure. I have **taken up Grammar**, Algebra, Physiology and Latin for my studies during the coming term.

Towanda is twenty **miles east of Troy**, a direct line of stages running between, and a trusty stage-driver (lucky for me).

I must close and save some for next time. Expecting to hear from you soon, I remain as ever

Your affectionate Brother,
PHILIP P. BLISS.

KINMUNDY, ILLINOIS, July 9, 1868.

MY DEAR MOTHER:

I have not heard anything from you since we came West. Phe and Mate have both written; Mr. Youngs also, but you have not. We hope you are well, and, if so, I think you are becoming quite *worldly* not to write to any of us.

We have all good health and times. Warren is in good spirits as usual. We have six hours' singing per day. But oh! how warm the weather!! Heavy thunder showers also. Expect we'll be here till July 24th; then go up the Mississippi River to Winona. Pray for us that we may have a pleasant and prosperous journey. Almost every Sabbath I go out to address the Sabbath Schools and sing with them. In several towns I have held children's meetings at five o'clock, Sabbath, trying to do something for the cause of the Master. If He shows me the way for work in this direction—and *because I like it*, I think He will—I mean to give some considerable time to it, and I write especially to ask you to pray for me in this field of labor, the Sabbath School. Pray that I may be blessed in leading the children to Christ, and glorify God, not myself.

July 9th, 1868.
July 9th, 1838.

———

30 years !!!

Do you remember thirty years ago? Well, I don't curse the day, as Job did. No; I've been so brought up and so blessed, that it is a good thing for me to live, and yet I may say "to die is gain."

I'm growing old ! but, I'm not sorry. What! sorry to think we are "Almost home ;" nearer the "shining shore." Nearer through the swamps and snares of this life, nearer the bounds of life eternal? No, I'm not sorry ! Roll on, Roll on. Good bye. Be faithful. Trust in the Lord forever,

Your son,

P. P.

———

BUSHNELL, ILLINOIS, January 10, 1869.

DEAR MOTHER :

This is the Lord's Day, but between the services it seems right and proper to write to you.

'Tis very pleasant ; not a cloud to be seen, no wind stirring, all is peaceful ; the town is quiet, and the bright sun is shining. How this day reminds us of that eternal Sabbath, the rest remaining for the people of God. I suppose Pa Young is at home to-day, and has told you all about us. Truly the Lord has been very good to us the past year, and we trust Him for the years to come.

I hope you, too, have enjoyed yourself better and are rising to higher life and attaining greater spiritual growth than in years before. I make it my daily prayer that you may be *contented*, established in the faith and filled with the love of God.

Your letters for a few months past, and Mr. Young's report in particular, lead me to hope your last days will be your best. God grant it !

I think we may be home in May. Then what shall I bring you? I think you have been a pretty good little girl, and anything you want, ask for it !

Lou is writing to Phe. We are both in the best of health. Lou never had so good health, she says, since she can remember.

There goes the bell ! So good day for this time. May the Lord's word comfort and sustain you and us.　　　　Your own big boy,

P. P.

CARTHAGE, ILLINOIS, January 29, 1869.

DEAR MOTHER;

This is Sunday, a quiet room, good dinner, pleasant day and sleepy wife—Lou is most sick—all favorable for letter-writing.

My mind, for a few days past—though I have been unusually busy—has dwelt considerably on the departed days and friends. Four years ago! How swift the years go by. Yet, I don't believe I would recall them, or, if in my power, stay the flight of time.

One of Pa's prayer meeting expressions used to be "improve the time." This is what we need to do, then the future has no fears, the past no regrets.

How about "tin wedding?" Don't you think 'twill be nice? We couldn't *afford* a wedding when we were married. Now I've tried the goods and think I've found a choice article; so I want to celebrate. Had we better have it in A. P.'s new house, on account of more room—that is, if they'll let us? Of course you need not say anything of this, to them, or any one else, if you please to keep it.

May the Lord give you grace for all your trials and save us all in Heaven.

Your big boy,

BLISS.

FAIRBURY, October 31, 1870.

DEAR PHE & CO.

How do you do? and how do your women folks do? Did Lou tell you of my silver-tipped "baton" present? Having much 'cess and such good times. Wish you and Mate could tend my big conventions all the time. I often thank the good Father for giving me voice and talents in my profession. How much better for me that He led me out of the humble life in which I was born, and I hope better for the world and His cause. I am glad I have such a good sister, too. You always remind me so much of Pa. If we all had his faith and trust—such humility! but I am glad and thankful we were always poor; and oh, we begin to see and feel, how much we owe to Pa for his example and influence. We may be in better circumstances, but we can hardly hope to lead a better, purer, more zealous Christian life. Only if we can meet him "where the wicked cease from troubling, and the weary are at rest"— one of his favorite passages. May "Our Father" bless you all.   P. P.

CHICAGO, February 19, 1871.

MY DEAR MOTHER:

I wish I might have written you on your last birthday, which I see by the record in Pa's old Bible, was February 16th, 1805. Seventy-six, ah, no, I mean sixty-six years old! Well, the Lord be praised for giving me a mother so old and so great and good. I thank Him daily for early influences intended to lead me to Christ. For, whatever of poor advantages, small houses, plain living, threadbare, patched clothing, back-woods society, and unpleasant recollections of my childhood I have to cherish, this precious thought—my parents prayed for me, even before I knew the meaning of prayer, and they consecrated me to the Lord and His service, nor can a prayer, earnest and heartfelt, ever be forgotten before God. I feel the answer to prayer every day.

Am just home from Sunday School; six hundred and eighty-five present; the Holy Spirit was there also. Pray that the Lord will bless me in the work. Pray for my assistant officers, for the choir, some of whom are not Christians. Pray, too, for L. M., a young lawyer, almost persuaded, and for C. A. Pray, too, for Mr. S., who "can't quite come;" he knows the way. These three I am very anxious about, but many are seeking the kingdom, and I believe these will yet be saved. Jesus seems very precious to us in our home; we talk of the Lord, and I love to feel as if He were one of our family—really our Father.

I meant to tell you all about our new house, and describe our daily life, how we get up at six; milk our cow, by setting a pail on the back steps with a ticket in it (8c. a quart); shake the grate so the fire starts; make tea, coffee or chocolate, sometimes tea and coffee or chocolate, then buckwheat cakes—good ones—flour from Rome, Pennsylvania, country butter, and beef or veal. The market man comes twice a week and gets our order for whatever we want, and sends a team around with it free of cost. Our fuel is quite a bill; the rent forty dollars; so our living is very nearly one hundred dollars a month—just about the same as boarding, and so much nicer. Then we've just bought a P. Annie. Yes, sir, after waiting twelve years, I thought I must have one.

The bell is ringing for evening service, so I must go. Now don't scold me for waiting so long, nor for writing so much. I am very busy on The Charm, a copy of which I shall send you as soon as out. Phe must have the first, as she named it. Write often. Lou joins in love.

P. P. B.

---

67 Washington Street; Chicago, August 4, 1871.

Our darling friend, sweet Mrs. Case,
The image of your smiling face,
With rosy cheeks and eyes so bright,
Seems ever pleading : " Write, do write."

Since we received your friendly letter,
My darling wife has grown much better ;
Enjoys the bliss of bed and table,
But yet to write seems hardly able.

Ah, with what joy would we 'uns greet you,
If at the Normal we could meet you !
What " shakes," and " thrills," what cordial k——s,
In case the Cases blest the Blisses.

Of course, we'll have you at Gustavus',
But oh, from dusty, long rides save us—
" To your house ?" yes, 'tis our decision,
Provided you have *large* provision.

> This open question I must pop:
> You didn't tell me where to stop.
> If at Burghill, or if at Greenville,
> Or leave the R. R. at that Mean ville
>
> Where, one cold midnight, I remember,
> We were dumped out—but then, September
> Will be more pleasant. My intention
> Now is to have a loud convention.
>
> Good-bye, our love to Mc. and Addie;
> Be a good girl and mind your daddie.
>
> B. P. P.

CHICAGO, Dec. 8, 1871.

DEAR FRIENDS:

Thought maybe you would like to hear a few words from us.

We have been roaming as usual, only a little more so. For instance, in the last three weeks we have visited Philadelphia, New York, New Haven, Albany, Providence, Boston, and Portland, Maine.

We left Portland Wednesday morning and arrived home late Thanksgiving eve. So we gave our thanks while traveling. We think we have so much to be thankful for. The Lord has been very good to us, and we have done so little in return.

Oh I did not tell you what we have been doing East. Mr. Bliss has been singing with D. L. Moody in his fire meetings. Mr. Moody is trying to raise money to rebuild his Mission Sabbath School.

We have had a splendid time. You remember how we talked last summer, about going to the Jubilee next spring. It is rather uncertain now whether we can afford it or not; but we shall see.

Are you coming to the Chicago Normal next summer? If so, we shall hope to have you with us some of the time.

We have not much that is elegant here now, but we have the most "magnificent inelegance," that the world has ever known. It is almost a miracle how the people could put up so many little "shanties" in such a short space of time.

So you see Mac's folks. Remember us to them. Mr. Bliss says ask if Mr. Case opens his conventions with prayer.

That the good Lord may keep you, and bless you and yours, is the earnest prayer of your friend,

LOU BLISS.

Remember us to father and mother, brothers and sisters. Don't forget to write.

CHICAGO, January 29, 1873.

DEAR BROTHER C. C. C.:

How is it with thee? And thy darling Annie *e*? Just about now **you are** preparing for Baconsburg, and Mr. Seward.

Do you know my wife actually proposed—as I have to go East in a few weeks,—that we come to B. and attend your Convention! Had it not been for an impudent Iowa town calling us away the same week, I do believe we'd a been thar! If this reaches you in Convention don't stop singing—Go right on with "The Multitude of Angels"—and at recess squeeze Mr. Seward's hand awfully for me. Don't promise him to be at Binghamton this summer *all the time;* come to Chicago *some*.

Are full of business of all kinds—Conven and S. Sch.—(which means Sunday School).

Mr. Young's wife's brother is with us this winter, kind o' helping round.

How are the dear friends Mac and Addie? Bless their hearts!

Boston Jibulo is rather doubtful since the fire. I'll tell you, instead of going there, you *all* come here and get used to the climate and city before the Normal. I want to see you very much and tell you how we love you! What's the use keepin' such things to one's self all the time? Seems as if our friends are leaving us every day for the "other side." We must talk fast, the boat is coming.

Love to Pa Williams' folks. Do your best. Live near the Lord. Farewell.

P. P. B.

> KIND KASES:
> We wish ye well;
> Lou is lying loosely low!
> Big-eyed Baby PAUL prospers,
> "Sunshine" smiles soothingly.
> "P. P. Jr." jolly;
> "P. P. Sr." silly!

[N. B.—That last line is composed for the occasion by Mrs. P. P. Bliss.]

What I mean to communicate is the good news that all is well. Only I have to go to Monmouth Monday for a Convention. I don't want to leave home one bit, but Brother Hanchett—you remember him—says come. Chicago seems to me very pleasant and friendly, as all the world ever has.

Wish you lived here. Adieu.

I must go and sing to baby. He likes me; you would like him. Come and see.

P. P.

CHICAGO, 11, 9, 72.

DEAR BROTHER C. C. C. c. c. c. c c.

Your $40 favor received this day.
Blessings on ye both.
Grace, mercy, peace, joy,

> Love, gladness, beauty,
> Happiness, cheerfulness,
> Comfort, voice, business,
> **Wife**, friends, classes,
> Oysters and tight pants
> Be yours forever.

P. P. B. & Co. are, as usual, digging ditties at my desk. Choir splendid. S. S. ditto. The Lord's work going on surely. Wife not very comfortable—hopeful always. A teacupful of love as strong as boneset to each of ye.

Our *horse* is no better, and now the stove's got it! 'twon't *draw*.

How's Greeley? Poor man. Hurrah for Black! Why don't Grant and May write to me? Tell 'em I have a tip of the old elephant's tusk on my desk and will call it "Mizpah," if Grant will find in Genesis what that means. Adieu, Adieu.

P. P. B.

CHICAGO, January 15, 1873.

DEAR MOTHER:

May the Lord be very near to you and bless your soul for the sweet, good letter we received to-day. Lou says that ever since we saw you last year, on the hill, and at Towanda, your letters have been splendid; and she never enjoyed a visit with you so much in the world as the last one.

Darling Paul, how you would love him! I just begin to appreciate what you have done for me! He is a nice, fat boy; sleeps and eats well; has a great big head, big blue eyes and indications of light hair. O. F. Young!

Lou says as soon as he can go out you shall have a picture. Warren manifested a great deal of pleasure, more than we expected. He often mentions him in his letters. Warren is still teaching in Southern Illinois, and can stay here in the West as long as he wishes; plenty of business for him.

I hope Willie Jennings will do well; and I can agree with you that perhaps he needs contact with the world and business. God bless him; and the more I can help him and other of my relations, the better.

You will find in a box sent to Towanda, a black dress; have it made "up and down," to wear to Chicago! Won't we have a good re-union, when we all get home to heaven? I so want to see Pa Bliss and Reliance—Jamie, and the blessed JESUS!!

Truth is: the mercy and favor of Our Father in Heaven seem continually shining on us, unworthy and unthankful as we are. Oh how we ought to praise and love Him. Help us.

Can't you and your folks find me some stuff for "Song Tree?"

Don't go to Boston Jubilee. I don't believe 'twill pay.

I'm glad I ever knew you.

P. P. B.

12 South Elizabeth Street, Chicago, May 24, 1873.

SWEET SPIRITS:

Tried and True, worthy brother and sister. Our partners in the ever-lasting inheritance. [How thankful ought we to be for such friends!] You speak of friends being convenient—"to pay in advance," etc. I believe it was some such unimportant matter that kept us from the "Feast—ival" at Cincinnati. But we are soon to have a "G. B." in Chicagano. Come and "burst."

My old mither and sister Jennings are visiting us for a few weeks. They both love you as well as they can till they know you better.

Yes, indeed, the Lord has blessed "Sunshine" greatly. Help us to praise Him for it. It's His book any how, and He should have the praise. No end of compliments for page 10.

The Paul boy is in his usual spirits—gay and blissful. Next Sunday, I think, he will put on his best (McGranahan's) robes and be baptized.

My "Joy" is full. Sunday School prosperous, thirty joined the church last Sunday. We are in our new basement. Kate Cameron died last week. We sung her "That City," from "Joy," at her funeral. May we all follow her.

AMEN.

[To Mrs. W. J. Crafts.]

Chicago, Aug. 7, 1873.

OUR DEAR SISTER SARA:

How kind of you to send a full volume of your sweet things when we know you must be very busy. You are not "our debtor," neither, indeed, can you ever be; our lives have been made sweeter and richer by your contact, and the oftener you come by letter or by bodily presence, the better for us.

Yes, thank you and your good mother (how we'd love to see her), the Eye Teaching came. It is a rich thing for me, and must do good. Dr. Vincent is jolly—great and good. Some people are great and good, but can't be jolly. I can't like them quite so well.

By the way, whence comes the song from which you quote,

Watching and waiting for me?

Bro. Hartley gave it all to me, but I am anxious to know if it is copyright.

No, I don't seem to rest much in hope of seeing a throng of heavenly ones waiting and watching for me—they might be in better business—nor of hearing echoes of my songs there. I want something better. About the best thing in Heaven seems to me will be eternal freedom from sin and Jesus' immediate presence.

There we shall see His face
And never, never sin.

If we can will write you from Rome, Pennsylvania, where we must leave Paul with his grandmother.

We have delightfully cool weather in Chicago this summer. Are very much occupied with our N. N. Musical Institute, which is a success.

> Good-bye—Bless you,
> 3 BLISSES
> love you much.

CHICAGO, Nov. 1, 1873.

DEAR PHE:

Eight years ago to-day, Towner, Bliss and wife, "Yankee Boys," arrived in Chicago. How God has blessed us all the way. Seems as if He picked me out from the beginning! He must have had His eye on me and on the work He was preparing for me when we lived on Elk Run. He has helped us so far, and surely He will not let go of us now.

More and more I am praying for one thing—Consecration to Christ. All *from* Him, all *for* Him, all to Him.

Aid me by your prayers. May you be a blessing to all and so be always blest.

> P. P.

CHICAGO, Last day of 1873. *Normal.*

PRECIOUS PHRIENDS:

Why didn't you stay a week with us? Come back *now*

I write on business—*Real " State."*

Do you wish to sell your puburban soperty at Ridgeland? I will give you $150 a foot for 135 feet! Provided you will take $13\frac{1}{2}$ feet! on Church Avenue at $1500 a foot in part payment. Seriously—help me to be thankful for about $500 *extra* copyright which came yesterday. God is and has been surprising me with such success. Help me to make it a *real* success—and not a hindrance to my own and others' *spiritual*—which is the *real* welfare.

My birthday verse is Prov. xxx 9, (beginning with the 8th verse). Please, if you have not seen it, let Mr. Case also see the inclosed criticism on N. N. M. I. concert. This is a little pleasanter, but oh, " what difference will there be ?"

I'd rather have a little girl or boy smile in my face and say, "I think you are real good," which means—though it may be not comprehended—" I think you are some like Jesus," than to have a column of high sounding praises in every newspaper in Chicago. " The things that are *not* seen are eternal," I tell you; " the kingdom of heaven is within," and let's you and I get as much of it packed up as possible before we take our long journey. Amen.

I am not forgetting the little songs for you and C. C.

> Forty Kisses
> From three ———

CHICAGO, February 7, 1874.

DEAR MOTHER:

I thank you for the Portage letter. It is a good one. You must have noticed that lately we do enjoy your letters more than we used to do. You will let me say it—that it seems to us your spirit grows sweeter, and your life more even and calm. It is not surprising that it should be so; for haven't you and your friends prayed for it? If we are in Christ, may we not all expect to grow more and more like Him? Let us try to live in the Vine and bear fruit to the honor of His Holy Name. You may be sure we shall pray for you, and I never can forget that you prayed for me and watched over me many years before I could pray for myself. I love to make mention of praying parents in my prayers and conversation. I feel the strength every day of the early religious training and surroundings—just as a man must be benefited all his lifetime by youthful physical exercise. I am determined the godly ancestry shall not stop with me, but that Paul shall be the subject of much prayer. He shall inherit a good fortune of faith, even if his worldly goods can be tied up in a cotton handkerchief, as mine were when I started for Troy.

Well, we are tired and sleepy to-night. The choir, about fifty in number, came in and surprised us last night; brought a big basket full of pop-corn, nuts and candy for their own refreshment, and a beautiful silver tea set, six pieces, tea and coffee pots, cream and sugar bowls, butter dish, and spoon-holder, frosted finish and finely lettered B. Cost seventy-five dollars. You may believe we were surprised and cheered. Bless their kind hearts! I don't know as I shall ever find such a good choir again. I told them, jokingly, if I'd known I'd got such a fine present, I might have resigned before! Now when you and Phee come to see us, we can give you better *tea*, maybe.

Good night, be good to yourself and Phe. Take care of little Phil, and I will remember you in my will.   P. P.

CHICAGO, February 13, 1874.

KOT OV KONTENT:

All well. Tried again to splash on to you at Conneaut or Burghill, and couldn't quite do it. Arrived home last Friday, and the choir had 'sprised us with a clothes-basket full of pop-corn, nuts and candy for themselves and a set of silver tea things—six pieces—for us. Bless 'em! So much I get for resigning. Who would not be resigned?

I go to Iowa next week, in the region of Br'n Waugh, Rheam, Turgeson, *et al*. Expect a good time. I just tell you we had a grand, good big convention at Honesdale, Pa., "175" singing "Hallelujah Chorus," "How lovely are the Messengers," "In Heavenly Love Abiding," etc. This was the country of my *beginning*,—a poor village singin' master. Now "the Professah from Chicago" with his accomplished lady, wearing better clothes and more hair, seemed to make a much profounder effect. I hope we were not vain, but we can't deny a *little* pride at our success.

Paul Bliss is the blessedest child, fat and healthy, good-natured as—as—his *paw*,—that's me.

Oh, I am writing some such good songs—of the prayer-meeting order—now-a-days.

16

The Lord has wonderfully blessed "Sunshine Songs." "Calling Now," I found at Gustavus', or rather at your house, do you remember? And that like Mac's "Heaven for me," has been sung and complimented very much in this country and in England. Bro. Sankey is doing wonders in Scotland, with Moody. Pray for me and my songs. If it does others half as much good to sing them as it does me to write them I am thankful.

To God be ALL the glory. Our church is to be re-dedicated Sunday. Dohn is to lead the music.

I know not what they'll do. More *showy* music was demanded, and I resigned. I must insist on plain music for devotion in public worship. And I can have no sympathy with operatic or fancy music for Sunday.

Pardon so long a letter; but I love you.

P. P. B.

DEAR   CHICAGO, Mch. 9, 1874.

Yours received and oh, how good it seems to have such a sister to write such letters. You'll never know how much you help me. Your sweet patient life—your abiding trust even in the thick darkness—and your earnest sisterly prayers all help me; and *I don't know how much*, either.

But what an accumulation of prayer must be before the throne for some of us. And then the dear Jesus praying for us—think of that! Earthly friends are good, but what a Friend we have above! Be sure you are remembered by us—but how much better by Him. Oh, surprising mercy! to love His enemies, to die to win our love. On His sweet word I'm resting, "I know no safer stand, not e'en where glory dwelleth in Immanuel's land."

I send a book in your name to W. H. The best book I've read in a long time—"Arthur Bonnicastle." I hope W. H. will succeed. He has the material, if he can only cultivate persistent, steady pluck; if he is not too much like his uncle. My prayers are for him ever.

Lou proposes to send you some things you need, if you will tell. A box worth a dollar or $1.50, wouldn't cost more'n 2s. for express.

She thinks she can buy things here cheaper than you can there. Make out a list from silk dresses down to sewing machines.

I go to Michigan Monday morning.   Yours all the way.

P. P.

CHICAGO, March 28, '74.

DEAR MA AND PHE:

How is it with ye? I have some news to say:

First, I am about to change—in fact, have changed my plan of work. Intending to write and sing Gospel songs in Gospel meetings, instead of Convention teaching. So giving *all* my time, voice and heart to the cause of Christ, *direct.* I've always wanted to do this, and now I can and must.

Oh! pray that God may use me and bless my songs (His gift) to the winning of many precious souls. Praise Him continually for selecting me, even me, out of such surroundings, and giving me such honor. You can't imagine how perfectly happy I am, and Lou too, already.

Major Whittle and I were at Waukegan three days and gained by the Holy Spirit thirty votes for Christ. He, too, has given up all for Jesus' service, and we shall likely go together a good deal. Pray for us.

Your devoted,
PHIL.

CHICAGO, June 11, 1874.

MR. AND MRS. CRAFTS:

Jude iid.

I was married before I was twenty-one. I pity poor folks who have to wait and wait! Much valuable time is lost by waiting.

But I thank Dr. Vincent for favor received, don't you? How I wish you would come and see the Blissful family. Why not? We have more room now than when you were here. Paul would say "De auntie" and "How do unkie." Yes, I know girls don't grow old so fast, if married—therefore I wanted you to marry.

Chautauqua? H'm! Michigan is a much beautifuller lake, and as to boat rides, etc., we hope to see some crafts here in Chicago, some day, perhaps a fleet of 'em.

Let us hear from you often, please. Who is this W. F. Crafts? What color hair? What church? Is he rich? Tall and handsome? Good affection, too?

Only may he be as happy in married life as has been his and your loving friend and brother,   P. P. BLISS.

Maj. Whittle and I are holding meetings, day and night, in the Second Presbyterian Church, South Side.

God is wonderfully blessing us in every way. Help us to praise Him for it.

I am preparing a book of Gospel Songs for our special use, and would be right glad to have you send a list of hymns and tunes which have been most successful in your experience. And above all, pray for the book. All the good in it must come from God.

CHICAGO, December 11, 1874.

DEAR MOTHER:

I beg your pardon for not sending your $2.00 sooner. I have been away from home and very busy in Gospel singing at Pittsburgh.

Lou telegraphed me Tuesday that she and the boys were both sick; so I came home. Will is almost sick, too. I've been flying around after a doctor, and got a good nurse. Sophy is a little better, so that she can help Annie, and now I guess we are all a little better.

I can tell you that this Gospel song singing and talking to people about

Christ and His love will be my business after this. Everything else is poor business. I am so thankful for what the dear Lord has done for me since last April. Nothing like it. How good God has been to me since first you knew me. Help me to praise Him, and pray for me, as I know you will while you live. Much happiness to you all.   Yours truly,

                                                          P. P. B.

                        GALT HOUSE, LOUISVILLE, KENTUCKY, Feb. 16, 1875.
DEAR MOTHER AND MATE:

   I can't wait—must tell you that the Lord has done and is doing a great and mighty work here. Thousands and thousands crowding daily and nightly to hear the old-fashioned Gospel of Christ. Three or four meetings daily; 200 or 250 arose for prayers Sunday night. This morning I had a glorious praise meeting in the hotel. Last evening, in the mass meeting in the hall, an immense opera house jammed full—2500 or 3000 people. Among those who arose for prayer, and went down into the inquiry room with me, and I trust gave her heart to the Lord, was—guess who? My heart is full as I write it—V * * * D * W * * * *! Hallelujah! There is joy in heaven.

   If all the meetings had been carried on and only this one result, how richly paid I would have been. Yet hundreds of souls just as precious have been saved, we believe. Oh! how good God has been and how precious Jesus my Master is to-day. I write in V * * *'s name, who sends her love to you all, and asks that you and I set apart Sunday, Feb. 28, to pray for her, and to praise the Lord for His goodness.

   Of course you will pray and praise for me. It is in answer to your prayers of years ago and to the prayers of him who now dwells in the glory land, that God has chosen me. Not a day, hardly a meeting passes but I think, and can it be that He has chosen me to be an instrument, a vessel in which to carry the water of life to perishing souls? Oh! pray daily that I may be a vessel sanctified and meet for the Master's use.

   I must be brief—want to go and call on V * * * and see if she is in the light this morning. Also want to write to Phe and Lou the news. Five meetings for to-day. I sing.

   All sick at home last I heard. Will had measles; babies exposed and Lou tired. I hope the Lord will take care of them all. I know He will. Love to all.   Joyfully,

                                                          PHIL.

                                                          APRIL 1.
DEAR MOTHER:

        *   *   *   *   *   *   *   *   *

   I send you papers of the meetings, so I needn't write you anything of them ; only must say 'tis a glorious calling to be a messenger for such a King and to carry such tidings, and to see so much success.

   Oh! pray for me while you live, and rejoice with me that God has set such honor upon me.   Pray that I have two things,—power of the Holy Spirit and a humble heart.

Love to all the dear ones.   I expect to come East—Syracuse, New York State Sunday School Convention, June 8.

Your happy boy,
P. P. Bliss.

664 W. Monroe, Chicago.

Dear Sister Phe:

Very pretty poetry you sent me.   Where did you get it?   The subject, "Hope," has always been my motto, and the Christian's hope!   It seems to me that I can see Pa now, as he used to stand up in the little old school-house and tell his friends and neighbors of his hope, "which was like an anchor to the soul, both sure and steadfast;" or, his hope finally to come off conqueror —"yea, more than conqueror through Him that loved us," or he hoped we would all "be up and doing," and hoped we would all meet him in "the bright mansions Jesus has gone to prepare."   Oh! how dark the world would be without "Hope."

Take fast hold of the promises—those blessed promises.   "If I go and prepare a place for you, I will come again and receive you," etc.   Let's not forget who said this; and won't He come?   We may forget *our* promises, but *Jesus* never.   *We* may get tired waiting, but He will come and "receive us."   Oh! be ready; and when I get to thinking about it I can't help saying—

> How long, dear Savior, oh, how long
> Shall this bright hour delay? etc.

Sing that as Pa and Ma used to, on a Sabbath morning, to the tune of Northfield, and think of me.

I hope we are getting nearer the kingdom,—making some little progress in Divine life; not as much as could be wished; but do you remember Gideon's band in Scripture, "faint yet pursuing." Oh, trust in the Lord, as Job says, "though He slay me yet will I trust in Him." Lord, give us all such trust, and save us through Christ our Redeemer.   Amen.   P. P.

I believe we should think of Jesus when we pray, as a dear friend really listening to us and ready to aid, not as some great power to be dreaded.   So let us come with boldness, liberty, freedom, believing His word and hoping in His mercy.   He likes to have us come in earnest, as the poor blind men came, saying, "Lord, if Thou wilt," and then He is ready to say "I will."

Chicago, January 9, 1876.

Dear Mother:

Happy New Year!   What different circumstances the different years bring us.   Where and how were we in 1866?   And January 1, 1856, 1846, etc.   This is, on many accounts, the best and happiest New Year we ever saw.   I cannot begin to recount the mercies of the past, nor do I appreciate the blessings of the present. I can only say, "The Lord is my Shepherd;" then I am His sheep, and because He cares for me I desire to live for Him. Amen.

We are all quite well. Paul and George are a little bad-coldish, but so as to eat and sleep; Will and Lou ditto. I came home from Milwaukee last night; have been there six weeks. The meetings for the past week have been greatly blessed. Many professed to accept the Gospel. Praise the Lord. Dear Bro. Whittle goes to Racine this week. I shall join him on Friday. Next week we go to Madison, the capital of Wisconsin, and the week after, the 25th, to St. Louis. Please pray for all these places. God will answer. I can testify to you that this life of service to Him who hath bought us is a very delightful one. My cup of joy has always been full, but in these glorious meetings it often runs over; and I have to-day, Sunday, been at home all day with my family, resting and rejoicing. Lou and I have had sweet communion with each other and the Lord. I am thankful for a wife who can enter into and share the joy of Christian consecration and service. Of course it is the greatest trial of our lives, so far, to be separated so much, but it seems to me especially hard for her. My time is so taken up with the meetings, going and seeing, etc., while she is left with the monotonous, every-day duties of home life, and that almost like yours, a widow. But nevertheless, the Lord has given her a cheerful heart, and she is just as content and reconciled as any one could be; says she would not detain me if she could, and prays, oh, so earnestly, for my success and safety. Again, I thank God for a praying wife and a praying mother. What would I have been but for both? The Lord only knows.

Some talk has been had of our coming to Towanda, but now it looks doubtful, at least for the present. If we go South, as invited, from St. Louis to Mobile, Montgómery, Macon, Savannah, etc., shall probably come around to New York or somewhere to meet Moody and Sankey, in March or April. This is all uncertain, but you can say to all who ask, We do not know. If the Lord approves of the plans, I am thinking of coming East about May and remaining till September or longer. Then you may not be at all surprised if on New Year's, 1877, my letter comes from England.

I have no plan nor wisdom. Where "He leads I would follow." Pray that "upper wisdom" be given us in all these things.

Owego, Tuesday.

DEAR CASE, SMACK & CO.:

I meant it, I wish I could be with you. My prayers and best wishes are for you.

In *Case* we can get home to your concert after next, *i. e.*, July 28, may I sing my Centennial Gospel Song and have the quartet names on slips inclosed? "Arise and Shine," not yet printed. Our little *vis* with you yesterday, only makes us hungry for more. Don't fail to go to Rome. We must not, cannot let go of you. Please write oftener the coming year than you did last.

I did not sleep a wink last night, went to bed about one. Stage came at 3.20. "Great is the Lord," and "The Lord is good, a stronghold in the day of trouble," and kindred themes kept running through my mind—and with my prayers and praises I could not sleep.

We go on to-morrow morning, and expect to get to New York the 25th.

Please may we find a love-letter from all of you at Biglow & Main's, 76 East Ninth Street, New York?

Yours in haste—a crowd of relatives are waiting—Yours as of old,

P. P. BLISS.

Lou joins in severest love.

May 8, 1876.

In regard to your convention, " I pray thee have me excused." *This* is the best kind of convention ticket, and I am full of engagements as long as I live.

TERMS : " Whosoever will may come."

INSTRUMENT USED—" The Sword of the Spirit."

TIME—" *Now* is the accepted time."

> " *While we were yet Sinners, Christ died for us.*" *Romans*, v. 8.

ACADEMY OF MUSIC.

GOSPEL MEETINGS,

7.30 P. M. each Evening, commencing Dec. 21st, 1875,

CONDUCTED BY

D. W. WHITTLE AND P. P. BLISS.

Singing by Chorus Choir conducted by P. P. BLISS.   Solos by P. P. BLISS.

ADMIT BEARER——WEDNESDAY EVENING.

In addition to Evening Services, a Noon Meeting will be held at the Academy of Music each day from 12 to 1 o'clock, a Bible Reading from 3 to 4 o'clock, and Young People's Meeting from 4 to 5 o'clock. Admission free WITHOUT TICKET. Tickets for Evening Services can be obtained without cost, upon application at Wisconsin News Co., of Pastors of Churches, or of E. Upson, Chairman Committee, Young Men's Library Rooms, at Academy of Music.

ROME, PENNSYLVANIA, May 8, 1876.

DEAR   AND

Yours received in Chicago. We didn't stop at Burgville. Put the two babies and two girls in a palace car in Chicago, and left the same car in Waverly, New York, for Towanda—our station. You may have heard of Towanda before.   Some second-class Normal is to be held there this summer; but 'twont be much of a concern 'cause my name isn't on the *circulaire*.

> Print, brother, print with care,
> And print " P. P." on your circulaire.

However I *may* be induced to smile on you during the term—if you give me my "Choice." While in Selma, Alabama, I received the information of Towanda Normal, and at once foresaw G. F. R., Mac, and Cases, *et al.*, spending a Saturday and Sunday in Rome—ten miles away—"praise meeting" in our church, etc. More than this, D. L. Moody writes me from Chicago: "I want to see you, and if you will tell me where you will be I will come and see you this summer." Wouldn't it be good to have Moody here when you are?

Our boys are pretty well. Paul is a little croupy, running out so much; but George seems better, right away. Wife is somewhat worn and wearied, but all things considered, we were never better off. Wish you were as well.

Love to all the dear Williamses.

Yours till we see you—after that we can't promise.

P. P. P.

- - - - - - -

KALAMAZOO, MICHIGAN, November 3, 1876.

DEAR MAMMA:

Let me give you a good morning kiss and wish you a "Merry November!"

Your last letter was received, I think, and I was glad, of course, as a good boy ought to be.

We have been here two weeks, and about the *best* two weeks we ever had. Your prayers are being answered, and I am thankful for a mother who prays. I hope my boys will remember with profit the prayers of their father and mother. Please to pray for them, and for those who have care of them.

We have been to Chicago meetings some, and sent you papers. Oh! what a privilege to live in these days and to be in any way connected with such a work of grace!

Do you enjoy anything or anybody this winter? How is your health and mind and spirit? Is it well with your soul?

Song of Solomon, ii, 14, is a sweet verse. It is the Lord speaking to us, His children. He wants us to look up and speak to Him. How good He is. What grace! what grace! I send you a song,

Hallelujah, what a Savior!

Mr. Sankey and I are to have a new book in January.

Now I must go to prayer-meeting. Guess you'd better direct to Chicago, Y. M. C. A.

Don't know how long we'll stay here, nor where we'll go next. Anywhere with Jesus.

Yours and His son,

P. P. BLISS.

JACK AND HIS SON,

Which amounts to Jackson, November 18, 1875.

Dear " Ma :"

This is our last week here ; next I may write you from Chicago. Yours received. I am sorry for your eye.

> Do not cry ; do not cry.
> For I hope it will be better
> By and by, by and by ;
> Wipe it with your little handkerchief,
> Do not sigh, do not sigh,
> You have eyes worth looking out of,
> So have I, so have I.
> Beams and motes are woful bothers,
> In your eye, in your eye,
> But a *bile* on yours or other's
> Is " too high ! "—far too high !

I sent C. W. a box of books, but hear nothing from it. Hope they've got 'em.

Thanks for the compliments to my boys. I think you and I have nice sons. I want to see my son P. P. Do you want to see yours ? Well wait till about Christmas, if the Lord will. Lou is making a worsted mat to put on our table. I'll have to go and get a table.

[Closed by Mrs. Bliss.]

Phil has been called away and his parting words were, " You finish this letter." The mat he spoke of is made of shaded worsted from a very dark scarlet down to a pink ; I think it will be very handsome. When I was keeping house I never found time for any fancy work, and now that I have a little time I am trying to improve it. We have sold or given away nearly all the things we had, so that when we go to keeping house again we will have to start all anew. I have kept my bedding, table linen, and silver, and about all the furniture we have is some clothes boxes. So if we ever do get a house of our own, I shall have everything new to start with.

We sent you a paper telling you all about the meetings in Kalamazoo. Whittle and Bliss are being very much blessed in their work. There are many precious souls born into the Kingdom every day. The Lord is very good to us. He keeps our children in such good health, and takes such good care of us. We get pretty homesick to see the boys, but must wait until about Christmas.

It is getting so dark that I cannot see ; so please excuse me,

Hastily yours,

Your Smallest Daughter.

PEORIA, ILLINOIS, November 30, '76.

DEAR MAC:

Yours with music came duly. Thanks. Have only time to acknowledge and hope to see you if we come to Rome, Christmas, as we hope to do.

Having most blessed meetings here,—still praying the Lord to send you into singing Gospel songs in Gospel meetings.

Glad you could call on my folks at Towanda; wish I could do as much for you. Wishing you a merry Thanksgiving and a Happy "77,"

Yours as ever,
P. P. AND LOU B.

At the time of writing the above letter, Mr. Bliss turned to his companion and said "Who is there that McGranahan could go with to sing the Gospel?" A few moments' talk followed, but no one could be thought of with whom he would be likely to go. One month from the date of this letter, Mr. Bliss was killed and these lines are now being added in Dubuque, Iowa; where Mr. McGranahan is singing the Gospel in meetings conducted by the companion to whom Mr. Bliss that day spoke. His prayers are answered.

A dearly loved friend of Mr. and Mrs. Bliss, in sending copies of letters, thus writes:

JACKSONVILLE, FLORIDA, Feb. 28, 1877.

Your letter with regard to the memoir you are preparing of Mr. and Mrs. Bliss came duly to hand. Am sorry I could not have replied sooner.

I am very glad that you have undertaken this, for I think thereby the world will know more of the character of one of the most unselfish, humble Christians I ever knew. One could not know Mr. Bliss well without being the better for it. He has helped me in my Christian life much. I have played for his musical conventions held in different times in Illinois, and heard much of his teaching in music for the past sixteen years, and the same lovely, simple faith has always been very apparent. My first acquaintance with these dear friends was in Warsaw, New York, my home before I was married, where Mr. B. was employed to lead the choir of the Congregational Church for six months. I belonged to that choir, and under his teaching was made to see *more* in every hymn sung than I had ever before imagined could be found in them. He was always careful to have every part of the choir's worship done in the most reverential, thoughtful manner possible. His Master's glory was always his highest aim. He has had great influence in his convention work, of late years. He always opened the morning session with prayer, followed by some devotional piece of music, which he would *always* use with good effect; and then a few words would fall from his lips upon the subject which was so near and dear to his heart—the saving of souls—and all eyes would moisten and hearts were touched in many, many instances.

I believe the Lord crowned with His blessing all these words. Mr. Bliss' pleasant, genial manner made him a favorite wherever he went, especially among the young; so every word spoken by him before the convention was treasured and *believed*. So he has been doing evangelical work for a good many years.

I have copied only such parts of Mr. Bliss' letters as might be of some use to you, knowing you will have no time to waste in reading anything else. I cannot let them go without expressing my thanks to you for this generous work you are doing. I, with hundreds of others, will be so glad to have such a memoir. I cannot cease regretting that so many letters which might have been so useful now are destroyed. Our peculiar circumstances of giving up friends and home in pursuit of health called forth many letters, beautiful letters of loving sympathy, ever turning our thoughts to the Great Healer, and always telling of his own great joy and perfect happiness in working for the Master. It was his *real, natural* life. His father was just such an humble earnest Christian before him.

I have been pained by mistakes made by the press, especially in one case where he was said to have been a Christian for the last six years, and another saying his wife taught him his first lessons of Divine love. She was a loving, faithful wife, but *her* rich Christian experience was developed under *his* influence, instead of as the press stated. N. E. M.

The following are the letters from Mr. Bliss to which Mrs. M. so feelingly alludes :

DETROIT, MICHIGAN, October the last, 1874.

OUR DEAR BROTHER AND SISTER:

Surely no name is too sacred to represent the relationship, though the many, many miles stretching between us seem to make us very *distant* relatives. How much you are both in my thoughts and prayers. It *is* sad to say "good-bye."

Your penciled note gave us great pleasure, although a portion (" for me ") had been omitted. Surely our past acquaintance warrants the supposition that anything, everything, we may write, will be perfectly understood and gladly received by each other. Never destroy, copy, or restrain anything suggested in regard to any member of the Bliss family.

While this is being written you are being whirled rapidly away, westward, chatting gayly of the aunt-elopes or Buffalo (Bills), plowing snow banks, eating venison, or, it may be, sending back a thought or word to "664," "Gospel Songs," "Paul" and his " corner," etc., etc., while here, in the study of Rev. Arthur Tappan Pierson, Pastor of the First Presbyterian Church—a mighty man, a perfect scholar and such a genial affinity—these lines are penned to you, though the hour is taken from the noon prayer-meeting. *Four meetings a day* leave little time for anything else. So this may be regarded as home missionary work!

You will not expect much in this letter concerning Chicago: a very tender feeling is awakened by the name; a gentle "redness of eyes" is induced by thoughts of wife and Paul and George. Yet the mighty question of my dear Master's business engages with a profound interest my *whole soul*. While the souls of men are dying, and the good news of the glorious Gospel will be so eagerly listened to, it is no time to hesitate.

Dear Lou is trying hard to say, "Go, and God speed thee," and her true woman's nature *is* being so ennobled and consecrated that, with no less love for me but so much *more* for the blessed Jesus and His sweet service, her heart has heaven's own rest of peace.

Morning prayer meeting at eight o'clock, attendance from 100 to 250, led by Whittle, Bliss or some other preacher. Requests by the dozen are read, one at a time, and prayer, silent or audible, offered for each one.

Five persons arose for prayer this morning; groups of six or more remained to talk or pray together. Noon meeting daily at Young Men's Hall. Whittle leads to-day. Bible reading every P. M., and to-day a children's meeting at 3; Gospel meeting at 7.30 (prayer meeting at 7); and oh, how you would enjoy seeing and helping on such a work. Incidents? Details? Where to begin, is the only question. Last evening two girls came up to me to "talk religion," *just in fun!* 'Twas a painful sight; my heart was grieved—the Holy Spirit, oh, how much more! This morning one of them came to prayer meeting and spoke of it with grief and penitence. One of the first families have a "high-toned" girl who hasn't spoken to her father for three years! She is asking prayer; but we told her this morning, How can you ask prayer? how can you pray with such a heart? Scores are being converted—hopefully, joyfully, scripturally converted. Praise ye the Lord.

Two weeks more here; then we go to Pittsburgh. Pray for us there. December or January will probably bring us to Boston, Massachusetts.

Anywhere with Jesus.

You will now be released, as the time for children's meeting is near. Let us live near the Lord, be happy, trustful, bold, earnest, *real* Christians. Serve Him who *saves us*, because we *are* saved and not *to be saved*.

Your names are in my prayers.

Very sincerely, your brother,
P. P.

MILWAUKEE, December 30, 1875.

Our meetings here are good. All the churches united, crowds attending, and many professing to be saved by believing the Gospel, the gift of God. How I do love to offer it as a free gift and hear the delightful reply, "Why, if my debt is paid, and God says it is, I must believe it or make Him a liar." "I accept Jesus as my Savior." "Is *that* the way to be saved?" "I'll live for Him who died for me," etc. etc. No joy in this world like this service.

Mrs. M. introduces another letter with the following prefatory note, and tells us the origin of "When Jesus Comes:"

The following is from our last letter from Mr. Bliss, written a few days before his death. You will probably remember the ride to which he alludes, about the bluffs and cemetery of Peoria. A few years ago while visiting us at Peoria, we took the same places in, in an afternoon drive. It was on a lovely October day; the air was hazy and dreamy, and all nature was clothed in her brilliant fall colors, making the cemetery a most charming picture. We drove slowly, winding about from path to path, now on the hillside, now in the valley, all keeping perfect silence. We all seemed to feel the same quieting influence. As we left the carriage to go into the house, Mrs. Bliss burst into tears. We went into the parlor together, Mr. Bliss going directly to his own room. While in the parlor, Mrs. Bliss told me what beautiful thoughts she had been having of her babe in heaven, (it was the fall after the birth of her first child,) and said she had never enjoyed a ride so much. All the surrounding circumstances had seemed to make her feel an unusual peaceful resignation to the loss of that child. Before long, Mr. B. came down with a slip of paper in his hand, saying, "Girls, I want to read to you what I have here. See my child that was born of that ride. I have never had more peaceful, enjoyable thoughts than this afternoon." Turning to me, he said, "Nett, I shall *never* forget that ride." Then he read to us, "When Jesus Comes." I have the same slip of paper now, and I need not say, I prize it.

ROME, PENNSYLVANIA, December 20, 1876.

We are home for a week or so; expect to leave the family all here Saturday. Probably return to Chicago December 30.

On my table lie the proof-sheets of "Gospel Hymns No 2," a proposition for a Canadian copyright, and an invitation for Whittle and Bliss to come to London, England, all of which engage my consideration and prayerful thought. I think we may go to England about May 1st. Don't ask me if I shall leave my wife and boys. Pray for us in song prayer with thanksgiving.

The meetings at Peoria were very satisfactory. All the churches united, and many professed to accept the "gift of God."

May the Lord give you great peace and rest. May all our lamps be trimmed and burning "When Jesus comes." Oh, how we missed you at Peoria, on our ride round the bluffs, cemetery, etc. I wanted to see "Wib," but failed.

May the new year bring you abundant blessings.

P. P. BLISS.

CHAPTER XXII.

THE following letters, and extracts from letters, are kindly furnished by a Christian lady, years ago a teacher of Mr. Bliss,
his first instructor in music, and for whom he always entertained
sentiments of the highest esteem, gratitude and affection, and whom
he was led to correspond with in a peculiarly confidential manner
concerning his spiritual life and plans of work for Christ, seeking
her counsel and sympathy.   This lady thus writes:

Away back in 1857 I first met Mr. Bliss when he entered the Collegiate
Institute at Towanda, in which school I then had charge of the department
of music. His complete attention and excellence in the singing class brought
him especially to my attention and esteem, and my every remembrance of him
at that time is laden with some grace or goodness of character. Always in the
true place at the right time, noble, modest and courteous, and of wealth of heart
and soul he possessed a princely store. A pure, fresh, sweet life consecrated
thus early to the Lord, unostentatious but sincerely glad to be heard in supplication or praise and ofttimes in the midst of professors and pupils, I have heard
him in such humble, reverent prayer that I knew he had learned of Him who
alone giveth such understanding. I do not know that any of his private letters
are to have a place or part in the book which you are helping to prepare,
but if I may modestly and unknown to the public help you in the least particular to catch any new or more beautiful picture of our lamented friends, I
shall be satisfied. Perhaps in lifting the veil from a life so loyal and devoted
to Christ, so faithfully tender to wife, children, home, and friends, you may find
in these extracts a few gems which you may like to put upon the golden thread
which is to hold the picture of a man so royal and grand, so loving and sweet.
After long years of separation, after he had gained new friends, new dignities
and new honors, as well as superior mental and spiritual attainments, he came
back to find me, with the gratitude and simplicity of a child, thanking me for
what I had done for him and begging still to call me "teacher," which name
I find in the last letter he wrote to me. In his wonderful friendship and

fidelity, I have found strength, peace and comfort. Always in my greatest need his letters came, and if in my invalid days I was ready to weep or faint or mourn, I had remembered some word or hymn or benediction of his and found courage and peace.

The following are quotations from Mr. Bliss' letters:

Kot of Kontentment, October 6, 1871.

Had I received your kind invitation sooner, and had the health of Mrs. B. been sufficient, you would have seen us on the recent trip East. We spent a Sunday in Owego, and are now safe at home again; but my wife is not well. She has been *down* the valley and almost across the narrow stream. No; I don't like such figures. The blessed Lord has led us *up the hill*, and by the gift of suffering made this poor life more glorious and heaven even dearer. How glad I am at your saying "Jesus the best of all." May you continue to rest in Him; whether living or dying, be "to" Him; whether here or yonder, be *with* Him. If you have received the "Charm" I sent you, let the "Light in the Valley" cheer you, "Over Yonder" win you, and "Jesus Loves even Me" entertain you. The Sunday School and choir and convention work to which I have been called seems to prosper. Conventions every week somewhere; Sunday School, 709 last Sunday. Pray for your pupil, that his life may be to many what yours is and has been to him.

[The winter after the great fire, 1872.]

Forgive me, but I had a real good cry over the pleasant memories of your last letter, and since then have been laughing at your mistake in supposing me to be anything else than the overgrown, awkward boy you used to be kind to. Please don't talk about our being on ahead of you and beg for us to wait for you. The best thing in your letter, the best thing about any of us is the reflection of the dear Savior's love. Oh, isn't it the name above every name—precious Jesus! yes, indeed, we have hugged the interests of the Redeemer's kingdom close, and if I could tell you, but I never *can here*, how His loving arms here encircle me and mine.

Our little "Kot of Kontentment" is on the West Side, nearly a mile from the burnt district. The music books, instruments, sheet music, etc.—the earthly substance in which my plans centered—all gone with the Opera House. Of course we lost all—insurance in "home companies"—but I can't say we've suffered anything by the fire. Good health and plenty to do; lots of friends, voice and faith; what need I more? Now I'll let you rest. Only pray to-night for me, that God may use me more and more for His kingdom. Good-bye. Wait. Won't we have a good song when we all get *home?*"

December 22, 1873.

I am glad you are only six years ahead of me. If I live fast, maybe I can quite come up to you yet. I honestly think it's beautiful to grow old—one can appreciate good things and avoid bad ones so much better.

And now, my sister, poor as is the prop, unsafe as may be the arm, it will be joy to think you do so lean upon it; to think that you believe in me enough to let your tired heart rest in unquestioning confidence, if it may, in my sympathy. I do feel sometimes that for Jesus' sake, I'd like to bear some- body's burdens, my way is so pleasant, and my life work so agreeable. I can only say He leadeth me beside the still waters. And yet I would not boast of myself. 'Tis not that I am strong ; more likely 'tis that He in tender mercy spares my sad ruin which His omniscience knows a little load would cost.

I have an offer to lead the music in San Francisco Tabernacle, Handel and Haydn Society, & Co., at a salary of $3,000 in gold. Do not press me for rea- sons for not going. I only mention this to you because I know you will rejoice in anything like my prosperity.

Wife and Paul send much love and unite in an invitation for you to come and see us.

Now I must go. Good bye. I'll send you a new song in a few days. So help me by prayer and pen, dear friend, and so use me, heart, hand and voice, as He would have you. Be sure that your influence from my first day at T. till now, has been only helpful and Christian. My music is the better and purer, my life brighter and my heart stronger and larger for your share in instructing me.

January, 1874.

If the dear Lord so wills it, I'm coming to see you some day, and you shall again be my teacher. I have only "Sunshine" and "Joy" in my heart and life, and if I might know Him who has given by sharing the gift, I shall be the happier.

CHICAGO, March 10, 1874.

PRINCESS LOUISA :

Your chatty communication containing the " personal heart " letters of the far away E—— is before me. I can't now remember much of her spirit. However, these are beautiful Christian letters. A rich and varied experience was necessary to develop such a heart. I'll send some music as you direct. This, I must say, is another apology only for the elegant, elaborate letter I owe you. Going, Going, G——, and my train leaves in twenty minutes. But between true friends there can be no debit and credit system. Believe me, if we had called at your house, or if ever you do come to our " Kot ov Kontent " there'll be music or would have been time improved. Bah ! what an awk- ward sentence ! I'll keep close to the shore after this.

So we are well, happy, cheerful, content, peace like a river. Wish you the same now and ever. I am flying from Iowa to Michigan and stop in Chicago for one night to sing my new song, " Work and Pray," at a women's temperance

MRS P P BLISS

PHILLIP PAUL

GEORGE GOODWIN

Mrs P. P. Bliss & Children.

song, at a Union Temperance mass meeting. I believe in women, prayer and God ; so there's only one **side** for me in the great crusade.

George Rodgers, of England, gave **one** of his world-renowned lectures on the "Tabernacle," **in our** church last evening, and I sang a new song for him, "Wishing, Hoping, **Knowing**." I have a **very** winning **call** to London, England, for **this summer**, to sing "Gospel **Songs**." Shall I go ?

Wife **and Paul send much** love.—If, **when I come home, I can** "**steal a while away**," **you may get a letter**, song or sermon.

Till then as ever, Blissfully
Yours.

March 31, 1874.

My dear wife is **fully** my equal as a performer and far superior in matters of taste, criticism, etc. You mistake when you suppose criticism "hurts" me. *True as I live*, **I don't** want to know the favorable things said about **me**, nearly so much as **I desire** to hear objections.

Since writing **you before, the way has been very** clearly **made known to** me and my wife, **for my immediate future.** We have long prayed God to lead **me into the widest field of efficient labor.** He has repeatedly come near to us **in His** delightful, *conscious* manifestations, and now I am fully persuaded He **calls me to** give my time and **energies to writing** and singing the Good News. **I am** constrained, by what Christ is and has been to me, to offer all my powers **directly** to His sweet service. **Beginning with this** desire, prompted, I am sure, **by the** Holy Ghost, I am willing—*we* are **willing**—to leave ourselves where we **always** have been, **in our** Father's **loving hands.** He has led us in spite of our plans into all and only pleasant and prosperous ways. It's no time to distrust **or question now.** Pardon me if this all sounds like "cant," to you. My **meaning is to be** honest and real. Pray for us, if you can, that I may be **honored by** "helping Jesus." Major Whittle goes with me to **preach the Gospel while I** try to sing it. Our only aim, sincerely, above all else, **is to win souls to Jesus Christ.**

Yours, in His love,
P. P. B.

July 20, 1874.

I did not **see the appropriateness of my trying to write, as** my wife ought to. Of Paul I can never tell **you one half.** He is (and always has been) "just **the** right **age** to be interesting ;" **has twenty or thirty** teeth —a large head, brown hair, chubby **hands, big feet, of course—a perfectly** healthy, happy **boy.** Can say "Papa's chatterbox," "Mamma's pigeon," and can tease most effectually for—"Nandy !" Mrs. Bliss is in excellent health and spirits, as **usual.** As she is not to read this, I must say she is an extraordinary woman. **You** don't know many women of such unselfish devotion, sublime faith and **child-like trust.** She lives so near **the Lord** that **I ought** to be a good man.

17

Humanly speaking, my life would have been a failure without her. God bless her. I am engaged to write and sing Gospel songs in this country this fall and winter.   Yours for Lou,

                                                        BLISS.

                                                  August 8, 1874.

DEAR SISTER:

I am just home for a day from the State Convention of " Y. M. C. A," Aurora, Illinois, and go Monday to S. S. Teachers' Assembly at Chautauqua Lake, New York. I wish you were to be there. I wish you could have been yonder. But I mind me of a convention soon to be called " of all kindreds and tongues and nations," where the theme will be " Hallelujah to the Lamb." To that our ardent souls aspire. During that grand convention I'll tell you how good God has been to me and mine.

Dear wife desires me first of all to thank you for the kind letter, and to say for her that she is not feeling quite well these days, and begs you will excuse her from writing.

Our Paul boy is just all we could wish, every way, and I perceive we are coming to think quite a good deal of him. If and if we could " come to the mountain," about September, I am sure you would be happy. Pardon me for writing on my business paper, but I want you to hear about Gospel Songs, etc.

Are you teaching, gardening or what? You wouldn't send me a picture of yourself, so 1 of course had to make one: Age, 40; complexion very fair; height, 5 ft. 2 in. ; weight, 122 lbs ; hair inclining, ———— ; teeth good ; mouth large ; lips thin, and smiling eyes, blue, large and watery ; dress neat and a perfect fit ; carriage erect and easy ! How's that? 'Twould all be impolite in me but for old acquaintance's sake. However, this "tabernacle" will soon be "dissolved," it's the *other* house I'm most interested in, and I can see that in every utterance of your pen, "the things that are not seen *are* eternal," aren't they ?—What trifles engage the attention of the king's children ! How we dishonor our loving Father by making so much of every thing else and so little of His blessed word and kingdom. I know 1 do—God forgive me.

Specimen "Gospel Songs" inclosed. Pray for them and us. 2 Cor. ix, 8 = the seven *A*'s.   Yours in Him,

                                                        P. P. B.

                                                  March 18, 1875.

Major Whittle and I had a series of wonderfully successful Gospel meetings in Louisville, Kentucky. We go to Cincinnati, Ohio, March 23. Pray for us and write me there, please, care John Church & Co. Wife and sons are well and happy and would be so glad to have you come and visit us. Why not ? The front chamber will be all ready painted, papered, etc., by the time you'll get here and this. I'm away from home much of the time. The piano, a glorious upright, is here, and you may have access to a musical library —considerable.

Are you in the midst of maple sugar, etc.? When we come to Owego again, "It may be for years," etc.

This singing and talking about the Good News of a present, perfect, free salvation and justification by faith is so popular and attractive I don't believe I shall ever find time for any thing else; and seems to me it's needed. How much of everything else we hear preached, and how little Gospel.

I sent you papers from Louisville, will also from Cincinnati. Wife unites in love unchanging. Please to rest in it.   Yours ever,

P. P. B.

The following letters were written by Mr. Bliss to his nephew, who is frequently noticed in the preceding chapter, by his initials "W. H." This nephew was a member of Mr. Bliss' household for some two years during his absence as an evangelist, and was regarded by Mr. and Mrs. B. almost as a son.

ORLAND, INDIANA, December 11, 1871.

DEAR NEPHEW:

Your good long letter came two days ago. It is a good composition and shows a spirit of trust in the Lord and at the same time a desire to help yourself, which, if continued, must lead to a successful life.

I am so glad for you that a way is so pleasantly opened for your schooling. God bless you in it. As to "agency" or similar means of raising money, I am not very favorable to the sort; still you might try, after study hours, some physical labor would seem better. Let me make a proposition if you are quite *sure* that your school is the thing and that you will *stay* through. I will pay your tuition for you. Then perhaps you can earn enough to clothe yourself. Of course 'twill be better for you to try (as I know you will) to be helping yourself just the same. If you would as soon, I'd like to have you ask *me* for money at any time instead of borrowing elsewhere. DON'T GET IN DEBT.

You ask my advice. Be easy in old clothes, don't mind any large, coarse boots; stand up straight, look pleasant, speak more cheerfully. I know you will succeed as long as you read the Bible and pray much. Watch and pray.

CHICAGO, November 22, 1872.

DEAR WILLIE:

May yours be a happy Thanksgiving day; will it help to make it such if I tell you that Aunt Lou and I have been talking a good deal about you, and concluded to say you may expect $10 a month from us after December. That is, the first January, 1873, and on the first of each month of the year, I will send you check for $10. God bless you with it, my dear boy, and may your mother's prayers be answered.

Would it be well to keep a strict cash account? Prove to us all that *you can* keep out of debt.   As a business matter it is always right for us to recommend what we think is a good thing.

In the things of the Kingdom we should do with our might.   I'd be glad to have you look at Congregationalism—that is, I am so happy in this work and with this church, I am desirous of opening its doors to my friends. Did you ever **say to what** denomination you belong? Of course you should have a choice, and learn to love your own, and labor for its **good**.   May the Lord guide you into all truth.   Pray it earnestly and **often**.

Aunt Lou **joins in** love.

P. P. B.

CHICAGO, October 15, 1873.

DEAR WILLIE:

I did not receive the letter you mention. I would advise you to teach this winter.   Your record of work is a good one.   "Do not be discouraged" is cheap and common advice, but I know you and I will often be discouraged. Prayer, asking for faith, and reading the promises are my remedies.   Be sure, my dear boy, God has great things for us to do and to be.   We are all praying for you and watching.   Farewell.

Your uncle
PHIL.

CHICAGO, February 10, 1874.

DEAR FRIEND AND NEPHEW W. H.:

How do you do by this time? You must not think you have been overlooked, forgotten, nor slighted.   I have been trying to ascertain what might be the best thing to write. Of course I am not competent to advise ; every one must decide and act for himself.   This has been a hard lesson for me to learn, and I've not yet graduated in it.   Still, we can by suggestions, etc., often assist each other in making conclusions. So I will speak quite freely as we have talked.   I have a great deal of faith in you, to begin with ; or, to speak more properly, I've a strong faith in God, and believe He will by various means develop you and in answer to prayers *make the most of you.*   You and I may sometimes complain of a lack of opportunities ; or regret inabilities, when, if we labor and patiently wait, it will appear that "God's ways were best."   If we admit that in advance, and then are willing to be led, we certainly must come into a cheerful content ; for of course we desire the *best* in all things.   I am not sorry to hear that you are with your Pa in the woods ; for 'twas with him in such places, *I* learned a great many useful things, and received a good education.   One thing I am glad to say—"Doc." as we used to call him, always had a good word of cheer for a fellow, and never by word or example led us boys astray.   He was a kind, hard-working, pleasant man, whose influence was always on the right side.

After you wrote to me about "medicine," I wrote to Dr. Anderson—and also went about this city to learn what I could of the project. The matter, as you proposed it, did not shine very brightly to my eyes; so I've looked about in other directions. **What would you** think of going into a drug store for a time? **Or have you abandoned this line of** thought entirely? If in mental and spiritual **matters you can be as thorough as you are** in physical (chopping and sawing **for instance), you'll succeed. And that is what we** are expecting of you, old boy! *Purpose—Pluck—*PUSH! *Faith in self, in friends, in God ; Pluck to plan, to push, to plod.*

[The poetry is original and composed for the **occasion ; please commit it to** heart and commit your heart to it.] I thought **of you and prayed most earn-** estly for you as we came through Wellsville. **In fact I looked for you a little ;** didn't know but maybe you'd happen down by the depot.

Well, really, you must pardon me for such a long letter, **and I haven't said** anything yet. **We are all** well—that begins to sound **like a letter—Paul is** awake as usual ; **Aunt** Lou **in the** bedroom with him ; **Warren off down town** somewhere ; Chicago lively **and lovely.** Won't you and your **Pa** come out and make us a visit? I tell **you, we'd be mighty** tickled to have you. The old ladies switched Chicago **in good style, and we weren't** ashamed of them. I guess we could get along **with you. Come and try it.**

I go to Iowa next week. **This convention business keeps me sliding in the** season of it. **God bless you. Let me hear from you.**

Truly your Uncle
PHIL.

May 15, '74.

DEAR BEARDLESS BOY :

Sorry you're sick ; "**Beware of dogs.**" Phil. iii, 2.

Guess you worked too **hard moving us.** I am writing up in the beautiful study which I found all papered and carpeted and in order waiting for me, last week, when I came home from a Gospel meeting **trip.** Oh, my boy, I rather guess I've a wife as is a wife. God bless her this minute.

What a blessed trial that Mansfield experience was. **How did Jennings stand it ? Did he show his Bliss ? or did he at the hotel kneel down and say,** "all right ; *all things* work together for good ?"

Of course we are happy and all pretty well. **Paul** has another tooth and Phenie another dress. House in good shape. I spent a very interesting hour in the barn to-day, sawing and splitting the kindling boards you hauled. I had to think of you considerably. **Old Mr. Young, "O. W.,"** is around yet ; he seems very feeble; don't get in till midnight sometimes, poor fellow !

Maj. Whittle and wife **come to tea and we have** a Gospel meeting on West- ern Avenue this **evening. Expect a good time.** We go to Whitewater, Wisconsin, next week ; **will be there, probably,** when you read this. Pray for us. Well, good day, 3 John ii. P. P. B.

DETROIT, October 9, 1874.

DEAR WILL:

Don't you begin to believe that I don't think of you every day? I believe in you and in the **power of** prayer and a life of faith. **You must succeed, and in order** to **true** success, **if** you would enter into the kingdom **of heaven, or of science** or greatness, you must become as a little child—humble and **teachable, desirous** of being led. I trust you have this spirit in a good degree; keep **it; pray for** more faith and trust. Don't apply yourself too closely to books and such. Don't stay too long in the rat-pit. Make haste slowly. Save time by waiting for some things. Save health. Confide everything to your loving Aunt Lou. She's a faithful friend, **and though her corrections** may seem grievous, who wouldn't be *correct?*

The **meetings are immense.** Crowds **and crowds—many** standing all through, **and many had to go away** from the door **of one of** the largest churches **last evening. Your prayers are** being answered. **Praise** God for it. To Him be *all*, ALL the glory. Amen.

his
UNCLE   ×
mark.

DETROIT, November 17, 1874.

DEAR W. H. J:

You are in my thought and prayers daily. I am anxious that your sojourn in **Chicago** shall do all for you, in every way, **that** we hope or God intends. I **need** not say to you, and yet it is a pleasure, your aunt and I are " **glad you came.**" Of course I am away so much. *The* important thing **to me is that you make it** pleasant **for** her. *She* says you do *that*, **so I am** content. **Thank God. Only don't let the** mental do injustice **to your** physical and spiritual energies. A *holy* man means a *whole* man—symmetrical, well-balanced; so have a look, **my dear boy, each day,** into all things concerning the " full man." Confide all **to Him who careth for you.** Pray **for much. Be courteous** to all, familiar with **few, intimate with none.**

Say to **the girls that we will be** home to breakfast Friday morning and that Mr. and **Mrs.** Whittle **will probably be with us, at about** 9 o'clock. Don't forget this.

I am glad to hear so good a report **from the Bliss boys.** Aunt Lou arrived this morning and surprised me on my return from prayer-meeting. I am very glad she could come.

The meetings go on grandly; many souls daily profess Christ, **and the** church more and more revived. **I have** some thrilling incidents **to relate, when I come home.** Pray for the meeting at Dr. Goodwin's church for Sunday **evening next.** Read this little **book** carefully and hand it **to** some friend. **Good bye.**

Your loving Uncle,
P. P.

LOUISVILLE, February 25, 1875.

DEAR WILL:

Put in your vote for Aunt Lou to come next week, if she don't come before, —and she can just as well bring a baby or two as not. Plenty of room and servants here, AND *I want to see 'em ;* I'd like to look in at you to-day. Wish you could come to one of these glorious meetings; but pray on. The Lord is doing a mighty work here. Praise Him. Here's a letter from Harry Moorhouse, the "boy preacher." I pray for you ; so does Major, every day, and I believe you are being led of the Holy Spirit. Let us ask God to correct and direct us ; and then be very careful to recognize and follow His leadings. We need to ask wisdom daily, and He says " *it* shall be given him," Math. vii, 7, and James i, 5. Now ask.　　　　　　Hastily but heartily, Yours,

UNCLE PHIL.

NASHVILLE, May 10, 1875.

DEAR WILL :

I don't blame you, 'tis too bad ! Pardon me. Your letters are good and helpful. Your diagnosis of sin, etc., was a good thing, and I used it. No use to try to tell you of our glorious meetings. The papers poorly do that. Oh, pray on for me, that I may be humble and empty, fit for use. Your opinion of Aunt Lou is quite correct. I believe you are to give her a great deal of comfort in answer to prayers for you. Fight on, my brave boy. *Faith* is Victory. Take good care of your health and don't study too close. Send your Aunt Lou to this sunny South, if you can. Bite Paul if he bites George. Yes, I send papers to Allegany. Telegram just received from Montreal, asking us to stop there a week or two on our way to London. Answered we'd come for a few days, beginning June 15, the week after New York Convention. God is *so* good to us, and His work so precious. You must excuse me if I talk that as you do medicine. Success to you. Live near the Lord, " Looking unto Jesus."

NASHVILLE, May 12, 1875.

DEAR WILL :

If your Aunt Lou is not here by the time you get this, you need not read it ; for I'll be so disappointed. I'll be ill-natured and won't mean it. I hope you are now about getting on the street cars to go to depot, so she'll be here to-morrow night. My heart is all flatting out, I think, for want of a wise woman to hold it together—what do the doctors call it, home-sickness ? The climate is beautiful here—weather still cold and healthful. If the Lord had sent the usual warm weather, all say our meetings would, hnmanly speaking, have been much less successful. The people here are so cordial and intense. You must never speak harshly of rebels again.

[This letter commenced by Mrs. Bliss finished by Mr. B.]

MEMPHIS, TENNESSEE, Saturday, 1875.

DEAR WILL :

We have just returned from a delightful boat-ride on the grand old Mississippi. It was cool on the boat, and we all feel greatly refreshed. We saw them land a mule, which furnished fun enough to last your uncle and Major a whole year.—And now she is interrupted and this mule continues. We are just wallowing in strawberries and cream ; only the berries are a little sour and the cream is skim milk. Bouquets are coming in by the basket-full. Aunt Lou has been sick as a Swede for two days; better now. I am well, but it takes two collars a day to keep me singing.

Your letters rejoice our hearts greatly. It is in answer to many prayers that God is giving you peace, and I expect you to grow in all grace. God grant it. Application is the sure road to success. Stick to your team.

Yours joyful,
UNCLE PHIL.

ROME, Friday, 1875.

DEAR ONES ALL :

I wonder how you all get along so well as you seem to; but "God is great and God is good." We pray for you every day. Received your telegram and the dear boys' pictures last night ; we are very thankful. The picture of Paul is splendid. I think George looks a little as if he were attending clinics, but am glad for as good a likeness as this. You may get this after we come home, so I'll be brief. Expect us Thursday, if not there before.

A great and powerful work of grace has begun here ; we all know that God is with us, and souls are being gathered into the fold. Of all the places in the world where I'd love to work for Christ, this old home of ours is the most interesting. Oh, how good it is of my Master to let me tarry here for a few days in His sweet service. May He abundantly reward you for helping us. It is all for His sake. To Him be the glory. Amen.

P. P. B.

CHICAGO, October, 1875.

I suggested to Mrs. E. Willson to come West by way of Wellsville and call on you 'uns. Maybe you've planned to go to Towanda ; if so, so. Do what and go where you think best, only *always* remember Psa. xxxii, 8. In *everything* believe that He has proved it to you and me. It will be an awful sin for either of us to ever doubt it.

How precious Christ is to me to-day. He has been here in the study all the morning. He is looking over now as you read this—He says, "Fear not, only believe," and I hear your answer, "Lord, I believe ; help Thou mine unbelief." Amen.

P. P. B.

ST. PAUL. October 30, 1875.

Aunt and I expect to enjoy your success. To see you as the happy proprietor of a first-class pill-shop, and a leading scalawag in your bloody business. Go on, I may be sick myself, some day, and you may save me an immense Dr. bill.

I tried your R— for my boil; **but what will** now "amuse" **me? I have** *two others!* Will send two or three papers,—to give away. I have **sent to your** mother and mine, **etc. The snow has** stopped falling, but **'tis cold and** dreary.

An old man told **us** this morning in prayer-meeting, that "the Gospel net is being **drawn in; some** self-righteous **fish will flop** over the top of the net, and some **low mud suckers creep** under; **but a great haul is sure!"** The last night in St. Paul was glorious; **but between two verses of a song** Whittle told them if they smelt fire 'twas some papers in the hall below. **'Twas a narrow** escape. Some dresses, carpets, etc., burned, **but no alarm sounded, or a fearful** calamity might have prevented this letter. **Give thanks for this.**

P. P.

MINNEAPOLIS, MINNESOTA, November 10, 1875.

DEAR WILL:

I am as well as could **be expected. Aunt Lou came this** morning while **we** were at prayers. I expected her on the **West Wisconsin** Road, arriving **at 8.40,** instead of which she came on the Milwaukee Road at 7.30. She had **to run all** over town to find me, but I was rather pleased to be found. She has now had her breakfast, and when she gets her hair combed up, we think she will look pretty decent, for a Chicago creature! Says she had a pleasant trip, but thinks *home* is pleasant, too; and if I'd come home 'twould be better yet. I am delighted with the report she brings of home affairs, including W. H. Surely prayers are being answered, and you and I ought to have more faith.

The meetings are going on lively; increased interest; good **results. Don't** know when we may come home—perhaps Monday, maybe Friday, watch!

Aunt says tell you that the woman you saw on the train had a cancer; been to Chicago to consult doctors. They pronounced her incurable, and she comes home to Minneapolis to die.

How thankful we all ought to be. God is good. Let us *live* as we talk— praising Him who owns us. I want to write to Roxie and Mr. Maynard; so you'll excuse brevity. Pray for us.

Your unctious Uncle,
P. P. BLISS.

MILKY WALKY, December 8, 1875.

WEAR DILL:

I hope you are as **well as I am;** but what shocking "bad weather," as we say for Rush. Really I **think we** should never find fault with the weather. Fault-finding rarely pays, except **with** *one's self,* where 'tis hardest to find. You have wondered, in a letter, how we could even "endure" you as you were last year. Let me assure you of continued "endurance," and I expect an increased interest in you and your welfare. 'Twill be a sad termination to the Jennings and Bliss alliance, the day that we find a tendency to deceit and falsity on either part. True friendship is honest. We hope to see you through your studies and in good condition as to heart and life. I believe you desire to be ALL that 'tis possible; so we will help you all we can, to retain all of nobility of character in all things, and to choose all principles of truth and excellence from the various channels opened up. I hope you will not adopt a habit because I have it, nor because any one else has it, but from choice—because it is *good*. Of course we will see things in you to criticise; shall try to do it kindly, for I know you want it done; and may we all be as little children; then only can we successfully enter any kingdom of usefulness and peace. God bless you.

Of the work here I'll only say it is better, apparently, than in any other place we have ever been in for the first week. Yet this is a German city—a phlegmatic people—a very "hard place." But so much the more need of work; so much the more honor to Christ in the victory. Four meetings daily, and from twenty to forty professing Christ every day. The Jews are growing more and more approachable and tender, which makes me hope the Lord is the nearer. The Gentiles are rejecting the Gospel according to Scripture. Then the Jews shall be gathered in according to Scripture. "Oh, let my lamp be burning when Jesus comes," is my prayer.

Of course I must be allowed to enclose a considerable deal of love to be handed over to my dear boys, Paul and George. I hope their mamma will have started for "Milwaulkey" before you get this. "Remember me" also to Mrs. Maynard, Phenie and Annie. Good P. M. Whittle has gone to Bible reading. I must go to young people's meeting.

Your loving Uncle,
P. P.

St. Louis, February, 14, 1876.

DEAR "COUSIN WILL:"

A happy day to you. Pardon my neglect; but of course a letter to your aunt is intended for "family use" generally, and so when I hear from her I hear from you as well. Your interests are ours,—and ours, I hope, are to some extent yours. Am glad your folks are coming into Wellsville. It looks to me as if the Lord might be taking this way to prepare a place for you, and especially to have a home at last for your father and mother. They seem to need one, and never have had one. Let us pray the Lord to lead in all our plans and theirs, constantly

The papers are so full of Babcock and whisky trials and tribulations, that they have no room for report of our meetings. Three to five thousand souls every day; fifty to one hundred asking prayers, daily; and individual souls hungry for conversation privately, *personally*, is the condition of things from my stand point. Our prayers and expectations are that this last week will be the best of all. Pray for us daily

I have been to the Missouri Medical College, where the boys at first made fun, extemporized burlesque Whittle and Bliss meetings, sung Gospel songs, etc. Now they are decidedly serious. All come to the **Rink.** Some happy young converts. One said if we'd continue another week he believed the whole college would be converted. **They** have earnest, bold Christian professors. I also had the opportunity of reaching one hundred and fifty young ladies in a seminary with good results.

You gave me a good illustration of salvation, sanctification, etc., in that story of the poor, weak boy who only needed good food to make him well. Watch for some more such.

Give my regards to Roxie and see that she is fed on the Bread of Life. We must try to help our friends to be happy, joyous Christians. "The joy of the Lord is your strength." Always rejoicing, I am your loving

UNCLE PHIL.

MOBILE, March 11, Sabbath.

DEAR W. H.:

All well. Why don't you one of you write a word, at least, "All well," every day? The last we heard was written Tuesday; most a week, and we get anxious.

The work here is the greatest and most apparently successful of any we ever had. Crowds at every meeting, and many seeking the truth. Young people's meeting P. M. is mine; over one thousand in attendance and one hundred or one hundred and fifty standing for prayers. Isn't it good? I read a part of Iona's letter, and had prayer offered for her, and I think her letter helped to decide many souls. It might not be best to tell *her* so.

The weather here is a failure, orange groves a fraud and the bananas a humbug. Oh for 664! You may look for a package of overcoats and underclothing at Revell's the middle or last of next week. We expect to go to Montgomery Saturday, and begin there Sunday; so address us accordingly; here till the 18th, if by telegraph; by mail until the 14th; then to Montgomery, Alabama. We feel confident, from all advices, that you are getting along nicely and we expected you would when we left. Our prayers are heard in the morning and at evening for you all. Here is a ticket for George, and a picture for Paul. Aunt and the Whittles join in love to you all.

Lovingly, your Uncle.

MONTGOMERY, March 20, 1876.

DEAR WILL:

Yours received. Good. **Your throat is** doubtless measly. Am encouraged about you and your studies. **I BELIEVE IN YOU,** or I'd never have sent for you. You will succeed, and, I expect, be a glorious **man,** an agreeable companion and friend, a good doctor and a pride and joy of all the family. We are praying for you to be *all* that is possible; and though you and I have some mean flesh in us, God's grace can overcome it. Think often of **Christ as a** personal friend and helper, and less of self or what man can do. Our meetings are glorious. The

Lord is very near to us and all things are working together. The city is being flooded with circular letters — one kind to Christians, one to unbelievers. A mighty work is begun. Your prayers for us all are being answered. Don't let go of us.

Think will be home about April 10th, or 15th. I don't dare to say much about it, or you couldn't read my letter, for the tears would blot it so; and Aunt Lou has reception from 12 to 1 and she hasn't time to cry. But we love our home and friends. Our boys, dear Paul and George, God bless them and you this minute.

Your loving Uncle,
P. P. B.

Mont-gum-or-rye, or Gum Mountain, March 24, 1876.

DEAR WILL:

Sorry you're sick. I should be more inclined to employ you to look after my health when you've learned to take care of your own. We are well. Three little words, but how much they are worth; we don't begin to appreciate them, I am sure. Your good letters from home cheer and quiet us in our home-sickness.

The good Lord is greatly blessing His work here; we never had more blessed meetings anywhere. He is also supplying our wants in other ways, bountifully, for which please help us to praise Him.

Good letters from the Homer House. Thank 'em; also the 664 folks. Bless 'em all.

Your
U. P.

Chicago, June 1, 1876.

DEAR WILL:

You remember I had to take what was the sunny side, this morning, but now, at 4 P. M., I'm all right. So in life's journey, bravely endure what you can't cure; your shady side is coming by and by. I've no excuses for writing to you so soon; only to reassure you of our real love for you, both for our relation's sake and your own sake. I am asking the good Lord, who has so lovingly led me, lo, these many years, to guide you fully. Ask Him all about your plans. Seek to honor Him in all things and He will bless you. Turn squarely away from every known evil way of thought and action. Ask the Spirit to search you and reveal yourself to yourself; then "Look to Jesus." Believe in your Aunt Lou. Be as good to her as you think of; she's worth it. She *did* favor my coming, or I'd not have been here to-day; which you can read and apply to yourself, too. If the way does not open for you to find some pleasant paying business here, I think you can go home if you don't more than pay traveling expenses. 'Twould do you and your folks all a great deal of good. That is why I proposed it—for the moral effect. You want to be all that is possible to your family. Those young brothers must know and love you, and personal worth, impress of character, is more than profession or money. Now talk more with "Aunt Lou" about yourself, your plans, and your future. Accept her suggestions. She is a safe adviser ; and be what you are capable of being—a cheerful, chatty companion, and a worthy Christian, pure and peaceable.

TOWANDA, June 16, 1876.

DEAR W. H.:

We had two glorious praise meetings at Rome, Sunday and Monday nights, and yesterday we came to Towanda with divided hearts—strongly convicted that there was work for us in Rome, yet irresistibly drawn toward our home and loved ones. We prepared for our Chicago trip, but prayed for guidance ; and went to bed at eleven, still undecided. Talking and praying at twelve o'clock, the minister from Rome drove up and said they had had two meetings that day and voted unanimously that I should return. We could not fail to recognize that as the answer to prayer, and so have decided to go back to what we believe to be the work the Lord hath appointed us. Souls are anxious and we have faith that a great blessing awaits our dear village of Rome. Pray for us.

Shall probably stay over Sunday and may not stop at Wellsville on our way home. If, for any reason, you think best, telegraph to Towanda, Pennsylvania, and Aunt Lou will start any day for Chicago straight. Hope the girls have got dresses all made and will have a nice time at the picnic. I wish they and my two boys were here. The Lord reward Mrs. Johnson for her care and love to us. Tell her " inasmuch as ye have done it to the least of these, etc." And now adieu. Bless you. I will write your mother to-day, and I think I'll call on Dr. Anderson, and see him and his plan for you.   UNCLE PHIL.

Chicago seems now to come into our programme about Thursday or Friday of next week ; but sooner, if any of you say so.

The following letters I received from Mr. Bliss during 1876 ; the last of them being written two weeks previous to his death :

ROME, PENNSYLVANIA, May 4, 1876.

DEAR WHITTLE :

I hardly know where to direct, but I must write to you. We had a most delightful trip from Chicago. The weather was just right, car comfortable, children as good as two good kittens, and " all things worked together for good." Had a blessed visit over Sunday with my sister, in Wellsville, New York, and a union praise meeting of power in Beecher's church there. Arrived safely home, May 2d. George seemed a little tired with the journey, but is getting rested and happy. I, the undersigned, took a dawful cold id by head, cubbing hobe frob that warb clibit. Am getting room, etc., ready to begin work in earnest next week. I wish you were all here with us and could stay here all summer. But if the Tabernacle needs you—and I don't believe the Lord will let you go there unless you are needed—then that's the place for you. May His presence ever go with us both. Amen. In regard to book, etc., my only thought is to write all summer, if the Lord will please to send me some good hymns, then His wisdom in regard to publishing. I thank you for your interest in me, and hope I shall do nothing to disappoint or grieve you, or especially to grieve my Master and yours. I said to Church about what you and I agreed upon, *nothing definite;* but in general a book for our work would be wanted next season, and I wanted him to see Moody.

My wife has been quite sick, wearied and worn—though not worried—by the journey. Picking and packing is hard work. She has lain in bed all day, but is well enough to laugh at the newspaper article and your joke on the parasols, which, she says, reminds her of the five dollars you owe her since we left the Battle House.

Yours resting,
P. P. B.

ROME, PENNSYLVANIA, May 11, 1876.

DEAR BROTHER:

Nothing special, only yours received. All well; I like hymn of "Hope in His Mercy" very much; shall set it soon and sing it some. Am surprised to hear of Moody running off to so many conventions, etc. Have asked him to give us a little time on his way East, or I'd come to him.

We think George is improving. He eats and sleeps Blissfully. Paul has all sorts of circuses with pigs, calves, dead chickens, mice, snakes, lizards and other " nice pets," much to his mother's consternation.

I have declined eight invitations (all I've had). Am determined to rest and write all summer. Had a good visit with my mother, yesterday, in Towanda. My wife, Lucy Jane, is usually busy buying carpets, curtains, paper, furniture, etc. She says I can't stand it and I ain't a-goin' to. I reply, with my proverbial complacency, "All right."

Had a good prayer meeting last evening and read together, Psa. cxix, 1 to 8, also 97 to 104 and 129 to 136, " Look and be merciful," " Words giveth light," " Make thy face to shine." May the Lord give us all light, " more light," Father Love used to say.

Love to dear Abbie, May, baby and all; Charlie may wait.

Yours when you want me,
P. P. B.

ROME, PENNSYLVANIA, June 16, 1876.

DEAR BROTHER:

Yours received. We haven't any earthly house yet. Had a pleasant trip to Chicago, while there and return. Found the boys and girls all right.

Think Monroe street more **desirable** than Adams. I have many letters to answer, but in a lot 60x325 **would have** plenty of room for croquet.

The weather is quite **warm here, and** the taxes in Chicago are **nearly as** high as at Lake View!

Had a good **letter** from Brother Sankey, but I wouldn't want to live on a cross **street or in a south** front. Vincent **wants you at** Chautauqua, the last three **days.** I think I will be thar, **if we get our** house furnished. I want a large dining-room and a bath-room ten feet square.

Augusta is reported to have paid Moody $1,500 and the papers say he deserved it. Would you want a Mansard or a barn to hang your clothes in?

I received $100 from Augusta and if you did $200 there, my part is $60, please endorse $40 on the you owe me; and if our house has a study with east windows in it, I shall be satisfied. Paul is out with Grandpa, mowing the front yard, but I don't believe we'd ever be contented on the South Side; do you? You said "twelve alsos in 8th Romans." I can't find but eleven. To-morrow is picnic, but I can't afford time to go. I want a house near the street cars. My mother and Mr. Jennings are here; we are having a family gathering. Take your **wife** to Chicago and Chautauqua. I'd be willing to go a little **west of Wood street on Monroe or Warren avenue.**

Tend to your part of the horse, and don't be running off to conventions, female prayer-meetings, etc. We might make a bedroom of the back parlor. Give our love to Charlie. Mail and Way. I'll be glad when we're in it and it's paid for.

"Tell him to keep cool and get rested for next winter," my wife says. In fact, she says so much, I fear I may have mixed up some things she says about our Chicago home with my letter to you.

ROME, PENNSYLVANIA, August 22, 1876.

DEARLY BELOVED BROTHER:

Your pome is quite overcoming. My time is too precious and the game too insignificant to reply in kind. Am bent on a month of quiet; so let me alone.

Just replied to Mrs. M.'s cordial invitation to visit them in N. "No," to J. C., who offered to come to Towanda to see me. "No," to a Canadian camp-meeting. No, I have not committed myself to C. or anybody else for anything except the Lord and you.

Nothing about book from Bro. Sankey or Moody. I agree with you about book and everything. I guess Moody will let G. H. and S. S. alone as it is.

Wife is good and I am glad. All things are working together. Have planned to leave the boys here with Grandma and Aunt Clara, this winter, so wife can go with me. Sent all of our folks (six) to Centennial yesterday for a week. Boys are doing finely.

Where are Charlie and May? Wait, like yourself, deserves spanking. Same to your wife.   Yours infirm,

P. P. B.

TOWANDA, Sunday, December 17, 1876.

DEAR WHITTLE:

We are within ten miles of the boys, arrived here at two o'clock this morning, four hours late; so are spending this Lord's Day with my sister, where my dear old mother is "waiting." I am glad for a day with her who gave me my first music lesson. And she is enjoying us so much. We remember you in our morning prayers. Suppose Chicago is all settled. Nevertheless my feeling is the same, though my faith, I hope, is stronger. If He says go I'm ready.

N. B.—The Lord is your Shepherd. He will carry you through. Hope your wife is better. Dear child! may the Lord bless her to-day. We hope to go to Rome to-morrow. Shall look for a letter from you soon. I hope the Lord will lead the meeting at P. Give our regards to the "singers as well as the players upon instruments" who are there. Also to the Grier House, Tyngs, Reynolds, "Hams," etc.

In peace I go,
No fear I know.
Wish you the same,

P. P.

CHAPTER XXIII.

A FITTING close to these memoirs is the contribution here made to the memory of Mr. Bliss, by friends who were very dear to him, and to whom he was very dear, and with whom he was in peculiarly pleasant relations, writing songs of praise to the same blessed Redeemer and Lord, sending out the messages of the Gospel on wings of music to the ends of the earth, These friends have kindly taken the hymns that were written by Mr. Bliss during his last days, and for which he had not prepared music, and their compositions, with his words, are here for the first time published, by consent of John Church & Co., by whom words and music are copyrighted.

Very kind and loving have been the messages that these brethren have sent with their music. "I thank you for the privilege," writes dear Mr. Lowry. "Dear Bliss —very gladly, very cheerfully, anything you want," was the tender reply of Root, Palmer, and all who were asked to make this contribution to the memory of their loved friend and brother. "Anything I can do for dear Bliss' orphan boys or for his family, count on me to do it," was the immediate reply of Doane ; and so this tribute comes from full, loving hearts. No thanks are expected by any, but to all this acknowledgment of their kindness is due and is gratefully rendered. Surely, those called of God, and honored with such a glorious mission, are yoked together in much to call forth mutual praise and prayer.

Another Soldier Fallen.

In Memory of P. P. Bliss.

Verses by E. E. REXFORD.   Chorus and Music by G. F. ROOT.

Con Moto.

Copyright, 1877, y John Church & Co.

I Believe.

"Lord, I believe; help Thou mine unbelief."   Mark 9,—24.

P. P. BLISS.   Rev. R. LOWRY.

My Redeemer.
P. P. Bliss.
James McGranahan.

1. I will sing of my Re-deem-er And His won-'drous love to me;
2. I will tell the won'drous sto-ry, How my lost es-tate to save,
3. I will praise my dear Re-deem-er, His tri - umph - ant pow'r I'll tell,
4. I will sing of my Re-deem-er And His heav'n - ly love to me;

On the cru - el cross He suf-fered, From the curse to set me free.
In His boundless love and mer-cy, He the ran - som free-ly gave.
How the vic - to - ry He giv-eth O - ver sin, and death, and hell.
He from death to life hath brought me, Son of God, with Him to be.

CHORUS.
Sing, oh! sing, of my Re-deem - er, With His
Sing, oh! sing of my Redeemer, Sing, oh! sing of my Redeemer, With His

blood He pur-chased me, On the
blood He purchased me, With His blood He purchased me; On the

cross He sealed my par - don, Paid the
cross He sealed my pardon, On the cross He sealed my pardon, Paid the

Repeat P. P. after last verse.

debt, and made me free, And made me free, and made me free.

Copyright, 1877, by John Church & Co.

276

Within, About, Above.

P. P. BLISS.

T. C. O'KANE.

Tell Me more about Jesus.

P. P. BLISS.

JAMES McGRANAHAN.

What wilt Thou have Me to Do?

P. P. BLISS.

W. H. DOANE.

Georgie's Welcome.

Words by P. P. Bliss, upon the birth of his little boy, George Goodwin Bliss.

"And whoso shall receive one such little child in my name, receiveth Me." Matt. 18,—5.

P. P. BLISS.   JAS. McGRANAHAN.

280

Wise to Win.

P. P. BLISS.
C. C. CASE.
Slow.
1. God of wis-dom hear my cry, Heal this bro-ken heart;
2. To Thy work I glad-ly go, Mas-ter, lead me on;
3. Winning wis-dom have I none, All must come from Thee;
CHORUS.
Weak and sinful, Lord, am I, Strength divine impart. By the
Of Thy grace the world must know, Trophies must be won.
Thine the power, and Thine alone All the praise shall be.
wa - - ter of Thy word, wash me, wash me
By the wa-ter of Thy word, wash me from
from all sin; By Thy Ho - ly Spir - it,
from all sin By the Ho-ly
Lord, make me wise, yes, wise to win.
Spir- it, Lord, make me wise, yes, make me wise to win.

Only a Little.

Only a Little. Concluded.

Constrained by Love.

I Trust, O Lord, in Thee.

P. P. BLISS. J. R. MURRAY.

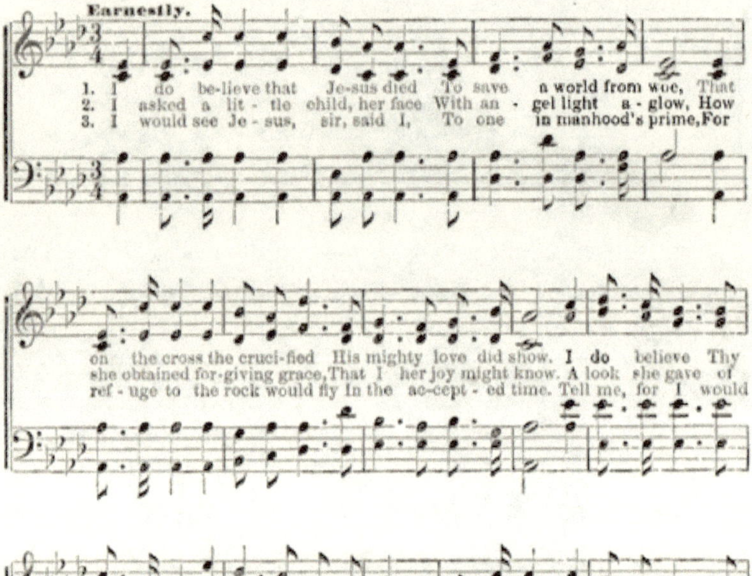

4.

Dear aged pilgrim, drawing near
To death's dark, shadowy vale,
How dost thou "read thy title clear?"
Does saving faith avail?
He answered as he neared the shore,
And earth's lights grew more dim;
‖: Forever and forever-more,
I rest it all in Him. :‖

5.

Jesus, Thou Son of God, to Thee
I breathe this prayer sincere:
Thine, Thine forever would I be,
O save me now and here.
It was Thy plan and not my own
That Thou shouldst die for me;
‖: Thine is the power, and Thine alone,
I trust, O Lord, in Thee. :‖

Stand Still, O, Child of God!

P. P. BLISS, finished by Major D. W. WHITTLE.   GEO. C. STEBBINS.

285

Arise, Work and Pray.

"The effectual, fervent prayer of a righteous man availeth much." Jas. 5,—16.
"And I will show Thee my faith by my works." Jas. 2,—16.

P. P. BLISS.   Mrs. C. H. SCOTT.

The Good News.

The Good News. Concluded.

When My Weary Hands are Foided.

"When thou passest through the waters, I will be with thee; and through the rivers, they shall not overflow thee." Isa. 43,—2.

Words written by P. P. BLISS for I. D. S.   IRA D. SANKEY.

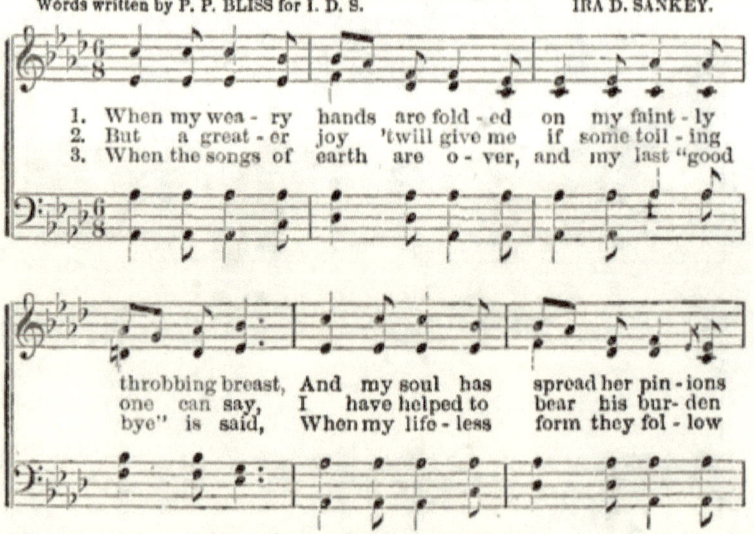

When My Weary Hands, etc.   Concluded.

4.

But if one poor tired wand'rer shall be guided home by me,
'Twere a grander, nobler monument throughout all eternity;
And to Him shall be the glory, unto whom all praise is due,
For the love that hath redeemed us, and hath made my Heaven two.

5.

When among the ransomed millions, by His grace redeemed I stand,
Then **my** song shall swell **the** chorus of the glad triumphant band;
Oh, how sweet will be the resting, when my conflicts all are past,
Oh, **the** mighty "Alleluia" of our victory at last!

Copyright, 1877, by John Church & Co.

289

CHAPTER XXIV.

THE railroad train on which Mr. and Mrs. Bliss rode to their
death left Buffalo, New York, on Friday afternoon, December
29, 1876.   At eight o'clock that evening, while approaching Ashtabula station, and crossing a ravine, the bridge gave way, and the
train, with its precious freight of human lives, was precipitated to the
bottom.   Fresh as is the memory of this horror in the minds of all,
the newspaper accounts given at the time will be read now with
renewed interest, and fittingly form a part of the record made in
these pages.

[Dispatch to the Chicago Tribune.]

ASHTABULA, OHIO, December 30, 1876.

The proportions of the Ashtabula horror are now approximately known.
Daylight, which gave an opportunity to find and enumerate the saved, reveals
the fact that two out of every three passengers on the fated train are lost.   Of
the 160 passengers whom the maimed conductor reports as having been on
board, but fifty-nine can be found or accounted for.   The remaining 100,
burned to ashes or shapeless lumps of charred flesh, lie under the ruins of the
bridge and train.

The disaster was dramatically complete.   No element of horror was wanting.   First, the crash of the bridge, the agonizing moments of suspense as the
seven laden cars plunged down their fearful leap to the icy river-bed ; then
the fire which came to devour all that had been left alive by the crash ; then
the water, which gurgled up from under the broken ice and offered another
form of death ; and, finally, the biting blast filled with snow, which froze and
benumbed those who had escaped water and fire.   It was an ideal tragedy.

The scene of the accident was the valley of the creek which, flowing down
past the eastern margin of Ashtabula village, passes under the railway three
or four hundred yards east of the station.   Here for many years after the Lake
Shore road was built there was a long wooden trestle-work, but as the road
was improved this was superseded about ten years ago with an iron Howe truss,

built at the Cleveland shops, and resting at either end upon **high stone piers,** flanked by heavy earthen embankments. The iron structure was a single **span** of 159 feet, crossed by **a double track** seventy feet above the water, **which at** that point is now from **three to six feet deep,** and covered with eight **inches of** ice. The descent into the valley on either side is precipitous, and, **as the hills** and slopes are piled with heavy drifts of snow, there was no little difficulty in reaching the wreck after the disaster became known.

The disaster occurred shortly before eight o'clock. It was the wildest winter night of the year. Three hours behind its time, the Pacific Express, which had left New York the night before, struggled along through the drifts and the blinding storm. The eleven cars were a heavy burden to the two engines, and when the leading locomotive broke through the drifts beyond the ravine, and rolled on across the bridge, the train was moving at less than ten miles an hour. The head lamp threw but a short and dim flash of light in the front, so thick was the air with the driving snow. The train crept across the bridge, the leading engine had reached solid ground beyond, and its driver had just given it steam, when something in the undergearing of the bridge snapped. For an instant there was a confused crackling of beams and girders, ending with a tremendous crash, as the whole train but the leading engine broke through the framework, and fell in a heap of crushed and splintered ruins at the bottom. Notwithstanding the wind and storm, the crash was heard by people within-doors half a mile away. For a moment there was silence, a stunned sensation among the survivors, who in all stages of mutilation lay piled among the dying and dead. Then arose the cries of the maimed and suffering ; the few who remained unhurt hastened to escape from the shattered cars. They crawled out of windows into freezing water waist-deep. Men, women and children, with limbs bruised and broken, pinched between timbers and transfixed by jagged splinters, begged with their last breath for aid that no human power could give.

Five minutes after the train fell, the fire broke out in the cars piled against the abutments at either end. A moment later, flames broke from the smoking-car and first coach piled across each other near the middle of the stream. In less than ten minutes after the catastrophe, every car in the wreck was on fire, and the flames, fed by the dry varnished work and fanned by the icy gale, licked up the ruins as though they had been tinder. Destruction was so swift that mercy was baffled. Men who, in the bewilderment of the shock, sprang out and reached the solid ice, went back after wives and children and found them suffocating and roasting in the flames. The neighboring residents, startled by the crash, were lighted to the scene by the conflagration, which made even their prompt assistance too late. By midnight, the cremation was complete. The storm had subsided, but the wind still blew fiercely, and the cold was more intense. When morning came, all that remained of the Pacific Express was a winrow of **car wheels, axles,** brake-irons, truck-frames, and **twisted rails** lying in a black pool at the bottom of the gorge. The wood had burned completely away, and the ruins were covered with white ashes. Here and there a mass of charred, smoldering **substance sent up** a little cloud of sickening vapor, which told that it was human flesh slowly yielding to the corrosion of the fire. On the crest of the western abutment, half buried in the snow, stood the rescued locomotive, all that remained of the fated train. As the bridge fell, its driver had given it a quick head of steam, which tore the drawhead from its tender, and the liberated engine shot forward and buried itself in the snow. The other locomotive, drawn backward by the falling train, tumbled over the pier and fell bottom upward on the express car next behind. The engineer, Folsom, escaped with a broken leg ; how, he cannot tell, nor can any one else imagine.

There is no death-list to report. There can be none until the list of the missing ones who traveled by the Lake Shore Road on Friday is made up. There are no remains that can ever be identified. The three charred, shapeless lumps recovered up to noon to-day are beyond all hope of recognition. Old or young, male or female, black or white, no man can tell. They are alike in the crucible of death. For the rest, there are piles of white ashes in which glisten the crumbling particles of calcined bones ; in other places masses of black, charred debris, half under water, which may contain fragments of bodies, but nothing of human semblance. It is thought that there may be a few corpses under the ice, as there were women and children who sprang into the water and sank, but none have been thus far recovered.

[Dispatch to the Cleveland Leader.]

The haggard dawn, which drove the darkness out of this valley of the shadow of death, seldom saw a ghastlier sight than was revealed with the coming of this morning. On either side of the ravine frowned the dark and bare arches from which the treacherous timbers had fallen, while at their base the great heaps of ruins covered the one hundred men, women and children who had so suddenly been called to their death. The three charred bodies lay where they had been placed in the hurry and confusion of the night. Piles of iron lay on the thick ice, or bedded in the shallow water of the stream. The fires smouldered in great heaps, where many of the hapless victims had been all consumed, while men went about in wild excitement, seeking some trace of a lost one among the wounded or dead.

The list of saved and wounded having been already sent, the sad task remains of discovering who may be among the dead. The latter task will be the most difficult of all, until the continued absence of here and there a friend will allow of but one explanation—that he was among those who took this fatal leap.

All the witnesses so far agree to the main facts of the accident. It was about 8 o'clock, and the train was moving along at a moderate rate of speed, the Ashtabula station being just this side of the ravine. Suddenly, and without warning, the train plunged into the abyss, the forward locomotive alone getting across in safety. Almost instantly, the lamps and stoves set fire to the cars, and many who were doubtlessly only stunned, and who might otherwise have been saved, fell victims to the fury of the flames.

On the arrival of the Cleveland train, the surgeon of the road organized his corps of assistants, and made a tour of the various hotels, where the wounded were attended to, such help being given to each as was possible. The people of Ashtabula lent a willing hand, and all that human skill and money could do to save life or ease pain was done. The train which came from Cleveland for the purpose was immediately backed into position, and long before daylight the least wounded were being prepared for transportation to Cleveland, to be sent to hospitals or their homes.

The scenes among the wounded were as suggestive almost as the wreck in the valley. The two hotels nearest the station contained a majority of these, as they were scattered about on temporary beds on the floors of the dining-rooms, parlors and offices. In one place, a man with a broken leg would be under the hands of a surgeon, who rapidly and skillfully went at his work. In another, a man covered with bruises and spotted over with pieces of plaster, would look as though he had been snowed upon, except when the dark lines of blood across his face or limb told a different story. In some other corner, a poor woman moaned from the pain which she could not conceal, while over all there brooded that hushed feeling of awe which always accompanies calamities of this character.

Towards morning, the cold increased and the wind blew a fearful gale, which, with the snow, that had drifted waist-deep at points along the line, made all work extremely difficult.

At 6 o'clock, the beds in the sleeping-car of the special train were made up, and such of the wounded as could be moved were transferred there.

The story of most painful interest to *us*—to all who will read this book, and all who knew and loved P. P. Bliss and his wife—is that told by Mr. J. E. Burchell, partner of Mr. B. F. Jacobs, of Chicago, who was on the ill-fated train. We give his account in full :

There were eleven cars on the train that left Buffalo at two o'clock Friday afternoon. There were two engines, three baggage, one smoker, two coaches, three sleepers and one parlor car. I should judge there were 250 passengers. We pulled out of Buffalo in a blinding snow-storm, an hour late, and ran at the rate of about fifteen miles an hour until about an hour, or may be only half an hour, before the accident, when she slacked up to about ten miles an hour. The second engine was taken on at about Dunkirk. Just before reaching the bridge, the snow was very heavy, and at that station near by, the name of which I have forgotten, there was every danger of being snowed in. We had lost an hour and a half from Buffalo to the bridge.

Before reaching the bridge, I went through the train and noticed that the coaches and the smoker were filled. The smoker did not come in its regular order. There were two passenger coaches ahead of it. Next behind the smoker was the parlor car, in which Mr. Bliss and his family were, and I noticed it

was one-third full. I was in the car behind the parlor, and my car was filled
Behind that were the three sleepers, which were also nearly filled.

We neared the bridge at about 7:45, though due at Ashtabula at 5:15. East
of the bridge the country is rolling, and beyond the creek it grows more level.
We ran on the structure at a rate of about ten miles an hour, and the whole
train was on the bridge when it gave way. The bridge is about two hundred feet
long, and only the first engine had passed over when the crash came, the weight
of the falling cars nearly pulling back the locomotive that had passed over.

The first thing I heard was a cracking in the front part of the car, and then
the same cracking in the rear. Then came another cracking in the front louder than the first, and then came a sickening oscillation and a sudden sinking,
and I was thrown stunned from my seat. I heard the cracking, and splinter-
ing and smashing around me. The iron work bent and twisted like snakes,
and everything took horrid shapes. I heard a lady scream in anguish, "Oh!
help me!" Then I heard the cry of fire. Some one broke a window and I
pushed out the lady who had screamed. I think her name was Mrs. Bingham.

The train lay in the valley in the water, our car a little on its side, both
ends broken in. The rest of the train lay in every direction, some on end,
some on the side, crushed and broken, a terrible but picturesque sight. Below
were the water and broken ice; seventy feet above was the broken bridge.

Mrs. Bingham sank down in the snow and I went back after my coat.
Securing that, I went to her and carried her, with a dozen stumbles and falls,
up the bank. The snow in the valley was nearly to my waist, and I could
only move with difficulty. The wreck was then on fire. The wind was blow-
ing from the east and whirling blinding masses of snow over the terrible ruin.

The crackling of the flames, the whistling wind, the screaming of the hurt,
made a pandemonium of that little valley, and the water of the freezing creek
was red with blood or black with the flying cinders. I did not then know that
any lives had been lost. All had escaped alive, though all were bruised or
injured. The fire stole swiftly along the wreck, and in a few moments the
cars were all in flames. The ruins covered the whole space between the two
piers, the cars jammed in or locked together. One engine lay in the creek,
smashed to pieces, the ruins breathing steam and fire.

I carried Mrs. Bingham to the only house near by, and which appeared to
be an engine-house. I was completely exhausted, and remained there forty-
five minutes, when the injured began to arrive. I think there were fifty-two
brought in alive, but one or two died after their removal to the town, where
they were subsequently taken. The town was about a quarter of a mile
distant.

I did not go back to the wreck, but from the engine-house door I could see
into the ravine, and the fearful scene it presented. The sight was sickening.
The whole wreck was then on fire, and from out the frozen valley came great
bursts of flame. There were crowds of men there, but the fire beat them back,
and they could do nothing. The wounded were lying around in the snow, or
were laid on stretchers or taken on the backs of men and carried up the bluff.
The spectacle was frightful, but those who had gone to assist worked steadily

and well in spite of the intense heat. They carried away all who could be rescued, and then waited mournfully for the flames to subside, so that bodies might be taken out. As fast as the injured were secured, they were taken to the hotel. That was some time before anything could be done, for in thirty minutes after the fall it was impossible to get near it for the fire. I think it likely that a great many were buried under the cars, and lost in that way.

The hotel was about a quarter of a mile from the creek, and as the long line of stretchers and stout men bore the sufferers along, the stormy air was filled with moanings of anguish. At the hotel, the wounded were kindly cared for. Physicians and surgeons were early on hand, and every effort was made to relieve the sufferers. One lady, whose foot had been crushed, was carried shrieking in labor pains to the little hotel, and during the night she gave birth to a child.

From the top of the bluff to the water's edge it is, I should think, from seventy to eighty feet, and along that bluff there ranged lines of excited men looking down on the burning, helpless agony below. It was a heart-rending scene. The mangled, bleeding bodies writhed in the terrible tortures around them. Some died with prayer and some with shriekings of woe on their lips. Some were caught in the iron and woodwork, and held while the flames crept upon them and burned them in the very sight of cool, rippling water. As they died, they fixed their bloodshot eyes longingly upon the snow that beat pitilessly down, and lay white and beautiful on their smoke-blackened faces. The fire crept steadily on through the snow flakes, leaping from one mass of ruins to another, licking up the blood as it passed along, and crushing out human lives as remorselessly as it curled around the stubborn woodwork.

When the train fell, Mr. Bliss succeeded in crawling through a window, supposing he could pull his wife and children after him. But they were jammed fast and every effort of his was unavailing. The car was all jammed up, and the lady and her children were caught in the ironwork of the seats. Finding that he could not save them, he staid there with them and died.

Most all the passengers who escaped did so by way of the windows. There was no egress at the doors, for the stoves were there. One lady was pulled from a window, and almost every stitch of clothing stripped from her, and when they were taking her out the rescuing party could hear the screams of women and children for aid, but could render them no assistance.

Those who came from the wreck said they could see into the cars and could see the charred trunks of those who had been literally burned to death. They described them as wholly unrecognizable beyond identification, and presenting the most ghastly scene they had ever looked on. Some of the unfortunates were burned literally to ashes, and in some cases only calcined bones were left to tell that human beings had ever been there.

Of the fifty-two taken from the wreck, all were more or less injured, and about forty of them dangerously, if not fatally. I don't remember any names. I was badly shaken up and bruised, and I think there was only one man who was as little hurt as I was.

There was a fire-engine there, but there was no hose. I think the fire lasted about an hour, and by that time all the cars were burned. I don't think any one was taken out alive after the fire. I am fearful that all who were not saved before the flames got headway perished in the general conflagration.

I should say there were at the least reckoning one hundred and fifty persons killed outright or burned to death, and this in spite of the fact that some of the officers claim that there were only one hundred and sixty-five on the train.

I don't know the name of a human being among the killed, except Mr. Bliss and his family, and I don't know the names of any of the injured. All along the road coming from the scene are anxious men, fearful that friends or relatives were on the train and killed or injured. Perhaps some of them may yet hear of deplorable losses, for the railroad officials admit that there were over one hundred killed.

Fortunately, the dear children of Mr. and Mrs. Bliss had been left at Rome, and *they* were safe. The father and mother "went before" them into the valley of the shadow of death.

CHAPTER XXV.

IN MEMORIAM—FEELING AND GLOWING TRIBUTES, IN POETRY AND PROSE, FROM EDITORS, CLERGYMEN, SINGERS AND FRIENDS, TO THE MEMORY OF THE DEPARTED SONG WRITER.

FROM various sources we select a few of the many good things which have been said of Mr. and Mrs. Bliss since the sad event of their death. "None knew them but to love them; none spoke but to praise them."

The editorial columns of the Chicago *Inter-Ocean* contained the following glowing tribute to our friend, written while it was still supposed that Mr. Bliss' children were among the lost at Ashtabula:

P. P. Bliss, the song writer, the author of "Hold the Fort," "The Armor-Bearer," "Almost Persuaded," and scores of other popular songs, was on the train that went down with a crash to terrible destruction at Ashtabula. He was coming from the holiday meeting at his old home, with its tender memories clinging to him, to hold a grand praise meeting in Chicago, to which he was looking forward with all the wholesome enthusiam of his stalwart, Christian manhood. Moving along a line leading from joyous scene to pleasant duty, he was stopped midway to die with wife and children; to die in an attempt to save those he loved from a terrible fate.

This horror of a railroad disaster has darkened many a home; in the case of Mr. Bliss it destroyed one—blotted it out as with a thunder crash. The catastrophe has depressed the public, a public already sore to the heart's core over the Brooklyn theater disaster; but in the death of Mr. Bliss it touches chords that bring it home as a family grief to every church and Sabbath School in America and England.

Mr. Bliss was the song writer of the church and Sabbath School. He stood prominent among those earnest workers who have invested Sabbath School music with the cheerfulness, lightness, brightness and briskness that were wanting in the old hymns, and who have added to them new pathos and tenderness. His works were songs rather than hymns, and they were written under the inspiration of the ideal song writer. In words and music his compositions were adapted to the longings and wants of those he desired to reach. The illustrations were familiar, the methods were striking, the sentiment was an echo of the feeling in his own heart. He seized quickly upon incident or figure, or story, and turned it to good account. Catching suggestions from the actual life of the people, his songs and his musical compositions came to the masses as revelations. The relation of an army incident suggested "Hold the Fort." It was written on the impulse of the moment, and it has traveled the world over. It has been translated into not only nearly all the European languages, but into Chinese and the native languages of India. It is not too much to say that it is popular beyond any other Sabbath School song of the age. And with it travel others almost as popular; " What Will the Harvest Be?" " Almost Persuaded," " Only an Armor-Bearer," etc., etc.

When we remember that every child, from the lisping four-year-old to the youth of fifteen or eighteen, is singing in Sabbath School and home, " Only an armor-bearer proudly I stand," and that not only in home and Sabbath School, but at political meetings, people have been shouting " Hold the fort, for I am coming," then, and not till then, do we realize how near this man, whom we of Chicago knew so well, was to the people at large. And when we read these songs and hear the simple music, we go further, and realize how much he has helped all people, but particularly the young, toward a better life.

Mr. Bliss was a fine specimen of the vigorous and robust man. He was gifted with a sweet voice and an attractive manner. He carried into his musical work the martial bearing and movement of the commander in a great crusade. This spirit breathes along his lines and swells in all his music. Children caught quickly this heroic spirit. His military figures found the nation responsive. He is never, in any composition, at a halt. He is always marching forward or struggling upward. There is always the suggestion of the leader's plume to the front; there is always a purpose, a hope, a promise, a resolve, at the heart; there is always present the spirit that moves masses to responsive or heroic moods, or that pathos that calls out the best there is in man. Hence the popularity of Mr. Bliss' compositions, and, more important, the good influence they have exerted.

As with Mr. Moody, the people of Chicago have watched the course of Mr. Bliss with peculiar interest. Those earnest in Christian work observed with pleasure his growing toward the conviction that he must enter a wider field. They were familiar with the doubts in his own mind, which went down one by one under the resolve that he must do his whole duty, and they have rejoiced over the good results of his work. And this class of earnest workers, numbering in its ranks Mr. Moody and many of the ministers of the city, have seen with clearer vision than the masses the spirit and purpose of Mr. Bliss. They have known him better and have understood him better than have the people at large. But to all he has spoken as a friend; and standing appalled before the Ashtabula horror, many will turn shivering to the picture of the song-maker struggling to save his wife and children. And then will come that vivid picture of his own:

On, like a fiend in its towering wrath,
On, and destruction alone points the path;
Mercy! O heaven! the sufferers wail—
Feeble humanity, naught can avail.

So he went down to death. And of this sudden coming of death he has said :

> I know not the hour when my Lord will come
>   To take me away to His own dear home ;
> But I know that His presence will lighten the gloom,
>   And that will be glory for me.

People think and speak in formula furnished by this man now dead, and many will recall reminiscences of his home life that make very touching this picture of his terrible death. One of his intimate friends relates how many of his compositions, now famous, first found shape in his own home ; of how, with wife and children and a few chosen friends about him, he first sung the songs that were to be given to the world. And this friend tells of how the singer and his family rejoiced over the perfecting of some work that reflected an experience or trial or struggle or rejoicing that they themselves had lived through. The man spoke from the heart of his home, and no wonder he touched the popular heart.

In a sermon preached at Minneapolis, Minnesota, on the 6th of January, Rev. R. F. Semple, D. D., expressed himself as follows respecting Mr. Bliss and his work. Want of space alone prevents our publishing the sermon in full :

There are many stricken households, widely scattered, greatly mourning the disaster at Ashtabula bridge. Some of our number lost near kindred on that dreadful night : the joy of the marriage succeeded by the wail of death. And there was one widely known and greatly beloved. Hence, thousands in this and in other lands, as the electric wire flashed the sad intelligence of his decease, cried in the bitterness of their grief, "Alas! my brother."

Wherever the sweet "Gospel Songs" were sung, and especially where the voice of him who wrote them had been heard, there is sorrow such as has seldom been surpassed. With feelings of peculiar sadness, relieved only by the light from beyond, we who linger a little behind now sing,

> Down life's dark vale we wander,
> Till Jesus comes.

And hereafter, as we join in the familiar song, there will come to us thoughts of a night dark and stormy ; and as we look through the blinding tempest we shall see a noble form moving calmly on, and a manly face turned heavenward, and shall hear a voice of marvelous compass and sweetness singing, in trustful strains, mingling with, and rising above, the moanings of the wintry winds—

> Though the pathway be lonely and dangerous, too,
> Surely Jesus is able to carry us through ;

and then as the weary, blistered feet touch the heavenly shore, we catch the triumphant refrain—

Hallelujah ! 'tis done ! I believe on the Son,
I am saved by the blood of the Crucified One.

You all know to whom I refer. I have scarcely felt that I could trust myself to speak his name. I had come to know him intimately, and to love him
tenderly, and to confide in him implicitly. The brother beloved who had labored with him in Gospel services, and was competent to form a judgment of
his character, said of him, "He is the purest minded man I ever knew." There
certainly have been few so loving, unselfish and kind. He was singularly art-
less. He wore no disguise. In presence dignified and commanding as Saul
among the children of Israel, he was in spirit simple, and unostentatious, and
confiding as a child. His songs were like himself. They were the utterances
of his own great heart. They claimed no relation, and had none, to the measured and lofty poetry of the Homeric hymns. They were sweet lyrics rather.
The most intellectual were moved by them. The unlearned understood them.
They were fragrant with the love of Jesus, and I doubt not led many to Him.
Already they are sung in every land. Though born within the last decade, they
have overtaken the sacred hymns of Watts, and Newton, and Toplady; and
some of them will live as long. It was well said of such songs as "Hold the
Fort," "Almost Persuaded," "When Jesus Comes," and "We're Going Home
To-morrow," that, "As the years roll on, like the handsful of seed dropped in
the furrow, they shall yield increasing harvests, till from all lands and kindreds and tongues there shall come up a mighty throng to cast their crowns
at the feet of that dear Lord whose dying love it was our brother's highest
joy to magnify." And we fully accord with the judgment of another, that
"Evangelical song lost its greatest exponent when Philip P. Bliss staid by
the car in Ashtabula Creek," and burned to death in the fruitless attempt
to save his wife—an act characteristic of his affectionate and self-forgetful
nature.

This dear brother has sown seeds in the hearts of many whom I now address, which I fervently hope shall yet bring forth immortal fruitage in their
salvation. How tenderly did he speak to the young, of Christ, the children's
friend, and urge them to come to Him. How earnestly did he pray that they
might know Jesus, and rejoice in His light. The memory of those November
days will abide with us down to the winter of life, and we shall always be
thankful that our dear brethren in Christ, Whittle and Bliss, came this way;
loving evangelists, who pointed us to the wicket gate of Mercy, and bade us
hasten to it.

*   *   *   *   *   *   *   *

I recall a sweet and solemn service, when our dear brother and his equally
lovely wife sang together a hymn which was prophetic of their end—may it
be of our peaceful departure :

Through the valley of the shadow I must go,
    Where the cold waves of Jordan roll ;
But the promise of my Shepherd will, I know,
    Be the rod and staff of my soul.

Even now down the valley as I glide,
  I can hear my Savior say, " Follow me ; "
And with him I'm not afraid to cross the tide,
  There's a light in the valley for me.

Now the rolling of the billows I can hear,
  As they beat on the turf-bound shore,
But the beacon light of love so bright and clear
  Guides my bark frail and lone safely o'er.
I shall find down the valley no alarms,
  For my blessed Savior's smile I can see,
He will bear me in His loving, mighty arms—
  There's a light in the valley for me.

Dear brother and sister, sweet singers in Israel, farewell ! There is a strange stillness in the air since you went ; a strange sorrow in our hearts. But it is well ; for God hath done it. Perchance the day on which you left us was a festal day in heaven, and your voices were needed in the song of the redeemed. Farewell ; yet not forever. On some glad day, not afar off, we shall hope to meet you yonder :

Saved through the blood of the Crucified One.

From Rev. G. C. Waterman we have the following words of loving praise :

Philip Bliss was my friend. I loved him as a brother, and have good reason to believe that the love was returned in full measure. My acquaintance with him began a few years before he went to Chicago, and up to that time was intimate, so that a friendship struck its roots into our hearts which has lived and grown through ten years of separation. In those days he was engaged in teaching singing schools, holding musical conventions and occasionally giving concerts with Mr. John G. Towner, who was his first teacher in music. He was a frequent guest at my house, coming sometimes alone, sometimes with Mr. Towner, and sometimes bringing his wife with him, but always welcome. His personal appearance and bearing were such as to attract and win respect and friendship wherever he went. Nature had lavished upon him a profusion of charms. Not Saul or David was more eminent among his fellows for fine physique and manly beauty. Homer would have put him high among his heroes and described him with his choicest epithets. He was at once dignified and genial ; a subtle and peculiar grace, which never degenerated into softness or sickly sentimentality, invested all that he did or said. Behind this there lay, not quite concealed, no small amount of power. These qualities, in combination with the instructive faculties which he possessed in a high degree, fitted him in an admirable manner for the work of teaching in his chosen profession. There was running through his temperament a rich vein of genial humor, bubbling forth in all sorts of unlooked-for ways, in odd conceits and quaint terms of expression, in rhymes and jingles, which made him a most delightful companion and correspondent. In it all there was never a drop of scalding sarcasm, biting acidity or turbid foulness; it was always pure, sweet and healthful as the waters from the mountain spring.

After a few years of this pleasant intercourse, our paths diverged from the quiet valley in which they had crossed and recrossed so often, his to lead into the heart of the life of the West, mine to wind along in other humble retreats; but from time to time golden threads were thrown across the intervening space, slender but strong, holding together loving hearts in two circles. When at length the great sorrow of my life came upon me and death quenched the central light of my household, he poured out the wealth of his loving heart in words of tender sympathy, bidding me "lean hard on the great Burden-bearer," and helped me with a brother's strong sympathy. I have not seen him since he entered upon his active evangelistic work with Major Whittle, but have followed him with deep interest, and rejoiced in all that God hath wrought through them. Soon after he begun this work, two years ago this very day, January 13th, he wrote me thus: "Do I enjoy this Gospel song singing? What a queer question for a musical minister to ask! There never was anything like it. Certainly the Master blesses us greatly, even now; with greater experience and greater faith we are expecting the increase of blessing. * * * Still there's more to follow;" to this he subscribed himself, "Gospel Songfully Yours."

In the Peoria (Illinois) *Transcript*, we find the following, from Rev. A. R. Thompson, Pastor of the Second Presbyterian Church in that city:

> O, thou sweet singer! hast thou passed away
> 　While yet thy voice is lingering on our ear?
> Must hearts so full of joy but yesterday
> 　Give place to sorrow and the bitter tear?
>
> Is thy sweet life of love and song no more?
> 　Thy noble manhood scarcely reaching prime;
> Yet in its richness fertile with a store
> 　Of sacred melody and heavenly rhyme,
>
> No more, sweet singer! Oh these words "no more"—
> 　Thy voice shall thrill and soften every breast;
> Thy anthems sung, thy mission now is o'er,
> 　And thou hast gone to thy celestial rest.
>
> Tender and loving, song was but thy prayer—
> 　An inspiration strain from realms above—
> And in angelic music thou didst bear
> 　The soul's petition to a God of love.

Thy noble wife! of self the counterpart,
  Whose voice and being blended with thine own :
In counsel, love, encouraging thy heart,
  Till she, so loving, in thy nature shone.

Bright spirits both! your work on earth is done,
  Your memory in sweet song shall ever live—
Your life of faith and love ere now has won
  A crown of Him whose joy it is to give.

R. W. Morgan, editor of *The Christian*, published in London, England, discourses, in a letter to his journal, as follows, respecting the work of Mr. Bliss :

"And devout men carried Stephen to his burial, and made great lamentation over him." Something of this kind has been repeated here. The lamentation is over two of the sweetest singers in Israel—Mr. and Mrs. P. P. Bliss—without even the mournful satisfaction of carrying them to their burial. I scarcely know how to write the sorrowful tidings which I have to send to-day. I had gone to Canada for Christmas week, and returned on Saturday night (Dec. 30) to meet these friends in Jesus, and make some final arrangements as to their coming to England with Major Whittle in the spring. Though I had heard on the way of a frightful railway accident at Ashtabula, in Ohio, it did not occur to me that they would be traveling by that very train—the Pacific Express. But on arriving at Chicago I was appalled to hear that they had perished on the previous night.

I have already written of my sojourn at Peoria, where I spent a few days with them. Mr. Bliss was a saint indeed, and his wife a true helpmate to him. "A prince and a great man is fallen in Israel," and of him and his sweet wife it may well be added, "They were lovely and pleasant in their lives, and in their death they were not divided."

On Saturday night, Major Whittle, Mr. Farwell, Mr. Jacobs and others went to the scene of the accident, to endeavor to recover the remains, but a telegram to Mr. Moody says that most of the bodies recovered are quite unrecognizable; and there seems no likelihood of anything being found of this beloved brother and sister whom Chicago mourns, and thousands all over the land and through the world are mourning, and will mourn more deeply, as the hymns he wrote, and which they sang together, are more fully understood. Their bodies have probably been burned to ashes, but they are themselves transfigured, and to us the hymns are transfigured also. We have been saying one to another that, read in the light of this fiery translation, they seem all changed to prophecies. How differently shall we now sing—

I know not the hour when my Lord shall come,
To take me away to His own dear home,
But I know that His presence will lighten the gloom,
  And that will be glory for me.

> I know not the form of my mansion fair,
> I know not the name that I then shall bear;
> But I know that my Savior will welcome me there,
> And that will be heaven for me.

After the Chicago fire he wrote and dedicated to Mr. Moody the words and music "Roll on, O billow of fire!" the chorus of which must have come back with even more vividness in the fire in which he perished than when written in recollection of the fire from which he had escaped.

How much more tenderly shall we now sing that childlike carol which was the one that took the earliest hold of us at home—

> I am so glad that our Father in heaven
> Tells of His love in the Book He has given.
> Wonderful things in the Bible I see ;
> This is the dearest—that Jesus loves me.

It melts one's heart to think how, in the agony of that last hour, the husband and wife needed to cling, as to an anchor within the vail, to the assurance that, even in this terrible ordeal, "Jesus loves me."

After a visit to a beautiful cemetery in Peoria, Illinois, and with his thoughts specially drawn toward the "blessed hope, and the glorious appearing of the great God and our Savior Jesus Christ," he wrote—

> Down life's dark vale we wander,
> Till Jesus comes,

and although the death of the individual is not the coming of the Lord to receive His bride to Himself, yet what a sublime fulfillment did those simple lines receive on that dreadful night!

> He'll know what griefs oppressed me, ·
> When Jesus comes.
> Oh, how His arms will rest me,
> When Jesus comes.

And now that he is gone how inspiriting will be the war-song, as we think how, trusting in the living God, he held the fort in death!—

> Ho, my comrades, see the signal
>   Waving in the sky ;
> Reinforcements now appearing,
>   Victory is nigh.
> "Hold the fort, for I am coming!"
>   Jesus signals still,
> Wave the answer back to heaven—
>   "By thy grace we will."

A story was told yesterday of a missionary in South Africa going into a kraal to rest, and the first sounds he heard were from a Zulu singing this tune. So these stirring strains go round the world.

As we remember how our noble brother stood, and how he **fell, shall we** not mean something more than ever before in singing?—

> Dare to be a Daniel !
> Dare to stand alone !
> Dare to have a purpose firm !
> Dare to make it known !

To us here, it seems as if his patient and truthful voice was singing out of the darkness and terror of that wintry storm—

> Brightly beams our Father's mercy,
> From His lighthouse evermore ;
> But to us He gives the keeping
> Of the lights along the shore ;

and that he appeals, with outstretched hands, on behalf of others—

> Let the lower lights be burning,
> Send the gleam across the wave ;
> Some poor fainting, struggling seaman
> You may rescue, you may save.

For he met his end not far from the very spot (Cleveland harbor) where the catastrophe occurred, which, related by Mr. Moody, was the occasion of his writing—

> Trim your feeble lamp, my brother,
> Some poor seaman, tempest-tost,
> Trying now to make the harbor,
> In the darkness may be lost.

He was a man full of sympathy, and the wisdom of the truest Christian sympathy shows itself in the hymn in which he counsels the burdened one,

> Go tell it to Jesus, and all will be right.

Gently and lovingly he leads the mourner on :

> Go gather the sunshine He sheds on thy way,
> He'll lighten thy burden—go, weary one, pray.

And there is a moral grandeur in the self-sacrifice and generosity which he commends, and which were indeed but the reflection of his own inner life :

> Go bury thy sorrow, let others be blest ;
> Go give them the sunshine, tell Jesus the rest.

In the same vein of advancing experience is the familiar hymn which was suggested by Mr. Moody's address on Assurance—

> I *wished* He was mine,
> And then began *hoping* that Jesus was mine.
> I'm hoping no longer, I *know* He is mine.

20

At the Industrial Exposition at Chicago it was an every-day appointment "Meet me at the Fountain." Our sweet singer, his mind always set on the things above, caught up the words, and wrote—

> Will you meet me at the fountain,
> When I reach the glory-land?
> Will you meet me at the fountain?
> Shall I clasp your friendly hand?
> Other friends will give me welcome,
> Other loving voices cheer,
> There'll be music at the fountain?
> Will you, will you, meet me there?

I spent but a few days in his society, but the impression he has left upon my heart is well expressed in the question and the assurance—

> Will you meet me at the fountain?
> I shall long to have you near,
> When I meet my loving Savior,
> When His welcome words I hear.

And so I might go on, for "Still there's more to follow."

> Oh, the grace the Father shows;
> Oh, the love that Jesus shows;
> Oh, the power the Spirit shows!

This was his experience, and although the flow of his sweet melodies is stayed on earth, before the throne—drinking of the water of life which proceeds from the throne of God and the Lamb—he will praise on through the long day of his eternal life; and the refrain of the unfinished song through the ages to come will be—

> Still there's more to follow.

Perhaps it is well that the stream of song has been diverted to the heavenly land. We might have gone on asking for some new thing, thinking more of the songs than of the salvation of which they speak, and forgetting the Giver in the gift. Therefore the only wise God our Savior has transfigured those we have, and shown us depths of sacred tenderness, and love, and courage that we had only dimly seen before; and, thus enriching the songs we possess, He has caught up the singer to His throne and heart, while we are left to urge them that are

> Almost persuaded now to believe,
> Almost persuaded Christ to receive,

to yield, and say—

> Fully persuaded, Jesus is mine;
> Fully persuaded, Lord, I am thine.

And as one by one saved souls confess the Savior's name, our departed friend will remember that he said, and by the grace of God fulfilled his pledge—

> Surely my Captain may depend on me,
> Though but an armor-bearer I may be.

Now he is gone, and his memory is very fragrant.   We may write his epitaph in the words of Dr. Bonar's hymn, which Mr. Bliss had set to music, and the second verse of which is peculiarly suitable and true of his most unselfish life—

> So, in the harvest, if others may gather
> Sheaves from the fields that in spring I have sown;
> Who plowed or sowed matters not to the reaper:
> I'm only remembered by what I have done.

And no doubt can remain on any heart that there has been a full and blessed answer to the aspiration, which he had set to sweetest strains—

> And when, with my glorified vision, at last
> The walls of " that city " I see,
> Will any one then at the Beautiful Gate
> Be waiting and watching for me?

" And I heard a voice from heaven saying unto me Write, Blessed are the dead which die in the Lord from henceforth: yea, saith the Spirit, that they may rest from their labors ; and their works do follow them."—Rev. xiv, 13.

George C. Needham, the evangelist, wrote to a friend, soon after Mr. Bliss' death :

A great and sore trouble has fallen upon us. Messrs. Moody, Sankey, Whittle, Stebbins and others of us who were identified in work with our departed friend can only weep and mourn to-day, though sorrowing not as those who have no hope.

During the past three years, Mr. Bliss had been identified with Major Whittle in Gospel labors, and both men were the bosom friends of Messrs. Moody and Sankey. In personal appearance he was a fine specimen of a vigorous man. Large, well-proportioned, noble in presence—he never failed to produce an impression on the passer-by. Possessing princely manners, and imbued with a true spirit of the Christian gentleman, a man of rare worth and grace and spiritual attainments has passed from us.

Since the hope of our Lord's coming dawned upon the heart of our brother, he loved to speak of that prospective day. The last time I talked with him, he said he would interweave that truth into his new hymns, and so teach the people to look and wait for the Son from heaven. Many of his pieces are full of the gladness and the joyousness of that hope.

A year ago, during Mr. Bliss' life, Philip Phillips, the singer, wrote :

Mr. P. P. Bliss combines the rare gifts of writing and singing Sacred Song, and like Chicago, his home, has come into public favor rapidly, and while

young. He is an excellent Christian man, a member of the Presbyterian
Church, and about thirty-two years of age.   This present year he has resigned
his position as chorister of a large church in Chicago, and cast in his lot as
singer with D. W Whittle, as a lay evangelist.   They are at the present time
laboring in the Southern States of America. Mr. Bliss has brought out the
"Charm" and "Sunshine" of Sacred Song, and goes about literally as an
ensample of his book.   He is author of "Almost Persuaded," "Hold the Fort,"
"When Jesus comes," "I am so Glad that Jesus Loves Me," "Dare to be a
Daniel," "Only an Armor-Bearer," "What shall the Harvest be?" etc.

The following poem, by Rev. Arthur T. Pierson, D. D., of
Detroit, comes to us with the explanatory words of the author : "I
read at an immense mass meeting held here in the Opera House,
Sunday afternoon, the following impromptu verses, in memory of
P. P. Bliss.   A harp draped and adorned with floral decorations was
placed on the platform ; and knowing that this was to be, I framed
these verses after my morning service.   If you publish them, please
let *italics* go in, as I have interwoven strains from Bliss' favorite
songs, and the italics indicate them.   The haste in which they were
written will explain their crude shape, as I could not destroy their
impromptu character by attempt at revision.

> The harp of Zion's psalmist now is still,
>   Ten thousand eyes, in bitter grief, have wept,
> Because the hand that, with a master's skill,
>   These silver chords so long, so sweetly swept,
> Is turned to ashes in the fatal flames !
>   Because no more that voice Redemption sings
> And sounds the *Name* above all other names,
>   With whose high praises even heaven rings.

> The harp is still ! the harper is not here !
>   No more shall that anointed silver tongue
> Arouse the dull and inattentive ear,
>   And teach us how the *gospel may be sung ;*
> How poet's harp and heart, alike devote,
>   Both words and melodies may consecrate,
> Till Jesus' call may sound on every note,
>   And win the wanderer to the narrow gate !

> The earthly harp is still, but up on high,
>   Where everlasting anthems ceaseless roll,
> A golden harp, resounding in the sky,
>   Thrills with the triumph of a ransomed soul.

There, 'mid the host of the celestial choir,
  His *sorrow buried*, and his heart at rest,
He has " *more holiness*," his soul's desire—
  Safe in the arms of Jesus—on His breast !

Weep not for him, who now doth fully know
  The *depth of mercy* and the grace divine,
The blood that washed and made him *white as snow*,
  And sings with rapture—" Yes, *I know He's mine*,"
He leadeth him, He *guides him with His eye ;*
  Light of the world, He brightly beams on him ;
And, brethren, we *shall meet him by and by*
  When not a tear the ransomed eye shall dim.

Catch up and echo ye his trumpet tone :
  Let *whosoever heareth shout the sound ;*
We'll tell of Him who *saves* and *saves alone*,
  Till *sinners* shall *receive—the world around ;*
Shall shout *'tis done*, I too, *believe the Son—*
  Till *prodigals come home* and *kiss His feet*,
Till hearts emptied of self, by grace are won,
  Nothing but vessels, for *His use made meet*.

He'd bid us, could he speak, from mansions fair,
  Rescue the perishing—not mourn the dead,
Bid burdened souls dismiss their load of care,
  And know that *Jesus loves them*—for them bled.
He seems to shout, from over Jordan's wave,
  Hold ye the fort ! by help of grace divine,
Let lower lights be burning, you may save
  Some struggling sailor—if your light doth shine.

We will not weep ! *when Jesus comes*, we'll fly,
  Our weary souls shall rest ; *we're going home*.
He gave his life for us, why should we sigh ?
  For soon our weary feet *no more shall roam*.
We're coming to the cross, anew to be
  With Jesus crucified—that so, ere long,
We may the saints and our dear Jesus see,
  And join, with harps in hand, in that *new song*.

Harper's Weekly published an excellent portrait of Mr. Bliss,
accompanied by the following references to him :

Among the victims of the dreadful railroad calamity at Ashtabula were the
evangelist Philip P. Bliss and his wife. Mr. Bliss was the author of the

well-known hymn, " Hold the Fort." He was on his way to take part in the Gospel meetings at Chicago, where he was highly esteemed. Probably no modern hymn has been more widely sung in England and America than the one just named. According to the statements of those who were in a position to know, Mr. Bliss made a heroic effort to save his wife when he might have saved himself, and, failing in this, remained and died with her, the two offering their prayers together as the fatal flames approached them, like the old martyrs at the stake; and thus, united in life, they were not divided in death. Those who remain pursuing the work in which he was engaged have already provided the means for educating his children, two young boys, and bringing them up in the way their father walked, and for erecting an appropriate monument to the memory of this faithful pair. The death of Mr. Bliss has elicited throughout the country many expressions of sorrow. He was but thirty-eight years old at the time of his decease, and had only in the later years of his life become a proficient in music. Ten years ago, he entered the music store of Messrs. Root & Cady in Chicago, and remained there until the great fire of 1871. Since then he has been an active evangelist, and with Major Whittle has made long tours through the country. Some of his best-known pieces are, " Hold the Fort," " Pull for the Shore," " Jesus loves even Me." His songs have done much to popularize the religious movement of our day, which has so visibly affected the masses of the population in England, Scotland, Ireland, and the United States.

Simeon Gilbert writes to *The Advance* as follows :

The telegraphic announcement that Mr. and Mrs. P. P. Bliss were on board the fatal train which plunged into the gulf with that broken bridge at Ashtabula, Ohio, and perished with the rest, sent a pang of sorrow throughout the country. All who perished in that most appalling disaster left friends to mourn their loss and cherish their memory; but in the case of Mr. Bliss, whose hymns and tunes had made him a favorite in thousands of churches and with millions of Sunday School scholars, his mourners, on both sides of the Atlantic, are innumerable.

The life of Mr. Bliss was a voice—the voice of one singing, with a wonderful persuasiveness, of the " good tidings of great joy for all people." He wrote his own hymns, composed his own tunes, and sung them, too. During the past three or four years, his Gospel hymns and tunes, popularized partly by himself, and still more by his dear friend, Mr. Sankey, have been used oftener and by larger numbers than those of any other cotemporary composer. Being dead, he yet speaketh, and the circumstances of his death will give a peculiar sacredness to the songs and tunes which he has left us. No doubt some of them will, having met a special want in the development of the Christian life of the period, and served their temporary, but not on that account unimportant, use, pass away; but some of them, we are confident, will take their place among those which the church will not let die. Those who shall hereafter pause to trace the distinctive qualities, the *timbre*, so to speak, of the Christian life of this time, will note that what Charles Wesley was to John Wesley, Mr. Bliss has been to Mr. Moody.

The best of Mr. Bliss' hymns and tunes are simple and lucid utterances of the heart of the Gospel and of the Christian experience of those who put complete trust in Christ as a perfect Savior. Not keyed to the same pitch as Luther's famous battle-hymn, "A strong tower is our God," he yet gauged the popular temper and want of the churches equally well. The present more particularly aggressive form of evangelistic work owes as much to what Mr. Bliss and his singing co-laborers have contributed as to any other human instrumentality.

In George Herbert's "Country Parson," the parson preaching is told that he must first "dip in his own heart" his words before he speaks them. Mr. Bliss had experienced his own songs before he composed them. It is not claimed that he was a great poet, or that he possessed the genius for some of the sublimer strains of music, but he had the sense and the tact which are not often equaled in matching words and tunes, and suiting both to the popular requirement.

Mr. Bliss was only thirty-eight years old. He was born in Rome, Pennsylvania. His parents were very poor, and his early advantages were extremely limited. To the last, his admirable wife was to a singular degree his greatest helper. One of his first instructors in music was Mr. Root. Coming to Chicago some ten years ago, he was employed in the music establishment of Root & Cady. The great fire of 1871 dissolved that connection, and he has been wont to say that the fire was the making of him, setting him at liberty to devote himself to the special kind of work to which he felt himself called of God. His first church connection was the Methodist, but coming to Chicago he united with the First Congregational Church, Dr. Goodwin's, and was for a number of years both its chorister and Sunday School Superintendent.

One of the sweetest of the hymns and tunes composed by him is the one entitled, "When Jesus Comes." Among those most in use, and which have been most evidently blessed in the using are the "Hallelujah, 'tis Done!" "Calling now for Thee;" "Whosoever Will;" "That will be Heaven for Me;" "Hold the Fort;" "Once for All;" "We're going Home To-morrow;" the one so dear to the little ones, "Jesus Loves even Me;" "More to Follow;" "Where Hast thou Gleaned To-day;" "The Light of the World is Jesus;" "Let the Lower Lights be Burning;" "Pull for the Shore," and "My Prayer."

Last Sunday, in some schools, and we presume in many, the hymns used were exclusively those which Mr. Bliss has left us. The one beginning, "Free from the law, oh, happy condition," Mr. Moody thinks will live always.

Of late, as is well known, he has been the constant associate in evangelistic work of Major D. W. Whittle. No one can possibly feel his loss more deeply than our friend Major Whittle. They had seemed as necessary to each other as Moody and Sankey. At the time when he met his death he was on his way to Chicago to join Major Whittle in carrying forward the work in this city begun by Messrs. Moody and Sankey. The first report was that Mr. and Mrs. Bliss, with their two little children, were all caught up in an undivided group to their heavenly home. It was since ascertained, however, that the children had been left with their grandmother in Rome, Pa.

Rev. W. W. Patton, who knew Mr. Bliss long and intimately, thus speaks of his life and labors:

Among the many victims of the Ashtabula calamity, none will be more widely and deeply mourned than Mr. P. P. Bliss, who perished with his wife, their remains being entirely consumed by the flames. He was the author of the most popular of the pieces sung in the Moody and Sankey meetings in this country and abroad, such as " Hallelujah,'tis Done ;" " What shall the Harvest Be ?" "Whosoever Will ;" "More to Follow ;" "That will be Heaven for Me ;" "My Prayer ;" "Almost Persuaded ;" "How Much Owest Thou ?" and many others, both the words and music of which were composed by him. He also wrote the music to many others of the favorite hymns which are sung in those meetings. In addition to this, he was an uncommonly effective singer, having a rich baritone voice, well cultivated and full of expression.

Mr. Bliss was born in the wilds of Northern Pennsylvania, and was of quite humble extraction. He had but few advantages in early life. He married, young, a lady of his own social position, who had much strength of character, who through life was his unfailing good genius. "I owe everything to my wife," he once remarked to a friend. Mr. Bliss for a time was in the employment of the publishing firm of Root & Cady, Chicago, and held musical conventions at leading points through the Northwest. His early religious connections were with the Methodists; but, on going to Chicago, he united with the First Congregational Church, under the pastoral care of Rev. Dr. Goodwin, and became the leader of the choir and the Superintendent of the Sunday School, during a period of several years. Such was the kindness of his heart, the warmth of his piety, and the personal interest which he took in the members of the choir and school, that he won the affection as well as the regard of the whole church which now mourns him with a special sense of bereavement.

When Major Whittle, induced by the example and urgent entreaty of Mr. Moody and other Christian friends, surrendered his business and gave himself to the work of a lay evangelist, Mr. Bliss decided to become his fellow-laborer, and to "sing the Gospel," while Mr. Whittle preached it. And this he has done for the three past years with great success, visiting not only numerous places in the Western States, but also Louisville, Nashville, Atlanta, Memphis and other points at the South. Being tall and well-developed in his physical frame, with clustering black hair and a handsome face, and possessing easy and polished manners and a very joyous temperament, together with a wealth of sympathy, he impressed most favorably those who saw and heard him, whether in public or in private. His singing, like that of Mr. Sankey's, often led sinners to Christ, by its touching presentations of Gospel truth. He was not much of a poet, in the high sense, but he had a poetic susceptibility of feeling and an unusual skill in versifying evangelic doctrine in the very phrases of

Scripture, as also in adapting the music to the sentiment so as powerfully to impress the hearer. What multitudes have been thrilled by his lines

> Hallelujah, 'tis done !
> I believe on the Son ;
> I am saved by the blood of the Crucified One !

At the time of his death, he was announced to lead, at Dr. Goodwin's church, a " praise meeting" of the Sunday School, on the afternoon of the last Sunday of the year, and also to sing, at a later hour, in the afternoon services of the Tabernacle. It had been arranged that, after the departure of Moody and Sankey for Boston, Whittle and Bliss should take their places, and carry on the glorious work. But, so far as Mr. Bliss was concerned, this was not to be. He had long enough " held the fort," and was to be relieved from further earthly service. The last piece which he sang at the First Congregational Church, before he went East to spend the holidays with family relatives, began with the lines of his own composition :

> I know not the hour when my Lord will come
> To take me away to His own dear home ;
> But I know that His presence will lighten the gloom,
>   And that will be glory for me !

In the *Cumberland Presbyterian* " Mrs. E. C. D." pays poetical tribute to " The Sweet Singer."

> He came to " sing for Jesus," his armor shining bright ·
> We knew that we could trust him ; the Savior was his light.
> The weary wanderer, seeking peace, he guided to the throne,
> And the rich music of his voice was used for God alone.
>
> The willing servant of the Lord is lost to mortal sight ;
> To him, or us, no warning came ; God's will—it must be right.
> We shiver in our anguish, and the world's warm throbbing heart
> Hath felt the stroke of the angel wing that bore the cruel dart.
>
> We trust that in that bitter hour the struggle soon was o'er ;
> Perhaps he did not know 'twas death till on the other shore,
> Where with the darling of his heart so safely by his side,
> He only wondered and rejoiced that they together died.
>
> The pearly gate was open, they saw " the mansion fair,"
> And found the Savior " waiting, watching " for them there ;
> Waiting to bid them welcome home, to clasp them by the hand,
> And give them quiet, peaceful rest in the brighter, better land.

> The reason why the summons came, our Father knoweth well;
> We only know we miss him here; the rest we cannot tell.
> But let us to the mercy seat bring all this grief and sorrow,
> And wait to hear him sing again when we "go home to-morrow."

A gentleman in St. Paul, who took a deep interest in the meetings of Whittle and Bliss, which were held in St. Paul about a year ago, contributes the following:

The sad death of Mr. Bliss, the evangelist, the preacher of Christ's Gospel by song, has come to this city with peculiar force, and burdened many hearts here with the most genuine sorrow. It is, therefore, most fitting that some pen should strive to put into words that which so many hearts feel, and though any written tribute must fall short of adequate expression, still all who knew and loved Mr. Bliss will be thankful that the attempt was made.

We cannot in St. Paul speak of him as we knew him long ago; in other communities he grew up, and in other places had his most intimate associations. But he was nevertheless our fellow-citizen, our friend, our brother. In an emphatic and peculiar sense he had no continuing city; no West, no East, no North, no South could claim him. Wherever souls needed the divine blessing and comfort of the Gospel; wherever there were those whose sensibilities could be touched by the sweetest of music, the glad evangel of salvation by Christ—there was Bliss' home for the hour, the day, the week, the month. He counted all men for brethren, and his heartfelt desire was that all, like he, should turn their faces to the heavenly Jerusalem and, accepting the Savior, whose love he so sweetly sung, be ready at any moment for the summons which should call them to be its inhabitant.

Those more intimately associated in arranging the details of the work which Messrs. Whittle and Bliss engaged in in St. Paul will call to mind the circumstances under which we first became acquainted with our brother Bliss. It will be remembered how earnestly it was desired by the committee in charge that Whittle should not fail to bring him with him; how circumstances prevented this; how something in the services was missing till he came, and how all realized, after his coming, that Whittle had seemed shorn of a portion of his power till Bliss was present to preach by song the same Gospel he so earnestly spoke to the people.

All will recollect, too, the magnificent presence God had bestowed upon the man. It was attractive and impressive, drawing attention at once to the singer, and aiding the effect which his song had upon all who heard it.

How sweet and tender was his voice, like the spirit of the words which he wrote and of the music which he composed. How strong were his notes—like the splendid physique of the singer—like the deep feelings that were in his heart for the souls of those who listened.

Those brought into more familiar contact with Mr. Bliss will gladly join in ascribing to him a nature similar to his voice, both sweet and strong. It was, many think, in the incidental and less public services that his character shone out most clearly and appeared to the best advantage.

He has, ere this, greeted those in Heaven whose weary hours he cheered while in St. Paul by singing and praying beside their beds. No invitation to a service of this sort was ever declined; nay, more, he seemed glad of these quiet opportunities to cheer and comfort, and convert, no doubt, in many instances, his fellow-travelers.

At the County Jail; at the County Hospital; at the State Reform School he held little singing services, always striving to appear at his best and give those who heard him at these places the very sweetest of his efforts.

His modesty about his musical attainments was always apparent, but at no time more so than when in the praise-meeting, which he held while here, though the Opera House was filled by the hope of hearing him sing often, he did not give a single solo piece during the whole two hours of service.

It is needless that mention be made of his hymns and their music, both words and tunes having been written by him in many instances. In services almost innumerable, on this quiet Sabbath, they are being sung to the praise and glory of the God whom he served, and so is his highest ambition satisfied. So shall he live on earth as well as in heaven; so "being dead, he yet speaketh" in sweetest words.

One characteristic of these hymns in the light of his sad death cannot fail of notice. Take them up to select those appropriate to sing at a memorial service of him, and how fit are they. How often he sang

> I know not the hour when my God will come
> To take me away to his own dear home;
> But I know that His presence will lighten the gloom,
> And that will be glory for me.

Truly the call came suddenly, and the gloom was very heavy on that awful night, but he died realizing what he sang while living.

His last hymn in St. Paul contained this verse:

> For those who sleep,
> And those who weep,
>   Above the portals narrow,
> The mansions rise
> Beyond the skies,
>   We're going home to-morrow.

So it was to him and his wife but "going home." They were one by all the sacred ties of earth—one in holy purpose of blessing their fellow-men— one in the sad circumstance of death. God will take care of their children, for He never breaks His promises. So, dear brother, to-day in singing your hymns, we bid you farewell in our hearts till we shall meet "over there," and once more hear your voice still praising the Lord whose Gospel you so faithfully preached to us here in song.

At the session of the Plymouth (Ohio) Musical Convention, under the direction of Prof. H. S. Perkins, of Chicago, the following resolutions were passed :

WHEREAS, The dispensation of Providence, in the sad, heart-rending calamity at Ashtabula, Ohio, on the evening of December 29, 1876, in which occurred the death of Mr. and Mrs. P. P. Bliss, of Chicago, while in the zenith of their usefulness; and

WHEREAS, Fully recognizing them as worthy, valuable members of society and of the musical profession; also desiring to condole with the relatives of the deceased in this time of their great affliction, therefore, by the Huron County Musical Convention now in session at Plymouth, Ohio, be it

Resolved, That we have been greatly pained by the very sad and untimely death of Mr. and Mrs. P. P. Bliss, of Chicago, for whom we entertained the greatest respect and friendship.

Resolved, That our most heartfelt sympathies and condolence be extended to the widowed mother, sisters, and other relatives in this hour of their great sorrow and affliction; and that a copy of these resolutions be presented to the Chicago papers for publication, and a copy be transmitted to the surviving members of the family.

[Signed by Committee.] H. S. Perkins, Chicago; the Rev. J H. Gray Attica, Ohio; A. L. Simmons, Steuben, Ohio; H. H. Johnson, Havana, Ohio Thomas Parkison, Mansfield, Ohio.

Rev. J. B. Atchinson, of Detroit, after many warm expressions of his sympathy with the brother left here, writes of Mrs. Bliss as follows :

There is no man, living or dead, that ever exerted such a powerful influence over me for good as did Brother Bliss. My acquaintance with him for the past few years has greatly changed and directed my religious work, and, now that he is gone I feel his influence still. There were many sad tears in our home— where he and his wife had a hearty welcome—when the news of his death reached us. Only a short time before he died, I received a letter from him which is so characteristic of his piety, friendship, cheerfulness, wit and pleasantry, and in all such a striking coincidence, when considered in relation to his death, that I can but hope it may find a place in your forthcoming work. The following is a true copy :

PEORIA, ILLINOIS, December 1, 1876.

DEAR BROTHER :

Finally—AT LAST—IN CONCLUSION—Here's your " Open Window." Sorrow-*full* am I that I hadn't one before. 'Scuse me.

Meetings *good*—wish *you* the *same*. Wife is with me. Hope to go home Xmas.

Truly,
BLITTLE & WHISS

And it proved to be his "Finally—at last—in conclusion" to me. How literally were his hopes fulfilled, that he should go home Christmas, and what a proof is his signature of his very close relation to you and at the same time so characteristic of his pleasantries and cheerful spirit.

Dear Bliss! I almost hear thy bugle voice singing—

> O crown of rejoicing.
> O wonderful song,
> O joy everlasting,
> O glorified throng,
> O beautiful home,
> My home can it be,
> O glory reserved for me.

God bless you, my dear Whittle. My feeble prayers shall aid you all they can.

Yours in glad sorrow,

J. B. ATCHINSON.

At a conference, held January. 2, 1877 of the pastors of several Evangelical churches of Louisville, Kentucky, representing the Presbyterian, Methodist, Baptist, Episcopal and Lutheran churches, the distressing intelligence was communicated of the death of Mr. and Mrs. P. P. Bliss in the dreadful railway disaster at Ashtabula, Ohio. Whereupon Rev. Stuart Robinson presented the following memorial minute, which was unanimously adopted :

In view of the peculiar and interesting relations of Christian friendship between Mr. and Mrs. Bliss and our people, growing out of the labors of Messrs. Whittle and Bliss as evangelists, so remarkably blessed of God, among us, we deem it eminently appropriate that some formal public expression be given of our profound sorrow and our tender sympathy in the grief of the kindred and friends of Mr. and Mrs. Bliss under this most mysterious Providence.

We desire to bear an affectionate testimony to the signally elevated Christian character of these servants of Christ, so earnest and faithful, yet withal so modest and unassuming, and so wise in winning souls. We recall with gratitude to God the marvelous gifts and culture of the sweet Gospel singer whose strains were blessed of God as the means of comforting and edifying God's people, of encouraging desponding souls, of determining the halting, of directing the inquiring, and of awakening the souls slumbering in sin.

We can only mingle our tears in silence with those of the bereaved who, "with groanings that cannot be uttered," mourn that death should have come to their loved ones in a form so awful and distressing. "We are dumb. We open not our mouth because *Thou* didst it." Yet fully assured that this dreadful affliction that was for a moment "wrought out for them an exceeding and eternal weight of glory," we bless God, and we exhort these bereaved friends to bless God for His marvelous loving kindness in preparing them by His grace for so signally useful and blessed, though so brief, a career on earth, and for receiving the welcome plaudit, " Well done, good and faithful servants ; enter thou into the joy of thy Lord."

It is the sweet assurance of God's word, that not only "Blessed are the dead that die in the Lord," but also that "their works do follow them." Tens of thousands in the church on earth will continue to be blest through the works of Mr. Bliss. They will sing the Gospel songs with ever grateful remembrance of him who put into their mouths these new and beautiful strains, long after he himself, called by his Lord to " come up higher," shall be singing in strains ineffably more beautiful and glorious in the church above, with the one hundred and forty-four thousand and with "the harpers harping upon their harps," the new song before them.

STUART ROBINSON,
Chairman of Com.
J. M. MORRIS, Sec'y.

On the day following the memorial services in Chicago, the *Tribune* said, in its editorial columns :

The intense interest and deep feeling manifest at the various services held yesterday testify to the affection and esteem in which P. P. Bliss and wife were held in Chicago, and to the sorrow and grief of this community at their sad fate. At the meetings led by Mr. Moody and Mr. Sankey, at the Chicago Avenue Church and the Tabernacle, tearful tributes were paid by the co-workers of the gifted evangelist so suddenly removed from his chosen sphere of usefulness, and at Racine, Wisconsin, where Messrs. Whittle and Bliss had successfully carried forward the work of revival, memorial services were also held yesterday. It will be a comfort to many sorrowing hearts to learn, through the dispatch sent last evening to the *Tribune* by Major Whittle *from* Ashtabula, that the two sons of Mr. Bliss, who were reported as having shared the fate of their parents, are safe at Rome, Pennsylvania, not having been on the doomed train.

Henry Moorhouse, the evangelist, writes as follows :

My first acquaintance with dear Mr. Bliss was some seven years ago, when, accompanied by Mr. Moody and Mr. Herbert Taylor, I called upon him at his room, and was charmed by his sweet simplicity of manner and earnest love for the Lord Jesus Christ. At that time his hymns, which were very sweet, did not contain the same earnest, simple Gospel truths which afterward made them so solemn and so powerful in winning souls to the Lord Jesus. Year by year, as I again and again visited America, I saw him growing rapidly in the blessed truths of the Bible, and was greatly blessed and charmed by his company and conversation. During dear Mr. Sankey's visit to England, how wonderfully the Lord used those sweet hymns eternity alone can tell, as thousands of dear Christians have been cheered as we have sung together "I Know not the Hour my Lord will Come," and "Down Life's dark Vale we Wander till Jesus Comes," and other kindred hymns.

With all my heart and soul I sympathize with the dear bereaved mother and little children, and I joy and rejoice with dear Mr. and Mrs. Bliss, who now are safe within the vail and who to-day are with their blessed Lord who loved them and gave Himself for them.

Wirt Arland, an old school friend of Mr. Bliss, said of "Hold the Fort:"

The best known of his pieces originated in a vivid description by Major Whittle of the signaling from Kenesaw Mountain "over the heads of the rebel host." It has gone round the world and comes back in the Chinese tongue. It has been issued as a holiday gift book in elegant form by William F. Gill & Co., with appropriate pictures by Miss L. B. Humphrey and Robert Lewis, and finely engraved by John Andrew & Son. When we last saw him he had been to visit, with Major Whittle, the spot from which the message was signaled to the Commander fifteen miles distant—"Hold the Fort!" Picking up a bundle, he showed us three hickory sticks that he had cut on the mountain and said: "You see we still hold the fort. These are some canes that I am going to have mounted for my boys and myself. My boys are darling little fellows, and I have been feeling quite sad to-day, since I left them with their grandfather at Rome and have got to leave them behind as I go to Chicago."

At a later date, Mr. Arland wrote:

The winters are drifting like flakes of snow,
And the summers like buds between,

since we trudged that long snowy winter, twenty-one years ago, to the same school. The ripe fruit of his manhood was but the generous fulfillment of the early promise of a stalwart and genial boyhood, and that deep hearty voice that was loudest on the play-ground or in the songs of the noontide recess, but needed development to form that which fell with a powerful charm on hearts yearning for the peace that passeth all understanding. We met him for the last time at Elmira in October, and we felt that our friend had not changed, only ripened, and his fervent "God bless you, A——" as the Erie train drew up to bear him to Chicago, was the blessing of one we knew in the days when the principles of life are tried. His love of music was a prominent trait in his character, and many an evening have we sat and listened to his violin, wondering how he who then knew only how to play by ear could play to touch our feelings so wonderfully. He could not read music at this time. His rich, powerful bass voice was an unfailing help in the school music, and across all these years we can hear it as he sang:

> Shed not a tear o'er your friend's early bier,
>   When I am gone, I am gone
> Pause when the slow tolling bell you shall hear,
>   When I am gone, I am gone.
> Think as you stand by my half opened grave ;
> Think who has died His beloved to save ;
> Think of the crown all the ransomed shall have
>   When I am gone, I am gone.

Rev. D. W. Morgan, of Griggsville, Illinois, relates the following incident relative to Mrs. Bliss, which may be of interest to our readers :

I think it was during the summer of 1868, shortly after Mr. Bliss had begun to turn his attention to writing for our Sunday Schools, that I was in conversation with Mr George F. Root concerning him. We recalled several of his recent pieces, and I remarked upon his wonderful versatility of talent as a hymn writer, song writer and singer.

Mr. Root replied, with emphasis, "Yes, I consider Mr. Bliss as incomparably the rising musical man of our day. He is destined to more than fill the place made vacant by the death of Mr. Bradbury."

In Mr. Bliss' generous and enthusiastic acknowledgment of indebtedness to his noble wife for early encouragement in his musical tastes, he would speak of her selling the two cows which were part of her marriage patrimony to enable him to pursue his musical studies at Geneseo, New York. And that she was moved by a pure, wifely ambition to study and work in the same direction with him, that she might be his peer, or at least his constant sympathizer and support in musical endeavor, of this all are persuaded who have listened to her rich, trained voice in solo or accompanying the stronger voice of him on whom she leaned. But the following incident will illustrate the keen insight which thorough training and close observation had given her in voice culture—that which pertains to the use and abuse of the vocal organs. It was, perhaps, in November, 1869, when I was pastor of the Baptist Church in Gardner, Illinois. I had worked up a musical convention of two weeks for Mr. Bliss, who, with his wife, was conducting a similar convention in Peoria. I wrote them, as they were on the eve of coming to us, saying that I should await their coming and see them safely ensconced in our home, and see the convention started, but that I did not expect to sing a note nor preach a sermon for three months ; that I was under the doctor's ban, my throat granulated and bleeding and stubbornly resisting all treatment. My church had voted me leave of absence for the winter, made generous provision for my support, and advised me to spend the winter in the South.

Mr. and Mrs. Bliss came, and the first evening, as we were seated about the fire, Mrs. Bliss said : "Mr. Morgan, I don't think you need to go South for the recovery of your throat, nor even to give up preaching or singing. I think I can tell what is the difficulty with your throat, and can point out its remedy. 'Tis brought on by a vicious elocution. You are using an *assumed* tone of voice, and are probably unconsciously imitating some one's voice that you have admired. The *orotund* is not your natural voice. By its use you have brought an undue stress on the larynx and vocal chords, and they have yielded to over tension. Your remedy is to adopt, arbitrarily, a more *tenor* key of voice. Raise it at least two tones in conversation, reading and preaching." I thanked her, but replied that I thought her remedy altogether impracticable; that I could not take up at once another tone of voice. But she insisted that it could be done; that they would be with us for two weeks, would watch me closely and help to enforce the cure. I tried it, sang in most sessions of the convention, and preached the next Sabbath. My throat toughened and I have never from that day lost a religious or other service from diseased throat.

The hint may be worth the attention of other public speakers and singers.

Mr. Morgan adds: "I have long been accustomed to think of Mr. Bliss and speak of him as my *ideal* Christian gentleman—the most perfect specimen I had ever met."

21

CHAPTER XXVII.

THE village of Rome, Pennsylvania, contains a population of
about three hundred, and is located in the Wysocken Valley,
surrounded by high hills, and is about ten miles from Towanda,
Pennsylvania. The funeral services in memory of Mr. and Mrs.
Bliss were held on Sunday, January 7, in the Presbyterian Church,
of which both of them had been members during their residence in
Rome. Before the hour of service (11 o'clock), sleighs, from all
directions, coming over the hills loaded with the families of friends
and relatives from a distance, were arriving at the church. By
eleven o'clock it was crowded in every part. The following relatives
of the deceased were present: Lydia Bliss, his mother; Mrs. M.
E. Wilson and husband, and Mrs. Phebe Jennings and husband,
sisters and brothers; Wm. H. Jennings, of Chicago, nephew of Mr.
Bliss; Mrs. Andrus, sister of Lydia Bliss, with her son and daughter, the latter residing in Elmira, N. Y; the wife of Mr. McEwen,
who was present; Mrs. Betsy Allen, grandmother of Mrs. Bliss;
O. F. Young and wife, father and mother of Mrs. Bliss; A. P.
Young and wife, O. W. Young and wife, George R. Young, Mrs.
C. C. Barnes and husband, Mrs. J. L. Ellsworth, and Melita Young,
brothers and sisters of Mrs. Bliss; Nathan and Thomas Young,
Mrs. Daniel Pitcher, and Mrs. Dunham, uncles and aunts of Mrs.
Bliss, with their families; also several cousins and more distant
relatives were present. A remarkable fact in connection with this
large circle is that they are all Christians.

The services were opened by the reading of the hymn: " God is
the refuge of His saints," by Rev. Mr. Keatley, pastor of the Methodist church. Mr. and Mrs. McGranahan, life-long friends of Mr.
and Mrs. Bliss, and well known in musical circles, led the singing
of the congregation.

The following scriptures were read by the pastor of the Baptist Church : John xvii, 18–24 : Acts i, 7–11 : Acts vii, 55–60 : 1 Cor. xv, 12–23 and 50–58 : 1 Thess. iv, 13–18.

Prayer was then offered by Rev. G. W. Chandler, pastor of the Methodist Church of Towanda.

The hymn, " Rock of Ages " (set to music composed by Mrs. Bliss), was sung by the choir.

A report of a meeting held in Chicago, on the Sunday after the news of the disaster, was then read by Major Whittle, who made the following remarks, explaining the circumstances of the departure of Mr. and Mrs. Bliss from home and of his being on the ill-fated train :

We have to-day no remains of these beloved friends ; none will ever be found ; and I am asked to make a brief statement of the circumstances of their death. Mr. and Mrs. Bliss left their home the 30th of December and went to Towanda and Waverly. The last heard of them was a letter to the father on Thursday that they had bought tickets by way of the Lake Shore road, and expected to be in Chicago Friday night. The letter closed with the sentence, " God bless you all for time and eternity "—probably the last letter he ever wrote.

Mr. Bliss was expected in Chicago to help carry on the work of Messrs. Moody and Sankey. Saturday morning in Chicago, when I read of the terrible accident at Ashtabula, my heart was filled with fear, and I sent a telegram to Towanda to know whether they were there. It was some time before an answer could come. His friends supposed he was twelve or eighteen hours in advance of this train. During the day, while waiting, we went to the railroad office and tried to get dispatches from the train, but could only learn that it was a terrible accident, and that Mr. Bliss was not on the later train that left on Saturday afternoon. My alarm increased, but I could not take it home to my heart. But Saturday afternoon, a telegram was received from Mr Burchell, who knew Mr. Bliss intimately, saying that " Bliss, wife and children are among the dead." And we started immediately for Ashtabula. We arrived there on Sunday morning, and for three days I was there while the wreck was removed, and every search was made that could be to find some relic of these dear friends. The few bodies recovered were unrecognizable except in two or three instances. We thought then that the dear little children were there. And when the dispatch came from Towanda that the children were safe at home, I fell on my knees and thanked God that the children had been spared.

I came away Tuesday night. Everything had been removed. A stream of water five feet deep in the deepest and two feet in the shallowest part flowed by. The bottom was dragged. Eleven cars had fallen, one on top of another. The cars were broken in fragments. The lamps set fire to the oil. It was a fierce wind and a terribly stormy night. The woodwork, everything was burned, the iron melted and not a fragment of anything was left that we could find.

And so we are left here to-day with nothing of these friends but the thought of them in glory.

Mr. Burchell says he passed through the passenger coaches, and that at the last station before the accident "the snow was heavy and I got out," he says, "to get some sandwiches, and found the two ordinary cars crowded and the smoking-car full. The next, a parlor car, was one third full. Mr. Bliss and family were there. I was in the next car. Behind that were three sleeping-cars." He gave the statement "I believe Mr. Bliss got out through a window, expecting to get his wife and children through, but the car was blocked up and escape was impossible. I believe Bliss was burned to death trying to save his wife and children." This, he says, is his conjecture.

There is a story at Ashtabula of Mr. Bliss escaping and going back, saying his wife and child were in the wreck, and he would rather die with them than escape without them. I cannot find that this is true. That man had a wife and child there, and we know that Mr. Bliss had no child there. I suppose that some one seeing the man thought it was Mr. Bliss, and that gave rise to the supposition that the children were on board. We showed Mr. Bliss' picture to the passengers who were saved. We found one lady who recognized it.

As to how he came to be on the train : He left Waverly on the train which ought to have been at Buffalo at midnight on Thursday ; but it met with an accident twenty miles from Waverly, was delayed, and did not arrive in Buffalo until five o'clock—too late to make connection. He left that train at Hornellsville, probably thinking that as they could not connect, they would wait over and get a night's rest. I find his name at the Osborne House, Thursday night. He took the train in Buffalo Friday noon, and so was brought to Ashtabula to be in the accident. His trunk went on safely.

This is all we know of the story. We are here, a circle of friends and relatives, and I tell you the story as we know it.

A favorite hymn of Mr. Bliss "I know not the hour when my Lord will come," was then very beautifully sung by the choir. Mr. McGranahan, the composer of the music of this hymn, the words of which were written by Mr. Bliss, was so overcome as to be unable to conclude the singing.

An address was then given by the pastor of the First Congregational Church in Chicago, of which Mr. and Mrs. Bliss were members at the time of their death, Rev. E. P. Goodwin, D. D. For nearly three years Mr. Bliss had been chorister and Sunday School Superintendent at the church of which Mr. Goodwin is pastor. The following is Dr. Goodwin's address :

My friends, I feel that I have come here as a kind of representative of that great family that to-day all through the land bows under the grief that has gathered us, and mingles its tears and prayers with those of this dear circle.   Indeed, I seem almost to be a member of this household, so personal to me is this affliction.   This dear brother had been for years one with whom I had wrought for the Master in most delightful accord.   Our aims were one, our sympathies in unison, our friendship hearty, and one of these precious children bears, as you may know, my name.   I come hence not to speak in any formal way, but out of the depths of my heart to utter a few words of loving tribute to one whose character and work I delight to honor.

Let me connect what I have to say with two passages of Scripture, viz., Psalm cxvi, 15: "Precious in the sight of the Lord is the death of His saints." Rev. xiv, 13: "And I heard a voice from heaven saying unto me, Write, Blessed are the dead which die in the Lord from henceforth ; yea, saith the Spirit, that they may rest from their labors ; and their works do follow them."

Dear friends, God makes no mistakes.   He has made none in allowing the calamity which has gathered us here in sorrow, let us make none in reasoning about it.   The significance of God's Providences does not lie in what we think but in what God says about them.   In his testimony we can alone find sure anchorage for faith, sure solace for bereavement.   Our reasonings, apart from His Word, instead of scattering the darkness, often deepen it ; instead of lifting our burdens from our hearts, often magnify them and torture us with keener sense of helplessness.   We can as easily reason the darkness out of a room, as the darkness out of God's dealings.   We get rid of the gloom when we stop debate, open the shutters, and let the light shine in.   And we get rid of the gloom that enwraps us in these trial times of faith, when we stop arguing and throw open the windows of our souls to the light of God's Word.

The first thought, therefore, which I suggest in connection with this Providence is, that God's children are not to look upon death with dread, but to anticipate it with lightness of heart, and, by whatsoever form it may come, welcome and rejoice in it.   If the death of God's saints is precious in His sight, and the day in which it comes better than the day of birth, surely His children need not be dismayed ; much less need they go through life, as many do, oppressed and tortured by gloomy apprehensions of the last hour.   Where God's face beams, our faces ought to brighten.   Where God pronounces His benediction, and all the blessed of the Upper Presence join in special jubilee, we may at least dismiss our fears, and even though it be through tears, lift up our song.

I remember well when I could not say this.   Death was the one depressing, despairful word of all Scripture.   No sound ever sent such chills through my blood as the mournful knell that was wont to be rung out from the village church whenever there was a death in the community.   A funeral was of all places the place of terror.   The somber crape fluttering so forbiddingly at the door, the closed blinds, the hushed voices, the grave faces, the robes of the mourners, the tears and sobs, the sepulchral utterances of the minister, the mournful hymns—all this went to make a burial service distasteful and gloomy in the extreme.   From a child I never attended one, even of a relative, if it could be avoided.   This feeling was dominant for years.   Indeed, I was well on in the ministry, before the true teachings of Scripture were so apprehended as to break the hold of the pagan ideas which had begotten such dismay. But, thank God, the light of the Word as it is in these texts, and everywhere through these inspired utterances, came at last, and I saw death as a foe vanquished through Christ, its terrors all abolished, and the child of God privileged to go through life anticipating it as the hour of his grandest triumph, his highest exultation. Look now at the testimony of the Word. Even the Old Testament emphasizes this thought. The old patriarchs had no dread of dying. There is something beautiful even in the composure with which they heard the voice, and laid aside their tent-life for the better country. How significant the record that they "fell asleep," "were gathered to their fathers," "entered into rest." What more touching and home-like, and free from everything like fear, than the picture of a father, conscious that his last hour is close at hand, calling his children about his bed-side, declaring the fact of his near departure, giving them his dying counsels and benediction, and then quietly wrapping his mantle about him and lying down for the death angel to close his eyes. Take the death of Moses. First he was closeted with God! Then God rolled away the cloud from the mountain top, touched his eyes, and gave him a vision of that fair land, in all its length and breadth, which he had so coveted to enter. When He took him, as it were, in His arms, as a mother would take a child, and as the vision of the land of promise faded away, there came instead the vision of that other country, even the heavenly, of which the earthly inheritance was but the feeble type; and as its surpassing beauty burst upon his soul, he passed into the presence of the King and was clothed upon with a transfiguring glory. Who of us that would have drawn back dismayed from that dying hour, had it been permitted us to be there? Who that would have thought there was need of crape, or sable plumes, or melancholy dirges to befit that burial?

But Moses is no exception. Precious in the sight of the Lord is the death of every saint. And God putting underneath the everlasting arms, giving now our last earthward look over all that is loveliest and best, and then swinging the gates and giving us to stand within the city and join the everlasting song, what is this to all God's chosen but death stripped of its terrors, and the valley of the shadow transformed into the shining highway by which the children of the Kingdom enter into glory. By the witness of manifold Christian experiences there is blessed reality in this. How many times have we stood by the dying and seen the light of heaven break over the pale face, and all the lines of pain and trouble seem to be smoothed out as God has spoken to His chosen. And how many times have we seen the thin lips part while the countenance shone, and caught some feebly whispered word, jubilant testimony that death was robbed of its sting and the grave of its victory.

And this is the spirit of the Gospel. It knows nothing of dread, nothing of depression or dismay as connected with the dying of God's people. On the contrary every witness respecting it is of unqualified cheer. It is "falling asleep," "entering into rest," "going home," being "present with the Lord." It is hence that which is to be coveted, and to secure which is inestimable gain. Instead, therefore, friends, of going up and down in the world with despondency in our faces and wailings on our tongues because death confronts us and we cannot escape, let us know a more excellent way. Let us no longer borrow the eyes of pagan mythology and see death as a hideous demon roaming the earth for victims with an insatiate fury. Let us see him rather through the sweeter unveiling of the Gospel, a blessed angel of light come to set us free from burdens, toil, vexation, pain, everything that annoys, and to give us welcome into the ineffable and abiding blessedness of our Father's house.

It does not matter, as respects this sunny forelook, in what way death may come. We are wont to emphasize the terribleness of a catastrophe like this; and viewed in its physical aspects it is terrible beyond all comprehension. But this text-truth holds good, nevertheless. Can you imagine anything more torturing than the death that Stephen died; to be set up as a target for paving stones, and to have bone after bone broken and life fairly battered out? It makes one shudder to conceive of it. There must have been the keenest pain; but do you imagine Stephen's thoughts were absorbed in that? Ah, no. As the cries of rage rang in his ears, and the cruel missiles rained down upon him, there opened to him in the sky a vision of glory that made him forget everything else. He saw the heavens opened and the Son of Man standing on the right hand of God; and gazing upon that face, the face of his risen and glorified Lord, he no more heeded the crashing stones, no more the clamoring outcries, but with a prayer of forgiveness on his lips "fell asleep" as sweetly as a child.

Our brother's anticipations of death were all of this unclouded, hopeful kind. You find no word of gloom in his hymns, but when he touches the thought of death he almost invariably breaks out into a strain of peculiar exultation. Take that beautiful song, "That will be Heaven for Me," sung in the opening services. It reads like a prophecy, and it exactly represents its author's feeling.

> "I know not the hour when my Lord will come
> To take me away to His own dear home;
> But I know that His presence will lighten the gloom,
> And that will be glory for me."

Or take that other still more prophetic song, "There's a Light in the Valley:"

> I shall find down the valley no alarms,
> For my blessed Savior's smile I can see;
> He will bear me in His loving, mighty arms,
> There's a light in the valley for me.

Death, no matter what its form, had for Philip Bliss no terrors. He believed with all his soul, that Jesus Christ came to "abolish death," to destroy him that had the power of death—that is, the devil—and deliver them who through fear of death were all their life-time subject to bondage. Hence, though leading his life on in the daily expectation that the end might come, he was not only undismayed, but overflowing with gladness. I doubt not that if, after that terrific plunge, there was a moment of consciousness, his soul was full of peace, and was borne up in its chariot of fire with a shout of victory. And that serenity in facing death by whatever form it may come, and that triumph over it, it is the privilege of all God's children to have.

The other thought connected with these Scripture texts which I suggest is, that the kingdom of Christ is in no sense so related to human instrumentalities that when any of them drop out it suffers loss or hindrance. We are apt to think that it does. Our plans are largely conditioned by circumstances as to their results. If a crop fails, or a war breaks out, or a panic occurs, or sickness comes, our hopes are wrecked; and we are so conscious that we are hedged about by possible mishaps, and can forecast no plans which may not be frustrated, that we naturally think it must be so with God. Like us, He must have His forming times and seasons, must have His chosen instruments and agencies; and if these fail, there must be great difficulty in making their place good, and the kingdom, hence, be checked. We have a feeling that certain honored laborers are so thoroughly identified with the urging forward of the Gospel that they cannot be spared; that their place cannot be filled. Mr. Moody's words over the sad tidings were the instinctive utterance of thousands of Christian hearts: "Know ye not that a prince and a great man is fallen this day in Israel? Who shall take the place of this sweet singer, and carry on his noble work for Christ? It seems as if this consecrated voice and pen could not be spared, as if they had hardly crossed the threshold of their mission for the good of men and the glory of God." But I go back to the word of God, and the history of His church, and I say, God takes in all the meaning of this providence, and He has made no mistake. Suppose we had been among the chosen people when God called Moses up higher, and the question had been put to us, Can you spare Moses? Shall God take him and provide you with another leader? We should undoubtedly have made quick answer, "Spare Moses? the man whose counsel is as the word of the Everlasting One? him who communes with God face to face and holds back by his prayers the judgments we deserve? him who led us up out of Egypt, gave us our laws, our ritual of worship, and has brought us safely through all our enemies to the very borders of the land of promise! No, now more than ever we need him. The land bristles with sons of Anak, and is full of fenced cities, how can we possess it? We must have him for counselor, for intercessor, for captain of the host. Take any one else, but spare us Moses. If he be taken all hope dies." But God had other plans. He knew how to take Moses and yet provide for Israel so that they should go forward to the immediate possession of the land and the longed-for and abundant fruitage of their hopes.

Or, to put the case stronger, consider how indispensable, judged from a human standpoint, was the continuance in His work of the Lord Jesus Christ. He was the embodiment of the mind and heart of God. He knew all truth, and exactly how to unfold and apply it to men's hearts. He knew all wants, and woes, and wrongs, and was eager to put them all away. He was God incarnate, and down on men's level that He might feel the beating of their hearts, catch the cry of their need and break the curse of sin. How could He be spared, and men be equally helped, and His Gospel pressed on with equal potency? Who could open the blind eyes, unstop the deaf ears, empty all the hospitals, and asylums, and infirmaries as He did? Who could so unfold the words of heaven, bind up the broken hearts, cast out the evil spirits, prove to men that God had not forgotten the world nor had its control wrested from Him by the devil? Yet the work of Christ only spread itself over three and a half years; and before even that brief career is ended, we hear from his lips the strange words, "It is expedient for you that I go away."

But what was the effect of Christ's departure? Why, that after He left the world, there was more of Christ in it than before. The promise of the Comforter, conditioned upon His going away, was fulfilled, and the power of the Holy Ghost came upon the whole company of believers. And thus, while the Lord Himself ascends to heaven, there to carry on the work of His intercession for His Church, these anointed men and women, in whose hearts the one absorbing purpose is to magnify Jesus Christ, go out and are multiplied a thousand fold, and spread the knowledge of His Gospel to the very ends of the earth. Christ remaining in the world is a single personality, teaching, healing, saving, and keeping His band of followers clinging timidly to His skirts, only echoing faintly His words and repeating feebly His works. Christ gone from the world and ascended into glory is potentially Christ reproduced among all His disciples, and these going forth with unparalleled enthusiasm, boldness and power, preaching Christ's Gospel, re-enacting Christ's life among all the nations and ages. So is it of every great worker. When he seems to drop his toil, he only begins it. While he enters into rest, God takes up the work which he let fall, and sends it out with His indorsement to repeat and multiply itself while the world stands.

Do you suppose that when Charlotte Elliott wrote those words now so familiar in all lands:

Just as I am without one plea,

she dreamed of their destiny? She lived in one of the quiet, unknown hamlets of Old England; and hardly one in a score that sing this sweet song knows her name. But how God has taken that one hymn, born, doubtless, in the closet, and sent it round the world, and down through all generations to save souls and exalt Christ. So will it be of our brother's work. Already witness has come to us that these Gospel songs have been translated into Chinese; and not long since, a missionary in Southern Africa wrote home, that while on one of his tours to establish a station for preaching the Gospel, he heard what seemed familiar music in one of the native kraals which he was passing. Curious to know what was the occasion, he entered the hut and found the Zulu children all engaged in singing in their native dialect, "Hold the Fort!"

By a forelook kindred to this would God have us all inspired for our work. It may be true, it ought to be true of every loyal disciple, that the fruitage for Christ after death should be to that preceding it, as the harvests that wave over the prairies to the first handful of seed scattered thereon. And when such leaders as our brother are called home, not only will they being dead yet speak, but their very dying, instead of checking the Kingdom, shall urge it on.   There will be a Joshua to follow every Moses, an Elisha every Elijah, and working through all, the counsel that never knows defeat.

Turning now to some features of our brother's character which have impressed me, let me notice first, the wonderful sunniness or hopefulness which marked his life.   I think I might safely call him the most joyous Christian I have ever known.   It was a rare thing to see a shadow even transiently clouding his face.   I remember when he came to me with one of his Sunday School singing-books just ready for the press, and desired help as to a fitting name. While we were conversing, suddenly his countenance lighted up with the words, "I believe I have it: why not call it Sunshine?"   And some of you will recall how, on the cover there was emblazoned the full-orbed splendor of the sun.   So when the "Gospel Songs" came out, the cover bore the same device with an open Bible in the heart of the rays.   No symbol could have been more apt.   His life, if not always led on under a clear sky, always had the sun shining through the clouds.   Not that he was exempt from trials.   He had his share of earthly disappointments, and the keen discipline they bring.   He knew what it was to be misapprehended; to have mean and selfish motives attributed to him ; to be talked of as having a desire for self-glorification in leading the praise-service of the sanctuary ; to be accused of singing for pay. If any of you have known what it is to have the conceit fasten upon people's minds that you are other than you seem, sordid when you aim to be unselfish, hypocritical when you seek to be devout, you can understand Mr. Bliss' feelings under such imputations.   Yet he never gave visible token of it.   And he knew sore trials.   He knew what it is to stand by the bed-side of a beloved wife, and press the hand that seems growing chill with the frost of death, and be watching the face for the last look, and day after day looking for the dreaded end to come.   It was a marvel to me how he could go through this and be so calm. I thought it must be by a prodigious effort of will ; but I found, as I knew him better, that it was the consciousness of God's tender presence and upbearing love that sustained him.   His anchorage was within the vail, and he believed and proved that God would be as good as His word, and keep him in perfect peace whose mind was stayed upon Him.   So when the younger of these precious children seemed daily slipping out of his embrace, and he bent over the crib that he expected would so soon be empty, to take what might prove the last kiss, his hopefulness suffered no eclipse.   There seemed always to be an open door between his soul and the city of light.

As might be anticipated, his hymns and music are full of hope and exultation.   There is hardly a melancholy verse or strain among them all.   Almost invariably both songs and music swell and grow jubilant as they move on. Hallelujahs ring all through them.   And not a few, however they begin, land us in the glory of the better country before they close.   Glad tidings are indeed in them, and are their inspiration.

When the sweet singer put his magnificent voice into the rendering, charged with the fervor of his sympathetic soul, as it was his delight to do, they that listened had a hint of what the joy of the Upper Presence will be.   His buoyancy was contagious. I have known him, when a prayer meeting **dragged,** when very likely the minister was dispirited and others shared the **feeling,** to sweep his hand over the keys of the piano, and alike by touch and voice scatter the despondency as a burst of sunshine scatters fog ; and this because he sang as he felt. On one of the last occasions when he was with us, in a flying visit to our city made during his work as evangelist, he came in late and sat in the rear of the room. Espying him, I called him forward to sing the hymn entitled " My Prayer." He struck the piano keys, stopped, and reading the words in the latter part of the first stanza, " More joy in His service," said, " I don't think I can sing that as a prayer any more. It seems to me I have as much joy in serving the blessed Master as it is possible for me to bear."

And the very last time he was present in a prayer gathering, after listening to the testimony of a number of young converts, he stepped to the piano, and after a word expressive of his delight in hearing the new voices, he said he would sing a new song that he hoped would encourage those who had recently come out for Christ. Then in his own royal way, that thrilled every heart, he gave us " Hold Fast till I Come : "

> Oh spirit o'erwhelmed by thy failures and fears,
> Look up to thy Lord, tho' with trembling and tears ;
> Weak faith, to thy call seem the heav'ns only dumb ?
> To thee is the message, " Hold fast till I come."
>> Hold fast till I come,
>> Hold fast till I come ;
>> A bright crown awaits thee ;
>> Hold fast till I come.

This was his spirit always. Mr. Moody says God cannot use a discouraged Christian. If that be so, it is easy to see one prime factor of Brother Bliss' success in his work. He never lost heart, and so never compelled God to set him aside and use some one else.

And this is what the Master wants us all to be, what the world greatly needs to see,—buoyant, cheerful, singing believers. The current idea is that the religion of Christ is something burdensome, disheartening, a sort of sackcloth-and-ashes life, chiefly led on through humiliations, fightings, fears. Christian people are largely responsible for this. Like the children of Israel in the desert, we are always ready to murmur at the roughness of the way, the lack of comforts, the bitter handlings of Providence. Many grumble far more than they give thanks. They forget the daily manna, the sufficient grace, the fellowship of the Spirit, the better country. Oh, the darkness that settles on so many Christian faces, and the despondency that enwraps so many Christian lives. How little do we impress those that know us best as being the children of a King ! How seldom do they think of us as possessors of incalculable treasure, walking ever through green pastures, fearing no evil, having God's arms about us, and our faces shining with the joy of our communion with Christ and the anticipations of the glory that is only a few heart-beats away ! I fear that instead of this, as they see our somber faces and hear our dolorous witness, they think of treadmills and service under the lash. This ought not so to be. Dear brethren, let this life so overflowing with gladness help us to better things. Let it help us to that appropriation of our privileges as those who have been redeemed, delivered from condemnation, made now the children of God, the heirs of the kingdom, that shall banish doubt and keep the songs of jubilee breaking continually from our lips.

Another trait of our brother's character was his thorough unselfishness. It seems strange that he should have been even suspected of being sordid or eager for self-glorification. And yet there are those, as has been intimated before, that thought him covetous of praise and pay. Never was suspicion more groundless, nor was there the slightest taint of sordidness about him. When he entered upon his career as a Gospel singer, his profession was yielding him a handsome revenue, and (as his publishers have assured me) he was certain to realize affluence. He turned his back on these prospects, and like the brother with whom he was associated, he surrendered income and ambitions, and with a family to be cared for, unhesitatingly committed himself to a life that promised not a penny. And he never murmured, never was downcast and never regretted the decision. Some of the facts respecting this unselfishness are very significant as showing how completely this spirit ruled him. Take that grand tribute paid him by Mr. Moody in the Tabernacle at Chicago last Sabbath morning. He stated that the royalty on the Gospel Songs and Hymns amounted to $60,000. He proposed to Mr. Bliss that he should take $5,000 of this sum and provide himself with a home. Mr. Bliss promptly declined the offer. They had agreed, as he felt, that whatever income was derived from the books should be devoted to benevolent uses. And he added, that if his Master was able to go without a home, he was sure *he* could until some other way opened to secure it. Mr. John Church, the Cincinnati publisher of his music, said to me: "When Mr. Moody returned from Europe the last time, Mr. Bliss had nearly ready for publication a book which I am certain would have netted not less than $10,000 or $12,000. Notwithstanding, when Mr. Moody wished him to issue a volume jointly with Mr. Sankey for use in revival services, he at once complied, and without a word of regret over the great pecuniary sacrifice, transferred all his choicest songs and music to the new book." Such things were characteristic, not exceptional. He had what I fear comparatively few Christians have, a charity fund to which he sacredly devoted a given part of his income. I do not know what that proportion was, but it has come to my knowledge that on occasion it yielded $1,000 in six months. No matter what needs pressed, that fund was never invaded. And the significant thing about it was that it never seemed to run dry. He has put repeatedly into my hands sums ranging from $10 to $25 to be used among the poor. And when I expressed surprise at his being able to spare it, his reply was that God was very good to him and he never lacked. I have known him to hand his pocket-book to our church visitor after some recital of suffering or destitution, and tell her to help herself in behalf of those in need. I suspect that when the charity fund failed through the demands upon it, there was a fresh assignment of income. Would that more of the Lord's people would follow that practice.

Then our brother was always glad to lend himself to every service whereby he could lighten the burdens of any afflicted heart. He never spared himself in the line of ministering comfort at funerals, and services among the poor, and where the Shepherd had taken children to the upper fold. Now in the cottage of the day-laborer, now in the attics, or tenement houses where poverty and wretchedness abound, everywhere he was to be found scattering gloom, upbearing faith, solacing aching hearts, preaching Christ with the marvels of his song. How often as he sang have the tears and sobs ceased and the light broken in on the faces full of dismay! There are many homes where the music of that voice bringing God's comforts to the soul in its trouble, lingers in a memory that will never die.

So when our brother sang, as he so often did, by the bedsides of God's afflicted children, he was greatly blessed in bringing out the bright side of God's providences. I have in mind a sister to whom the night brings no darkness and the day no sun, who rarely missed a visit from this pilgrim singer when he was in the city. And I have it from her lips that when that silver voice rang through her heart, and set forth the Christian's hope and triumph, her repinings ceased, her depression passed away, and forgetful of herself she was filled with joyful thoughts of Christ, and with the spirit of acquiescence in His will.

Naturally this unselfishness found its highest expression in devotion to the work of winning souls. Always single-hearted, and faithful in using his opportunities for doing good, after he took up evangelistic labor he came to have a peculiar intensity of zeal in spiritual things. He hungered for more knowledge of Christ, more of the indwelling power of the Spirit, and this to the end that he might save men. In his later years, this desire was very marked. His testimonies in social meetings always emphasized it; his daily conversation had it for a constant theme; his appeals to Sabbath School children, his songs were full of it. Even his ordinary correspondence, not only that of a friendly character, but that relating to business, was permeated with it. From the letters I have seen, I am constrained to believe that during the last three years, those letters, of whatever kind, were exceptional, that did not contain some word of earnest witness, encouragement or appeal in behalf of Christ and His salvation. I saw, the other day, a purely business letter in which toward the end was a most affectionate entreaty to accept Christ and live for Him. I remember a letter to a member of the choir, in which he pressed upon her very earnestly the claims of her Savior, and she traces to that appeal the beginning of her life of faith. And how many of you can bear like witness to his solicitude for your salvation? In how many of your homes has he prayed during his transient home visits? With how many of you has he had personal interviews concerning your eternal welfare? How faithful he was to his Master and to you in these days of his last fellowship on earth. When he instituted those Bible readings and plead for souls, neither you nor he dreamed the end was so near, and that this was his last work for the Lord he loved. But if he had known it, wherein could he have been more faithful? Up and down this valley he went day after day, telling the old, old story, and seeking to persuade all who heard, to believe and be saved ; and, as I learn, nearly a score of new-born souls rejoice to-day in the hope of eternal life through these labors.

This was his spirit always. He never had a choir rehearsal that was not opened with prayer ; and the burden of his prayer was, that the singing might exalt Christ. In the center of one of the stained windows of the transept of the church was a large crimson cross, and around it the words, "God forbid that I should glory save in the cross of our Lord Jesus Christ." Mr. Bliss often called attention to that symbol and its motto, and said, "I am glad the cross is always before us when we sing. Let us seek to forget ourselves and magnify Christ."

A little incident that occurred at the time of the burning of our church, in January, 1873, illustrates this. The front gable of the church was surmounted by a large cross, and underneath it was an immense window studded with purple stars. As the flames rolled up from within, the starry emblazonry shone out very beautifully ; and when, climbing higher, they fairly garlanded the cross and, standing there among the gleaming stars, it seemed to dash the fiery billows back as with majestic disdain, the sight was grandly impressive. Coming up to a young man, a member of the Sabbath School, Mr. Bliss laid his hand upon his shoulder, and said, "James, why not give your heart to the Savior to-night ? Why not come to the cross this very hour ? See it yonder ! it was never so beautiful, never so dear to me as now." And I have it from the lips of the young man, now a member of the church, that those words on the pavement brought him to a decision, and then and there he planted the cross in his heart. So this dear brother wrought ever. And no words could more truly set forth the one absorbing purpose that ruled his life, than those of one of his later and most effective pieces :

My only song and story
Is—Jesus died for me ;
My only hope of glory
The cross of Calvary.

Would that the thousands of Christian people whose hearts are saddened by this providence, might, through it, come to know a spirit of like coveting of souls.

I name as a final characteristic that our brother was preëminently a singer of the Gospel. Taking both songs and music into the estimate, I think I may safely call him the Gospel singer of the age. Certainly I know of no one in the whole range of hymnology that has put Gospel truth into song with the clearness, and fullness and power which stamps the compositions of P. P. Bliss. Many of his songs, especially his later ones, are little else than Scripture versified and set to music. Take, for example :

"Jesus of Nazareth Passeth By,"
"Free from the Law,"
"Look and Live,"
"Whosoever Will may Come,"

"Hear ye the Glad Good News from Heaven?"

"Almost Persuaded,"

"Seeking to Save,"

"No Other Name."

There is Gospel enough in almost any one of them to lead a troubled soul to Christ. And in no hymns with which I am acquainted, not even Charles Wesley's, is the doctrine of salvation by the blood of Christ as the sacrifice for sin, so clearly stated, so fully emphasized; and no wonder—these songs were born in the closet and at the foot of the cross.

This is why, as Mr. Moody testifies, no songs so lay hold of people's hearts. In words and music they are surcharged with the very spirit of the Gospel. And herein lies the secret of the power which they are destined to wield in after years. Take the hymns that have wrought themselves imperishably into the affections of God's people, such, for example, as:

"Rock of Ages,"

"Just as I am,"

"Nearer, my God, to Thee,"

"Jesus, Lover of My Soul,"

"All hail the Power of Jesus' Name,"

and what is the reason of the place they hold? Obviously this, that they embody truths which go to the heart of the Gospel, truths that have to do with the most vital experiences of the soul in seeking and working out salvation. So of these songs of Philip Bliss. And this is why the Chinese and the Zulus sing them. They do not sing "Hail Columbia," or the "Star Spangled Banner." They do not care for the story of our native land; they have no interest in either its past or its future. But the story of Jesus Christ, of the Lamb slain that sinners might have pardon, that story finds a response in their hearts. They know they are in darkness. They know they are in trouble. They know the curse of sin binds its yoke upon their souls, keeps its cry of woe upon their lips. And when they hear these songs, they recognize the offer of help, the opening up of a way of deliverance. In a word, the conscious want of men the world over is Christ, and these songs preach Him. They press him so fully, that if a ship were wrecked among the South Sea Islands, where no missionary has ever yet set foot, and the survivors should have no Bliss, nothing but a copy of the "Gospel Songs," I should expect in five years to find churches and Sunday Schools and revivals and missions among the heathen round about.

They have been most wonderfully blessed already. At the farewell meeting in London, after the labors of Brother Moody and Brother Sankey were closed in that city, Lord Shaftesbury said that "if Mr. Sankey had done no more than teach the people to sing 'Hold the Fort,' he would have conferred an inestimable blessing on the British Empire." Mr. Sankey bears witness that these songs laid hold of the English people with wonderful power. Major Cole says, "the ragged children of London, children who are largely street waifs, living in the utmost ignorance and degradation, flocked to hear and sing these songs till they had ten thousand of them at a gathering. And to this day, they are to be heard on the streets, in the courtyards, stables, shops, factories, homes, everywhere. Mothers rock their babes to sleep with them alike among the rich and the poor. Nobility and peasantry find common inspiration in them, and to the suffering and dying of every rank they minister inexpressible blessing.

But their grandest work, at home and abroad, has been in preaching the Gospel and winning souls. Let me give a single illustration of many connected with the recent revival services in Chicago. One of the reformed inebriates says that he had been for years one of the hardest of drinkers. His friends had given him up as a hopeless case, and he had given up himself and expected to die as he lived, and meet a drunkard's awful doom. In this condition he came to Chicago, and one day, when more than half-intoxicated, wandered aimlessly with the crowd into the Tabernacle, and found a seat in the gallery. He was too intoxicated to know much about what was going on, and did not remember anything about the text or the sermon. During the evening, Mr. Sankey sang " What shall the Harvest be ? "   And when he came to the words—

<blockquote>
" Sowing the seed of a lingering pain,
Sowing the seed of a maddened brain,
Sowing the seed of a tarnished name,
Sowing the seed of eternal shame ;
O, what shall the harvest be ? "
</blockquote>

the singer's voice rang through the inebriate like a trump of judgment, and fairly sobered him. The conscience so long dead was roused and began to lash him with the words of the song. His wasted, wretched life passed in painful review before him. The promise of his youth blighted, the ambitions and hopes of manhood turned to ashes, his family beggared and disgraced ; his name a byword of shame, his friends among the pure and good all alienated and his fellowship only with the low and vile, his whole career one dark, damning record of folly and sin, and before him a gathering night of hopeless despair—he could not endure the torment of such a vision. It was hell before the time. So he went out and tried to drown the song in drink. But it would not die. It rang in his ears by day and by night, and forced him again and again to the Tabernacle. By and by his sin so burdened him that he went to Mr. Sawyer's inquiry room, and there God met him, took his feet out of the horrible pit, planted them on the Rock and put a new song into his mouth. And now he is doing with his might to help others bound by the same curse find the blessed liberty of the Gospel.

This is only one case of scores, that during this single revival have been led into the kingdom through the agency of these hymns. So it has been elsewhere, so it will continue to be. I believe, with Mr. Moody, that God raised up Philip Bliss as truly as Charles Wesley to save men by singing the Gospel. And herein lies the guaranty of a mighty harvest of souls in the days to come. Few of us have ever read John Wesley's or Isaac Barrow's sermons ; but there are none of us who do not sing Charles Wesley's hymns, and Isaac Watts' versions of the Psalms. The preacher's horizon relatively to the singer's is an exceedingly narrow one. He may reach the men of his city, his country, his age, possibly a handful in other lands and in after years; but the singer's voice ranges all lands, all ages. Not only does it not die, but it gathers potency with every cycle of years. Such hymns as Rock of Ages, Just as I Am, My Faith looks up to Thee, will be sung as long as there are saints to be helped or sinners to be saved. Every generation will only widen their influence and magnify their power as agencies which God delights to honor. I do not hesitate to say that some of my Brother Bliss' songs will go down the future side by side with these in their ministry of Christ and salvation. And the fruitage of his life before God called him, blessed as it was, compared with that which shall yet be garnered, will prove only as the first fruits to an ingathering that only the arithmetic of heaven can measure. He dropped the seeds by handfuls, but the harvest shall wave like Lebanon.

While I say these things, I do not forget how thoroughly identified with our brother in all his aims and work, was his dear wife, over whose early going home we both mourn and rejoice to-day. She not only cheerfully accepted the call of Providence which took her husband so largely from home, but with constant and potent aid of voice and pen she helped to crown his work with an abundant success. He appreciated such coöperation, and often recognized it, saying that he "was more indebted to his wife than any one else for what he was and what he had done." "Lovely and pleasant in their lives, in their death they were not divided." Their memories are alike precious, and their works will alike follow them.

In the mountains of the Tyrol, it is the custom of the mothers, and wives and children to go forth when the twilight gathers, to welcome home their husbands, and fathers and sons, from their care of the flocks up the mountain heights. And as they go they sing a strain or two of some national air, and then listen, till apparently from the clouds there float down to them the answering refrains, and they know that all is well, and that ere long they will see the faces and be clasped in the arms of those they love. Something so may we not venture to imagine it here. In the deepening twilight of our sorrow we lift our eyes to the uplands of the better country, longing for the fellowship of these dear departed ones. And as we look, the sweet strains they taught us and which we were wont to sing together, break instinctively from our lips, and lo, in the pauses of our song there seems to float down to us from the heavenly heights the refrain borrowed from our lips, "Watching and waiting for you." Dear friends, we are the pilgrims, and these who have gone before are the ones at home. And a little way on, a few more steps only of this rough and thorny way, after a few more pains, and griefs, and tears, and a little more blessed toil for Christ and for souls, we shall receive their welcome, share their joy, and abide in our Father's house forever.

I should be unfaithful to the spirit of my brother, and to the significance of this Providence, if I did not add a word of solemn admonition. Dear friends, you have been wont, some of you, to meet the appeals of the Gospel for your personal acceptance of Christ, with that old excuse, "when I have a convenient season." Very possibly you used it, or had it in your thought, when you

22

were pressed by my brother during these last meetings held here the week before he died. You may have sat where you now do, and as his loving eye searched you out, and his tender entreaty fell on your ear, you may have answered, " Yes, I ought to decide for Christ, I ought to make sure of the salvation of my soul, and when I have a convenient season, I will." Ah, that hoary lie, how many souls it has deluded into perdition. What a mighty witness this catastrophe to the Scripture doctrine—*now* is the accepted time. Suppose our brother had gone through that train on that fatal evening and said to his fellow-travelers, " We propose to have a little Gospel meeting in the parlor car. We will sing a few hymns, have a word or two of Scripture, and a few testimonies and prayers as any feel inclined. We should be glad to have you there." Suppose, further, that such a meeting had been held, and that just before the train reached Ashtabula, Mr. Bliss had said : " Friends, this has been a delightful hour. It has made heaven seem very near, and eternal things very real. It is not to be expected that we shall ever meet again, and now before we part, I feel impressed to invite any who have not yet accepted Christ, to receive Him now. Now He stands at the door. Now the Spirit calls. To-morrow may be too late. I will sing a little song and while I sing, will not those present without conscious peace with God, make the great decision." Then, after singing in his touching way " Almost Persuaded," imagine that just as the whistle sounded for their last stop, he closed the meeting. What various comments would have followed. Let us hope that there would have been one or two at least to accept the offered salvation and to pass from death unto life. But the greater number would doubtless have stood aloof. Some would have said, " This gentleman sings well, I should like to hear him in a concert where they had something besides hymns." Some, " This matter of salvation *is* of great importance ; I have often wished I were a Christian, and when New Year's comes round I believe I will set about being one in earnest." Others, "These evangelists are all alike ; they don't think it impertinent to interrupt a game of cards, as this one did ours, or a pleasant story, or conversation. Then they are always talking about 'blood,' and 'wrath,' and despair, and making every one feel so uncomfortable. I wish they would keep their religion to themselves." Possibly some would have sneered, and as they stepped on board as the train started from Ashtabula, said, " what folly to be frightened into getting on one's knees and crying for forgiveness here on the cars ! There will be time enough for that when we get home. They are having a revival in our town, and the true place to settle such a question is a church, or a man's home." Then a moment of adjustment to their places, the cards dealt, the books resumed, the jests exchanged, the storm noted and their watches examined to see how late they would be at Cleveland : then that terrific plunge— the convenient season forever beyond their reach !

Oh, friend, if you are here unsaved, let the voice of this dreadful calamity emphasize that one word *now*. The word of God has no invitation, no promise for to-morrow. Repent *now*. Believe *now*. Escape for thy life *now*. May God help you every one to believe this day on the Lord Jesus Christ and to be saved.

At the close of Mr. Goodwin's address, Major Whittle announced as a closing song a hymn that had just been found among Mr. Bliss' papers—probably his latest work—entitled "He Knows." He remarked that had Mr. Bliss desired to leave a special message of comfort to his bereaved friends appropriate to their present calamity, he could not have left anything more beautiful or more comforting.

> So I go on in the dark, not knowing;
>   I would not if I might;
> I would rather walk with God in the dark
>   Than walk alone in the light;
> I would rather walk with Him by faith
>   Than walk alone by sight.

Before the singing of the hymn Major Whittle briefly addressed the people as follows :

I cannot but say a word to God's people who are here in this village. It seems to me that Christian men and women here should consecrate themselves anew to God. It is not a light thing to have the providence of God come to any of us as it has come to you. You have had two of God's servants among you. Mrs. Bliss stood shoulder to shoulder with her husband, consecrated to God, ripening for Heaven ; a noble, Christian woman ; my sister in Christ Jesus. I loved her as I loved her husband. You have had these two servants of God and they have left their testimony here. Dear friends, I would not want to die in this village professing to be a Christian, and go up to God with a barren record.

Some of you went to school with them and know how right down thorough they were. Take up this work. Let the memory of this dear brother inspire us. Let his songs inspire us. His heart was here in Rome. He prayed for you here in Rome. He loved these hills. This valley was dear to him.

A year ago he started a union Sabbath School, for he loved the children. Consecrate yourselves anew to this work. Let his name be attached to a union Sunday School. And as the echo of his glorious voice has rung over these hills, may it never die away till we are called to meet him in glory.

You loved that noble man as a brother. You loved his wife, that dear, dear sister. You could not bear to have a word said against him. But you grieved Philip Bliss in the deepest sympathy of his heart. When he looked back upon these hills for the last time, he carried away an ache in his heart that many of you had a part in putting there. You never have given your hearts to his Savior. Philip Bliss loved Jesus Christ; and that anybody that he loved should not love Jesus Christ made his heart ache. All the best impulses of your heart are upon the side of Jesus. My friends, I beg of you in the name of Christ, in the name of Philip Bliss, in the name of his dear wife who grew up in your valley, and is now in Heaven, I beg of you, young women, young men, middle aged, give your hearts to God.

I do pray God that this may be a blessed day to this valley, to these pastors, and to friends all. And I want Brother Goodwin to lead us in prayer before we sing, that we may consecrate ourselves to the service of our Master, and that you will decide: I take Philip Bliss' Savior as my Savior, his God as my God.

The Elmira (New York) *Advertiser*, from which we have largely drawn for the materials for this chapter, says :

"The services were about two hours and a half in duration and were very solemn and impressive throughout. The many relatives of the deceased, and the fact of this having been the home of their childhood, and many present remembering them as schoolmates and early friends, made it seem to the whole community like a household grief. Never has any event in the history of this beautiful valley so profoundly moved its population. Mr. and Mrs. Bliss were enthroned in the hearts of the people. Their memory will linger long round those beautiful hills and among the people of the Wysocken Valley ;—the place they loved to call their earthly home. His last labor for the Master was done here. During the two weeks of his holiday visit he held almost nightly meetings and visited from house to house, inviting his friends to accept Christ. God blessed his labors, and a score or more during his visit turned to the Savior.

" At an afternoon service on the day of the funeral, many more who had been impressed during Mr. Bliss' labors publicly manifested their decision to accept Christ and commence a Christian life.

" By special request, a union meeting was also held in Towanda in the evening—a memorial service participated in by all the pastors and people. Rev. Darwin Cook, pastor of Mr. and Mrs. Bliss twenty years ago in Rome, who gave Mr. Bliss his first encouragement to devote himself to the composition of music, and who married them, was present and offered prayer. Upon invitation, at the close, a large number rose as desiring the prayers of Christians that they might enter into a Christian experience."

CHAPTER XXVII.

FOR the account of the memorial services held in Chicago, we are much indebted to the daily newspapers, and have in part adopted their language as our own, as it eloquently portrays the character of the services and the deep feeling betrayed by the people.

A large congregation assembled at the Tabernacle on Sunday morning, December 31, 1876. Mr. Moody had announced a sermon on "The Return of Our Lord," but from the drapery of mourning around the platform and the galleries, with its heavy lines and festoons of black and white, and the pure beautiful white crowns which stood upon the speaker's stand, it was evident that, instead of the coming of the Lord to us, the topic of the morning was to be the departure of loved ones to Him. The announcement in the papers that Mr. Bliss, with his entire family, had perished in the fearful wreck of the railway train at Ashtabula, Ohio, fell with such weight upon the ears and hearts of his thousands of friends in Chicago, that for hours it was impossible for them to realize it, or even to believe it to be true. But, if any of them went with lingering hopes to the meeting, one look at the great Tabernacle with its emblems of death overhanging the promises of eternal life which are inscribed on its walls, was sufficient to show that the only hope of ever seeing or hearing this sweet singer of our Israel again was in joining him on the other shore. Four crowns all together, and all for one family! Not often does heaven bestow so lavishly. One for Paul, one for "Paulina," one for the son who bore his father's name, and one for little George Goodwin ; these crowns are woven of pure white camellias and lilies, but those crowns are made of "glory."

While the congregation was assembling the choir sang softly and lovingly several of the favorite hymns written by the man whose name Death had written on the tablets of history, and whose record

God had written in the Book of Life.　Presently Mr. Moody ent
and, as all eyes were turned to see how this man, twice broken u
the weight of affliction since these meetings began, would
himself, and as all ears were listening for his first word in his ;
sorrow, he stood up in his place and, with manifest trouble to
back the sobs and tears, he repeated those words of David, " E
ye not that there is a Prince and a great man fallen in Isr:
Then, almost unable to speak for weeping, he said, " Let us lit
our hearts to God in silent prayer."　A long period of silence
lowed, broken at length by signs of overpowering emotion, ir
midst of which the voice of Dr. Chamberlain was heard g
thanks to God for the hope of eternal life, on behalf of this e
household who had been borne on angels' wings from the pla
terror and death up to the bosom of God.

The congregation then joined in singing: "In the Christ
Home in Glory there Remains a Land of Rest;" after v
Mr. Moody arose and said :

I was to take up the subject of our Lord's return, but I cannot contr
feelings so as to speak as I intended.　I will take up that subject at ai
time.　When I heard last night that Mr. Bliss and his whole famil
perished, at first I could not believe it, but a despatch from a friend who w
the train took away all hope, and left me face to face with death.　For the
three months I have seemed to stand between the living and the dead, and
I am to stand in the place of the dead.　Mr. Whittle and Mr. Bliss
announced to hold the 4 o'clock meeting in the Tabernacle to-day, and
Mr. Farwell, and Mr. Jacobs, and Mr. Whittle, with other friends, have go
see if they can find his remains to take them away for burial.　I have
looking over his hymns to see if I could find one appropriate to the occ
but I find they are all like himself, full of hope and cheer.　In all the y
have known and worked with him I have never once seen him cast down.
here is a hymn of his that I thought we might sing.　Once after the wre
that steamer at Cleveland, I was speaking of the circumstance that the
lights were out, and the next time we met he sang this hymn for me ; it
sixty-fifth in our collection ; let us sing it now.　It begins, " Brightly bean
Father's mercy," but still more brightly beams the light along the sh
which he has passed.　It was in the midst of a terrible storm he passed
but the lights which he kindled are burning all along the shore.　He ha
young,—only about 38 years old,—but his hymns are sung round the '
Only a little while ago we received a copy of these hymns translated in
Chinese language.

In spite of the mourning it is sweet to think that this whole family
away together, father and mother, Paul, only 4 years old, and little George

2 years old, all gone home safe together. There comes a voice to us saying, "Be still and know that I am God," but we know that "our Father doeth all things well."

The sixty-fifth hymn was then sung.

Mr. Sankey read from a letter he had received from Mr. Bliss near his old home in Towanda, Pa., in which his happy faith in God and his love for his dear old mother were sweetly expressed.

Rev. Dr. Goodwin, of whose church Mr. Bliss had for many years been a loved and honored member, then came forward and said:

Ever since these sad tidings came I have been trying to say, "Not my will, but Thine be done." I don't know of any death that has come so near to me. For years I have been almost as a part of that household; one of the little ones bore my name; we have worked and prayed together, and I have known very much of his heart in connection with the great mission of his life, and shared in his ever-increasing delight that God was using him and his music so wonderfully. It was hours after the awful news came before I could see any light, but at last I seemed to see a vision of a great praise service in heaven with Brother Bliss leading it—he was to have led a praise meeting at our Sunday-school this afternoon—and then I found light in this darkness. Out of the fifty Sunday-school scholars who are now waiting to be received into the fellowship of our church, there is hardly one but can bear witness to his helpfulness in leading them to Christ. This morning it seems wonderful to me that this whole family should be taken up together, all at once, to enter the world of praise and take up the new song; a full household now, for one had gone before. Out of this affliction has come to them an exceeding and eternal weight of glory, and so I begin to feel it, as well as say it, all is well, all is well. It is not that the Lord does not care for us; but "Precious in the sight of the Lord is the death of His saints," and "The day of his death is better than the day of his birth." Thirty-five times have I been called this year to comfort the mourning ones in my congregation, and the thought has come to me of a little praise meeting in Heaven to-day of those who have come up from that First Congregational Church. This is not the time to speak as I would like to speak, but this I can say, that no man is so identified with the work of the Lord but that God can glorify him, and still carry on the work. Here is that thirteenth hymn which Mr. Bliss sung for us the other night. He began by saying, "Brethren, I don't know as I shall ever sing here again (and he never did), but I want to sing this as the language of my heart."

"Let us sing that hymn," said Mr. Moody, which was done.

The next speaker was Rev. Dr. Thompson, who had only the previous evening returned from a double funeral service among his relatives in another State, to which he had been summoned by telegraph, and where he had been singing the hymns of Brother Bliss at the bedside of the sick at the very hour of the awful calamity. He has learned, said the Doctor, the form of his mansion fair, and the song that the angels sing. "A few days ago I received a letter from a friend who had been annoyed at the charge that Brother Bliss sang for gain, and desiring me to disprove it if I could; and when I spoke to him about it, he said, with a smile: 'I sing for Christ; I have not even a home to my name.' His songs are sung round the world, and it seems to me they are sung in glory, too. By and by the work of the preacher will be done, but the singing will go on forever; singing the name of Jesus and the triumph of the redeemed."

After further remarks by Mr. Moody, prayer was offered by Rev. Dr. Williamson, especially in behalf of the mother of the deceased. The twenty-second hymn was then sung—"We're Going Home."

Mr. Moody then appointed two committees; the first to raise money and erect a monument to the memory of the dead, consisting of Messrs. T. W. Harvey, J. V. Farwell, Henry Field, and J. D. Sankey. Mr. Henry Field, of Field, Leiter & Co., was appointed treasurer of this fund, to whom all contributions may be addressed. Mr. Moody requested that as there were so many who would want a share in this work of love, that none should give more than a dollar.

A collection was then taken for that purpose, the only one ever taken in the Tabernacle.

The other committee was to draft resolutions and communicate them to the friends of the deceased. It consists of the Rev. Messrs. Goodwin, Bishop Cheney, Dr. Parkhurst, Dr. Everts and Dr. Petric.

The benediction was pronounced by the Rev. Mr. Walker.

At the afternoon services, the Tabernacle was more than comfortably filled. Those who were there wore on their countenances a funeral aspect. Around the pulpit and along the gallery were long stretches of white and black muslin, festooned in grieving recollections of Mr. Bliss' untimely end. A spirit of sadness prevailed, and the religion that teaches that the death of good men should bring no mourning in its train seemed to bring very little consolation to the vast number of sorrowing friends, so sudden had been their bereavement.

The usual exercises opened with music.

> I gave my life for thee,
>   My precious blood I shed
> That thou might'st ransomed be
>   And quickened from the dead—
> I gave, I gave My life for thee ;
> What hast thou given for Me ?

Mr. Moody had hoped for some better news, he said ; hoped that it might turn out to be a mistake, but a late despatch from Maj. Whittle dispelled all this, and confirmed the first horrible report of the death of Mr. Bliss and his family, whose remains had been recovered though not recognizable.

Mr. Sankey sang "Watching and Waiting for Me," and the audience were still as death as the beautiful words rang out.

Mr. Moody said that he had looked forward to this Sabbath to hear Maj. Whittle preach and Mr. Bliss sing. Only Friday night he had told his wife that he was weary, and he anxiously awaited the rest this Sunday promised. But now he found he must take Maj. Whittle's place. Only one text suggested itself to him, and had been ringing in his head all day: "Therefore be ye also ready." He called on those who had heard him preach for three months to bear him witness that he had said nothing about death, confining himself to life. But it might be that before long God might lay him away, and send some one to take his place, and he could not forbear saying a word urging upon all the necessity of regeneration and preparation. His voice was more subdued than usual, and in all he said and in all his readings from the Scriptures, it came tremulously and mingled with tears. He spoke painfully and with difficulty, the words sometimes utterly unintelligible. "Be ye therefore ready. Don't put it off. There are some who may say I am preaching for effect and making use of this good man's death to frighten you." Satan might even say that of him and say it truly. He was preaching for effect, and he hoped the effect would be to save the soul of every human being before him. He felt that he must warn them—must warn them of the wrath to come and the death pursuing. That death hath sent many a warning during the year, and now an awful one had come. Many of them had looked down upon the dead faces and opened graves of departed friends. Would they not heed those warnings? Would they not heed this last one, that might be even nearer to themselves than any before? Death had taken them by surprise, and

had taken Mr. Bliss at the very time the speaker was writing out the
notices of Bliss' appearance to-day. He and his wife were snatched
from life. But they were ready. They might have suffered for a few
minutes, maybe for an hour, but when they reached heaven there
was none in all the celestial choir that sang sweeter or played better
on his golden harp than P. P. Bliss.

He would rather have been on that train and taken that awful
leap, and died like P. P. Bliss and his wife, than had them go as they
did. And every man would feel so who knew God and was ready
to die. Oh! might they profit by the calamity.

Mr. Moody prayed long and earnestly for the unsaved souls, and
invoked the richest outpourings of mercy on the obstinate hearts.
At times during the prayer he stopped for some minutes, utterly
unable to control his emotions.

Then came a silent prayer, during which about two dozen arose
on invitation, to be remembered in the invocation.

"Rock of Ages," sung by the congregation, closed the services.

The morning services on the same day, at the Chicago Avenue
Church—widely and popularly known as "Mr. Moody's Church"—
were conducted by Messrs. Moody and Sankey. Mr. Sankey sang
several of his Gospel solos, one, "When Jesus Comes," a favorite of
Mr. Bliss, creating a profound impression on the audience. The
whole service—hymns, prayers, and sermon—had reference to the
sad end of Mr. Bliss and the dreadful railroad accident of Friday.

Prior to the sermon Mr. Moody offered up a fervent prayer for
Divine help to sustain them in the sad bereavement which had come
upon them.

During the sermon which followed, Mr. Moody said:

This being the last day of the year, I had been looking forward to it as one
of the most solemn days of the year, and I had prepared some thoughts to bring
out on this occasion. But little did I think it was going to be as solemn as it
is. My thoughts have been drifted into another channel entirely. A text came
into my mind when I heard of the sudden death of Mr. Bliss and his family.
He was coming to the city to fill his appointment here to-day. He was to have
been with us this morning, and it seems almost as if I am standing in the place
of the dead. It is always solemn to stand between the living and the dead, as
a preacher does; but it is a great deal more solemn to step into a dead man's
shoes, as I feel to have done to-day. The text that occurred to me is in the
twenty-fourth chapter of Matthew and the forty-fourth verse: "Therefore be
ye also ready." Death often took us by surprise, but it did not find Mr. Bliss

unprepared. He and his wife had been ripening for heaven for years, and I have been thinking of that family before the throne this morning singing the sweetest song they had ever sung. We should profit by this awful calamity. God is coming very near this city; there was never before such an inquiring after God as there is now; and this last stroke of Providence ought to be a warning to every one to get in readiness to meet the Lord. If you do not take this warning I do not know what would move your hearts. There are three things every man and woman ought to be ready for—life, death, and judgment. Life is uncertain; no man can tell at what hour or in what manner Death may visit him. Accidents like the one which occurred Friday are by no means uncommon, and may strike down any one of us. It therefore behooves every man to place his trust in Christ, so that he might be prepared to meet Him at any moment.

On the evening of the 5th of January, an additional service was held at the Tabernacle. Inside the building there were at least 8,000 people; outside there were 4,000. The exercises were to be more than ordinarily interesting, for it was to be a song-service in memory of Mr. Bliss. Early in the evening the crowd assembled to pay their last tribute, anxious to assist in the rites. The Tabernacle was filled. The doors were locked. Those inside patiently awaited the exercises. Outside, the unfortunates pulled and pushed and crowded against the building and begged and implored the inexorable doors to open unto them. It was of no avail. Until the service was ended the disappointed held possession of the sidewalks, hoping to hear through the open windows, even if they could not participate.

The whole service was musical, with a brief introduction to the hymns by Mr. Moody and short prayers.

> Hallelujah! 'tis done, I believe on the Son,
> I am saved by the blood of the Crucified One,

and the congregation took up the chorus. "Hold the Fort" came next, the children singing the fourth verse and the choir the refrain. There were hundreds of young voices and they sang with a will. Mr. Moody related the circumstances under which the hymn was written.

"Beneath the Cross of Jesus," a hymn not so well known apparently as the rest, was sung exquisitely by Mr. Sankey. Then Mr. Moody prefaced "Roll on, Oh! Billow of Fire," with an anecdote of its basis. To the children again was committed the twenty-third hymn, "I am so glad that Jesus loves me." They sang sweetly, and at the conclusion there was a rattle of applause in the audience. "Whosoever will may come," brought the congregation to their feet.

"At one of the Expositions," said Mr. Moody, "a common invitation was, 'Meet me at the Fountain,' and upon this Mr. Bliss wrote the hymn, 'Will you meet me at the Fountain?'" Mr. Sankey sang it.

"Precious promise God hath given," and Mr. Moody read the twenty-third psalm, and Mr. Sankey sang, "There's a Light in the Valley for Me." "Weary Gleaner, Whence Cometh Thou?" Mr. Moody spoke of the Gospel meetings in New York, where the service had been entirely of song. He thought such meetings profitable. From a friend he had learned that the last seen of Mr. Bliss he had a Bible in his hand and was composing a song never to be heard on earth, only to swell the waves of music that roll across the Heavens. "Only an Armor-bearer Proudly I Stand," sang Mr. Sankey, the congregation joining in the chorus. "Fading Away like the Stars in the Morning," a rich, beautiful hymn, was exquisitely rendered by Mrs. Johnson, and Mr. Sankey followed with "Waiting and Watching," the most pathetic of all Bliss' music.

"Rock of Ages," to the music composed by Mrs. Bliss, and "Hold the Fort," were sung by the congregation as they dispersed.

CHAPTER XXVIII.

SO widely was Mr. Bliss known, and so warmly was he beloved, that the grief at his death was well-nigh universal among all professing the faith of Jesus. Not alone at Rome and Chicago, but at numerous other places, memorial services were held in honor of the dead singer. We have culled largely from the newspaper reports of these services, and present them here in connected form, as a part of the record this book was designed to perpetuate.

On the evening of January 21, a large congregation assembled at the Reformed Church in South Bend, Indiana, to attend the services held there in honor of Mr. and Mrs. Bliss, which were conducted by the pastor, Rev. N. D. Williamson. The songs sung were of Mr. Bliss' own composition, and were very effectively rendered by the choir and congregation. Two—" Eternity " and " Almost Persuaded " —were sung as solos by Miss Maud Wellman. The pastor enjoyed the personal acquaintance of Mr. Bliss, and the affectionate regard which he entertained for him was evident in the deep feeling betrayed by the tones of his voice in discoursing of his unspeakably sad fate. Many of the congregation also knew Mr. and Mrs. Bliss, and more than one gave evidence of tears to the manner in which their hearts were touched by the dreadful story. At the close of the sermon, Prof. J. Sydenham Duer read with tender effect the lines written on Mr. Bliss' death by Rev. Dr. Pierson, of Detroit, entitled " The Silent Harp." Hon. Schuyler Colfax had intended to be present and pay a tribute to the memory of Mr. Bliss, in lieu of which he sent a tender and beautiful letter, which was read by the pastor. Our limits forbid our giving it space.

Mr. Williamson selected as his text Revelation xiv. 13 : " Blessed are the dead which die in the Lord—that they may rest from their labors, and their works do follow them." We copy the greater portion of his discourse :

To " die in the Lord " is indeed blessed. But to die in the Lord it is not needful that you die in your bed, at the close of a wasting sickness, attended by skillful physicians, surrounded by tearful friends, and bearing witness with your dying breath to the mercy of the Lord. To die in the Lord it is not necessary to have your body garnitured by all the taste and skill that loving friends and experienced undertakers can furnish, nor to have it followed by a long train of relatives and friends, nor to have it deposited in the grave or the tomb amid the sobbing of the multitude, nor to have the spot visited by admiring friends during the years and centuries that follow.

To those who die in the Lord, death may come on the highway with thundering crash, with shrieks and moans, and suffocated breath, and mangled limbs, and frost, and fire, and storm-winds ; and it may turn the body into undistinguished ashes, mingled with the snows and waters, so that no friend who seeks them with the intensest gaze of agony, that he may bear them to their sepulture, and no admirer who would beautify the earth that covers them with garlands of gratitude, can tell where they are.

For even amid the tornado crash, the rending earthquake, and the consuming fire, the God of the elements and the God of grace can enwrap their souls in His everlasting arms of peace, and bear them with swifter than lightning wing into the realms of the painless and the glorified. And He can keep watch and guard over the ashes of their physical decay, until the dawning of the resurrection morn, when the power that made the God-like Adam out of the dust of the earth will restore them in Christ like forms of excellence and glory ! And the emphasis that such a departure gives to the faith and labors of a godly life, may carry the praises of the Lord, through the instrumentality of that life, infinitely farther on the broad world and down the reaches of time than a thousand peaceful death-bed utterances possibly could do. Yes ! those whose memories we honor to-night—who went into eternity on the sad evening of the 29th of December, from the Ashtabula bridge, amid the terrors and horrors of that carnival of death and destruction, without any premonition of the approach of the grim monster in his most hideous mien, and whose physical forms disappeared from human view in that valley of death as completely as that of Moses did on Mount Nebo when the Lord buried him—died in the Lord, and of them the " voice from heaven " is " heard saying unto me, write, blessed are the dead which die in the Lord ; yea, saith the Spirit, that they may rest from their labors ; and their works do follow them."

Professor Bliss and his wife went to Rome, Bradford county, Pa., to spend the holidays, preparatory to entering with Major Whipple on the labors of succeeding the brethren Moody and Sankey in the tabernacle work in Chicago. Their last visit in Rome was passed not wholly in tarrying with their relatives and friends, but in assisting in a series of religious meetings during the last week of the year. The last night Professor Bliss was in Rome, which was Wednesday night, December 27th, he sang a sacred song, the music of his own composing, and the words written by his wife, entitled " Hold Fast till I Come." As he was about to sing it, he remarked, " Here is a song I have never sung in public, and I don't know as I shall ever sing it again." This song is the last one we have heard of his singing in the earthly assemblies of the saints.

On Thursday morning, they left Rome. On Friday evening just before dark, Professor Bliss was seen by a passenger whose life was spared, sitting in a car by the side of his wife, with his open Bible on his knee, and both seemed intently engaged in the study of the Sacred Word, while he was composing a Bible song, which earth was never to hear. And this is the last we know of them in the body. The report that it was Professor Bliss who escaped from a burning car, and went back to rescue his wife, and perished with her, may be true; it would be just like his tender, generous, manly nature ; but we do not know.

The ill-fated train in which our friends had embarked, was made up of two express and two baggage cars, two day passenger cars, one drawing-room car, and four sleepers—eleven cars in all—drawn by two locomotives. As it was crossing the chasm spanned by the Ashtabula bridge, which was only about one-fourth the length of the train, the first locomotive had barely reached the farther abutment, when the bridge went down sixty feet, carrying with it the other locomotive and the cars that followed it; and then, oh, horror of horrors! the other cars, with their heated stoves, and lighted candles, and precious freight of human lives and hopes, went leaping down one after another, one on the top of the other, crashing through each other, and as they leaped headlong into the chasm, the fiery stoves went sweeping through some of them from one end to the other, with their ponderous, blistering force, crushing, mangling, and burning the hapless inmates. And soon the bright light, shooting its red glare heavenwards, told the watchers at the station—some of whom are with us to-night, who also had the blessed privilege of ministering there to the wants of numbers of the wounded—the story that was hissing with tongues of flame in the ears of the pinioned prisoners in the deadly gorge below, that the fire fiend was completing the work of the wrecking fiend.

What passed between our sunny-hearted friend and his noble wife in these moments freighted with the intensest terror that wreck, and frost, and storm, and fire can combine to produce, we know not. But we can imagine that whatever the number of moments they were compelled to await in that whirlwind of fire the summons home, they had grace to remember the song of their own they had sung two nights before:

> Oh, child, in thy anguish, despairing or dumb,
> Remember the message, Hold fast till I come!

And we can know that at whatever point before the completion of that great holocaust, their ransomed spirits left the mangled and charred bodies behind, they started singing :

> Where He may lead I'll follow,
> My trust in Him repose,
> And all the time in perfect peace,
> I'll sing, " He knows, He knows."

*   *   *   *   *   *   *   *

Had we the power to follow and witness the effect of the announcement of the tragical earthly end of these two writers of sweet sacred song, as it traveled and is traveling over the round world, what varied scenes of sorrow and regret would we witness! Here we see the brethren who have been his especial co-laborers, hasten to the scene of disaster as quickly as possible, in a vain anxiety to secure at least the bruised and mangled bodies of their dead friends for Christian burial. There we see the great tabernacle, with its vast assembly of eight thousand inside, and as many waiting outside in the cold in the vain hope of gaining entrance, filled and surrounded with mourners. Yonder we look upon the multitudes gathered at the home funeral service, where their last earthly ministrations were rendered. And on the Atlantic, and on the Pacific coast of America, and between, and over the waters to the east, and to the west, and the south, in Europe and Asia and Africa, the sad tidings bring regret and eulogy and grief to assembled thousands, and to solitary readers and hearers. The Christian songs that have belted the world with their melodies, have caused and will cause their writers to be mourned the world over. "Their works do follow them."

And words of sorrow for the dead, and of gratitude to God for what His servant and handmaiden have done in the realm of song, have been spoken in multitudes of places by the great and the obscure.

Mr. Williamson here continued as follows:

My personal acquaintance with Professor and Mrs. Bliss began in 1865, one year after he came to Chicago. His musical convention work here was done, I have been informed, in 1869. He began his purely evangelistic work with Major Whittle at the beginning of 1874, and had grown greatly in spirituality and force of character, as well as in breadth and power of influence. It was our earnest endeavor to secure his services, with those of Brother Whittle, for the series of union meetings just closed, but God so ordered affairs that the closing labors of his life were employed elsewhere, and we were saved the severity of the shock, which otherwise would have fallen on us.

Still God has come so near to us in this solemn providence, that it becomes every man, woman, and child who has heard the songs of this man and woman, to ask himself and herself, What good ought I to get, what good can I get from it to my immortal soul? If there should be one here who has not sung or heard the Bliss hymns and music before to-night, it will well become even such an one to ask, What good use can I make of those I have just heard? How much more should we do it, who have become so familiar with some of this music and have sung these Gospel Hymns so often?

A service in memory of Mr. Bliss was held at the House of Hope Church in St. Paul, Minnesota. There had been put upon the blackboard the words, "In memory of our brother Philip P. Bliss," and, the board being wreathed in evergreens and the evergreens sprinkled with white lilies, the whole formed a beautiful tablet. It was placed upon the wall behind the platform, and under it was a cushion of flowers and vines upon which it seemed to be resting.

In commencing the sermon, the Superintendent, Mr. Cochran, read the hymn, both the words and the music of which Mr. Bliss wrote, " When Jesus Comes," saying that in no better way could his memory be honored than by singing heartily the hymns which he wrote to the praise of God. The congregation, composed of the regular attendants upon the Sabbath School and those who had come in to participate in the services, then read alternately with the Superintendent the first eleven verses of 1 Thessalonians v., after which Mr. Charles H. Bigelow led in prayer. Then was sung the hymn, the words of which Mr. Bliss wrote to music furnished by another, " I know not the Hour when my Lord shall Come," after which Rev. Mr. Breed, the pastor of the church, addressed a few words " to the grown people present." He said he thought it was generally the case that the manner and circumstances of our death would generally be found in some measure to have been anticipated by the thoughts and works of our lives. He called attention to the fact that a member of this very church and Sabbath School, whom no one would have thought to be anticipating sudden death, but to whom death had come almost unannounced, by terrible accident, had marked in his Bible two of the verses which had just been read. " But of the times and the seasons, my brethren, ye have no need that I write unto you." " For yourselves know perfectly that the day of the Lord so cometh as a thief in the night." Those who had watched beside the death-bed of that young man have testified that he met his death, suddenly as it came, calmly and with full faith in his Savior.

So, in thinking of this sad death which came to our brother Bliss, and reading the hymns, could any one fail to be struck with their foreshadowing of the suddenness of his end. Those that have already been sung were examples of it, but perhaps the most striking, not only in its spiritual but physical aptness, was—

> Through the valley of the shadow I must go
> Where the cold waves of Jordan roll,
> But the presence of my Savior will, I know,
> Be the staff and support to my soul.

Literally, Mr. Bliss was called at death, to pass through a valley of the shadow, and literally the cold waves overwhelmed him upon that awful night.

And yet why should he or any of us be astonished at the suddenness of death, for do we not " know perfectly," as the Apostle saith, " that the day of the Lord so cometh as a thief in the night?" One remaining thought: the lesson to us of Mr. Bliss' life was to consecrate whatever talent God had given to us to His service. It was in his case a musical gift; he had fully consecrated it, and perhaps more than any other writer of sacred music of the century, his name and memory would live and his music be the means of converting souls to Christ for years and years to come.

After Mr. Breed had ceased speaking, Mr. Cochran said that what he had to say was to be addressed to the children present. He then reminded them how Major Whittle and Mr. Bliss when holding services in St. Paul had devoted part of their vacation day, Saturday, to holding a children's service; how the last one had been held in this very church the last Saturday of their stay in St. Paul. He then described how two children, 5 and 7 years old, had remembered the text from which Mr. Bliss had spoken that morning, making the five words which composed it answer to the five fingers of his left hand while he pointed to them with his right, and thus fixing them in the minds of the children. The text was, " Daniel purposed in his heart;" and after he had spoken from it he made a request of the children, and these same little children here in St. Paul had remembered this request, though it was made more than a year ago. It was that the children present should remember when they said their prayers at night to pray for Major Whittle and his (Mr. Bliss') little children, from whom they were so often and so long separated. The speaker felt sure that though Mr. Bliss' voice was forever silent in this world, yet if he could to-day speak from Heaven he would make exactly the same request, that the children of St. Paul and everywhere should pray for his little boys, who never again on earth would know a father's or mother's love, and the message he would deliver from heaven would be the same message he gave on that Saturday morning in this church, that all would imitate Daniel and accept Daniel's God in Jesus Christ.

Another memorial service was held in St. Paul, of which the following letter gives an account:

St. Paul, Minn., Jan. 31, 1877.

Maj. D. W. Whittle:

My Dear Brother—We had a memorial service in our little church (Dayton Avenue Presbyterian) which was to us very interesting. Mr. Bliss had

endeared himself to us not only by his sweet songs, **but our children had been to his children's meetings here in Saint Paul, and so nearly all of them knew him personally.** During our memorial service a boy 13 years old (son of Senator M.) arose and said **he wanted to bear** testimony to Mr. Bliss' influence **upon** him. He stated, **between sobs, that the singing of " I've Found the** Pearl of Greatest Price " **had been the means of leading him to the Savior.** Other incidents were given showing how warmly our people felt toward him. We do not forget your labors here, and it may cheer you to know that none of the boys and girls belonging to our Sunday School who were converted at that time have gone back again to the world. A boys' prayer meeting was started soon after you went away, and has been maintained ever since. May God prosper you in all your labors.   Very truly yours,   L. A. GILBERT,
Superintendent Dayton Avenue Sunday School.

At Louisville, Kentucky, the death of Mr. Bliss caused the most profound sorrow. His evangelical labors there created for him a general regard, while among those with whom he came in personal contact, he was held in affectionate esteem. As one of the local papers expresses it, the great success achieved in that city "was, as far as a religious awakening is concerned, something that surpassed all precedent. The singing of Mr. Bliss tended strongly to popularize the meetings, and his gospel songs are still used in many of our churches and Sunday Schools."

A memorial service was held at the Chestnut Street Presbyterian Church. The attendance, notwithstanding the rain and snow that checkered the weather's general inclemency, was so large that the seating capacity of the church was wholly inadequate to accommodate the congregation. The aisles and every vacant space were filled with stools and chairs, and many remained standing until the close.

After reading the parable of the fig tree (Luke xiii), the pastor, Rev. Mr. Simpson, proceeded to say that the words were peculiarly appropriate to the occasion for two reasons. In the first place, this was the fourth New Year's Sabbath he had spent among them as their pastor, and the words seemed to come with peculiar solemnity to all who had rejected his message: "These three years I come seeking fruit, and find none; cut it down;" while the interceding Savior pleaded once more, perhaps only once, "Let it alone this year also."

The parable finally presented the touching picture of the great Intercessor standing between the sinner and his doom, and pleading one more year's delay. How solemn to reflect that He only asked one year, and even that was not assured ; and after that even Jesus promised to cease to plead for the hardened and impenitent. Having at some length expounded these thoughts, he proceeded to the second and principal part of his discourse—in reference to the occasion as a memorial service. In the second place, he said, the parable had reference to two very sudden calamities that had occurred—the slaughter of certain Jewish worshipers by Pilate, and the destruction of eighteen by the falling of a tower in Siloam.

How suitably its lessons connected themselves with the many appalling disasters which had lately shocked the public mind; and how tenderly these lessons were impressed by the sad memories of the terrible death they had met to-night to improve. If any might have claimed exemption from such a fate it was one whose usefulness seemed scarcely in its prime, and if he were not spared how could the careless and indifferent risk delay?

Mr. Simpson then referred to Mr. Bliss' connection with the work in Louisville two years previously, and the loving recollections he had left behind him in hundreds of hearts. "The evangelists had always regarded it as the most cheering work of their lives, and hopes had been cherished of their return this winter. Their plans, however, had been made to spend the winter in Chicago, continuing the work Mr. Moody had begun, and then visit Europe in the summer, and begin the work in Great Britain."

The speaker closed by an earnest appeal to all who hesitated to accept the Gospel, to begin at once to seek the Savior, whose greater love and more terrible sacrifice for them had been feebly shadowed forth in this sad calamity. Mr. Bliss had died to save a dear wife, and failed; Christ had died to save His enemies, and, as a living, loving, pleading Friend, stood now at every heart, crying, "Behold I stand at the door and knock ; if any man hear my voice and open the door, I will come in to him and sup with him, and he with me." The noblest tribute they could lay upon the grave of their dear friend was to know that even his death and its lessons had led a great multitude of the unsaved to the Master he loved so well.

In response to this appeal, many persons rose in acknowledgment of their purpose to begin that night to seek the Savior, and after a solemn prayer for them, the service closed.

The First Cumberland Presbyterian Church, in Nashville, Tenn., was crowded on the occasion of the Bliss memorial services, even the space in the rear of the seats being completely filled. The exercises opened by a portion of the choir singing "Almost Persuaded."

Dr. Baird said that only a few years ago there was a new era in secular songs. People discovered that little children could sing, and from this sprang songs full of simplicity and truth, that were caught up and set the world on fire. He paid a touching tribute to Mr. Bliss, dwelling briefly on the striking simplicity of his character, his Christian earnestness and devotedness to the cause of Christ. The songs they would sing to-night were compositions of Mr. Bliss, in some cases both the words and music. The next song they would sing was probably at this very moment ringing along the streets of London and Edinburgh, and throughout America.

"I am so glad Jesus Loves Me" was then sung, and followed by a prayer from Rev. M. B. DeWitt, in which he alluded to the consecration on the altar of Christ, and the removal of the "Sweet Singer" and evangelist from his work in this world to take up his songs in Heaven. The song "Watching and Waiting" then followed.

Mr. DeWitt made a few remarks, and was followed by Dr. Baird, who offered a series of resolutions, which were adopted by a rising vote.

Rev. A. J. Baird, pastor of the First Cumberland Church, sends us the following letter respecting the above meeting:

NASHVILLE, TENN., Jan. 8, 1877.

MY DEAR BRO. WHITTLE:

Last night was a memorable evening with us. We held a service of song in my church in memory of our dear Brother Bliss. Our service consisted of prayer, a few remarks by different persons, but chiefly singing. The choir, orchestra and congregation joining. Oh, it was so sweet to recall the holy memories of the meetings held by yourself and our lamented brother. Many were there who were brought to the Savior during those meetings. Our songs were: "Almost Persuaded," "Waiting and Watching," "Jesus Loves even Me," "Hallelujah, 'tis Done," "Free from the Law," "When Jesus Comes," "That will be Heaven for Me," "Hold the Fort."

It is a joy to join with the friends in Chicago and elsewhere in cherishing the precious memory of our dear departed brother and sister.

A. J. BAIRD,
Pastor First Cumberland Presbyterian Church.

A commemorative service in honor of Mr. and Mrs. Bliss was held in the Presbyterian Church at Kalamazoo, Michigan, under the auspices of the Young Men's Christian Association. The arrangements for the meeting were in the hands of a committee of one from each of the co-operating churches. Abundant material for draping the church was loaned by several of the merchants. Mrs. Jas. Allen supplied the artificial flowers used, made the beautiful cross, crown and shield used in the decorations, and gave her aid, with Mrs. Frank Russell, Mrs. J. C. Burrows and Miss Smith, to the work of preparation. The skill and taste exhibited by these ladies betokened how much they had the subject at heart. The drapery of black and white extended fully around the church on the galleries, and was beautifully arranged in folds. The platform was arranged in nearly the same manner as when it was occupied by the evangelists, during their revival work in that city. An organ was placed upon it, with the motto Mr. Bliss had on his: "God so loved the world that he gave his Only begotten Son, that whosoever believeth in him should not Perish, but have Everlasting Life," forming an acrostic of the word "Gospel." The singer's chair was in the position as when used by him, and appropriately draped. The chair Mrs. Bliss used was elevated so as to indicate to the audience the place occupied in the choir by her. It was also fitly draped. The drapery was centred over the pulpit, and drooped to the doors on either side; and at the point of the draping over the center was a cross on a shield; underneath it, in large capitals, the title of the last song Mr. Bliss sang while in Kalamazoo—"Waiting at the Beautiful Gate." Over one door leading into the chapel was a superb cross; on the other, a crown. Everything betokened taste and intense interest for the work. The choir held the same position as before, with the change of the organ to the center. The organ representing Mr. Bliss' was silent. Prof. C. J. Toof presided at the other, and Mr. W. F. Leavitt, who rendered Mr. Bliss effective aid during his period of service there, took direction of the choir. The ministers present, the members of the choir and the ushers wore suitable badges of mourning.

Long before the hour of beginning the house began to fill rapidly. At the second ringing of the bell, it was tolled with thirty-eight measured strokes, that being the number of years of Prof. Bliss' life. By this time the church was filled to overflowing, and many were standing about the doors. The exercises were opened by the singing of the hymn, "I know not the hour when my Lord shall Come." Rev. Mr. Sherwood pronounced a brief and feeling invocation. "The Home over There" was sung, and the fifth chapter of Revelation was read (containing the words, "And they sung a new song," etc.) by the Moderator of the meeting, Rev. Jos. H. France. A prayer was offered by Rev. Dr. Hodge. Mr. Leavitt sang as a solo, with great tenderness and clear expression, one of the favorite songs of Mr. Bliss, " Oh, to be Nothing." The presiding officer then introduced the chief exercises of the evening with a short and earnest address, delivered with very earnest and effective feeling.

Capt. Ford, from the Committee on Resolutions, prefaced the report with an explanation that the Scripture used in the first sentence was the text of Rev. xiv, 3, taken in part as the basis of Hymn 44, in the Gospel Hymns, music by Prof. Bliss; that the reference to South Africa was called out by the reported singing of his hymns in the wilds of the Zulu country; the first quotation of poetry was from the 86th of the Gospel Songs, the older book of Mr. Bliss, both words and music by him; the text cited in the first resolution was the theme of Hymn 24, Gospel Hymns, words by Mrs. Bliss, music by her husband, from which the extract was made in the second resolution; the extract in the fourth resolution was from the 41st of the Gospel Hymns, words and music by Bliss; and that in the fifth was from the 79th hymn, music also by Mr. Bliss. He then read the resolutions, as follows:

Philip Paul Bliss and Lucy Bliss, his wife, have gone to sing, as it were, a new song before the throne — that song which no man can learn but they which are redeemed from the earth. Their tragic death overshadows the whole Christian world. From the north of Scotland to the Zulu huts of South Africa, from the Far East to the Far West—wherever their songs are sung, the poets and singers will be mourned. He, cut off in the prime of his splendid manhood, with all his great powers at their best; she, worthy companion of his joys and toils—have left time for eternity in the black gorge of death that opened at Ashtabula. At one dread plunge they went to make real the truth of his own sweet song:

Through the valley of the shadow I must go,
Where the cold waves of Jordan roll;
But the promise of my Shepherd will, I know,
Be the rod and the staff to my soul.
Even now down the valley as I glide
I can hear my Savior say, " Follow Me,"
And with Him I'm not afraid to cross the tide,
There's a light in the valley for me.

Like the singers of Nehemiah, Brother and Sister Bliss "kept the ward of their God." By the talents and abilities they consecrated to the Redeemer; by their pure, strong, unselfish Christian character; by the priceless service they have done and through the works they leave shall yet do in His cause among

men, they have **earned a** memory which **the world shall** not willingly let die.
Therefore, **resolved :**

1. That the citizens of Kalamazoo **and vicinity, so** lately blessed **by these sweet
singers,** do deeply mourn the bereavement of **their families and** friends, **and the
loss of** their living presence from the fields of Christian usefulness; doubting **not,
however,** that they were "willing rather to be absent from the body and to **be
present with** the Lord."

2. That our deepest sympathies, in this hour of trial, go out to the widowed
mother and sisters of the brother gone, to the parents of Mrs. Bliss, to the little
ones thus orphaned, to all other relatives of the sainted dead, and to the great
throng of friends who are bereft.   **May all remember that,**

> For those who sleep
>   And those who weep,
> Above the **portals** narrow,
>   The mansions rise
> Beyond **the skies,—**
>   We're going **home to-morrow.**

3. That the special and **fraternal** sympathies **of** this people be **extended to
the** friend and Christian **brother, the** companion and co-laborer of **the dear
departed,** Major **D. W.** Whittle, who loved them with a love like that of David
for Jonathan, "passing the love of women ;" and we hope and pray that he
may be upstayed by the Everlasting Arms, that the **blow** may be mercifully
softened to him by the Divine Hand, and blessed to the strengthening of his
heart and tongue for the great work that remains to him.

4. That, while this visitation of Providence seems **mysterious and dark, wo**
humbly recognize that "He doeth all things well."

> No darkness have we who in Jesus abide,
>   The Light of the World is Jesus ;
> We walk in the light when we follow our God,
>   The Light of the World is Jesus.

5. That the life and **labors of the lamented** dead shall be perpetual incen-
tives to the best work **we can do for the Master.**

> Sowing the seed with an aching heart,
> Sowing the seed while the tear-drops start,
> Sowing in hope till the reapers come,
> Gladly to gather the harvest home.
> Oh, what shall the harvest be ?

6. That the contributions of this community be respectfully solicited in aid
of the Bliss Memorial **Funds, now** being raised.

At the commemoration services at Peoria, Illinois, Centennial
Hall was crowded and many failed to find seats.   Rev. J. D. Wilson,
of Christ **Reformed** Episcopal Church, opened the service by asking
the choir to sing the hymn, "In the Christian's Home in Glory,"
after which Rev. **W. B. McIlvaine** led in prayer.

Rev. W. C. Mappin then read, as the scripture lesson, selections from the 6th and 7th chapters of Revelation, and the choir sung, softly and beautifully, the song, "Go, Bury thy Sorrow," and "When the Comforter Came," followed by a hymn that will always be dear to Peoria Christians, as it was written by Mr. Bliss in that city, viz.: "When Jesus Comes," beginning,

> Down life's dark vale we wander,
>   Till Jesus comes ;
> We watch and wait and wonder,
>   Till Jesus comes.

Rev. John Weston, of Calvary Mission, was the first speaker. He said:

We can almost see our departed brother as he sat and sang before us, but a few days ago, his whole heart in his song. He has gone home ; he was waiting and ready. What a gloom fell upon us last Sabbath, as the sad word came to us. So like the old prophet of old, he went home to heaven, not a vestige left of him on earth. Let a double portion of his spirit rest on us who are left. We ask why did God take His servant away so? It is not ours to tell, "God moves in a mysterious way." .The time will come when we shall see the wisdom of God's dealings with us. His glory shall be seen after all. It says to us, "Be ye also ready." Out of the dark valley comes the voice to us, be faithful and devoted to His service. Also a lesson to those who are not God's children. We would not bring our friends back. They sing the "New Song' to-night ; but to you who have no such hope the warning comes, "Prepare to meet thy God." You have heard him sing ; let his sweet voice invite you to follow him to his home in heaven.

Rev. Mr. Thompson, of the First Baptist Church, then spoke.

Mr. Bliss was a man of tender sympathy. Knowing sorrow himself, he felt for others ; feeling tenderly himself the love of Christ, he desired all others to know the same. A man of eminent abilities, he was humble and trustful, and gave all glory to his God. How his face would glow as he sang "Hallelujah, what a Savior." How my own soul felt as he sang his thrilling songs. I am told wherever he went in domestic life he left the savor of his Savior behind a consecrated life.

He is gone. We feel as if he was still needed with us. God can make his death more effective than his life. "He being dead, still speaketh." He speaks in song round the world to-night. It was said of Sampson "he slew more in his death than while living." How many may be brought to Jesus by what we call his untimely death. "He walked with God," and "he is not, for God took him." The Master has said, "Come up higher." One of his songs says, "We'll soon be at home over there ;" now he is there. Another, "I know not the hour," etc. He did not know the hour, but Jesus called and took him away in His own time. He knows "the song the angels sing" now. The last song our brother sung with us was the 22d, "We're Going Home To-morrow." Shall we meet *them* there when God calls us to meet all of those who have gone before?

The 22d hymn was then sung with deep feeling by the entire audience.

Rev. A. A. Stevens, of the First Congregational Church, next came forward and spoke tenderly and kindly of the dead singer. He spoke of the effect of his songs upon himself. "It seems as if we were just waiting for him to come in." He spoke specially of the songs, "Are your windows open toward Jerusalem?" and "The half was Never Told." Now he knows the whole of the glories of heaven. It is a blessed thought that our brother loves us still as he did when here. How bright the prospect of our meeting dear friends again in the better world. How it strengthens us for our work. If any shall linger now to accept Christ, how can they when they remember his love and prayers so recently for them? We cannot see all the plan, but we "know all things work together for good to those that love God."

Mr. Stevens spoke of the cheerfulness of Mr. Bliss — always cheerful. "We don't sing enough," said he. Let us cherish him because he was so much like his Master.

Rev. Mr. Wilson at this point led in an earnest prayer asking for all submission to the will of God.

Hymn No. 13 was then sung—

I know not the hour when my Lord will come.

Rev. Ira J. Chase, of the Christian Church, followed in some very appropriate remarks. He wondered what Mr. Bliss was doing when death came. He quoted Mr. Bliss' motto for 1876, "Be ye therefore steadfast," etc. It was his habit to select a text to be his motto for the year. Perhaps he was selecting his verse. Perhaps he was singing. At all events he was ready. I am glad those who have spoken have made it a practical matter with us all. What testimony will we leave behind us? Why don't you all prepare for the future? God calls to us. It is for each one to say, "Oh! to be 'waiting and watching' up there!"

Mr. Chase then read a tribute to the memory of the dead singer, written by some friend and given to him.

Rev. Mr. Wilson spoke, and asked to have "Watching and Waiting" sung, but those accustomed to sing would not venture to sing it. They could not, and No. 50 was taken in its place: "I will Guide Thee with Mine Eye."

Rev. H. S. Beavis, of Grace Church, was then called upon, and said : "Silence might now be golden." He could not soon forget the pleadings of this departed brother as he plead with the youth of our city. His is one of the lives that speak to us and bid us make our lives sublime. It tells us of the record we are to make. It seems as if it were cut short in the very midst of fire and storm. Bliss met trials and storms and overcame them, and speaks to us to go forward. He added enthusiasm and untiring industry to his energy, and added to all consecration to the Master's work. He breathed it in his prayer ; he carried it in his life; he sung it in his songs. Let us imitate him and make our lives beautiful, and leave behind us the fragrance of a consecrated life.

Rev. Mr. Wilson followed in an earnest and tender reference to the dead. We would not bring them back—he is happy now. There are some who might have come to Jesus if they could have heard another song. There is one hymn that has not been referred to to-night, "Hold the Fort." What joy the words "I am coming" brought to the beleaguered garrison at Allatoona!

"Hold the Fort" was then sung with feeling by the choir and entire congregation. After singing this hymn, Rev. Mr. Wilson asked Wm. Reynolds, Esq., to take charge of the meeting.

A request was made for all who had found Christ during the meetings held here recently to rise. A large number arose. "Now," said the speaker, "who will join these and decide now? While they sing a verse of Hymn 59, let them rise." Some arose, and Rev. Mr. Thompson led in prayer, asking that the death of those beloved ones might be the means of leading many to think of the awful future. After prayer, No. 15, "There is a Gate that Stands Ajar," was sung, and one of the saddest and most impressive meetings ever held in Peoria was closed.

The following extract from a private letter from Peoria, written previous to the holding of the above meeting, and soon after the reception of the news of the Ashtabula disaster, will be read with interest:

In every church in the city, yesterday, the sad tidings were told, and heart-felt, loving, stirring words were spoken, while we all wept together. Mr. Reynolds made most touching and thrilling mention in Sabbath School, asking those young people who had been brought to Christ through Mr. Bliss' meetings to rise. Over thirty arose to testify of what he had done for them. Oh! how many precious souls will sparkle as gems in his crown!

We conclude this chapter and the volume with a few letters from Christian friends and co-workers. The first is from Rev. Dr. J. H. Brookes, of St. Louis:

St. Louis, Jan. 1, 1877.

My Beloved Brother:

Since yesterday morning there has seemed to be a pall upon earth and sky. One of the Elders came to the study, just before the hour of preaching, and asked me if I had heard the sad news, and then told me with sobs that Bliss had been killed. The tidings stunned me, it was so unexpected, so impossible, my poor heart said.

Mention was made of the heavy loss the church had sustained when we met for public worship, and the tears of many attested the strength of the hold our dear brother had taken upon the affections of the saints here. Again we met in the evening, and remained in prayer and meditation upon the word, and singing many of the sweet songs Mr. Bliss had composed, until the old year had gone away and the midnight hour announced that we were entering upon a new year. Many were the allusions to Bliss and his family, and to you also, stricken to the ground by this sudden and appalling blow.

Oh, how my heart bled for you, as the thought of your loneliness and desolation of spirit and bitter disappointment occurred to me; but it only led some at least—no doubt many—to bear you before the Lord in fervent supplication. Surely He is saying to you now, as never before, "Be still, and know that I am God," and "What I do thou knowest not now, but thou shalt know hereafter." Yes, He will make this strange providence perfectly plain very soon, for, "Yet a little while and he that shall come will come, and will not tarry." It is the time, dear brother, for your faith to meet the deep darkness rolling over you with the cry, "Though He slay me, yet will I trust in Him."

A young man in his prayer, last night, referred to Bliss as having taught many of us to sing "Waiting and Watching," and now he is waiting and watching for the saints he had cheered on earth. Even so; he is just on the other side of the river, waiting and watching for his companion in testimony and service. Let us more and more be waiting and watching for that blessed hope, when at our gathering together unto Jesus, we shall meet our beloved ones who sleep in Him. Oh, in the presence of such a sore affliction, how our hearts cry out, "Even so, come, Lord Jesus!" How pitifully little the world seems! How contemptible, self! How near, eternity! How bright and glorious the home toward which we are traveling!

These hurried words have been written as fast as my pen can move, just to let you know that some of God's dear children in **St.** Louis have fellowship in your sorrow, and are bearing you up in their hearts in prayer. The Lord will bless this terrible trial in drawing you nearer to Himself, and **giving you more** singleness of heart.

In a common **grief, but a common hope, too.**

Yours in Him,   J. H BROOKES.

MILWAUKEE, Jan. 18, 1877.

MY DEAR BROTHER WHITTLE:

I have thought much **about you of late and especially since the death of our** dear friends, Mr. and Mrs. Bliss. We had had several very sad afflictions in our church, and this one of their so sudden departure, **coming at the close of the** year, made the year go out in gloom. I shall always remember the last months of 1876 as a time of abundant and almost overwhelming sorrow. How happily the year began — for me, at least — when we were working together in this hard field of Milwaukee. The work was a joy and it was a joy to see its results, though they were not such nor so large, seemingly, as we had wished. In God's sight they may have been far greater than the ones we had expected. In the first terror of the calamity of December 29, it was difficult to get near to the divine point of view. But we are doubtless now both calm in the view that the acts and the kingdom of our dear Father have all space and all eternity to interpret them. They are not to be judged by a single fearful night and a single dreadful ravine. The flesh shrinks from the thought of the bruised and mangled frames of those so loved, but the spirit of faith remembers One who was more bruised for our iniquities. And that God can use, in some mysterious way, the bruising of the body for the healing of souls, the great example of the wounded Saviour teaches us. It seems terrible to the shrinking flesh to think of **dying** by fire, but God has brought some of the richest blessings to His church through fire. God's beloved Zion owes much discipline of purifying and exaltation to this element of fire. It is the great law of the Lord, expressed most astonishingly upon Calvary, that the world shall be saved with suffering.

Thus the crushed and broken frame
Oft doth sweetest graces yield,
And this suffering, toil and shame,
From the martyr's keenest flame,
Heavenly incense is distilled.

The converts of last winter **stand well;** we are having some more continually, and I am hopeful of good results in the Sunday Schools. I wish I might have an afternoon's quiet talk with you. Do **you never** long for some quiet? I do, and think it necessary to the highest life of the soul.

With love,

GEO. T. LADD.

He Knows.

P. P. B.

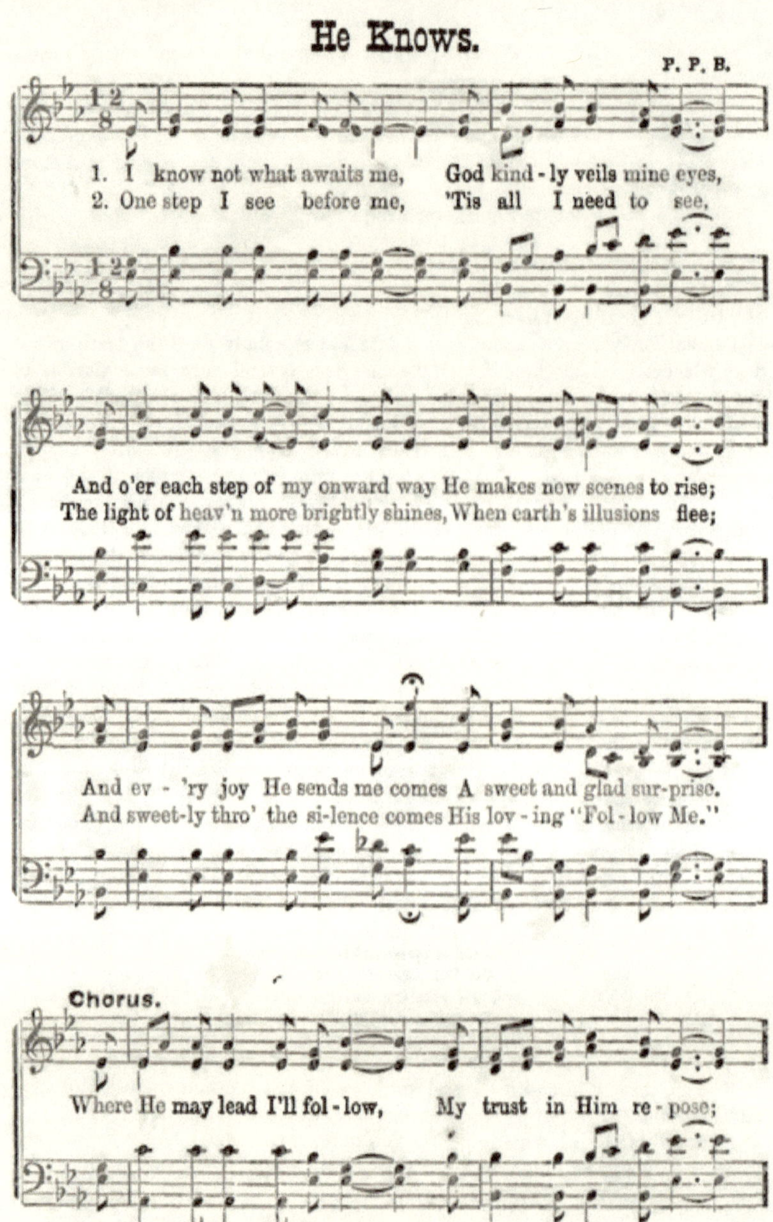

1. I know not what awaits me, God kind-ly veils mine eyes,
2. One step I see before me, 'Tis all I need to see,
And o'er each step of my onward way He makes new scenes to rise;
The light of heav'n more brightly shines, When earth's illusions flee;
And ev-'ry joy He sends me comes A sweet and glad sur-prise.
And sweet-ly thro' the si-lence comes His lov-ing "Fol-low Me."
Chorus.
Where He may lead I'll fol-low, My trust in Him re-pose;

He Knows.--Concluded.

3. O blissful lack of wisdom,
   'Tis blessed not to know;
He holds me with His own right hand,
   And will not let me go,
And lulls my troubled soul to rest
   In Him who loves me so

4. So on I go, not knowing,
   I would not if I might;
I'd rather walk in the dark with God
   Than go alone in the light;
I'd rather walk by faith with Him
   Than go alone by sight.